Big Chance Cowboy

TERI ANNE STANLEY

sourcebooks
casablanca

Published by Sourcebooks Casablanca, an imprint of Sourcebooks
P.O. Box 4410, Naperville, Illinois 60567-4410
(630) 961-3900
sourcebooks.com

Printed and bound in the United States of America.
OPM 10 9 8 7 6 5 4 3 2 1

For Stella; the best brown dog we ever had.

Prologue

Afghanistan, nine months ago

"HEY, COLLINS, ARE WE CLEAR?"

Marcus Talbott's voice crackled into Adam's earpiece, barely suppressed tension thickening the soldier's Kentucky drawl.

Tank snuffled next to Adam, tugging at his lead. "Hold back," Adam murmured into his mic. The dog hadn't alerted to explosives but continued to weave his head back and forth, every now and then pausing when he caught a hint of something that troubled his world-class nose. He didn't stop for long in any one spot however.

Adam forced himself to breathe in and out for a count of five and tried to let Tank take his time. Adrenaline and exhaustion fought for dominance in his blood, and it was only long hours of training and experience that kept Adam from urging Tank to give the all clear so the team they were assigned to could do their thing. Everyone was tired and ready to end this. Four other highly trained soldiers crouched close by, weapons ready to blast their target the moment Yasim Mansour showed his evil, drug-dealing, bomb-building self.

It would have been safer to make sure the run-down shack was clear of innocents, then blow the bastard up from a distance, but that wasn't an option. Mansour had important information about the next link in the chain of terror.

"If he's in there, he'll be in the back bedroom," First Lieutenant Jake Williams whispered through the airwaves. The kid was still wet behind his West Pointy ears but smart as hell. He knew everything there was to know about their insurgent of the moment, so Mansour would be exactly where Jake said he'd be.

It was up to Adam and Tank to make sure the path to the bad guy wasn't booby-trapped. And Tank, the chillest IED-detecting dog Adam had worked with, wasn't ready to stop searching. Tank raised his head, ears pricked, then sniffed at a shadow. He looked back at Adam as if to ask if he should keep going. Adam nodded, mentally promising Tank half of his own dinner tonight for working overtime on this mission.

"Come on, Sar'nt," Talbott urged.

Adam held up a hand that he hoped the team could see through the dim, dusty twilight, asking for patience. He and Tank had been assigned to this unit for a couple of months now, and the team knew how he worked with his dog, had accepted the pair as one of their own. Some of the younger guys treated Adam like a respected elder, but others, especially Talbott, added Adam to their own special brotherhood, which was probably why the lunkhead was screwing with him now.

"I've got a date with some pictures of your sister," Talbott continued. "So, you know..."

Adam sent another hand signal, one used for offering opinions to bad drivers and other assholes around the world. Tank was tired, damn it. So was he, and in no mood for Talbott's normally tension-defusing banter. Talbott chuckled in Adam's earpiece, about to continue, but then Jake spoke. "There's a light on in the back bedroom now. I can see two people. We need to get moving before they vaporize through a vent." These guys had more escape routes than a meerkat colony. "Can you give us an all clear?"

Adam considered the dog. Tank stared back at him, patient and trusting. He'd done his job, and it was time for Adam to do his part and make the final call.

Once again, Adam raised his hand, this time with the go signal. He clicked his mic and murmured, "Stay on the right." He summoned Tank to his side and waited for the team to silently enter the house and gather behind him. Adam and Tank would take point until they reached the end of the hallway, then Talbott would sweep around and kick in the door.

The door.

Why was there a door? Most of the rooms in these houses had curtains, if anything. It niggled at Adam, but everything made his hair stand on end these days, even someone knocking on the side of the damned latrine. There was a door because the bedroom wasn't really a bedroom. It was a command center for one of the biggest scumbags in the Middle East.

Talbott, no longer joking, jaw set, moved silently toward Adam and Tank. He was followed by Emilio Garcia, Max Zimmerman, and finally Jake, the young lieutenant.

The operation began like clockwork. The soldiers moved past each other in near-perfect silence, the only noise the sound of their own adrenaline-amplified heartbeats.

And then it all went to hell.

Later—days later—when the brass debriefed him, Adam said Tank suddenly started to freak out, barking and fighting the leash, and tried to run to the front of the line of soldiers. The dog knocked Talbott against a shelf on the wall. If that was what triggered the bomb or if it was the men in the room beyond, no one would ever know. The ensuing explosion blew every damned one of them into the street, and not a single man could remember exactly what happened.

Not Adam or Max Zimmerman, who each had a mild concussion and a few bumps and bruises. Not Marcus Talbott, with a cracked pelvis, knee, vertebra—if it was bone, Talbott's was broken. Not Jake Williams, who was in an induced coma following surgery to relieve pressure in his brain. And not Emilio Garcia, because he was on life support in Germany.

Why hadn't the dog alerted to the danger? Tank wasn't talking. He was lying under four feet of desert sand, his collar hanging from a post.

Chapter 1

Present day, just past the middle of nowhere, Texas

HOUSTON WAS THREE HOURS AND A COUPLE OF BROKEN dreams behind her when Lizzie Vanhook crossed the Chance County line, right about the same time the Check Tire Pressure light in her dashboard blinked on.

Crap. She'd been in the homestretch. There was something symbolic about an uninterrupted beeline home, to the place she planned to find her center of gravity. Maybe start doing yoga. Eat all organic. Drink herbal tea and learn to play the pan flute.

"Get over yourself," she said to the boxes and suitcases in the back end of the SUV. She'd do that getting over herself thing just as soon as she checked this tire at the truck stop.

Flipping the turn signal, she pulled into Big America Fuel and stopped near the sign for *Free Air*. She stepped out onto the cracked gray asphalt and bent to search for the pressure gauge her dad always insisted she keep in the pocket of the door but came up empty.

It's here somewhere. Lizzie would admit to giving a major eye roll for each Dad-and-the-art-of-vehicle-maintenance lesson her father had put her through, but she was secretly grateful. She was surprised Dad hadn't sent her text updates about the traffic report in Houston before she left this morning. There wasn't much going on in Big Chance, so he watched Lizzie's news on the internet and always called to warn her of congestion on the way to work. Her throat tightened when she acknowledged the reason he hadn't sent her a text today was because he was at the clinic in Fredericksburg getting his treatment. He and Mom might claim this prostate cancer was "just a little inconvenience," but Lizzie was glad she'd be home to confirm he was as fabulous as he claimed to be.

She abandoned the driver's side and went to the passenger door, hesitating when she noticed the dog leaning against the nearby air pump. The *big* dog. It was missing some significant patches of hair, and the rest was black and matted. Its *big*, shiny teeth were bared in what she hoped was a friendly smile. Its football-player-forearm-sized tail thumped the ground, raising a cloud of sunbaked, Central Texas dust. Lizzie sneezed. The dog stopped wagging and raised an ear in her direction.

"Good boy," she told it, hoping that was the right thing to say. It was one thing to misunderstand the intentions of a tiny fuzzball of a dog and need a few stitches. Ignoring a warning from something this size could be lethal. It had to weigh at least a hundred pounds.

She kept the beast in her peripheral vision while she bent to search for the tire gauge. *Ah ha!*

"Y'all need some help?"

"No!" Lizzie straightened and turned, the pressure gauge clenched in her raised fist.

"Whoa there!" A sun-bronzed elderly man, about half Lizzie's size, held his hands in front of him in a gesture of peace.

"I'm sorry," she said, relaxing slightly. "The dog—" She gestured, but the thing was gone.

"Didn't mean to scare you, darlin'," the old man said, tilting his *Big America* ball cap back. "We're a little slow today, so I thought I'd check on you." He indicated the vacant parking lot.

"It's fine," she said. She should remember she was back on her own turf, where it was way more likely that a stranger at a gas station really *did* want to help you out rather than distract you and rob you blind. "It's been a long drive, and I'm a little overcaffeinated."

"No problem. You local?"

"Yes," Lizzie said. Even though she'd been gone for years, it was about to be true again.

The attendant squinted at the tool she carried. "You got a leaky tire?"

"I don't know." She stooped to unscrew the cap of the first valve. "The little light went on while I was driving." *Nope.* That one wasn't low. She put the cap back on and continued her way around the car while her new friend followed, chatting about Big Chance. He wondered about the likelihood the Chance County High School quarterback would get a scholarship offer. Lizzie had no idea; she hadn't been keeping up. He speculated on the probability that the Feed and Seed might close, now that there was a new Home Depot over in Fredericksburg. She expected she'd hear about it from her mom and dad if the local place was closing and wondered if her friend Emma still worked there.

It had been ages since Lizzie had spoken to Emma, and a wave of guilt washed over her. After swearing to always be BFF's, Lizzie left for Texas A&M and only looked back on

Christmas and Easter. She'd gone to Austin for Emma and Todd's last-minute before-he-deployed wedding but hadn't been able to come home for Todd's funeral.

Finally, the last valve was checked, and she screwed the cap back on. She reached through the open window and dropped the tire gauge on the passenger seat while she said "Everybody's full. Must be a false alarm." She wrinkled her nose as she caught a whiff of the interior of her car. *Sheesh.* The service station probably sold air fresheners; maybe she should invest in one. Compared to the breezy, wide open spaces of home, her car smelled like an inside-out dead deer. She wanted to get home, though, so she decided to deal with it later.

"Well, everything's got enough air," she told the attendant. "I don't know why the light went on."

"Those sensors are a waste of time, if you ask me. You don't have nitrogen in there, like those fancy places put in, do you?" he asked, then launched into a diatribe about modern technology.

One of the things she'd not missed about Chance County was the tendency of the residents to ramble as long as possible when given the opportunity. "Well, thanks again," she told the man. "I've got to run."

It wasn't until she was backing out onto the main road that she realized the awful smell inside her vehicle wasn't just long-drive funk. There was something—something big and black and furry—sitting in the middle of her back seat, panting and grinning in her rearview mirror.

"Ack!" She hit the brakes, then jammed her SUV into forward and pulled into the parking lot again. She opened the door to jump out, barely remembering to put the SUV into park before it dragged her under. She finally whipped open the back door and glared at the scruffy passenger. "Out. You. Out."

She looked around frantically for the old man who'd been chatting her up, but he was nowhere to be seen.

The dog panted and tilted its head at her.

"Out. I mean it."

It wasn't wearing a collar, not that she'd reach in to grab him anyway, in case he mistook her hand for a Milk-Bone.

"Come on, puppy. Seriously. Get out."

The dog sighed and lay down, taking up every inch of her back seat.

She was afraid to leave the thing alone in her car, so she pulled her phone from her pocket and stood next to the back end. She Googled the number for the Big America station and waited for the call to connect.

"Y'ello," said the gravelly voice she'd been chatting with a moment ago.

"Sir, this is Lizzie Vanhook. From the air pump just now."

"Sure, darlin'. What can I do you for?"

"I'm right outside."

"I see ya."

She looked up, and sure enough, he was waving to her through the glass.

"There's a big dog in the back of my car."

"Oh, yeah," the man said. "He showed up here a week or so ago. Kind of invaded, so we've been calling him D-Day. Real sweet little guy."

She eyed the sweet *little* guy. *Uh-huh.* "Could you come help me get him out of my car?"

Laughter. "I don't think you can get that boy to do anything he don't want to do."

"But he's in my car."

A sigh. "Well, I've been threatening to call the animal control officer for a few days now, but I kept hoping his family would come looking for him."

"Don't you think the shelter would be the first place they'd go?"

With a snort, the man said, "There's only room for a coupla dogs over there. Don't even take cats. They'd probably have to fast-track that one to the gas chamber, seein' as how he's so big and would eat a month's worth of food at one meal. Besides, he's ugly as sin, with all them bald spots."

Right on cue, D-Day sat up and stuck his nose through the open window, giving Lizzie's arm a nudge and turning liquid coal eyes up to gaze at her. Reluctantly, she stroked his surprisingly silky head. And then she gave his ears a scratch. *So soft.*

D-Day licked Lizzie's hand. What the heck was she going to do with this guy? Mom and Dad weren't too crazy about dogs. Lizzie loved dogs, but Dean, her loser ex, had been unwilling to get a dog of their own. As a matter of fact, one of their biggest fights was the weekend she'd volunteered to babysit a friend's perfectly mannered labradoodle. Then, when Lizzie called her mom for support, she'd gotten an "I don't blame him. Dogs are a pain in the neck."

"I can't take this dog with me." Lizzie sounded defeated even to her own ears, which contradicted her plans for an optimistic return to Big Chance and a fresh start.

The attendant said, "I'll give the shelter a call. Shame, though. I think he's still a pup."

Those big black eyes stared up at her. D-Day needed a fresh start, too.

Lizzie decided that Mom would tolerate a canine house guest if Lizzie promised he was moving on. "Never mind," she said. "Thanks anyway."

Who did she still know in town who might take a dog? The Collins family came to mind right off the bat. Adam Collins specifically. *Oh no.* She wasn't going to start thinking about him, now that she was moving home. Not. At. All. And really, she wouldn't be running into him. It had been years since he'd joined the army, and his main goal in life, other than becoming a military policeman so he could work with dogs, had been to get—and stay—as far from Big Chance as possible.

She got back in the car, rolled down all the windows, and turned the fan to full blast.

"Listen," she told the dog, who leaned over the seat and licked her ear. "I'll bring you with me. But we're stopping to get you a bath at the car wash on the way through town right before we go to the vet. Then I'll find you a new home as soon as possible."

The dog barked.

"No. No dogs for Lizzie. I mean it."

"Beer, bologna, and white bread. That's all you're gettin'?" The middle-aged grocery clerk—her name tag said *Juanita*—glared at Adam as though he'd personally offended her. "How's a big boy like you gonna survive on that?"

Adam fought the urge to wipe away the cold sweat that

had broken out along his hairline in spite of the frigid air-conditioning inside the Big Chance Shop-n-Save. He'd about reached his out-in-public time limit. *Don't snap her head off. Just smile politely.* She was simply being friendly, in that judge-everything way people had in Big Chance. "Well, ma'am," he found himself explaining, "it's just me, and…"

"Hmmph." She crossed her ample arms instead of scanning his food items.

Come on, he silently begged. *You don't really want to see me go into full frontal meltdown, do you?* He looked around for a self-checkout, but the store apparently hadn't been upgraded since he'd left for the army, and it was old then.

The clerk—Juanita—peered at him now, eyes squinched up to inspect him. "You're that Collins boy, aren't you?"

I used to be. "Yes, ma'am," he said.

"I heard you was back. Holed up out there like some kinda hermit on your granddad's ranch. You know he used to come in here and talk about you like you was the second coming of Patton."

He was momentarily stunned that Granddad had spoken of him at all, much less with pride. For Granddad, the greatest praise he'd ever offered Adam was "Well, you didn't fuck that up too much, I guess." Maybe it was just as well that his grandfather had lost most of his grip on reality these days, because he wouldn't even be able to say that much about him anymore.

Adam told Juanita, "Thank you. That's nice to hear."

She shook her head. "So sorry for how he's gotten to be. He was a good man in his day."

Granddad was something, all right. "Yes, ma'am. Thank you."

"Your sister's doing a good job with him, though."

"Yes, she is." Unfortunately for her. The war Emma had fought at home, while Adam was deployed, was as bad as anything he'd suffered overseas, and she wasn't free yet. If only he'd known how bad things were here, he could have... what? Gotten out sooner? Not reenlisted—twice? He didn't know if he could do things differently, because until that last mission, finding IEDs with his dog had been the one thing he was good at.

Now here he was, sweating through his clothes in the grocery store, wanting nothing more than to get back to hiding out in the place he'd avoided for the last twelve years, at least until he could move on again.

Juanita still hadn't scanned his loaf of bread or his lunch meat. Or—*please, God*—the beer. The country music playing on the intercom seemed to get louder, even through the buzzing noise, which Adam knew didn't exist anywhere but in his head. The sound, always present at a low hum when he was in town, intensified. He inhaled on a count of ten and exhaled.

"Sooo..." He waved at the supplies, hoping to get checked out and into his truck before his vision narrowed any further.

"You still in the army?"

"No, ma'am."

"You were in a long time."

"Yes, ma'am." Hell, he'd planned to stay in the military until they pried his dog's leash from his cold, dead hand, but that wasn't how it had worked out.

She nodded. "You need some meat. Homer!" she barked over her shoulder at the elderly man standing a few feet away.

Adam flinched at the volume. Nothing compared to an IED or gunfire but jarring in its own way.

"Yep?" Homer moved a step closer, tilting his head in Juanita's direction.

"Go get some a' them pork chops, and bring me a couple big Idaho bakers. Oh, and a bag of that salad mix!"

Homer nodded and shuffled off.

"Ma'am, I don't need—"

"Yes, you do. You can't keep that fine body strong on nitrates and Wonder Bread."

Adam snorted. He wasn't having any trouble staying in shape out on the ranch. There was enough work to be done that he could sweat from morning until night for a year and not finish all the hammering and scraping and scrubbing.

"Am I right?" She raised her eyebrows. "You need to keep up your strength."

Homer thunked Juanita's order down on the counter.

She pushed the twelve-pack toward Homer and said, "Take this beer back to the cooler and bring me a gallon of that sweet tea."

"Really, I—" Adam reached for his beer, but the old man was already staggering away under its weight.

Juanita shook her finger at him. "No ifs, ands, or buts. You get some good food in you." She stopped then, her eyes wide and sympathetic. "Unless…you don't have anyone to cook it for you, do you?"

He assumed she meant a woman. But instead of mustering some righteous feminist indignation on behalf of his sister and all the women he'd ever met, he just felt tired. It was good that he lived alone—no one besides himself to make miserable. "I do know how to cook, Miss Juanita. I don't do it much, though."

Juanita snorted. "That's ridiculous. What do you eat for breakfast? You're not buying any oatmeal or even Pop-Tarts." She held up a hand. "Don't tell me you eat at that cesspool diner at the truck stop out on 15."

"No, ma'am." He'd tried it once, in the middle of the night, figuring that would be a safe time, fewer people. Something about the vacant, litter-strewn parking lot reminded him a little too much of his time in the desert, though, so he hadn't been back.

"Well, that's good, anyway," Juanita said. "But you better not be going to that superstore over in Fredericksburg, either. They got radiation in their eggs, you know."

"Really?" Adam didn't mind a little radioactivity. It was a failure to find the right balance of desperation and anti-anxiety meds that had him stuck buying food in Big Chance instead of going farther away, where no one knew his name or cared what he bought to eat.

Juanita smiled and slapped the counter. "You know what? You gotta get offa that property. Bein' alone ain't healthy. You come on to town some Saturday night. There's movies in the high school gym, bingo at the Catholic church, and there's gonna be a big shindig on the Fourth of July in the square. There'll be a band and dancing and food trucks and everything. There's all kinds of unmarried women there, just dying for a big strong man to take care of. Some of them girls are divorced, but don't let that stop you from givin' 'em a chance. They probably know how to cook, too."

"I've got a lot of work to do out there at the ranch. It

keeps me pretty busy." And away from town with its memories. Although, if he did wander through the town square
one night, he wouldn't run into anyone he'd thought about
over the long nights in the desert. Last he'd heard, *anyone*
was seriously dating some land developer mogul-type and
living the big life in Houston.

Homer returned with the jug of tea, plunking it on the
counter next to the paper-wrapped bundle from the butcher
and several plastic containers, one containing something
green that he leaned to look at—beans?—and one full of
coleslaw.

Juanita nodded. "That's better."

"Can I keep my bologna and bread?" Adam asked.
Maybe he could get out of here with his bachelorhood
intact if he hurried.

"Fine. But you better not come back in here and buy
more of that crap."

The chances he'd be back soon were getting slimmer by
the minute, and a grab-and-go convenience store diet was
looking better.

He gathered his bags and stepped into the already
oppressive early summer afternoon. His white pickup truck
sat alone in the parking lot, and only a few cars passed by.
Big Chance was still more or less alive—there was someone down near the vet's office—but most people had the
sense to stay in their air-conditioning today. A plastic grocery bag blew from between two buildings and did the
twenty-first century tumbleweed thing down Main Street
toward him. He put out his foot and caught it on the toe of
his boot. He bent over and pulled the plastic free, wadding
it up and shoving it in his pocket while keeping an eye on

the street. A quiet neighborhood wasn't any less likely to wield danger than a busy market place, but it was easier to avoid distractions.

Except for the activity two blocks away, where a woman struggled with what was probably a dog but looked more like an elephant calf. It wasn't stupid, whatever it was, and it barked in protest. *Smelled one veterinarian's office, smelled them all*, it seemed to be saying, and no one ever saw the vet just for the treats and pats on the head. Adam suppressed a pang of longing—dogs had been a big part of his life for as long as he could remember, but the smarter, more experienced part of him was glad he didn't have the responsibility and problems anymore. The woman shook her head at the dog, a move that seemed familiar. He couldn't see her face, but when she tripped over the dog, who had stopped to sit in the middle of the sidewalk, there was something about the way she tossed her hair as she laughed that took him back.

Back to memories of the night before he went to boot camp, when he'd kissed a girl in the dark summer night. Kissed her and touched her and *wanted* her like he'd never known was possible. He'd never had any doubts about joining the military, wasn't afraid of basic training, knew how to handle himself, but that night, holding Lizzie Vanhook in the moonlight, he'd felt a trickle of regret and longing for what he was leaving behind.

A car door slammed nearby, jerking him back to his own space. With a hot prickle of anxiety, Adam shook his head and turned toward his truck. Time to make tracks back to the ranch and get back to work. He'd promised his sister he'd stop and visit Granddad this afternoon, but he'd been in the presence of humanity for long enough.

He glanced back down the street, but the woman with the dog was gone. Just as well. Lizzie would never have settled for the likes of him, and now he was even less respectable than when he'd been the kid with dog crap on his cowboy boots, who thought this little redneck town was the worst place in the world. He'd had no idea how much worse the outside world could get. As of now, Big Chance was just one more reminder that the kid he'd been hadn't turned into the man he'd expected.

Chapter 2

"ELIZABETH MARIE! IF THIS THING ISN'T OUT OF MY house in the next two minutes, I'm going to drag it into the front yard and lasso it to the next car that drives past!"

Uh-oh. Mom sounded a little…shrill. *D-Day, what did you eat now?* It might be time to get him out of the house for a while, take him for a ride. Lizzie wanted to look at some of the properties her dad's real estate agency was listing. Since he didn't seem to have the energy to think about work right now, she wanted to step up and help.

She grabbed her car keys, purse, and the leash. "Come here, D-Day!" She headed toward the dining room, hoping the dog had learned his name since the last time she'd tried it, forty-five minutes ago. "Come on, buddy!"

"Elizabeth…" Mom's voice was lower now, almost calm, which was possibly even worse.

"Coming!" She broke into a jog and skidded around the corner to find the source of the chaos. "Come on, D-Day. Let's go for a ride!"

But D-Day wasn't interested in a ride. He wanted in on Mom's Big Chance Hometown Independence Day planning party, which consisted of seven other local ladies, a pitcher of margaritas, and enough diet-busting food to fill the Astrodome. This last part was clearly what D-Day was most interested in, because he stood perfectly still, his enormous face resting on the edge of the dining room table.

Meanwhile, her mom's friends began to gather around Lizzie.

"Oh, Lizzie, it's so lovely to see you back in Big Chance," one woman said. "I'm so sorry things didn't work out for you in Houston," she added in a stage whisper. "But don't worry. You'll find someone else."

Lizzie smiled as politely as she could, desperate to escape the inquisition. She clipped the leash to D-Day's collar and tugged, but he didn't move.

"It's so nice that you're willing to help out at the agency until you're able to settle down," another woman said.

Until you find a husband to support you, she knew the woman meant. She didn't need to *settle down* for that. "I'm just glad I could be here to help out." Lizzie gritted her teeth. "Come on, D-Day."

He didn't budge. Worse, he'd locked eyes with Ms. Lucy Chance, supreme goddess of the universe herself. The older woman sat frozen, a half-bitten miniature quiche hanging from her creased, orange lips.

Seriously? Could he choose a less appropriate target? Ms. Lucy held most of Big Chance, Texas, in the palm of her hand. She had more dirt on the residents than anyone else in the county. She was also the president of the Third Savings Bank of Big Chance (no one knew if there had ever been a first or second), and Third Savings was the only bank in Big Chance. Ms. Lucy knew who charged porn sites to their credit cards and who bought seventy-five boxes of Thin Mints last year from the local Girl Scouts. As far as Lizzie knew, Ms. Lucy didn't use her power for evil, but the threat was always there, and no one wanted to tip her over the edge.

"What the tarnation *is* that?" the old lady whispered, not looking away from the dog.

"D-Day." The dog ignored Lizzie and licked his chops, sending a string of drool flying over the crystal dish of trail mix.

"Good Lord," Mom swore, swept the bowl out of sight, and grabbed the lemon squares before they got contaminated.

D-Day seemed to grin at Ms. Lucy. The dog, who might be a Great Dane/buffalo mix, weighed more than Lizzie did, and *she* was no delicate flower. If she got into a tug of war with him, she'd lose. "Come on, buddy." She had to get him out of here before something awful happened.

But then Ms. Lucy asked, "Can I pet him?"

"Uh…sure." Lizzie nudged D-Day with her hip, and he obligingly stepped over to the older woman, who reached out to stroke his giant head.

As a side effect, his back end started wiggling with delight. Hoping to avoid a tail-induced accident, Lizzie said, "D-Day, sit." At which point he rose onto his hind legs and planted his front paws on either side of Ms. Lucy's Jackie Kennedy pink skirt.

"D-Day, no!" She pulled back on the leash as hard as she could without strangling him, but he didn't move. "D-Day, down!"

Nothing.

"Come on, D-Day. Let's go, big guy. Seriously." *Crap.* She'd promised herself she'd never beg a man for anything. Did begging a male dog count? "I'm so sorry, Ms. Lucy. I'll save you." Somehow. And then maybe her mother would forgive her for ruining her party, and Lizzie would magically lose thirty pounds *and* win the lottery.

Coiling the rope around her fist, she reached for D-Day's collar, intending to lever his giant body off the woman's lap and wedge herself between them. But before she could get into position, she heard something.

A giggle?

Holy crap.

Ms. Lucy was *laughing* while D-Day licked her. And not just her face. He lapped at her from collarbone to hairline, and Ms. Lucy had her hands in the patchy fur around his neck, hugging him.

Lizzie tried again. "Let's go, D-Day."

"Noooo!" Ms. Lucy begged. "He loves me! He's just a big old wubba dubba boy, isn't he?" she asked, kissing D-Day back. Fortunately, she didn't seem to be using as much tongue as the dog.

While Ms. Lucy made googly eyes at D-Day, Mom took Lizzie's arm and hissed, "You've got to get rid of this dog."

"I'm sorry, Mom. I'm trying to get him to behave. I really am."

"I see that, but it's not working, and he's simply too much for you to handle."

She opened her mouth to argue, but the fact was, Mom was right. But who was going to want to adopt a dog with the body of a *T. rex* and the mindset of a Jack Russell terrier? "I'll figure something out."

"Elizabeth."

What now?

Mom was looking pointedly at D-Day's underside.

"Yeah. Okay." Lizzie prepared to put her weight into moving the dog this time, because she'd seen what Mom was staring at. D-Day was clearly at least as enamored of

Ms. Lucy as she was of him, because he was humping the dickens out of her right leg. "Let's go, dog. I really mean it this time."

With a long, lingering look in Ms. Lucy's direction, D-Day followed Lizzie to her car.

"What do you say, D-Day? Want to go meet a friend of mine?" Lizzie asked when he'd jumped into the back seat.

Mom had said Emma Collins-Stern still worked at the Feed and Seed down on Main Street, and Emma's family had trained police dogs when they were younger. Even though they hadn't seen each other in person for a decade, Lizzie hoped Emma would help her out. Maybe even let D-Day stay at the ranch for a while.

Lizzie drove down her parents' street and turned onto Main, passing the old Dairy Queen, which, along with the Feed and Seed, Todd's parents had owned, back when he was Adam's best friend and not Emma's husband.

And there she went, thinking about Adam again. Her secret fantasy knight in dusty cowboy boots. At least that's how she'd thought of him until she'd thrown herself at him and chased him away. She shuddered, slamming a lid on that embarrassing memory and focusing on the now. Seeing Emma would be fine. Adam was probably still in the army, and if not, he'd have moved as far from Big Chance as possible.

He always swore the last place he'd spend his life was the ranch where he and Emma had grown up after their parents died.

Going to visit Emma would be easy-peasy. No worries.

Lizzie didn't see Emma when she finally wrangled D-Day into the Big Chance Feed and Seed. This may have been because she'd only spoken to her friend a few times on Facebook over the past ten years or so, and Emma didn't post pictures of herself. Heck, her profile picture was her first day of kindergarten.

Also, D-Day, yanking Lizzie six ways to Sunday, had her a little distracted.

She went into the store looking for the quiet, bookish girl with the long black hair, heavy eyeliner, and thick glasses she remembered.

A young woman with a blond buzz cut, countless piercings, and electric blue eyes glanced up from a ledger on the paint counter.

"Is Emma Collins here?" Lizzie asked the punk pixie.

"Maybe."

D-Day chose that moment to spy something at the end of the aisle he needed to investigate at warp speed.

"Damn it, D-Day!" Lizzie yanked the dog's leash, but he didn't stop, dragging her halfway through the store, until the clerk stepped around the counter and said, "Down," in a calm, authoritative voice.

D-Day immediately dropped to his haunches.

"I'm so sorry," Lizzie said. "I'm trying, but I can't control him to save either of our lives."

"I can see that," the other woman said, laughing. She straightened and met Lizzie's eyes. "You're going to have to get a handle on that."

"That's kind of why I'm here." A tingle of recognition swept over her, and Lizzie looked more closely at the girl— woman. "No way. Emma? It's you! It's me. Lizzie."

"I see that, too." Emma grinned and reached over the dog for a clumsy hug. "I'd know you anywhere."

"Really?" Lizzie was surprised. "Sometimes people don't." As Dean had pointed out every chance he got, the years hadn't been kind. Nor had Doritos and M&M's, her comfort foods of choice. Of course, he'd met her after she'd starved herself half to death and was running 10Ks every weekend. The snack foods came back into her life after they'd been dating a while.

"Are you kidding?" Emma laughed. "You're prettier than you were back then, if that's even possible."

Whatever. Lizzie didn't want to get into a reality smack-down in the farm supply store, so she let the over-the-top compliment pass. "So how are you? What are you...up to?" She didn't add, *you know, since your high school sweetheart drove off a bridge?* Or better yet, *How's your jerk-face stud muffin of a brother? The one with the giant chip on his shoulder? And by the way—will you help me train my dog?* Not a good way to resume a friendship.

Emma's smile chased away the flash of darkness that flitted through her eyes, and she spread her arms wide to indicate her surroundings. "Living the dream of single, successful girls everywhere."

"That's, um, that's great." Lizzie glanced around the nearly empty store and wondered how the place managed to stay open. Especially with shrines to a dead soldier hanging from every available bit of wall space. The shelves might be nearly bare, but the walls were covered with photos of the late Todd Stern, mostly either in his football uniform or his army uniform.

"Yeah," Emma said. "I'm really grateful to the Sterns for

this job. After they had to sell the Dairy Queen, I wasn't sure if they'd keep me on here."

After an awkward pause, Lizzie said, "I'm really sorry about Todd. I'd have come back for the memorial service, but I was out of town when I heard."

"Thank you. And you sent flowers. That was nice. It's been hard, but I've been keeping busy. It really is okay." And the way Emma said it let Lizzie know that while she would probably never be over Todd's death, she was getting by and didn't want to talk about it right now. "What's going on with you? Last time I saw a Facebook update, you and Dean were just getting back from a Caribbean cruise."

"Oh." Lizzie's shoulders slumped. "Yeah. That was pretty much the last time I had anything positive to say on social media. Dean...moved on to 'other opportunities.'" *Found a thinner, prettier girlfriend.* "And I've moved home." *Given up, tucked my tail, and skedaddled.*

"Is that a good thing?"

Lizzie gave a quarter of a second's thought to how much Dean had hurt her and another quarter to how much more peaceful she'd felt after deciding to come back to Big Chance and said, "Yeah. It is. There's nothing for me in Houston, and my dad needs help here. It seemed like a good time for a fresh start." And maybe she'd be better at life here than she'd been there.

Emma's musical laugh contrasted with her hard-ass look. "There's *nothing* fresh in Big Chance." She sobered slightly. "I heard about your dad. Prostate cancer? That sucks."

"Yeah, thanks. His prognosis is good, but"—*he seems to have lost his will to live*—"he's got a long road ahead of him."

Emma started to speak, stopped, then said, "I was going

to offer some sort of 'Gee, this might be a good time for him to retire while you sashay to the helm of the family business' optimism, but the market here doesn't exactly support a lavish lifestyle."

Lizzie shrugged. "I don't care about lavish. The Lifestyles of the Rich and Feckless demographic I worked with in Houston wasn't exactly where I fit anyway." *To put it mildly.* She needed to change the subject, so she asked, "How's your grandpa? Does he still have the ranch?"

A shadow crossed Emma's features, and Lizzie regretted the question. Before she could apologize, Emma said, "No. Granddad and I are living in the little house in back of the store." She pointed toward the rear exit. "He's got dementia, and the ranch got to be…not safe. So we're here in town, and Adam's staying out there."

Adam.

Lizzie had been carefully not thinking about him for at least ten minutes, and she'd never thought he'd be living in Big Chance again. What was he like now? Her teenage dreamboat, becoming a studly soldier turned—what? "Is he, uh, still in the army?"

Emma blew out a frustrated breath. "No, he got out a few months ago. He's been living alone on the ranch, hiding from the universe, I think."

"That's too bad." Though maybe he'd taken off his camouflage and put his Wranglers back on. She suppressed the shiver that ran through her at the thought of seeing him in either. Or nothing.

The conversation lulled, and D-Day saw a new opportunity to escape. Lizzie dropped her purse to grab his leash with both hands while her belongings scattered across the floor.

"Here," Emma said. "Let me take him while you gather your stuff."

"Can you take him until, I don't know, until he's a good dog? I could use some help."

Emma looked like she was going to laugh off Lizzie's request, then realized she was serious.

"I wish I could. But Granddad takes up all of my spare time. We haven't had dogs since, well, since before Todd died."

"I'm sorry."

"Yeah. Me too," Emma said, squatting down to rub D-Day's ears. "Sometimes I miss working with them. It's so...straightforward, I guess. In the moment. You can't worry about other stuff when you're focusing on a dog and he's focusing on you."

Lizzie didn't know what to say, not sure if Emma was referring to the tragedy of watching the man who'd raised her disappear before her eyes or if she was talking about Todd, or both. And of course, Emma also worried about Adam. She'd mentioned he'd retreated into himself out at the ranch. He'd been to war, and that must have messed him up plenty. Lizzie thought of the earnest country boy he'd been in high school and wondered if he'd lost his optimism.

She tried to push Adam's memory away. That was a long time ago. She might remember the way she'd made a fool of herself over him, but he'd no doubt forgotten her existence. Instead, she said, "Do you have any suggestions about what I should do with D-Day? Mom's already threatened to sell him to a glue factory if I don't keep him in his crate all the time."

Emma raised an eyebrow.

"Well, she'll call animal control, anyway."

"Oh, you can't do that!" Emma looked at her like she was about to drop her grandmother off at Walmart and not come back. "I mean, I'm all for crate training a dog, but not if he's never going to get out and have a life."

"I know. And I'm determined to make sure he has a life. I really didn't want to keep him, but I can't find a shelter within a hundred miles that has room and won't promise not to kill him."

"How long have you had him?"

"I found him a few days ago. Or rather, he found me. I stopped to check my tires, and he climbed in the car and wouldn't get out. The clerk said he'd been hanging around for a couple of weeks. He's not a bad guy," Lizzie told her. Honestly, the ugly beast had started to grow on her. "But I'm staying at my parents' house right now, and they aren't fans of big dogs." *To say the least.* "Aaaand he eats everything in sight. Like furniture. And car parts."

"You do need help," Emma told her.

"Yes. I do." It had been foolish to take on the responsibility for a dog when she'd soon be so busy helping her parents, but what was she supposed to do? Leave him on the side of the road to starve or get hit by a semi?

The doors of the store slid open as someone walked by and triggered the mechanism. A white pickup truck passed, and Emma narrowed her eyes in its direction. "I have an idea."

"Yeah?"

"Yeah." She looked at her watch. "I get off work in ten minutes. Our neighbor Mrs. King stays with Granddad while I'm at work, and she's usually willing to stay a little longer. Do you have the next hour or so free?"

Lizzie was afraid to hope and afraid that Emma's idea was going to make her—and a certain army veteran—very uncomfortable.

Chapter 3

ADAM DID *NOT* SHRIEK LIKE A LITTLE KID WHEN THE trickle of lukewarm water flowing over his head and shoulders turned arctic. He uttered a few high-pitched yet completely manly curses and rinsed off as much soap as he could before his balls completely retreated inside his body. He reminded himself to be glad that Emma and Granddad were living in town in relative comfort while he tried to add sweat equity to a worthless, run-down ranch and appreciated the solitude.

So when he turned off the water and stepped out of the chipped, claw-footed tub, he was surprised to hear a feminine voice from somewhere outside.

"Sit," he heard his sister say, followed by a bark in response.

Oh hell no.

He should have known she'd show up here, since he hadn't stopped at the farm store while he was in town, but bringing a dog here to torment him was just twisted. He looked around for a pair of clean gym shorts with no luck. *Eh.* It was only his sister. Pants were overrated anyway.

Wrapping a towel around his hips, he padded down the steps, dripping water on the warped pine floors the entire way. They'd get refinished eventually, just as soon as he fixed the roof on this old house, painted it, cleaned up the yard...

He was about to open the front door when he heard another female voice outside. Emma wasn't alone.

Ditching the towel, he found a pair of sweatpants in the pile of clean laundry on the couch and shoved his legs in but gave up trying to tighten the knotted drawstring. They hung low around his hips, but since nothing crucial was exposed, they'd have to do.

This wasn't a good time for company. He glanced around the inside of the house at peeling paint and grime-encrusted windows. The view outside wasn't much better, though. Invisible from the road, the dilapidated house faced north toward an ancient barn filled with deserted kennels. The neutral territory between was a quarter of an acre of lawn, er, *weeds*. Rounding out the areas that needed to be cleaned up were a horse shed and paddock that had never, at least not in Adam's time, held a horse.

A loud *bang* was followed by two softer knocks. "Adam! Are you here?"

"Yeah." He was going to let Emma have it for not calling before she visited. He threw open the door and stepped onto the porch. "Dammit, Emma, I thought I told you—"

Emma's presence was a dim shadow in his peripheral vision as Adam stared into the familiar liquid-brown eyes of his dirtiest midnight fantasies.

Lizzie Vanhook. It *had* been her on the street the other day.

He should say something, like *hello*, but a black blur bolting into view caught his attention. Before he could react and get the women to cover or even warn them, he was slammed sideways and tackled to the porch floor.

Deeply familiar impulses prepared him to neutralize the threat.

"D-Day, no!" Lizzie yelled, and her husky voice cut through Adam's narrowed focus. *Dog.* It was a dog. Straddling Adam's legs and playing tug-of-war with the drawstring of his sweats. Another, older instinct arose from Adam's addled brain, and he gave the command before he even realized he'd opened his mouth.

"*Down.*"

The dog dropped to its belly, right on top of Adam.

"Omigod, I'm so sorry." Lizzie knelt next to Adam, tugging ineffectually at the dog's collar. "Come on, D-Day. Get up. Come on."

Her hair was shorter and streakier than he remembered. She was definitely more grown up, in a very good way. She was a prettier, curvier version of the girl he'd tried to leave behind, and every bit as tempting. But she smelled as sweet as she had the last time he'd seen her.

She noticed his examination, and her expression shuttered.

Turning to Emma, she said, "I don't know if this is such a good idea."

So she was still pissed about the way he'd run off from her the night before he left town.

If only she knew how much more painful that had been for him. Surely, she—what was she doing here anyway?

"Li—" He cleared his throat, masking his uncertainty by shoving the dog off and getting to his feet. "Lizzie."

If she was surprised at his chilly reception, she didn't show it as she rose and moved back a step. "Hi, Adam." Her voice was a little lower, richer, than it used to be. She gave him a quick up and down look, masking her expression, but he felt the judgment anyway. "How are you?"

Lizzie was here. With his sister. And a dog. Which remained in the down position but managed to army crawl right against Adam's leg. He fought the urge to shove the thing away.

Lizzie had retreated to the edge of the porch, arms crossed over her middle, looking like she'd rather be anywhere but where she was. At least she'd gained some self-preservation since he'd last seen her.

"What are you doing here?" He finally pulled his brain together enough to ask. "What's going on?"

"We need your help," Emma said, seemingly oblivious to the fact that he and Lizzie were both uncomfortable.

"What? No." He shook his head but had to ask, "What kind of help?"

"We need you to be a foster parent," Emma told him. "You're out here alone all the time, and it's not good for you. You need company."

He deliberately didn't look at the dog, but a chill ran up his spine anyway. "I don't need company," Adam protested. "It's really good for me to be alone out here."

"No. It's not. You need a companion, and we happen to have one for you."

Nope. No way. He stared at the beast grinning up at him, enormous pink tongue dangling. Adam looked away.

The dog sat up and shoved its head into Adam's crotch. *Pet me.*

Adam stepped back. The dog got to its feet and followed.

"What *is* that thing?"

"That's D-Day," Lizzie said, a note of defensiveness in her tone.

"But what is it?"

"Well, the vet thinks one of his parents was a Rottweiler," Lizzie said.

"And the other was, what, a mastodon?" The dog responded to that remark with an enthusiastic bark and another crotch nudge. Adam shoved its head away.

"D-Day, come here," Lizzie pleaded with the dog, tugging ineffectually at its lead.

For crying out loud. She was beautiful but clueless when it came to dogs.

Before he could stop himself, he took the leash and reminded the dog to sit. It sat. Adam and the dog both worked on instinct—he to lead, the dog to obey the alpha—but he'd sworn off this job. To distract himself from his own contradictory behavior, he asked Lizzie, "What's wrong with its hair? Why is it half bald?" The thing had huge bare spots.

"The vet thinks he had mange, and someone tried to treat it with a home remedy that killed the parasite but also killed the hair."

Adam's gut roiled at the thought of some of the things he'd heard of people doing to their pets, through ignorance, cruelty, or neglect. Nothing like the dogs he'd worked with in the army. Those damned things were treated better than most Thoroughbred racehorses. At least until their handlers got them killed.

The dog nudged his leg, big black eyes rolled up in supplication.

"Down," he commanded, and the dog flopped to the porch floor, staring at him with a vague semblance of adoration.

"See? He does all that stuff for everyone but me," Lizzie huffed, hands on hips. "This is why we need your help."

And yeah, he noticed when she stomped her foot and produced a nice jiggle.

From the corner of his eye, he caught his sister's smirk. He glared at her.

"Here's the deal," Emma said. "Lizzie can't keep him at her parents' house because he's a little more dog than they can handle."

Lizzie shrugged. "We don't have a fence, and he's still mostly puppy. He needs somewhere he can get some exercise. I can't keep him."

"Take it to a shelter," Adam told her.

"Not an option," Lizzie said, shaking her head.

"He'd be killed before we got out of the parking lot," Emma added. "Neither the county nor the city has the funding to run a no-kill shelter."

A memory came to him then, of Lizzie marching through the halls of Big Chance County High School, carrying a clipboard to collect signatures for some cause or other. "Why don't you work your student council magic and get a new one built?"

She lowered her chin and scowled at him from under her eyebrows. "Even if I had that kind of pull, it's not going to solve my problem today."

"I can't help you." He wouldn't back down, either.

"I'm going to find him a new home. I'll post something online tonight, but could he possibly stay with you for a while?" Lizzie asked. "I'll come out and take care of him as much as I can, and maybe…" She bit her lip. "Maybe you could teach him some basic obedience? That would sure make it easier to find someone to adopt him."

"I don't think so," Adam told her, trying hard to ignore

the fact that the woman whose memory had warmed many cold desert nights was standing inches away, more enticing than she had been in his exceptionally vivid dreams, and volunteering to visit him—well, visit his property—on a regular basis.

She sighed—a tad too dramatically—and said, "If you won't keep him, I'm going to *have* to take him to the shelter. My mother threatened to poison him if he chewed up anything else in the house. And then when he tried to get romantic with Ms. Lucy's leg in the middle of Mom's Fourth of July party planning meeting, the camel's back broke."

Adam caught himself before he actually smiled. He remembered Lizzie's mother with her perfectly arranged blond hair and always tidy PTA president appearance, giving him a polite but cold smile when he picked up his sister at their house. And Lucy Chance. That sourpuss had been old as dirt when he'd left town. How could she possibly still be alive?

"I'll pay for his kibble and clean up after him," she assured him. "Whatever you want."

He raised an eyebrow, and her lips parted—to offer what?—but she closed her mouth, much to his disappointment. Not that he'd take her up on anything—hadn't Emma said she was engaged or something?—but the recluse gig was boring sometimes. He could use some new fantasy material.

Both women tilted their heads, and he could practically hear the "Pretty please with sugar on top?" that Emma had always tried to use on him as a kid. And then, Lizzie and those open, trusting eyes transported him back to the swing in her side yard all those years ago, looking down at the girl who was way too good for him, begging him to spend the last few hours before he left town with her. But this time, she was asking him to take care of her dog, and he was the last soul on earth she should want to get care from.

Damn it. Emma knew why he didn't want a dog, and she was being manipulative. Well, he wouldn't be yanked around like that.

"I'm really involved with getting this place back in shape," he pointed out. Knowing he should have stopped with *no*, he went on, "There's no way I can give a dog the attention it needs and do all this work." He gestured at the disaster around them.

Sensing weakness, Emma came in for the kill. "Lizzie already said she'd come out to feed and walk him. She just needs somewhere to keep him until he's got a new home."

"I'd really appreciate it," Lizzie said with her refined twang. "I felt so sorry for the poor guy, starvin' to death there on the side of the highway, and—" She cut herself off. "Anyway, I really would appreciate it. I'll make sure he's no bother. If it gets too bad, I'll…I'll call animal control myself."

Lizzie's eyes echoed her experience with disappointments, and he hated that at least one of them was his own fault, but like that long-ago summer night, he knew he had her best interests at heart. He had no business working with dogs, and seeing her here every day, knowing he couldn't take another taste of those long-ago kisses, would be torture.

If he'd ever had the upper hand in this situation, he'd lost it when he'd given that dog its first command, but he wouldn't surrender easily.

"I can't train it."

But once again, Emma had an answer. "What if Lizzie

trains him, and you just tell her how? That shouldn't take you away from your incredible *Rehab Addict* activities." She glanced around the property with a critical eye for his lack of progress.

"I can do that," Lizzie said, a little too quickly. "I'm working for my dad, but I've got a really flexible schedule."

He exhaled and looked around at the ranch. His sanctuary. Could he deal with Lizzie and her peppy energy out here all the time?

He'd hurt her feelings back when they were younger. Turning away from her had been the right thing to do at the time.

But that was then. Now she just wanted him to teach her to train her dog.

"I bet Granddad would come out here and teach her," Emma threatened.

He shot her a glare. Granddad *would* come here and criticize and find fault before wandering into the bushes, looking for the refrigerator. There was a reason Adam suffered through visits in town, a reason that included keeping Granddad the hell away from the ranch.

Emma's mouth tipped up in a smile. She had him.

Fine. "Nothing fancy. You learn 'sit,' 'stay,' 'come,' and 'don't eat shit you're not supposed to.'"

"Oh, thank you," Lizzie breathed, and he felt a little rush of…something. Something light and unfamiliar.

"Seven tomorrow morning. I spent ten years getting out of bed before dawn to take care of dogs. *I'm* not doing that again."

"I'll be here at six thirty."

"You can feed the dog and get it out of the kennel when

you get here." He pointed at the barn where Granddad had built a series of indoor-outdoor enclosures. "Put the food on the porch for now. I'll find something raccoon-proof before I go to bed."

"Okay."

The stupid dog rested its head on his foot.

Damn it. *No.* He wasn't going to like the damned thing. He was only keeping it from the pound.

As he stood on the porch, holding the leash and watching his sister and the girl he couldn't forget drive away, he tried not to notice that he hadn't had anything close to a panic attack the whole time he'd been talking to Lizzie. As a matter of fact, the anxiety that had tried to take him down when he first saw the dog had left before it got a toehold.

"That was…interesting." It was all Lizzie could think of to say when she and Emma were in the car and on the road back to civilization.

"I thought it went pretty well," Emma told her.

"You did?" Lizzie thought Adam seemed about as happy to see her as he'd be to see the IRS.

"Considering what a grump he can be, he was practically like that teapot lady from *Beauty and the Beast.*"

The round little teapot lady was hardly who Lizzie thought of in reference to Adam. It was hard to believe, but Adam—who had been cowboy sexy in high school with his rare but wicked smiles and hooded gaze—had become a mash-up of the Incredible Hulk, Captain America, and the *Men's Fitness* Cover Guy of the Year.

He'd traded that slouchy cowboy thing he'd had going on for military straight, badass, and simmering danger. His short, dark-brown hair made her fingers itch with the need to touch. But he'd nailed Lizzie with a narrow blue-eyed stare that confused her because it held both hunger and rejection.

Well, she'd been there, done that, and was home in Big Chance for a new start, not a rerun. She was no longer a simpering teenager with a huge crush on her best friend's older brother; she was a professional woman with ambitions and self-respect. She'd spend time around him working with the dog, but she didn't have to let him twist her in knots.

"Seriously," Emma continued, "he's in better shape than a lot of guys who deployed." She hesitated, a faraway sadness making a brief appearance before she refocused on the road. Lizzie suspected she was thinking of her late husband. "War messes people up." Emma waved her hand as though to brush the statement away.

"That really sucks." Lizzie didn't know what else to say. She'd read enough to know that PTSD, if that was Adam's issue, affected everyone differently. "Is he getting help?"

Emma gave a short laugh. "If he was, he wouldn't tell me about it. He won't admit there's anything wrong, even though he can't be in town for longer than ten minutes without sweating through his clothes. He almost never leaves the ranch. And did you see the bags under his eyes? I don't think he sleeps, either." There went that dismissive hand wave again. "I'm probably just hypersensitive."

"Because of Todd?"

Emma nodded. "He shouldn't have enlisted at all, but his daddy and granddad both served in the army, and he idolized Adam. Then I...I told him I thought he should do it. It wasn't a good thing. He came back all kinds of messed up, but I didn't realize how bad it was until it was too late. I should have stopped him."

"It's not your fault."

Emma shook her head and ran a finger under a very shiny eye to keep her mascara from running but then jerked that hand back to the steering wheel. "Oh shit!" An old white pickup shot out of a gravel cross street and swung right in front of their car. With a squeal of brakes, Emma yanked the wheel and honked the horn. The truck sped away, leaving them stopped in the middle of the road in a cloud of dust.

Panting, Emma gripped the steering wheel, staring after the disappearing vehicle. "You okay?"

"I think so." Lizzie's heartbeat said otherwise.

Emma took a deep breath as she released the brakes and cautiously accelerated.

"I guess I forgot how everyone drives out in the country."

Emma harrumphed. "They're not usually crazy like that, not coming out of Mill Creek Road. It's too torn up and full of potholes."

"Is that old farm that Mitch Babcock's family owned still out here? Back in the day, no one lived there, but it had a creek and a couple of big fields. I mean...of course the land is still there, unless it got sucked into another dimension."

"Well, I'm pretty sure the land didn't get hoovered up by aliens. The property still runs up against the back of our ranch. But something happened to the Babcocks a year or so after we graduated. Someone put a No Trespassing sign at the farm, and the next day, the Babcocks' house in town went up for sale."

"No kidding." Lizzie hadn't heard any of this from her parents. "Do you know why?"

Emma shrugged. "Someone said Mitch's dad got caught embezzling money and they had to sell all their stuff before they left town."

"Huh." Lizzie looked back over her shoulder, where the turnoff disappeared into the dust. "Remember how, in high school, kids went out there to...do things?"

"Things?" Emma shot Lizzie a sideways glance.

"Well, I never did," she said primly. She would have. Especially if she'd been able to convince a certain Adam Collins to take her out there with him, but she'd never gotten an opportunity. He wasn't exactly friends with Mitch, though, so he probably wouldn't have taken her if he'd wanted to.

Emma laughed. "Todd and I may have gone a couple of times, but I don't think anyone goes out there now. At least not like we did in high school."

"What, kids don't sneak out to party anymore?"

"Ha. I don't think they sneak, and I don't think they go out. They just do stupid stuff at home."

"Lazy bums."

"Right?" Emma grinned.

"When I was little, my dad used to drive by there and tell me all about how my great-something or other grandfather discovered gold in that creek. I don't think anyone lived there even then. Obviously, *someone's* still going out there. I wonder who owns it now?" An idea began to take shape in Lizzie's mind, and she reached for her bag. Earlier this morning, her father had given her a few folders from the real estate office of properties he wanted her to look into. She'd only glanced at them before shoving them in her bag—she'd been distracted by a certain large dog. But now, she remembered seeing something about a property out here. She flipped through the top folder until she landed on a sticky note that said *Make sell sheet for 9873 Wild Wager Road.* "Oh." Now she recognized the address.

"What's wrong?"

9873 Wild Wager was where she and Emma had just seen Adam. Why wouldn't Emma have mentioned a plan to sell the ranch? Would Adam sell it without talking to his sister about it? *Could* he? "Uh, nothing," she finally said, flipping through some more pages. "Just something I forgot to ask Dad about earlier."

Lizzie changed the subject then, asking about the Chance cousins, because she'd heard that Joe Chance, who had been their class president, was now the mayor.

While Emma filled her in on years of gossip, Lizzie closed the folder. She'd find out who was officially listing the property and why Emma didn't seem to know anything about it.

Chapter 4

"I'M SO GLAD YOU LISTENED TO REASON AND GOT RID OF that horrible dog," Mom said as she dumped artificial sweetener into her coffee. "You're going to be so much happier without that responsibility. Now you can focus on living up to your potential."

"No pressure," Lizzie muttered.

"What?" Mom asked.

"Nothing. I'm just glad to be home," she said more loudly and hugged her mom.

"I'm glad you're here, too."

They did seem to appreciate her help, and that made Lizzie feel good. She looked forward to making them both proud of her. Nothing to distract her except the small matter of a large dog who'd cried as she'd driven away from him yesterday and the cranky cowboy holding his leash.

"Is Dad up yet?" she asked. "I wanted to go over some of these notes with him."

"Here I am." Dad shuffled into the kitchen in his ancient terry cloth robe, the one Lizzie had bought him at least fifteen Christmases ago. It seemed bigger than it used to.

He leaned over Lizzie's shoulder to peer at the open folder, then turned to pour himself a cup of coffee. "That's the old Collins place. What about it?"

"Put that down." Mom opened the refrigerator, took out a bottle of water, and placed it in front of Dad, taking his coffee. "You know you can't drink coffee on treatment days. It'll make you sicker than a flea after getting dipped."

"I'll get sick anyway," he groused, then asked Lizzie, "Why are you looking at that?"

"I'm going out there this morning, and I wanted to know who called you about listing it."

"Why do you have to go there?" he asked.

"Adam Collins is keeping D-Day for now."

Mom harrumphed but didn't comment.

"Since I'll see Adam, I thought I'd find out what price he hopes to get." And why it was being sold, not that it was any of her business.

"Too bad that stream from the Mill Creek farm doesn't run through the Collins place," Dad commented. "That would make it a lot more valuable."

"For cattle?" Lizzie asked. "I know there are about fifty acres, but I'm not sure much of that's good for grazing, if you're thinking someone might want to lease it."

"Exactly," Dad said. "The creek is unreliable anyway, which is why my great-grandfather gave up his gold claim upstream and moved to town, back in the day."

"That, and there wasn't any gold," Mom added.

Lizzie thought again of the discussion she'd had yesterday with Emma, when that truck had come out of Mill Creek Road. Was the creek still running there, even occasionally? Was it still a place kids might like to swim and catch tadpoles? She shoved the idea flickering in the back of her mind deeper for the moment. There was an inaugural dog training session to get through first.

"I guess I should take a look around so I can make suggestions about what work needs to be done out on the

Collins place before it's listed." Dad didn't sound too enthusiastic, but Lizzie took hope from the fact that he was at least still acknowledging he had a business to run.

"I'll take lots of pictures," Lizzie assured him.

He opened his mouth to protest, but Mom shoved a piece of toast in with a wink at Lizzie.

"I tell you what, Dad. I'll take notes and photos of everything I think you should see and even stuff I think you don't, and then if you feel better, you can go out with me later in the week."

"We'll see." He shrugged. "Depends on how much life this treatment sucks out of me."

As fear bloomed in her chest, she forced herself to hold her smile. "Great. It's almost a date." She figured that was as close to a commitment as she'd get right now. She slung her bag over her shoulder, the weight of her camera and notebook banging against her hip. Grabbing her coffee and car keys, she moved toward the back door. "I'll talk to you later."

"Will you be here for dinner?" Mom asked before she completely escaped. "We won't be back from the clinic in time for lunch, but I'm making liver and onions tonight."

"Oh. Gee. I'll have to let you know. I might have a... thing. An appointment." She didn't look back to see Mom giving her the "I know you're lying" face and instead made a beeline for her SUV.

"That's okay. I'll save you a plate if you can't get here," Mom called through the slamming screen door. "Be careful!"

Lizzie unlocked the driver's side door and got in. Her old cowboy boots looked unfamiliar as she pressed the brake and started her car. Unfamiliar but very right with her favorite jeans. Not that it mattered. She didn't have to impress anyone today.

Anyone but Adam Collins, her evil brain pointed out. Would he like her just as well in jeans, or would he prefer her in the fancier stuff she'd worn when she lived in Houston?

No, he wouldn't like her in anything, she told herself. That didn't mean he'd like her in nothing—it meant he wouldn't be interested. Which was exactly what she wanted.

Lizzie was glad, too. She was. She really was.

Adam was staring at the cracks in his bedroom ceiling when Lizzie's tires crunched over the gravel driveway. He wasn't ready for this. Not for getting out of bed or for dealing with that dog, which had cried for an hour last night after he'd tried to leave it in the barn. He'd finally given up and brought the thing inside to sleep in a crate, but only because the caterwauling was about to give Adam a panic attack— not because he gave a damn about the dog's feelings, alone out there with no other animals for company.

He ignored the sound of toenails rattling the metal bottom of the crate as he stumbled to the bathroom.

The four minutes of sleep he'd managed to get had been populated by explosions and body parts—both human and canine—flying into his face. He could have taken a pill. The VA docs had given him a pharmacy's worth of choices, but none helped, and some made the nightmares worse. He brushed his teeth, then shoved his head under the faucet to rinse the sweat from his hair. Finally, he grabbed his best threadbare towel and rubbed his head, opened the bath-room door, stepped into the hallway, and crashed right into a warm, soft body.

Adam jumped back to avoid bulldozing Lizzie and the dog as surprise, which felt too much like fear, shifted into the default emotion, anger, which escaped through his mouth. "*Damn* it! What are you doing?" His voice was huge in the tight space. D-Day leapt and barked at the end of the leash.

"I'm sorry," Lizzie squeaked, eyes wide as she flattened herself against the wall.

Regret flooded through him, although he told himself that he should feel glad about scaring her. Then maybe she'd stay away.

He took a long breath, trying to slow his beating heart, and stepped back into the open bathroom doorway. "What are you doing?" His voice was still sharp.

Something pressed against his leg. Apparently, the dog didn't have Lizzie's sense, because it nudged him with its big nose and grinned. The dog rolled to its back, exposing its belly in hopes of a good scratch. *Dumb ass*. It should have every hair on its body raised in an attempt to look bigger and badder to threaten the asshole who had just yelled at its mistress.

He gritted his teeth. He didn't want any dog right now, much less one that didn't know how to act like a soldier. He reminded himself that he was in a totally different sit-uation—he was home. Not some half-burned-out village teeming with insurgents waiting to blow him up. And this dog was going to be trained to be a loving pet, not a single-minded warrior.

"Are you okay?" Lizzie had moved closer, laying her

hand on his arm. The contact wasn't unpleasant, and he didn't flinch, as he did when most people got within touching distance. As a matter of fact, her soft skin against his felt nice, almost cooling his overheated insides. Of course, now that he'd noticed, he stiffened.

She stepped back as though she'd been burned. Flash frozen, more likely. "I shouldn't have barged in," she said, "but I couldn't find D-Day in the barn. I was afraid he'd escaped, but then I heard him bark inside. When you didn't answer, I figured it would be okay to come in and get him for breakfast and potty."

Speaking of which, the dog had given up on that belly rub and gotten to its feet. It pranced around, looking a little anxious.

"I had the water on. I didn't hear anything." Obviously. "Take him outside. I'll be there in a minute. After I'm dressed."

He knew he was being an ass, and he was also suddenly, uncomfortably aware that he was standing in the hallway outside his bedroom in nothing but his boxers. And Lizzie had noticed, too.

Great. Both times he'd seen her so far, he'd made a half-naked fool of himself.

He cleared his throat. "Just so you know, I don't always run around mostly undressed." Not that he needed to justify himself. *She* was the intruder here.

Her lips tilted up. "That's good to know. So next time I come over, you'll be lounging about in your fuzzy footy bunny pajamas?"

His mouth almost won the fight and cracked a smile, but he managed to only grunt.

"We'll wait for you outside," she said.

"Good." He gave her a nod and stepped toward the bedroom but did make a last-second turn to watch her walk down the hall.

Chapter 5

Five minutes later, and Adam was dressed, not in footy pajamas, but jeans, boots, and—God help him—one of his granddad's old plaid flannel shirts. His clean laundry pile was officially gone. The only other clothes he had were military issue and still stinking of desert and other things he didn't want to think about. He made a mental note to order shirts from Amazon. Hopefully something a little less late-eighties ranch hand.

When the screen door screeched, Lizzie and the dog both turned their heads to look at him. She smiled, tucking her hair behind her ear with the hand that wasn't holding the leash. He wondered if her hair still felt as silky as it looked.

He blinked to clear the thought of his hands pushing her hair back and said, "Let's get started."

At the sound of Adam's voice, the dog leapt toward him, eager for whatever exciting thing he might have to offer.

"D-Day, no!" Lizzie said, hauling back on the leash as hard as she could, but the dog kept going and yanked her forward so she had to trot behind him.

"Damn," he muttered and then more loudly, "D-Day, stop!" as he moved toward the pair, hand raised to signal the dog to stop.

Of course, the dog didn't understand that and decided the hand was a chew toy, but at least Adam managed to grab the leash—and Lizzie—before she was dragged farther through the gravel-strewn yard. She stumbled against him, and the warm heat from her body was a Taser, jolting his libido. He released her as soon as she regained her balance. *No touching the nice lady.* She might be even hotter now than when they were younger, but she was also even further out of his league now than she'd been back then.

He focused on the dog trying to drag him anywhere but right there, gave the leash a forceful tug, and said, "Sit."

Startled, the dog looked up at Adam, then away. It casually, *slowly* lowered itself to its haunches as though the motion was its own idea.

"Good." He nodded at the dog.

It started to get up.

"No," he said, giving another yank. "Sit."

It sighed and sat.

"Good."

It started to rise again, but after another "No!" and a firm pull on the leash, it surrendered and remained sitting.

"Shouldn't you give him a cookie or something?" Lizzie asked, arms folded, lips pursed.

"No," Adam said, once again reminding the dog to sit when it decided to stand. "You might not always have a treat with you when you need it to obey you, and if you've got it trained to work for praise, you'll be better off."

"But that's harder," she argued.

"Maybe a little, at first. But this dog, it just wants attention."

She snorted. "And free rein over the earth."

"Well, it doesn't get that. It's got to learn that you're the one who provides everything good in the world, and you can take all that away if it doesn't do what you want." He noticed she frowned every time he called the dog *it*, but that was just too damned bad. Granddad had always said the best way to keep emotional distance from a dog was to keep *it* an *it*. Adam hated when the old man was right.

Lizzie raised her chin with determination. "All right, what do I do?"

"You take this." He led the dog over to her and handed her the leash. "And practice walking around. Every so often, stop, give a 'sit' command, and wait a second. If you don't get a sit, give that leash a firm pull, say 'no,' and repeat 'sit.' Don't move again until you get what you asked for. Then you can say 'good dog.' Make sure you say 'okay' to release it before the dog's allowed to get up."

She looked down at D-Day, who stood panting expectantly. "This ought to be interesting."

He thought so, too, but didn't tell her that. "I'm gonna work while you practice. I'll check on you in a few minutes."

He escaped to the dim confines of the barn where he found the ladder and dragged it outside. Might as well see what was needed for the roof. It wasn't going to order its own new shingles.

He planted the ladder next to the house and climbed up, gazing out beyond the house and barn.

There were fifty acres, mostly overgrown scrubland, but still space, stretched in a long, narrow rectangle away from the road.

After she and Todd moved in with Granddad, Emma had tried to keep things cut back, but after Todd died and Granddad got worse, she gave up. The weeds were winning again. It was a pathetic sight.

The old farmhouse where he and Emma had grown up was nothing special. It wouldn't even qualify as a farmhouse, at least not in any kind of architectural way. It had started out as a one-level cottage. The second story had been added sometime around when his father had been born and then divided into a master "suite" and two small bedrooms when Adam and Emma had come to live with Granddad.

There was a poured concrete slab in front of the house, which Emma had insisted should be a real porch. She'd convinced Adam to help her, and they'd spent their weekends building a roof and railings. That roof was now a little saggy, but considering it had been built by a fourteen- and sixteen-year-old with scrap wood scrounged from around town, it didn't look all that bad.

The roof itself, however—the whole thing needed to be replaced. That was going to make for fun in the Texas summer sun.

Adam's attention was diverted from calculating square footage of shingles by Lizzie's progress with the dog. It wasn't going well. She did everything technically right but was still too wishy-washy in her commands, and the dog had her number. It seemed obliged to forget everything it had just learned.

Meanwhile, Lizzie was being…*Lizzie*. Determined to get it right, her persistence tinged with good humor.

She told the dog to sit, turned to see if Adam was watching, and smiled. The dog, knowing her attention was diverted, got to its feet and tried to make a break for it.

"D-Day, knock it off," Adam snapped, stepping down from the ladder. The dog looked around…*Who, me?*…and bolted for him.

Lizzie squealed as the leash was yanked from her hand.

"Down!" Adam hollered, as a hundred pounds of brain-less exuberance leapt to tackle him. He stepped aside and grabbed the leash. "Damn it, dog, I said *down*."

It looked at him with surprise. *You talkin' to me?* It sat down as though that had been its intention all along.

"Try a little fetch in the paddock," Adam suggested, pointing Lizzie toward the fenced-in area next to the barn. He led the dog over and let it in through the gate. If this training session didn't improve, he was going to have to take over, and that wasn't on his agenda. He'd once taught dozens of young MPs to handle bred-to-be-headstrong Belgian Malinois, but one reasonably mature female and an eager mutt had him ready to scream.

This had *not* been a good idea. He still wasn't exactly sure how he'd gotten roped into this madness.

Yet he found himself leaning against the fence next to Lizzie while the dog scrambled around the enclosure, chasing after the big rubber Kong toy that they took turns throwing.

"Thanks again for doing this. I know it's an inconve-nience." Lizzie's big brown eyes tempted him to say that he was glad to have her there, in spite of his intentions to stay here alone until he could leave Chance County.

He shrugged. "Emma would never forgive me if I let a dog get sent to the gas chamber."

The corner of her mouth rose as she looked at him, con-sidering. "You're a good man."

No, he wasn't, but he wanted to believe her. Three deployments, God knew how many explosions, body parts, screams, whimpers—the past ten years almost disappeared when she looked at him like that. He went back to a long-ago summer night, leaning against an old wooden swing that still held the day's heat, looking at her, bending toward her—*No.* Not going there.

He forced his mind back to the present, chalking up his reactions to nostalgia. It made sense—a burnout like him *would* want to dwell on the rose-colored past. Besides, didn't she have a boyfriend somewhere nearby?

"It's going to take you a lot of work to get that dog in shape to be adoptable," he told her instead of going down any dangerous roads.

She nodded, her smile ironic...and kissable. "It's going to take *me* a lot of work. I have a feeling you could do it in less than a week."

If she kept looking at him like that, he was going to do it in twenty-four hours, just so she wouldn't have any more reason to come out here and torture him, but then he'd have to break his self-imposed moratorium on dog training. The no dog rule or the no people rule—which one was more important to follow? He'd have to navigate among people soon enough when he sold this place and figured out what to do for a living.

He supposed that if she was going to be around, he might as well practice interacting with normal folk. He threw out what he hoped was a reasonable change of subject. "Why did you come back to Big Chance? Last I heard, you were living in Houston with some fancy real estate mogul."

She rolled her eyes. "Dean. He's—*was*—my...boyfriend, fiancé, partner, whatever. The important part of that sentence is *was.*"

And there went one reason he had to keep his mind off

Lizzie and her kissable lips. He reminded himself there were a few others, like she was out of his league, he was a plane wreck with no little black box, and oh yeah, he was getting the hell out of Big Chance—out of *Texas*, as soon as he sold this ranch.

"Anyway, I came back because my dad's sick and he needs my help. Dean and his king of the universe attitude are what made it easy to leave Houston."

"If he was such an asshole, why did you go out with him?" Why was he being nosy? Oh yeah. Trying to interact with normal humans.

"He wasn't always a jerk. I mean, he didn't *seem* to be at first. We started working together at the same firm right out of college. We hit it off, started flipping houses, and it was like, 'Housing crash? What housing crash?' One thing led to another, we started dating, and then—" She shook her head.

"And then what?"

"His idea of what constituted a partnership didn't align with mine. He decided his role should be He Who Only Communicates to Criticize and that mine should be She Who Doesn't Complain or Eat Popcorn with Butter."

"Popcorn with butter?" he asked.

"Dry without salt if you have to have carbs at all," she said, holding her arms out from her body and looking down at herself. He looked, too. She was curved in all the right places, as far as he was concerned. Being pressed against those soft thighs, belly, and breasts would be heaven.

He cleared his throat. "No popcorn would be a deal breaker for me," he said.

She laughed. "There were a few other little issues, like

infidelity and excessive prevarication, which put the final nails in the coffin."

"'Excessive prevarication?' Fancy."

"It still makes him a lying jerk."

"I know," he said, and he also knew that her flip explanation hid some serious hurt. Her self-confidence had taken a major tumble. "You want me to go kick his ass for you?" He was only partially joking.

She shook her head, but he thought he saw a hint of pleasure under her bitter smile. "Nah, there'd probably be a police report, and I'd have to testify on your behalf, and I'd rather not have to see that jerk ever again."

Adam once again found himself fighting the urge to smile. "So you ran away and came back here where you can be more successful?"

She snorted. "I don't know if *success* is what I'll find here."

In spite of himself, he asked, "What *do* you want?"

She looked at him for a long moment and nodded. "You know what I want? I want to live my life on my own terms. I want cold beer in the afternoon, after a full day of hard work at Vanhook Realty. I want my mom and dad to be proud of me. I want to wear cowboy boots every chance I get, and I want my damned dog to find a good home."

Well, that was a mouthful. Adam's brain buzzed with a connection. "You're going to work for your dad?"

"Already am."

"That's, um, that's great." He remembered now she'd mentioned that yesterday. It hadn't occurred to him until this moment that she'd be involved in selling the ranch.

She followed his train of thought. "I get the impression that your sister doesn't know you're listing this place?"

"No, and if you don't mind, maybe you don't have to mention it to her just yet?"

She raised an eyebrow. "Doesn't she have some say in the matter?"

"It's in my name."

"Okay, technically, it's none of my business. If the deed and all the financial statements have your name on them, then you can do whatever you want with the place. But isn't she taking care of your grandpa?"

Adam sighed. It was really Emma's story to tell, but Lizzie would hear some version from the local gossips soon enough. "Yeah. Here's the deal. Before Todd died, they lived out here, helping Granddad take care of the place. Todd... got into some financial trouble. Emma called and volunteered to sign over her half of the ranch if I'd help them out. Granddad had put this place in our names when he realized he was getting forgetful, so she basically sold me her half for enough money to pay Todd's debts."

Lizzie didn't blink. "Okay, so this place is yours."

Not even close. He'd never have accepted Emma's shares of the ranch if he could've convinced her to take the money free and clear, but his sister wouldn't accept a handout. "The money I gave her wasn't enough to cover half of what this place should be worth. I don't want much for myself, just enough to leave town, but I need to make sure we make enough on the sale to get Granddad proper care." He shook his head. "Anyway, I owe it to Emma to make life a little easier."

He could see by the softening on Lizzie's face that she understood.

"Don't get all mushy. I'm not a goddamned hero," he

told her. "I just want to get out from under this place and get away."

She nodded. "Okay. I'll sell the hell out of this place— it's the least I can do to repay you for helping me with D-Day. And I'll keep my mouth shut until you're ready to tell Emma what you're up to, but you'll have to come clean before it officially goes on the market. There are no secrets in Big Chance."

"Don't I know it."

They stared at each other for one beat too many.

She looked at the dog, which had laid down nearby to chew on its toy. "I told my dad I'd take some photos while I'm out here this morning, but I'm going to have to do that another day. I've got to get back into town to print Mom's fliers for the Independence Day thing and then schedule a closing for a house Dad sold in town. Can I leave D-Day in the yard?"

"Yeah, I'll get some water out here in a few minutes." He hesitated, then said, "And thanks for keeping this stuff under your hat for now. I don't want Emma to have to worry about helping out around here." *Or to talk me out of leaving.*

She shrugged. "I understand."

He wasn't sure if she did or not, but before he could clarify things, his cell phone vibrated like a damned grenade, making him jump as music blared from his pocket.

"'Uptown Funk'?" She raised her eyebrows. "I took you to be more of a Jason Aldean kind of guy than Bruno Mars."

"I don't even know who Bruno Mars is. A friend—a guy I served with—programmed that for himself," he told her, then he slid the button on the screen to answer. Marcus Talbott didn't call unless it was mission critical. "S'up?"

"I lost Jake." Talbott sounded out of breath and anxious, not like his normal chill, top-of-the-universe self at all.

"What do you mean, you lost him? Just ask at the nurses' station. Maybe he's getting some kind of test."

"We're not at the hospital," Talbott said. "They discharged him yesterday. I brought him home with me, made a Walmart run, and when I got back, he was gone."

"Well, call the police, and tell them—"

"No, I found him again."

"Okay…"

Talbott was the easygoing member of the unit, but he had his panties in a wad now.

Lizzie was listening with undisguised interest.

Talbott went on, "I got Jake back, but he won't talk to me. He's sitting on this park bench, pouting like a damned ten-year-old."

Adam pinched the bridge of his nose. "Let me talk to him." Talbott was a hell of a friend and one of the best soldiers Adam had ever worked with. But away from the army, he might not be able to look after himself, much less someone like Jake, who had left a significant chunk of his brain in Afghanistan.

He sensed a change on the other end of the call, but there was no "hello."

"Williams? Jake?" Adam asked. "That you?"

"Yeah."

At least he was using words and not grunts. From what Talbott had said in a previous conversation, getting Jake to talk at all was a challenge some days.

"You okay?"

"No."

Lizzie shifted, concern knitting her brow.

Adam tried another tack. "You want to tell me what's wrong?"

"No."

Okay, now what? "Why did you leave without telling Talbott where you were going?"

"I...wanted beer." Jake spoke carefully, but his speech was clear.

Talbott said something in the background that sounded like "What's wrong with my hard lemonade?" and Jake responded, "It's pink!"

Adam guided the conversation back onto the topic. "Okay. You wanted to get some beer. Will you go home with Talbott now?"

Silence filled the line.

"Jake?" Adam prompted.

"Sar'nt, the carryout's...only two blocks." Jake spoke tight and low, addressing Adam by rank. "I could see it from...the porch. But I couldn't find my way home." In the soft words, Adam heard a lifetime of fear and despair in his friend's voice.

"What can I do to help?"

Talbott was back on the line. "Better clear off some floor space, Sar'nt. We'll be there in about a week."

Chapter 6

THE SUN HAD BARELY BEGUN TO BURN OFF THE MORNING dew when Lizzie settled onto the front steps of the old ranch house, enjoying the last few sips of her coffee while she waited for Adam and D-Day to join her. Summer had spread its fiery breath over south central Texas, but this morning, spring gave a valiant last gasp.

The days had settled into a not-terrible routine. As Lizzie promised, she hadn't said anything to Emma about Adam's plans, telling herself she didn't want to burst her friend's bubble, but it could have been that she wanted to imagine Adam staying in Big Chance forever. He was holding up his end of the agreement, and she spent a chunk of each day researching properties similar to this, comparing prices, making notes of more stuff for Adam to fix before they listed the place.

Training had been going okay-ish. Lizzie now understood what she was supposed to be doing with D-Day. D-Day understood, too, though he didn't always cooperate. Adam provided dog handling advice, usually from a distance. Maybe today would be the day that Adam called D-Day *him* instead of *it*, but she wasn't placing any bets. In spite of the fact that he was allowing the dog to stay in the house, he rarely looked at the dog or called him by name.

D-Day was no worse for being treated like an unwanted stepchild. He clearly adored Adam. Maybe *because* he was so distant. Lizzie snorted. Kind of like her. She couldn't seem to stop watching Adam or trying to make him smile, no matter how hard he clenched his jaw in her direction when she teased him.

A clatter of toenails and cursing signaled D-Day and Adam's arrival at the other side of the screen door. Lizzie got to her feet and tugged the legs of her shorts into place.

"Sit," Adam ordered. D-Day had learned that Lizzie's arrival meant not only breakfast but fun and games, so instead of sitting, he barked and leapt into the air with a wiggle. His landing made a thump that reminded Lizzie to have the house's foundation inspected.

"Good morning," she said through the door. "D-Day, sit."

D-Day stopped wiggling, which was better than nothing, she supposed.

Adam nodded and, if she wasn't mistaken, smiled slightly. At least he wasn't scowling. Lizzie was starting to think that he occasionally forgot he hated the world and appreciated her company. As long as she didn't forget that she wasn't going to get attached to him, they'd probably get through this dog training and ranch selling process in one piece.

Bang! D-Day leapt with both feet at the door.

"Sit, damn it," Adam said, though the curse lacked heat.

The dog jumped a few more times, then stopped and raised a doggy eyebrow at Adam as though to ask why he didn't open the door.

"Sit."

D-Day pranced a little more.

Adam crossed his arms and waited.

Finally, D-Day must have realized he had to do

something different to get what he wanted and slowly lowered his back end about a third of the way to the floor inside.

Lizzie laughed at the pleading look of *Isn't this close enough?* in D-Day's eyes. "You're going to have an accident on your hands if you're not willing to give a little," she warned.

Adam glared at her and then refocused on the dog. "Sit," he repeated.

With a sigh, the dog sat, but the second Adam reached for the door latch, he began to jump and bark again. Adam moved back from the door.

D-Day stopped, looked at Adam, then sat down.

They repeated this a few times until finally D-Day gave up and stayed sitting while Adam opened the door.

"Okay," he said.

The black blur nearly knocked Lizzie over on his way to the grassy area at the side of the house.

"Wow, I'm impressed," she said.

"Just takes an extra minute or two of patience," Adam told her, holding the door open and stepping back, an unspoken invitation, which she accepted.

"Patience is not my strong point."

He quirked his mouth. "I noticed."

The dog finished his business and notified the humans by slamming full force into the now-closed screen door. Adam flinched at the crash but then stepped around Lizzie and stared down at D-Day, who panted, happily oblivious that he'd offended anyone. After a long pause, he circled once and sat.

"Good dog," Adam said, opening the door to let the dog in.

"He must know his breakfast depends on you," Lizzie said as she followed Adam and D-Day toward the kitchen.

"Along with patience, Dog Chow's a good tool," he agreed. He pulled out a rickety wooden chair for her at the scarred oak table.

She sat and gazed about the dated but spotless room. *Mental note: Suggest removing at least half of the chicken-themed canisters, dishcloths, and salt and pepper shakers.* Lizzie had a hard time imagining Emma cooking in a virtual henhouse, but Adam explained that his grandfather would never let them change things, because their grandmother had decorated this room.

D-Day barked a reminder about breakfast. Adam gave him the evil eye. D-Day sat. Food *was* a powerful motivator.

"It's nice that you're letting him sleep in the house with you," she said, trying not to picture Adam, all rumpled from sleep, stretched out next to the big dog, though she knew there was a crate upstairs where D-Day slept.

"I figure since you want to train it to be a lap dog, it should learn some house manners." He scratched the bridge of his nose. "Besides, it's getting hotter in late afternoon. I don't feel like putting air-conditioning out there for one dog. Next owners might not want to keep kennels in the barn."

"There wasn't air-conditioning out there when your grandpa kept dogs?"

"Nah. Said it made them weak. Just had a few big fans. But even the army dogs get cooled kennels whenever possible." He pointed at D-Day. "And that's not even close to a military working dog."

D-Day shifted impatiently but didn't move from his hopeful seat.

"Why do you call him 'it,' instead of 'him'?" she asked. She was on a roll with pushing Adam's conversation skills this morning.

"Best way to keep from getting attached," he told her, the skin around his eyes tightening as his expression dulled. "You should do that, too. Remember that it's a dog, not a person. It's equipment."

"*Equipment.*" She gaped at him. He really had locked himself down. "I don't believe that."

He shrugged, and apparently the subject was closed, because he turned away to open a cabinet. He scooped a generous heap of kibble into a bowl, which he put on the floor. D-Day vibrated with need, and when Adam said, "Okay," he dove in with gusto, crunching loudly enough to cover the silence.

Determined to have a normal conversation, Lizzie fished around in her brain for something to talk about. "Don't you have friends coming to stay?" she asked. What little she'd understood from Adam's end of the conversation last week led her to believe that a couple of his army buddies were heading his way.

"I think they were just blowing smoke up my ass," he said, then added something that sounded like, "I hope."

She'd asked Emma about his friends the other night when they were drinking pink wine and watching *Downton Abbey* with Granddad (his choice!), but Emma said Adam never talked about them.

D-Day finished breakfast and flopped onto the cracked vinyl floor with a sigh.

"Do you still talk to people you served with a lot?"

"Not very often." And then *that* subject was closed, too, because he asked, "You want something to drink?"

"I give up," she muttered under her breath. *Whatever.* She'd already wasted too many years trying to get a man to communicate. Holding up her insulated mug, she said, "Sure. I can always use a refill."

"I'm sorry, I don't have any coffee," he said, then scratched his jaw and wrinkled his nose. If he wasn't so freaking sexy, standing there all beard stubbly and bed heady, she'd have said it was cute. "Actually, I don't have tea or soda, either. You want a beer?"

She laughed. "No, thanks. I'm good, but you go ahead."

His mouth barely tipped up at the corner. "I can probably wait a couple more hours."

His eyes held hers, and her heart gave a heavy thud before he looked away. Did he almost just flirt with her?

The whine of the dog, sitting in front of his empty food bowl, broke the suddenly awkward silence, and Adam shoveled more kibble into the bowl while the dog dug in.

Lizzie cleared her throat. "We should talk about a timeline for listing this place. I still need to get some pictures for my records, but I'd like to wait until you've got the cosmetic stuff done before we do official photos." She glanced around and tried to figure out how to stage the over-decorated but otherwise under-furnished living space. "Once you've painted and removed a chicken or fifty, the kitchen will be fine." She looked through the archway at the threadbare couch and pitted coffee table. "But the living room's gonna need some help."

"What, *early millennium pathetic bachelor pad* doesn't cut it for home buyers?"

She laughed, surprised at the rare display of humor. "Well, I'm sure it works for a certain segment of the population, but it might be good to broaden our options."

"So what does that mean? Do I need to buy more furniture?"

She eyed the chipped walls. "You don't have to get new stuff. We can move around what you've got and borrow a few things if we need more."

"There's a ton of antique junk in the horse shed," he offered. "Emma put most of our grandparents' furniture out there when she moved to town with Granddad."

"Great. We can look through it and choose a few things. I don't want this to be a lot of work for you, but I know you want to get as much as you can for the place."

"So you're confident you can sell it, huh?"

She pushed down the always-present niggle of self-doubt. "Oh, we'll get it sold." She wasn't quite sure how, but she'd promised to help him, and she would. "Just get the work done."

Instead of answering, he asked, "Are you ready for your lesson?" and grabbed a leash from the hook by the back door. He clipped it to a newly enthused D-Day and, after waiting for a sit, opened the back door, and everyone trooped outside.

"What are we working on today?" she asked.

"Leash walking."

Lizzie stretched her arms apart and did a couple of big circles in the air to loosen up. "Let me at him."

Forty minutes and a lot of frustration later, Lizzie saw it. From the corner of her eye, Adam smiled as she tried, for the four millionth time, to get D-Day to heel.

She stopped and narrowed her eyes at him. "Are you laughing at me?" D-Day also seemed to be laughing from the far end of his leash, at which he pulled with all his might.

Adam scratched his jaw. "I think this dog might have a harder head than you."

"What's that supposed to mean?" she asked.

"Just acknowledging your dedication to lost causes."

She didn't think he meant just the dog. Was he a lost cause? The remaining shred of her that wasn't cynical seemed to hope not.

In spite of himself, he showed endless patience for helping her work with D-Day, even though he still insisted on calling him *it*.

She'd also noticed that while he said he wanted to fix up the ranch, to sell it as soon as possible, he'd been meticulously scraping and sanding every board on the house for the past week. Of course, maybe she could have mentioned that a quick coat of paint would have been more than sufficient.

Adam put the sandpaper down. "Why don't you try to take him around the yard again?"

"D-Day, heel," she said and tried to keep her arm from being dislocated when the dog took off at a sprint. Reeling him back in, she groaned. "Aaargh. I don't know if he's ever going to get this."

Adam harrumphed. "You saw it heel for me."

"I don't understand why he *won't* do that for me." A hint of tears threatened to burn the back of her sinuses.

Adam picked up on her frustration, because he said, "Maybe it's time for a break."

A break sounded really good. But... "I can't just give up. Then he'll know I'm a pushover."

"True, but you can make it do something easy. Then it'll know you're happy, and you'll both feel better."

She knew when she was being patronized, but at least he wasn't dismissing her abilities. She sighed and held out her hand toward the dog. "Sit."

D-Day hesitated for an instant, as though to make sure she knew he was only humoring her, scooted his long front legs toward his back legs, and sat.

"What a good fuzzy wuzzy poophead you are," she cooed, ruffling the dog's ears. "I'm so proud of you for taking up space and adding to the carbon footprint with your millions of calories of puppy chow per day!"

The dog grinned, giant tongue lolling halfway to the ground.

"Attagirl," Adam told her, and his praise made her want to lean against him and nuzzle that stubbly chin. Dear God, she was turning into a dog.

"You did okay," he told her now. "It's going to be hard, but you're as stubborn as the dog, and that's half the battle."

"What's the other half?"

"Time and patience. If you get the patience part down, the time part will be shorter. And you need to be in charge. Dogs can tell when you're insecure and take advantage of that."

It was embarrassing that he'd seen through her so easily, and she felt her mouth tighten. She'd always been insecure but had usually been able to fake it well enough to get through what she wanted to do. Having to tuck tail and flee Houston had put a serious dent in that skill.

"Let's get a drink," Adam suggested, indicating Lizzie should lead the dog into the barn. The kennels inside sat empty but clean.

D-Day zeroed in on a big pan of water and began to slurp with gusto.

She'd left her coffee mug on the kitchen counter. "I don't suppose you have a glass out here or at least a hose?" she asked as she hooked the human end of the leash over a hook on the wall and ran her hands over D-Day's patchy fur. The dog leaned against her as she caressed him.

She looked up at Adam and caught a flash of longing in his gaze, but was it for her or the dog? Whatever it was, she doubted he'd let himself go after it.

Which was fine. D-Day would find a loving new home, and she didn't want Adam to want her. She was not in the market for a man. Especially one who was packing up to move on even as he fixed up his family home.

"If you don't want to drink out of the bowl, how about a lukewarm bottle?" He handed her a plastic water bottle from a case sitting on some crates. "Sorry. Forgot I had water out here when I offered you beer." He unscrewed the cap from one for himself and took a long drink.

"I'm still alive," she said, though she drank greedily. "Speaking of carbon footprints," she commented, "I understand the new mayor—remember Joe Chance?—he's started a recycling program. He's got shipping containers set up behind the middle school, and on weekends, you can drop off all kinds of things, even computer parts."

"I recycle," he said.

"I see that." She looked around at the pile of trash bags—filled with plastic bottles and aluminum cans—that filled one corner of the barn.

"I was going to make a trip to town later this week."

Lizzie decided not to push. Emma mentioned that he

was uncomfortable even talking about going to town. "I can take a load if you like." It seemed like the least she could do, since he was helping her with the dog.

"I can do it," he said a little too quickly.

"Okay."

He polished off his water and screwed the cap back on. "Watch this." He scrunched the bottle.

D-Day, who had finished his drink and moved on to licking his own butt, left his fun and turned an alert ear toward the sound of the plastic. Adam squeezed again, and the dog leapt to his feet, straining at the leash.

He handed Lizzie the bottle. "Try this as a reward."

Lizzie was as interested in the new development as D-Day. She took the bottle, accidentally brushing her fingertips against Adam's wrist during the transfer. An arc of energy as potent as a shock but much more pleasant ran along her arm. She was tempted to touch him again and see if it felt as good the second time but was afraid it would be even better.

Adam pointed at D-Day. "Get its attention and give a command."

Refocusing on the dog, she scrunched the bottle and spoke. "D-Day."

The dog looked at the bottle.

"D-Day."

He reluctantly tilted his head up a degree, meeting her eyes for an instant.

She made the wonderful, amazing, scrunching plastic sound again, and the dog quivered with excitement.

"D-Day, sit."

This time, the dog looked at her, sat, and waited.

She made one more scrunch and handed the bottle to the dog.

He pounced on it, took it into his mouth, bit down a few times, tossed it in the air, repeated the process.

"That was great," Adam told her, bending to take the bottle back from D-Day. "You don't want to let it get all chewed up."

She did *not* look at Adam's butt when he bent over. And *oh, no*, he did *not* catch her looking.

He blinked away what might have been a twinkle in his eye and indicated the mountain of plastic bottles. "Until I get to the mayor's fancy new recycling dumpsters, you've got plenty of training toys."

She grinned. "Now all I need are pants with giant expandable pockets to carry empty water bottles around with me. That would look awesome."

He raised an eyebrow, as though picturing her with giant lumpy water bottle thighs.

She shook her head. "I'd better get out of here," she told him. "Let you get on with your home repairs."

He turned and looked at the half-scraped house. "Gee, thanks."

Chapter 7

ADAM AWOKE SWEATING AND PANTING, THE REMNANTS of a dream hammering at his awareness. Unlike the normal nightmare involving his teammates, his dog, explosions, and blood, this time, Lizzie's luscious, naked self had been spread beneath him. He'd been about to enter her hot, willing body when the crash of tires braking hard in gravel heralded oncoming danger. A locomotive bore down on them. He'd tried to pull her away from the impending crash but couldn't hold on.

Deep breath. Okay. Slowing the heartbeat. It was a dream. He blinked, trying to clear his way back to the *good* part, but a slamming car door refired his waking adrenaline surge and told him the first sound had been real.

Damn. He rarely slept more than a few hours at a time and got laid even *less* often—in his dreams or otherwise. What asshole was out here at this time of—he looked at his watch—9:30 a.m.? He really *had* slept.

A movement near his legs startled him. He jumped out of bed and turned, pulling up short before he slammed a fist into the intruder.

The dog stretched, yawned, and tilted its head sideways as though to ask if everything was okay.

"What the hell are you doing in my bed?" he asked it. In the week and a half it had been at his house, the stupid thing had weaseled its way from the barn to the crate and the crate to the bedroom floor because its whining and howling was loud enough to wake the neighbors—and the nearest one was three miles away. But this bed-sharing thing? That was too much.

The dog wagged its tail, swiping a pillow onto the floor in the process.

"Get down." He pointed at the floor. D-Day licked Adam's hand, then took its sweet time reaching two long front legs over the edge before jumping down and bounding to the window. It shoved its nose beneath the bottom of the blind and barked a greeting.

Adam padded to the window, pretending not to hope it was Lizzie, but then remembered the reason he was oversleeping in the first place was that he'd offered to take morning dog duty. She had an appointment in town with the Brunch Bitches, as she called her mother's Fourth of July party-planning group.

He was almost afraid to look outside to find out who was here, but he raised the blind anyway.

A gleaming white Camaro Z/28, vintage #beforehewasborn, sat in the barnyard, sunlight glinting off of the windshield. The thing had a metallic red racing stripe along the side and major chrome on the wheels. To complement the obnoxious train-whistle horn, bass from some long-dead metal band thumped from subwoofers loud enough to set off a seismograph. Adam wondered if it had a neon undercarriage light, too.

Holy shit. They were here. A couple of solid bangs on the front door below triggered a burn in his gut. He considered locking the door and pretending to be gone. He couldn't deal with this right now. He wasn't ready, would never be ready to face his mistakes.

D-Day leaned into his side, and Adam absently reached down to stroke the dog's ears.

Talbott and Jake were his two best friends, and he'd promised that if *any* of his guys needed anything, they could come to him. Talbott said he and Jake needed help. It was time to pay up.

With a deep breath, he slid the window open to let the warm morning breeze flow over his skin, then called out, "Talbott, you motherfucker, get off my porch before I call the sheriff!"

He heard a deep, rich laugh, and then a headful of stubby black knots appeared from beneath the cover of the front porch as Marcus Talbott stepped into the yard. He looked up at Adam and grinned, spreading his arms wide, and in a really bad John Wayne voice, drawled, "We're here, Hoss!"

Adam hadn't heard the nickname Talbott had saddled him with—so to speak—in a long time, and it sounded good. "What did you do to your head?" Adam asked.

Talbott ran a hand over his hair. "I'm growin' dreadlocks."

"I hope you aren't giving up your day job, because you've got a way to go before you can join any decent reggae band," Adam said, then winced. Talbott's day job was non-existent, since his injury last year had sidelined him from active duty.

Optimist that he was, however, Talbott just grinned and turned to limp toward the car, waving his arm in an exaggerated *Come on!* motion.

D-Day pranced next to Adam, clearly excited to meet new people. "All right," he told the dog. "But you've got to get your leash on."

It seemed to understand, because it scrambled down

the steps and stood still in the living room while Adam got the lead connected, then waited politely for permission to go out. "Okay." He gave the dog time to take a leak in the bushes next to the porch, then walked to the car.

Talbott was leaning into the driver-side window, talking to someone in the passenger seat.

The dog couldn't resist and stuck its nose right between Talbott's legs, surprising him into bashing his head as he jerked upright. "What the hell?" He put one hand on his head and the other on his lower back as he pulled away from the car window.

"I'm sorry, man," Adam said. "This one's got a way to go. I shouldn't have let it get up in your business like that. You okay?"

Talbott saw that Adam was looking and jerked his hand away from his back. "I'm good. I didn't know you were working with dogs again."

Adam wanted to drop the leash as fast as Talbott pretended his back didn't hurt. "I'm not. Doin' a favor for a friend is all."

"Huh." Talbott patted the dog. "You're an ugly son of a bitch, aren't you?" D-Day licked Talbott's hand and nudged him for another pet, making him laugh. "That's one of the best things about dogs. You can say anything you want, as long as it's in the right tone of voice." He leaned back down and spoke into the car. "Come on, Jake. Get out here and say hello to Sar'nt Collins."

After a second, the passenger door opened, and another man hesitantly stepped out, squinting into the bright Texas sunshine. Adam's heart lurched when he saw how much his friend had withered during his hospital stay. An inch or two taller than Adam's six feet, the young lieutenant had been built like a linebacker, possibly because that had been his position on the United States Military Academy football team. Now Jake's shoulders seemed to curl in, hunched in case a strong wind tried to take him out. Worse was the enormous scar snaking over the left side of his head, like a giant question mark shining through the growth of short dark hair.

Adam's chest locked up, not allowing air in or out. His vision began to fade around the edges.

He fought the anxiety. Jake's injury wasn't a surprise. He'd seen him in the hospital months ago, swaddled in bandages like some kind of comic book character. He hadn't seen him since, because he was afraid. Afraid to see what he'd done. Well, he was seeing it now.

The brass, his team, everyone agreed that there was no way to know why Tank had missed the bomb that blew them all up, but Adam knew. He was to blame. He'd pushed the dog too hard or wasn't paying close enough attention. That was why Talbott limped and threw out his back at the slightest wrong move.

It was why Adam hadn't visited either of them after that first time in the hospital. Why he'd hoped they weren't serious about coming to visit him at the ranch.

Vaguely aware that D-Day was pressed against his legs, Adam was surprised to realize that he had his hand on the dog's head, stroking its ears. And even more surprised to realize the panic attack receded to a dull ping at the edges of his awareness. D-Day barked, drawing Adam's attention down, away from Jake. The dog panted and head-butted his leg. *Yeah, okay*, he thought. *Get your shit together.* He ran his hand over the dog's head. He couldn't change the past, but he could atone for it.

Jake slammed the car door and lurched a few steps away, carefully straightening his right arm and unclenching his fist until he stood straight, almost at attention. The contrast between Jake and Talbott had never been more noticeable. Where Jake was pale, whippet-thin, and well over six feet tall, Talbott was dark, barely six feet, and heavily muscled. A few ruptured discs and a rebuilt knee hadn't stopped him from working out. Hopefully together they could inspire Jake to eat a little more and regain some muscle.

"Lieutenant Williams, how's it hanging?" Adam asked as he stepped around the front of the car.

Jake nodded and slowly held out his hand for Adam to shake. Adam took it and slapped him on the shoulder.

"It's nice to see you, Sar'nt," Jake said.

"Screw nice." Talbott shook his head. "Dude. How could you lose your sense of direction and still be too polite to be real?"

Sober as a drill sergeant, Jake said, "At least I can still dance."

"Oh, now that's just mean," Talbott shot back. "You can't dance to save your life. My grandma dances better than you, and she's been dead for ten years."

This was familiar. *This* he could deal with. "Children," Adam warned. "If you can't get along, I'm going to have to have your moms come get you."

Even though Adam had been teasing, he noticed Jake's smile lose some of its luster.

"We're just fine," Talbott said, a note of warning in his voice. "Batman and Robin. The Green Hornet and Kato."

"More like...the Two Stooges," Jake added carefully, and the tension ebbed.

"So how about a tour before we unpack all our stuff, Hoss?" Talbott suggested.

The Camaro's back seat seemed to be packed full. Adam's earlier anxiety began to resurface. "Um, exactly how long are you two planning to stay?"

"Well, Hoss, you did say that if we needed anything—anything at all—you were here for us. Right now, we need a place to live."

Adam didn't have a chance to wrap his mind around that before D-Day began to bark and jump, practically whining with excitement.

"What's wrong with your dog?" Jake asked.

"Company's coming," Adam said, and sure enough, Lizzie's car came into view.

"Oooh, company," Talbott said, waggling his eyebrows.

Adam rolled his eyes and walked toward Lizzie as she parked and got out. "I thought you had a meeting this morning."

"I did," she said, stopping to rub D-Day's ears and accept a few kisses. "But Ms. Lucy's having a flare-up of gout and wanted to get home, so we got through everything fast. I thought I'd come out and spend a few minutes with you. I mean with D-Day. And you. To take some pictures of the property. Before I have to go to the office."

Adam fought down the pleasure he felt at her slip of the tongue and weak excuse for visiting. He didn't want to want her, but he'd come to look forward to her visits over the past week or so.

"Are these your friends?" Lizzie asked, taking the dog's leash and looking over Adam's shoulder.

"I guess so," he groused, but he had to admit that as much as their presence jacked up his tension in some ways, he was really damn glad to see them, to see men he knew how to talk to. How to be around. "Jake, Talbott, come here and meet someone."

"Howdy, ma'am," Talbott said with a toothy grin. "I'm Sergeant Marcus Talbott. Sar'nt there calls me Talbott, but all the ladies call me Marcus. And this is Jake—Lieutenant Jacob Williams."

"Hi, Marcus, Jake. I'm Lizzie Vanhook." She held out her hand, and Talbott shook it. Jake nodded his hello at Lizzie but maintained some distance and didn't speak.

"Lizzie, huh?" Talbott turned to look at Adam over his shoulder. "Dang, Hoss, you never told us you had a pretty little cowgirl waiting for you at home—or are you new on the scene?" He winked at Lizzie. "In which case maybe you're not too permanently attached to Sergeant Grumpy Pants here."

"Oh. No. We're not…I mean—" Lizzie stuttered.

No, they weren't, and he needed to remember that and ignore the niggle of disappointment he felt at her denial. "She's Emma's friend."

"In that case, do you have plans for dinner?" Talbott asked.

Lizzie giggled. *Giggled.*

Adam took a deep breath and counted to ten.

"So that's a yes?" Talbott pumped his fist. "Sweet! I've still got it."

Lizzie coughed but didn't look at Adam before she said, "No, I can't have dinner. Thank you anyway. I'm, uh, actually, uh, here to see the dog and on a professional basis. I'm a real estate agent," she explained, "and Adam's generously helping me with D-Day until I make other arrangements."

"Ah. I see." Though Talbott's sideways glance at Adam suggested the conversation about Lizzie wasn't over. "Well, it's nice to meet you, Miss Lizzie. And if you change your mind about dinner, you'll know where to find me."

"I'll keep that in mind," Lizzie said. "I'll take D-Day to help me get measurements," she told Adam.

"Good luck with that."

She grinned, and they shared a moment in which Adam had a brief, terrifying glimpse of what it would be to parent a preschooler with a woman he loved.

He turned to face his guys. "What can I carry?"

"Here." Talbott popped the trunk and hauled out a couple of big-ass duffels. "Jake, can you get the fast-food trash out of there while we grab the bags?"

Jake looked like he wanted to protest, but instead, he nodded and bent to riffle through the interior of the car.

"Trash cans are next to the barn," Adam told Jake before grabbing a couple more bags and nodding Talbott in the direction of the front door.

"So you like her, huh?" Talbott dropped a sleeping bag inside the door to the one extra room with a bed and came to join Adam at his bedroom window a couple of trips later.

Adam didn't answer. He was watching Lizzie tell the dog to sit while she juggled camera, notepad, and measuring tape to record the dimensions of the shed. It held broken farm implements and old furniture right now but had a horse carved into the top half of the split door. When they were little, Emma had liked to open the top half and hang out of it, pretending to be that talking horse from the old show on Nick at Nite.

"Lizzie's pretty hot," Talbott continued as though Adam hadn't been ignoring him.

"It's not like that," Adam protested, though he had dreamed of her last night—naked, sweating, crying out in his arms.

"So it's cool if I use my magic on her?"

"No. Not cool." The thought of Talbott working his stud muffin thing on Lizzie made something unpleasant shift in his gut. "She's not your type."

"Uh-huh, sure. Whatever you say." Talbott laughed and smacked Adam on the back.

"So there's only one extra bed up here," Adam said, pointedly avoiding the protest-too-much zone about Lizzie. "I hope Jake's okay with the couch." Without discussion, they'd put Jake's things in the living room, where he'd only have to navigate the stairs at shower time.

"He's totally fine."

"He doesn't look it. He's"—Adam didn't know the right words but waved his hand over his face—"kinda blank."

Talbott squinted into the distance before saying, "He's different, but he's in there. But hell, we're all different, right?"

Adam thought about the Jake Williams from *before*. The kid had been all kinds of eager when Adam met him. They'd both been newly assigned to the unit. Williams was still a wet-behind-the-ears junior officer and an all-around good guy. He'd managed to be decisive and clear when he gave instructions while maintaining an "I'm new here so I'm going to ask a lot of questions" demeanor—a difficult feat for many seasoned officers with more fragile egos.

The dog barked. For a second, Adam imagined he heard Tank, but it was just D-Day, trying to convince Lizzie to play instead of sitting quietly while she tried to work. The enormous puppy was like a canine prophet to remind Adam of his failure.

As though reading his mind, Talbott tossed out some bullshit wisdom. "Jake's different, but he's working on finding a new normal. It'll be good for you two to hang out. He's tired of me following him around, so you can take a turn, and you'll feel better if you can see him getting better."

"I don't need to feel better," he told Talbott. That was impossible. Not because he felt great but because his feelings didn't matter. "What about you? How are you?"

Talbott looked like Adam asked if his pantyhose were too tight. "I'm fine. Just gotta keep up with the exercises, and I'll be back in action before you know it."

Adam didn't comment.

"Jake's gonna be okay, too," Talbott said. "That's why we're here. He needs a place to be a man. We can't baby him."

"Okay." They'd figure it out. "What about you? You don't need your sleeping bag."

Talbott seemed torn but then said, "I know, but my back still gives me twinges now and then. Sometimes I do better sleeping on the floor." His normally relaxed smile had a few faint cracks. "But I'm doing a shit ton of PT, physical therapy *and* training, and in a couple of months, I'll get the docs to sign off and let me get back to active duty."

Adam was doubtful. He'd seen the X-rays after the explosion. The man's body had been broken, and parts had been displaced. Adam suspected there were more than a few back twinges at play in his friend's reluctance to sleep in a bed, but he didn't push. "If anyone can do it, it's you, man."

"You just have to work your ass off and keep thinking positively." Talbott tapped his head. "In the meantime, we're going to get Jake back on his feet."

"Whatever you need. Both of you."

What Talbott had said earlier was true. Adam *had* pledged to do anything in his power for the two of them. For any of his brothers-in-arms, but especially Talbott and Jake, who were the direct victims of Adam's own screw-ups. He'd feed and clothe them forever if necessary. If only he could do something for everyone who had been hurt in that blast.

"Have you talked to Garcia's wife?" he asked.

Talbott nodded. "Yeah, we stopped to see her on the way out of Virginia. She's okay. She and the kids are living with her sister. There are only four little Emilios running all over the place, but it seems like twenty."

"Damn. The last one is a boy, too?"

Talbott laughed. "Yeah. Poor woman. As though having one big Emilio wasn't bad enough, she's got to deal with his clones for another eighteen years or so."

The reality that Celeste was going to have to raise four boys without their father swamped Adam, and he nearly staggered under the weight. He'd struggled without his own dad, but at least he had a few great memories. The Garcia kids wouldn't even *remember* their dad. He looked at Talbott and said, "I wish—"

"Don't. It's no good. We do what we can. The army's doing its share, and Celeste's got her mom living nearby. That's more than a lot of people can say."

"Are your mom and dad…"

"Yeah. They're fine. They've got half a dozen little grandkids—not by me—running around Kentucky, stirring things up. I was talking about Williams."

"Oh." Adam didn't know what to say. All he knew about Jake's family was that they had money and weren't thrilled with Jake's career choice. "What's the deal?"

Talbott went to the door and looked to make sure no one was listening out there. He closed it and lowered his voice. "Seems Daddy Dearest won't let Jakey come home. Says he made his choice when he left for West Point, and he's got to live with it. His mom disagreed, wanted him to come home, so they compromised. Daddy Warbucks will pay for a caretaker or a *home* but won't let him come home."

"They want to put him in an *institution*?" Adam was horrified. "Is he that bad?"

"Absolutely not." Talbott shook his head. "He's got issues, though. Can't find his way out of a paper bag. Something… geographical dis-anterio-something, the doc said."

"Will he get better?"

"Yes," Talbott said decisively. "It just takes time and work. His speech is a little fucked up, too—it takes a little bit to get his brain in gear—but he's as smart as he ever was. Probably smarter. He's moving a ton better, too, but he says people stare at him now, and he's sensitive about that."

And his parents didn't want to be seen with him. "That's such bullshit."

"I know. I told him he should work that attention from

strangers like a boss, but he didn't even smile. He seems to think chicks won't dig him."

That wasn't what Adam thought was bullshit, but he didn't say so. Of course, he didn't want his friend to feel inferior; considering what he'd sacrificed, he should feel *better* than most people. It was Adam's part in the tragedy—and his own inability to fix it—that ate away at him.

For once serious, Talbott said, "He hates that he needs help, but he can't live on his own—not yet. The thought of him living in some institution or group home or whatever—I couldn't let that happen."

"No," Adam agreed. "You can't. *We* can't."

"If nothing else, we've got to see if we can make him smile again."

Adam sighed, knowing he'd made this decision before Jake and Talbott had even arrived, and said, "I need some help around here. I'm going to sell the place, but there's a shit ton of work to do in the meantime. Maybe some good hard manual labor—whatever he can manage—will get him in a better place."

"Thanks, Sar'nt."

"Yeah." Adam hoped he wasn't setting them all up for more pain.

Chapter 8

A FEW DAYS LATER, LIZZIE SLOWLY BUMPED HER WAY down Mill Creek Road to satisfy an urge that had been percolating in the back of her mind. It had moved forward, waking her this morning like extra-strength Starbucks. She probably should have driven her own SUV instead of her mom's little Prius, but Dad said he wanted to get her oil changed, and she never turned down someone who remembered she should do maintenance.

Her phone buzzed for the fourth time in as many minutes, so she slowed down even more and answered. "Hi, Mom."

"Lizzie, it's your mother."

"Hi, Mom," she repeated, because apparently answering a phone with caller ID and saying *Hi, Mom* wasn't enough to prove she knew who was on the other end of the line.

"Where are you? I've been calling since you left the house."

Which was ten minutes ago. "Were you calling to find out where I am?"

"Don't be a smart aleck," Mom said. "I was worried when you didn't answer."

"I was driving. I'm still driving, but I'm going slower now, so I answered."

"Oh." Mom digested that and said, "I want to know if you'll stop by Ms. Lucy's on your way back to town to pick up her Festival Crafts and Prizes Company catalog.

We're going to order flag kits for the little ones for the Fourth."

"You know you can find all that stuff online, right?" Lizzie asked, scanning the side of the road for the entrance to the old Mill Creek farm and trying to dodge the potholes Emma had warned her about. "You don't need a paper catalog."

"Yes. I'm fifty-five, not ninety-five," Mom snapped. "But Ms. Lucy is…well, if she's not ninety-five, she's close, and she doesn't trust the internet. She's flagged the kits she wants me to buy, and I hoped if you were going to be out, you might be able to stop over there."

Lizzie thought about coming up with an excuse, because the last time she'd stopped by Ms. Lucy's home, the older woman had held her hostage for an hour asking detailed questions about D-Day, his training, what Lizzie thought the dog's breed might be…

She slowed the car to a crawl through the oppressively overcast afternoon. A few brave butterflies swooped along the fence line, but otherwise, there was no movement out here. Not even a tiny breeze. *Where was that lane?*

"Earth to Elizabeth."

"Sure, Mom." Lizzie checked the clock on the dashboard. After this, she'd have time to stop by Adam's place to check on D-Day (yeah, that was why she was stopping out there, *the dog*), and then get to Ms. Lucy's. "You can tell her I'll be by about four thirty."

"Thank you, sweetheart," Mom said. "I really appreciate how much you're doing to help us right now."

"I'm glad I can do it," Lizzie assured her and ended the call. She was really happy to have a role both at work and with her mom's civic projects. She'd accomplished more in the few weeks she'd been home than all the years she'd spent in Houston, and she was excited to get even more connected through this possible Mill Creek project idea she kept turning over in her mind.

Thinking about connections made her think about Adam, who was working hard to stay distant from people. She'd seen him laugh and joke with his friends this past week, but even when he was with them, he'd get a faraway look in his eye.

And then she'd see him watching her, but any time she thought they were about to have a real conversation, he would pull back and make some excuse to walk away.

A few twists and turns later, a mile or two farther from the turnoff than she remembered, she saw a vaguely familiar space between two fence posts that looked like it had been driven over sometime recently. Remembering the obnoxious truck that had nearly run into Emma and herself a few weeks ago, she hoped whoever had driven out here wasn't still around. Maybe she should look into MMA training. And a Taser. And pepper spray. A former military policeman with a bad attitude wouldn't be a bad addition, either.

Of all her options, she figured pepper spray was a better bet than the MP. Adam would find something much more important at the ranch that had to be fixed *immediately*.

Well, screw that. She had a monument to build to her father's heritage and no time to chase around a grump, no matter how sexy he was.

Distant, difficult, and damaged—*no, Lizzie. Bad.*

Her car bumped and scraped over a rock before rattling over a rickety wooden bridge.

The lane dipped and then rose, turning a bend before revealing the remains of a barn and part of a large open area where a house once stood—one she'd heard was haunted. Beyond the barnyard was a line of brush, behind which, she remembered, was a field that sloped down to the creek. Lizzie braked to take a photo through the windshield. She'd look more closely later, but it should be easy enough to knock down or rebuild the barn, depending on what she wound up doing, if she managed to get support for her idea and could figure out who owned the place now. Her records search had come up empty. No one had paid taxes on it in at least ten years, but no one was being charged for delinquency, either. It was like the place didn't exist.

Someone had been here, though. The rocky, weedy yard had been mowed. Not yesterday or even the day before, but it wasn't completely overgrown. Goose bumps rose in a wave over Lizzie's skin. Tire tracks from a recent trespasser were one thing. Evidence of maintenance was a total mystery.

A few high-wind storms had battered the old barn until it tilted and collapsed on one side, so now it was more of a lean-to. The burned-out footprint of what had been the farmhouse was now a charred wasteland, complete with a gaping, black hole for the cellar.

She put the car in park and made some notes with estimates of distances and area. Birdsong floated through the open window along with the warm summer breeze and the scent of wildflowers.

She was sketching out her ideas for improvements when she heard the sound.

What was that? A high-pitched whine came from the

vicinity of the burned-out house. It was probably the wind hitting something the wrong way, she told herself until she heard it again. There was something in that big hole in the ground. A tickle of apprehension skittered along her spine. This was the part of the movie where the intrepid babysitter goes downstairs to find out why the electricity went out, only to come face-to-face with a guy wielding a fire ax. And the intrepid babysitter doesn't even have pepper spray on her key ring. She should forget her harebrained scheme and drive away.

So of course, she got out of the car and took a few steps toward what was left of the farmhouse. She stopped to listen again but heard nothing. No whimpers, cries, or swelling organ music signaling it was time to turn back before she hit the point of no return.

Well, crap. She picked her way through the charred remains to the edge of what used to be the basement.

The hole in the ground wasn't empty or filled with charred house parts but instead held some sort of a cage. A ten-foot-high chain-link fence divided the near side from the other, where steps led down from ground level. What in heaven's name had the owners stored here? Psycho killers?

The wind shifted, swamping her senses with an ungodly stench. Something rotten and animal waste. Dog, if she wasn't mistaken. *Oh no.* Had someone kept dogs down here? All alone on the edge of nowhere?

Then she understood. She'd seen photos on the news, part of a story about pit bulls. This was a dogfighting ring.

The sound came again, from a corner of the basement that was shaded by the angle of the sun. There was something there. It looked like a scrap of carpet.

Lizzie stepped around carefully, squatted down to peer over the edge, and caught her breath. Staring up at her with one shining eye was a white dog. The other side of his face was a swollen, bloody mess, but the square head was clear. A pit bull lay on his side, next to a pile of rags. His heaving chest was covered by skin that stretched taught over meatless ribs. "Hey, buddy. What happened to you, huh?"

The pile of rags moved, and Lizzie realized the dog wasn't a *he*. The dog was a *she*, and she had at least half a dozen puppies desperately trying to nurse from her starving body.

"Who the *fuck* could do something like this?" Talbott asked it out loud, but all of them were thinking it as Adam stood with his two friends and Lizzie on the lip of the pit.

Compared to the shit they'd seen in Afghanistan, this was nothing. The human misery they'd witnessed on a daily basis should have made them immune to one banged-up, hungry dog and a few extra squirmy blobs of fur.

Instead, Adam's blood boiled on behalf of the poor things. He barely heard Lizzie when she said, "Thanks for coming. I didn't know what else to do. They're stuck down there, and I couldn't leave them to go home and get a ladder. I felt bad enough about having to go out to the road to get a signal to call. Not that I did anything helpful, standing here wringing my hands—" she broke off.

Adam squashed the moment of pleasure that her first thought was to call him and said, "We're here now."

The dog whimpered, and his focus shifted to thoughts

of chaining some nameless, faceless asshole to a stake and leaving him there, because that was surely what had happened to the dog. They'd found remnants of a bloody rope near the barn. The other end was attached to the dog's collar.

"She must have been tied to that post by the barn and chewed her way free so she could try to have her pups somewhere safe," he said. "I wonder if she *fell* in this hole, based on the way her front leg's bent."

"What about her eye? Do you think she hit it on something when she fell?" Lizzie asked.

Adam looked at her and saw the hope there—that this was a mistake, and the dog was in this situation by accident. He wanted to lie to her, to make up something innocent. She deserved that kind of world, but he couldn't give it to her. Returning his attention to the dog, he said, "This place has been used for dogfighting, and that one was probably bait, left behind because no one had the balls to put her down after they let her get chewed up."

He heard Lizzie's shocked breath, but he wouldn't comfort her and say everything would be okay. That dog was in terrible shape, and the likelihood she'd survive her rescue was slim. The pups' chances weren't much better, especially if they couldn't find a surrogate to nurse them.

"What's the plan, Hoss?" Talbott asked. "Do we call the dogcatcher?"

Lizzie said an emphatic "No," and followed with, "They'll put her down. We have to at least *try* to save them." She looked at Adam like she believed he could not only save the dog but get the earth to spin backward simply by flying fast in the opposite direction.

"I don't have bolt cutters with me, so I don't think we can get through the fence they used to section off the room. It makes more sense to climb down in there and hoist them out," Adam said. "Let's see what I've got in the truck." Not much, he feared.

Lizzie's panicked phone call had scared him enough that he'd barely thought to grab Jake and Talbott on the way to the truck. The guys had given him enough bullshit teasing about why he was running off in the middle of a video game because some girl called that he'd only grabbed a crate and a few other things, convincing himself she was overreacting.

Until he'd seen the dog.

The next thing he knew, Adam was being lowered on a makeshift rappelling harness into the cellar-turned-deathtrap while Lizzie crouched over the corner where the dog lay whimpering and watching the activity with one hopeless eye. "It's okay, Mama," she said. "We're gonna help you. It's gonna be okay."

The sound of her voice seemed to keep the dog distracted while Adam caught the crate that Jake lowered to him.

He wrapped a sweatshirt he'd found in the back of the truck around his arm as a homemade bite sleeve. He crept toward the dog, moving slowly but steadily. He didn't know how aggressive this pit bull might be—had she been trained to fight? Even if she hadn't, she might be in enough pain to go for anyone who tried to touch her or her puppies. "It's cool, Mama," he said, echoing Lizzie's comforting words—he could remind himself later that dogs *weren't* people.

He put the crate down and opened it, taking out the

bowl and bottle of water he'd had the presence of mind to include. He held the protected arm out to shield himself as he poured an inch of water into the bowl and pushed it toward the dog.

She didn't even look at it. *Not good.* He unwrapped the sweatshirt and put it aside. The next issue was how to move her, when he had no idea how broken her body might be.

He looked up where Lizzie, Jake, and Talbott watched silently. Deep inside, he knew he should still be wary. The dog could use her last breath to attack him if she thought her pups were threatened, but he had to get her out of this hellhole now or bury her here.

He slowly reached a hand out toward the dog. She lifted her head and sniffed his hand, then lay it back down. He put his hand in the water and dribbled a few drops onto her mouth. Her tongue barely moved, but she did seem to try to swallow, so he did it again. And again.

"Come on, Mama," he coaxed, taking the half-full water bottle in hand. "Let's try this." He poured a few drops onto her jaw, and she tilted up her chin, apparently realizing this was real, drinkable water. He gave her a steady stream of water, which she began to lap. When the bottle was empty, she turned to the bowl and took a few more laps until Adam took it away. "That's enough. We don't want you puking."

Up close, her injured eye was a festering mess, covered with flies and smelling of decay. She was *rotting*. The puppies couldn't have been more than a couple of days old, tiny and blind. It would be more merciful to put the whole family down right here.

"It's okay, babies. Adam's gonna help you," Lizzie whispered.

No, Lizzie, he thought. *Don't count on me for this.* He wasn't fit to take care of the half-grown dog and two broken-down soldiers already on his doorstep, much less a needy pit bull and a litter of newborns. Even if they survived, they'd need round-the-clock attention. This was a damned lost cause.

Lizzie watched Adam scan the area around him before pulling his T-shirt over his head with one arm.

"Damn, Hoss, this isn't the time for your Chippendale's act," Marcus Talbott said, but when no one responded to his attempt at humor, he asked, "What do you need us to do?"

Adam shook his head but didn't answer. Instead, he continued his steady murmuring to the mother dog while he carefully eased the shirt under her body. He bent down and slid his arms under her and lifted her so gently, Lizzie might have thought the dog was weightless except for the shifting of his muscles beneath the tattoos covering his back as he worked.

He maneuvered the dog into the plastic kennel and scooped up the pups in two big hands, putting them on the old sweatshirt and then next to their mother before looking around to make sure he hadn't missed any. Finally, he latched the door and stood.

She wasn't sure, but she could have sworn she heard him say, "Okay, honey, we've got you now," but when he finally looked back up at Lizzie and his friends, his cold, emotionless mask was firmly in place.

"Jake, toss me the end of that rope," he ordered and tied

it to the handle on top of the crate. "Okay. Slowly now." He lifted the crate and didn't relinquish his hold on it until Marcus lay on his stomach and reached into the pit to steady it while Jake pulled it the rest of the way up.

Lizzie felt completely useless, but they seemed to know what they were doing. Like they'd mounted a few rescues together before now.

As soon as the dogs were on high ground, Jake joined Marcus on the edge of the basement to reach down for Adam's hands, pulling him up far enough to grab a few handfuls of sod and pull himself the rest of the way out.

His big, muscled body shone with exertion in the midafternoon sun, and he gave Lizzie a slight nod that made her shiver in spite of the heat.

She cleared her throat, breaking away from the intensity of his gaze, and bent to look into the crate, trying not to gag at the smell. "How many puppies?"

"Six. Don't know how many will make it, though."

"I called Rob Chance while I waited for you to get here. He and his vet tech are expecting us."

Adam nodded with a heavy sigh, as though resigned to seeing this rescue through to the end.

She looked from her mom's little car to Adam's big white truck.

"What if Talbott and Jake take your car to the ranch, and I'll take you and the dogs to the vet in my truck?" he asked.

"You must be psychic," she said.

"Or psycho," he muttered but lifted the dogs into the back seat of his roomy old pickup truck. Louder, he said, "Why don't you sit back here so you can talk to them, keep things calm?"

That was a good idea. Otherwise, she'd worry about them the whole way to town.

"We'll feed the semi-hairy beast his supper," Marcus assured them, opening the driver's door of Adam's truck.

"Thank you," Lizzie said. "Not just for feeding D-Day. For—"

"Yeah, yeah," Marcus told her, waving her thanks away.

Jake, who hadn't spoken the entire time he'd been there, opened the passenger door and said, "We'll see you…and the puppies…later."

Lizzie took it as a positive sign that Adam didn't even pretend to fight about giving the new little family a home.

He sighed and pointed at his friends. "I don't know when we'll be back, but when these dogs get there? You assholes are on midnight kennel duty."

Chapter 9

LIZZIE STROKED HER HAND OVER THE MOTHER DOG ONE more time before a technician lifted her from the examination table. The poor thing seemed to be lost between exhaustion and terror, and Lizzie's heart squeezed. "Bye, Mama," she said as another tech gathered the pups and all were taken to the back room to be treated.

Adam leaned against the wall, arms crossed, glowering. He'd been the poster boy for *rude* from the moment the veterinarian came into the room.

Rob Chance, the vet in question, tucked his stethoscope into his pocket and said, "We'll get some IV fluids into her tonight and start trying to feed her. We'll take a look at her in the morning and know if she's strong enough for general anesthesia. We need X-rays for that leg, and the eye's probably going to have to come out."

"*We* really appreciate that you stayed late to help us," Lizzie told him, trying not to glare at Adam.

"No problem. It was a stroke of luck that you got there when you did. I don't think she'd have made it through the night."

Lizzie shuddered at the thought of those poor puppies starving to death next to their dead mother.

"What do we owe you?" Adam asked, the first words he'd deigned to utter. Was that his problem? He was worried about the cost? Lizzie should have made it clear that she'd take care of the bill—it was *her* rescue.

But Dr. Chance shook his head. "Let's see what we go through in the way of meds and supplies. I'm not going to charge you for my time. I hate these fu—dogfighting rings. I thought we'd chased them out of the area, but they're like cockroaches."

"That's very generous. How early can I call to check on them?" Lizzie asked.

"I can call you after I've had a chance to examine her. This is your cell number, right?"

Adam was almost through the door—what was his hurry?—but stopped and came back to Lizzie's side. She ignored him and answered Dr. Chance. "Yes, that's my cell, and my parents' home number is on there, just in case."

"You've got mine on there, too," Adam pointed out. "My schedule's flexible. Call me first if there's a problem."

Lizzie gaped at him. *Really?* He'd spent the entire trip to the clinic and the whole visit acting like this was all a big waste of time, and now he wanted to be Johnny-on-the-spot in case of a dog emergency? He was so weird. He'd refused to look at the dog or her babies after getting them into the crate but constantly asked her to check on them during the ride to town.

"Should we stop and file a report with the sheriff while we're in town?" Lizzie asked when they got to Adam's truck.

He looked toward the center of town, then shook his head. "Let's call them later. I've had about enough of Big Chance for one day."

Lizzie realized she should have been more sensitive to

his triggers—like driving through town. She softened over his reaction in the vet's office. "Let's get out of here."

He nodded and unlocked the door for her.

"That was really nice of Dr. Chance, to donate his time like that," Lizzie said, once she'd buckled herself into the passenger seat. She made a mental note to find a way to do something for the staff of the veterinary clinic as soon as she could. Cookies? Dog biscuits and cookies?

"Yeah," Adam said. "Really nice. Especially the way he took your phone number."

Wait. *What?* She laughed. "You think he was *hitting* on me?"

"He's thinking about it," Adam told her, backing on to Main Street.

"I don't think so." She ran through the visit in her head. She didn't know him very well. He was a Chance, but she wasn't sure which branch—not a sibling of Joe, the mayor, she thought. Probably a cousin. She'd first met the young veterinarian when she'd brought D-Day in for a checkup, and he'd been friendly and chatty. Today, he'd seemed enthusiastic and more than willing to stay at the clinic for an extra hour until she got the dogs there. "Well, you know…I do have this effect on men who care about animals," she said, though her sarcasm was probably lost on Adam.

He grunted.

Okay, maybe not a *positive* effect on all of them. "Take you, for instance," she continued. "I seem to have the effect of making you grumpy."

"You seem to think I'm someone who cares about animals."

"You don't?"

"Not more than the average person."

"I'm pretty sure I remember that you were a dog-handling MP in the army, right?"

His nod was more like a shrug, but she decided not to let his reticence deter her. She'd heard him talking to the mama dog and had even seen him pet D-Day a few times.

"Maybe you should get a job with the sheriff's department here. Be a K-9 officer."

He snorted. Lizzie noted that his eyes were on the road, but his attention seemed to be far, far away. "I don't think so."

"Okay, I guess you've done your share of protecting and serving. You're certainly entitled to do something else if you want. You'd be really good at managing...something."

"Not," he said, then looked like he wished he could eat his words.

"You're totally a leader. That's why Marcus and Jake came to you."

"Talbott and Jake need somewhere to stay. I owe them—" He cut himself off. A muscle in his jaw twitched as he braked at the stoplight in the center of town.

"Maybe you could be a high school teacher."

He shot her an incredulous look. "What?"

"You have that natural alpha dog thing going on. Kids would love you. After all, you're good at making D-Day behave."

He snorted. "Anybody can do that."

"I can't."

"That's because you don't command respect."

His words stabbed her. "I don't?"

"No. Everything you think and feel is broadcast across

your face, through your body language. The dog can sense your insecurity."

A wash of something similar to shame spread over her. Was that true of everyone in her life?

Adam went on. "You need to practice being in charge. You've got too much 'Oh, D-Day, you're such a sweet boy' going on." His voice went up and got all squeaky when he mimicked her, but then went back down. "He doesn't respect you."

"Oh." She wanted to deny it, but Adam was right. And not just about D-Day but about her relationship with Dean, her career—heck, everything to this point. Good thing she wasn't interested in getting involved with Adam, because she'd be horrified if she thought she'd acted simpering and weak in front of him, too, inviting him to walk all over her.

Bummed, she pondered her failure as she stared at the dying rays of the sunset, reflected in the windows of the mostly empty businesses in the center of town.

Ah, hell. He'd hurt her feelings. Again.

It was more evidence that he shouldn't be around people, except that, damn it, today had been different. Even when he was having a stupid attack of jealousy, he hadn't had a whiff of the tension that normally tried to paralyze him every time he came to town. For that matter, he hadn't been as jumpy as usual lately.

He was struck by the realization that it had something to do with Lizzie, with the way she was around him. And it wasn't how much he wanted to touch her every time she came near. Sure, imagining her naked kept him distracted, but he'd gotten with a few willing women since he'd been back in the USA, and not even sex could drown out the worst of the shit that went through his mind. It was Lizzie. Even though he'd been a total ass to her more than he cared to acknowledge, she neither fawned all over him—like having been to war and getting a bunch of people blown up was some sort of amazing feat of manhood—nor did she tiptoe around, waiting for him to explode. She talked to him, she teased him, and she seemed to think that he had something to offer.

Unless he'd just alienated her completely.

A faint sniffle reached his ears, and he risked a glance to see that Lizzie was staring out the side window. He had to fix this.

There. To the right was Dairy Queen. His parents had always taken him and Emma for ice cream when they were having a hard day. Call him cowardly, but he couldn't face riding the next twenty minutes to the ranch stuck in a car with a woman crying over something he'd said.

He turned on the blinker and slowed.

"What—what are you doing?" Lizzie asked.

"I'm hungry."

"You want to eat here?"

"Why not? It's open. They have food." He pulled into an empty slot and turned off the engine.

He took his wallet out of the center console, leaned forward to shove it into his back pocket and reached for the door handle, trying not to remember the good times he'd had when Todd worked here. How he'd planned to meet

Todd here the last night he'd been in town and instead found himself at Lizzie's house.

What they'd done and not done on that swing in the dark, and how strongly those moments clung to his memory bank. They hadn't actually done *it*. He'd had plenty of actual sex both before and after that little non-event, and she'd have found someone else to help ease her ache. Dean? Some fraternity dick wherever she went to college? Her high school prom date?

"Who did you go to prom with?" he asked, interrupting her in the motion of opening her own car door.

"Huh?" She turned to look at him.

Her hair swung around, and he caught a whiff of that familiar scent, the scent that took him back to before. When he only *thought* he was jaded and bitter.

"Never mind." It wasn't important. Not as important as the curve of her thigh on the upholstery of his truck right this minute, her smooth skin, the quizzical smile she sent his way.

When they got to the front of the restaurant, he reached around her to open the door, appreciating the way she seemed to fit right in his negative spaces, even though they weren't touching. They were in town, too. Adam should have begun to sweat and prickle by now, but he felt pretty okay.

At least until he got a load of the couple in line ahead of them—especially the guy.

Adam stood next to Lizzie, trying to peruse the menu board while they waited for the couple to finish arguing about their order. They were young, Adam thought, but each had a few miles on them. The woman was pregnant, her enormous belly a contrast to her thin arms and legs, making him think of the starving dog they'd just left at the vet's office. She bore several amateurish tattoos. There was an angel on her right upper arm, a cross on her left forearm, a cartoon character on one calf, and some writing—a date—on the other thigh.

The young man was even more inked up. Elaborate sleeve tattoos covered each bare arm, and large gauges pierced each earlobe. He was medium height—maybe five eight—and wiry. It was neither his body nor the tattoos that stirred Adam's threat receptors, however, but the air of edgy discomfort emanating from the girl.

"Come on. Just decide," the guy urged. "Either a hot dog or a sundae."

The young woman rubbed her belly tiredly. "Fine. Give me a hot fudge sundae," she told the counter worker. She added a sharp glare at her companion. "A *small*. Please."

Adam stepped toward the row of freezers displaying ready-made ice cream cakes and novelties, uncomfortable standing in the middle of the store with the giant plate glass window to his back. Lizzie shot him a glance, then turned her attention to the menu board. The kid turned, eyes resting on Adam appraisingly. He lifted his chin in a barely perceptible greeting and reached under his shirt.

Oh no. He was about to pull out a gun.

"Hey!" Adam grabbed Lizzie's arm and pulled her next to him, ignoring her gasp of surprise. He stepped forward just as the kid produced…a wallet.

A freaking *wallet*.

The girl, her boyfriend, and the kid behind the counter all stared at Adam as though he'd grown an extra head—one with horns and green hair. The cold acid sweat that had been waiting in the wings broke through, and Adam's skin burned. Lizzie shifted, and he knew she was looking at him, but he ignored her. No way did he want to see how she took his overreaction. *Think*, he told himself. *Breathe.*

"Hey," he said and cleared his throat as though that would blow away the haze of terror and embarrassment from his mind. He reached for his own wallet. "We're, uh, celebrating. Because…I won the lottery. Lizzie said I was stupid for wasting my money on instant tickets, but I promised myself I'd buy dinner for the first people we saw if I won. So I'm buying. Get whatever you want. Add it to our bill."

To his amazement, Lizzie joined in his charade. "Are you getting a chili cheese dog or a regular one?" she asked the astonished pregnant girl. "Because if you're getting chili cheese, you have to get a cotton candy Blizzard to go with it. The Oreo one is good, too."

"Umm…okay," the girl said. "Yeah. Chili cheese dog, please." She looked at Adam, like she expected him to start laughing and rescind his offer, but when he didn't, she turned back to the cashier and said, "And an Oreo Blizzard."

"Dude, are you serious?" the baby daddy asked Adam, probably terrified his girlfriend was going to order half the menu and then stick him with the bill.

"Of course he's serious," Lizzie told him. "What about you? I bet you're a chicken finger guy. That's what Adam likes, right, babe?"

Adam didn't speak again until they'd taken their food to the picnic tables in front of the restaurant. He put their trays down. "I forgot napkins. I'll be right back." In about two steps, he was back inside the Dairy Queen.

Lizzie settled onto the picnic bench and watched through the smudged glass as he reached one long arm over the back of the nearest booth to raid the dispenser on the table. He appeared to have lost none of the muscle he'd built as a soldier.

She already found him distractingly attractive, even though he usually seemed to wish *she* were anywhere else but with him. Unfortunately for him, the hot-guy-to-the-puppy-rescue thing this afternoon and tonight's sensitive generosity made her want him more, no matter how much she'd tried to avoid it. With everything on her plate—taking over Dad's workload, worrying about Dad's cancer, worrying about Mom's worry over Dad's cancer, D-Day, and the idea she had for the Mill Creek property—she didn't have time to moon over Adam every time he took a breath.

Or shoot her an actual *smile* as he pushed the door open on his way back outside.

A honk sounded, and she turned to wave goodbye to their new friends, Clint and Crystal, as they backed out of their parking space. Lizzie hoped their rattletrap vehicle would get them wherever they were going. If not, there were at least a million more beat-up white pickup trucks they could choose from as a replacement. This one was almost identical to the one that had whizzed out of Mill Creek Road that day she and Emma had taken D-Day to Adam's place.

Clint and Crystal sent them a wave as they rumbled

past, and Adam stared at them until they were safely around the corner, then took a deep breath and sat down across from her.

"What's the deal with all the white trucks?" she asked Adam as he handed her a small mountain of paper napkins.

He snorted. "According to Emma, when the economy went bust a few years ago, Big Chance Chevrolet had just ordered a fleet of new trucks for some business that was moving into town. The company went bankrupt, didn't come here, so the dealer had a fire sale."

As if to punctuate his story, another beat-up white truck rolled by, engine coughing and gagging. Adam stared at it until it was out of sight.

"Thanks. Are you sure you want to sit out here?" she asked.

"Yeah. This is great." He wiped his forehead with the back of his wrist and unwrapped his chicken fingers.

He started to take a bite but then stopped. He looked away, out into the Texas night, then met her eyes and said, "Thanks. For going along with that."

She was momentarily stunned, had been prepared to pretend nothing had happened. But since he was talking, she said, "No problem. For what it's worth, that guy seemed creepy to me, too."

He didn't comment, just took another bite.

"Does that happen often?" she asked.

He stopped chewing for the briefest instant, then swallowed and shrugged, shoveling another piece of chicken into his mouth.

Well, all-righty, then. *Not* okay to talk about. "Sorry.

I don't want to make you uncomfortable. Just trying to understand."

"Nothing to understand." He was so nonchalant about it that she almost believed she'd imagined his tension a few minutes ago, the air that quivered electrically over hard muscles as his breath had gotten choppy. That *had* happened.

"It really was nice of you to pay for their food. That poor girl looked like she hadn't had a full meal in nine months."

His only response was a grunt, then, after a moment, "Are you going to eat those?" he asked, indicating her fries.

"Be my guest." She snatched the last bite of hot dog from the basket and shoved the remains of her dinner in his direction. "Well, anyway," she said, "you're good with dogs *and* people. I don't know why you wouldn't want to keep working with them. Maybe you could open a dog training school. Teach people like me to handle their exuberant pets."

He heaved out a heavy breath. "I don't work with *pets*." He said it with a slight derisive curl in his upper lip.

Yes, he did. He worked with *her* pet. Well, her sort-of pet, anyway. "What's wrong with *pets*?"

"*Pets* take up space. A real dog is equipment—it does something useful."

"Okay, then. You can train police dogs or airport drug-sniffing dogs."

"Not gonna happen." He took a long drink of his Coke and said, "You forget. I'm moving on as soon as the ranch is sold."

"What are you going to do?"

He shrugged. "I've got a few options."

Well, that was informative. Fishing around for a change of subject, she said, "So Jake and Marcus are nice."

A grunt.

"I take it you were all in the same, um, unit? Platoon? Whatever?"

"I think 'whatever' might be a good name for it. We did a lot of work together in the Middle East." Adam sighed and rubbed his hand over his face. "And then we got blown up together."

The blast from that statement was too powerful for Lizzie to look at directly. "That's, um, quite a bonding exercise." *Oh geez*. What a stupid thing to say. She opened her mouth to apologize, but then he spoke again.

"You have no idea."

"No. I don't."

"One guy, Emilio Garcia, died, left behind a wife and four boys. Max Zimmerman got burned pretty badly. You've met Jake, who had a TBI—traumatic brain injury. Can't find his way out of a cereal box now and has trouble communicating, along with some physical stuff." He spoke as though he were reciting a grocery list. "Talbott's back is completely jacked. He fakes it really well, but he takes a ton of meds, and it's probably going to get worse as he gets older, though he won't admit it. He works out like crazy to try to keep it strong, but I think he might be making it worse." He stopped talking and gathered their trash.

That couldn't be the whole story. "And you? What happened to you?"

He didn't meet her eyes when he said, "Nothing."

"Nothing at all?"

"That's right," he said. "Are you ready to go?"

Chapter 10

ADAM WASN'T SURPRISED THAT LIZZIE DIDN'T SAY MUCH on the ride from town to the ranch, since he'd weirded out and then shared a chunk of his shitty history, but she also hadn't gone running into the night to get away from him.

And now, instead of the buzzing, prickling anxiety that normally swamped him when he thought about that last mission—or any mission, for that matter—he felt a different kind of tension. He felt as if his skin were reaching out into the air, searching for something, almost like anticipation.

It didn't help that the truck was filled with Lizzie. Her scent, her energy, her *self* all combined to tease him.

It was probably some new post-traumatic flashback endorphin thing caused by the stress of eating chicken fingers after almost going SWAT team on that kid in Dairy Queen. Lizzie was probably quiet now because she was thinking up an excuse for canceling future dog training appointments. *Good.* She should.

There were his old friends, self-loathing and pessimism.

He was surprised when she spoke. "Do you think those two were from Big Chance?"

He switched topics gratefully. "The pregnant couple?"

"Yeah."

He thought about it. "I don't know. The kid looked kind of familiar, but I don't know why I'd recognize him. He'd have been in preschool when I left town."

"You never came back at all?" she asked.

He felt her watching him but knew his face wouldn't give anything away. "Not really. Coupla times to see Granddad and Emma. Didn't come to town." Except one Christmas. He'd been so full of himself and his ambitions. Halfway through MP school, ready to walk up to Lizzie's front door and ask her out on a real date. He'd stopped in to the Feed and Seed to see Todd first, though. He'd been about to ask about Lizzie, when there she was, walking past the store— snug and dry under an umbrella with Joe Chance, who was home from Loyola for break. "Why didn't things work out with you and Joe Chance?" he asked before he could stop himself.

"Huh?" A quick glance showed him a mask of confusion. "Joe Chance?"

"Yeah. You know, the mayor? Football captain, student body everything?"

"I don't know what you're talking about."

He wasn't about to admit that he'd watched her, arms wrapped around one of Joe's, talking and laughing while Adam's heart thudded heavily once or twice before leaking out onto the floor. "I, ah…I thought I remembered hearing you were going out with him."

She was quiet for a while, but her gaze peppered him with questions. Finally, she said, "Nope. We hung sometimes when we were both home on vacation, but it wasn't, like, *romantic* or anything."

Shit. *Shit, shit, shit.* Adam swallowed twelve years of regret that tried to suffocate him. He'd thought he was being all adult, staying out of the way because she was with a better man anyway.

"Someone really said we were going out?"

He cleared his throat. "Yeah. I think Todd said something."

"Well, he was wrong. Joe fell in love the first week of college. His girlfriend told him she was pregnant right before Christmas break that year, and he proposed to her the day they got back to school. I even helped him pick out an engagement ring."

He shook his head. "No, I don't remember hearing anything about that. I was pretty busy."

"Hmm."

What did *hmm* mean?

"Well, anyway," she said, as though their conversation hadn't been detoured through chapter 19 of *Adam's Fucked Up History*, "I just wondered if those two had grown up here or if they moved here for some reason."

"If you see them again, you can ask." He sounded abrupt, even to himself.

Lizzie didn't seem offended, though. "I certainly can."

She sounded so prim and certain that Adam stopped mentally beating himself about the face and head long enough to laugh. "Why do you care?"

"I don't know. Why *do* people live in Big Chance?"

"They're too dumb to chew through their ropes?"

She snorted. "It's not that bad."

He didn't reply.

With a sigh, she said, "Okay. It's not like there are tons of great jobs here, and we're a million miles from anywhere with employment opportunities. So if they didn't grow up here, what would make someone choose to move to Big Chance?"

"I can give you a million reasons to leave, if you want."

"You're not helping," she said, giving his shoulder a playful punch. "I'm trying to brainstorm about bringing new people to town and keeping the people who are already here employed and contributing to society."

"I might be the pot calling the kettle black," he said, "but those two didn't strike me as a couple who are going to be joining the Chance County Chamber of Commerce anytime soon."

"Yeah…but at least he wasn't stupid enough to hold up the Dairy Queen."

He caught her slight smile and raised eyebrow from the corner of his eye and *wasn't* overcome with shame over his near miss. Actually, he felt a strange sort of acceptance. Emma would tell him he was being afflicted with the *feels*, and he wasn't sure he liked it, but it beat cold sweat and stomach cramps.

Lizzie went on. "Anyway, I doubt stealing the cash there would have been worth the trouble. Surely, we can attract a slightly better—or worse, as the case may be—class of criminal."

He burst out with a laugh. "Is your goal to get Big Chance on the *U.S. News and World Report*'s list of best small towns for high-class criminals?"

She grinned. "It's a start."

"Your mind goes some interesting places." And he was tempted to follow.

"I guess I was thinking that, with the possibility of dog-fighting going on near your place and people who can't afford date night at Dairy Queen, Big Chance might take more work than I expected."

"More work? What do you mean?"

She hesitated. "This probably sounds stupid," she finally said, "but I always thought Big Chance could be restored to its former glory as somewhere people visit, instead of a struggling collection of businesses threatened with extinction by the big box stores..." she trailed off. "Yeesh. I sound like a brochure."

Adam chuckled. "What kind of former glory? It's been like this as long as I can remember, except there were a few more places to eat and shop."

"Apparently my great, great something or other grandfather came here in the mid-1800s to help build the town. It had been a trading post when Texas belonged to Mexico, and then after independence, it was a stagecoach stop, and then a railroad stop for all the farms that started to grow up around here. And at some point, someone found gold in the Mill Creek."

"In Texas?"

"That's the story my dad tells. Apparently, that's where the Babcocks—remember Mitch? That jerky guy?"

Oh yes. Adam remembered Mitch Babcock. Though he'd use a stronger description than *jerk*.

"Anyway, I think that's where the original Babcock made enough money to buy the land for the Mill Creek farm once the gold was panned out. I don't think it was a huge gold rush, but it did give Big Chance a short moment of notoriety as a party town. Saloons, gunfighters, the whole shebang. But then there was a drought, and the Civil War happened, and everyone kind of forgot about the gold. My dad's done a ton of research about the history, and I think it would be cool to see the whole area come back to life. I'd love to—" She shook her head. "I don't know. Do something that would bring people out here because it's a neat place to be."

"That's, ah, ambitious," he said. He could almost picture it. "How is this going to work?"

"In stages. First, we need a community gathering point. They're gonna build a new courthouse in town, and that'll use up the space in front of the current one. The reason I went out to the Mill Creek farm in the first place today was because I wanted to see if it can be turned into a park with a historical side, to show the geology of the area, the natural resources, then teach people about which groups of Native Americans lived here before the gold miners and the cattle ranchers and farmers." Lizzie pointed over her shoulder. "Downtown's got such cool retro potential. If it were an attractive place to live, more business might move in."

He snorted. "You want to make Big Chance a tourist destination? You think you can drive commerce here?"

"Well, maybe." She tensed, and he figured she thought he was about to crap on her idea.

It was his turn to surprise her. "I think that's awesome. If anyone can do it, it would be you."

"Oh." She blinked. "Thanks."

He meant it, too. She had some sort of force field that attracted people—and it wasn't just him. Talbott and Jake liked her—which, yeah, could be marked up to sex appeal—but Emma, who he was pretty sure was straight, mentioned Lizzie every time he spoke to her, and that girl at the Dairy Queen had started spilling her whole life story as soon as Lizzie asked her name. No, it was some sort of magic Lizzie mojo, and Adam wasn't immune to it.

"So tell me why you're so anxious to leave," she prodded. "Is it the job market or something else?"

"I never wanted to stay here," he told her, the old fears and heartbreak swelling in his chest and spilling out. "It's stupid, but living here in Big Chance meant our parents were never coming back." He couldn't believe he'd said that, but Lizzie seemed to draw out the dumb-ass confessions. Why hadn't he kept her at arm's length?

"I'm so sorry," she said, no condescension or pity in her voice but empathy in the way she touched his arm.

He lifted his hand to run it through his hair, gently brushing her away and missing the heat the second it was gone. "I was a pretty angry little kid, and I blamed the place, because I couldn't blame the people."

"Your mom and dad?"

"I said it was stupid. Their car wreck was an accident."

"And we have no control over accidents."

Like not finding a bomb before half of everyone you cared about got blown up. Fortunately, the mailbox at the end of the ranch's driveway came into view, and he was saved from responding.

She'd certainly managed to push all the man's painful memories into the light tonight, hadn't she? *Way to build a friendship, Lizzie.* Especially when he was so supportive of her half-baked ideas for Big Chance. Should she apologize? Before she could come up with the right words, they were at the ranch, and Adam was stopping his truck next to her car.

The house was dark, save for a bluish light flickering

through the living room windows. When Adam cut the engine and turned off the headlights, the yard was plunged into near complete darkness. When she got out, however, her steps around the front of the truck were lit by the moon that hung heavily over the trees. Crickets sang and a frog called out for a mate from the brush.

"Wow," she whispered, looking up. "The stars are really bright."

"Yeah, it's pretty dark out here," he answered, closing the driver-side door and stopping a few feet away from her. "I should get one of those automatic lights on top of the barn."

The real estate agent in Lizzie should have agreed, but she waved up at the incredible celestial show spread above them, and said, "But then you wouldn't be able to see that."

Adam didn't answer. When she looked at him, she saw that he was watching her, inscrutable as always. The moonlight made the angles of his face sharper, the planes harder, his eyes dark and dangerous. She couldn't look away.

She licked her lips, and he tracked the motion, his chest rising and falling as the night air grew thicker.

"Listen, I don't usually—" he started.

"I shouldn't have—" she said at the same time, and they both broke off, letting the night sounds fill the space between them.

He took a step closer, and her breath stuttered. He was so strong and handsome and *alone*, and she wanted to touch him, to reach into his heart and let him know that he didn't have to shoulder all the burdens that he carried, but she knew he wouldn't welcome that from her.

Yet she couldn't turn away, couldn't keep herself from looking at his lips, from noticing that he glanced at her mouth, too.

A sudden splash of light from the front of the house broke through the darkness and shattered the moment.

"Hey, did you guys pick up any beer on your way through town?" Marcus called.

"No, but there was almost a whole twelve-pack in the fridge this morning," Adam said, stepping back.

"Yeah, well, something happened. You might have a gremlin or something. Oh shoot. Is that the real estate agent with you? Lizzie, just pretend you didn't hear that. We'll get the exterminator out, and it won't be a problem."

"I don't know if I can get an exterminator to get rid of pests that big," Adam muttered.

"Hey, watch out!" Marcus's silhouette jerked back as excited yipping broke out and the black blur that was D-Day galloped through the darkness.

"Sit!" Lizzie barked out without thinking, and as proof that small miracles do occur, D-Day heard and all but skidded to a stop inches away from her toes. "Good boy," she said, giving him a quick ear rub.

"How are...the puppies?" Jake asked, following Marcus onto the porch.

"I think they're going to be okay," Lizzie answered. "The vet said he'd call with an update tomorrow morning."

"That's good," Marcus said, then pointed at Jake. "This guy's so worried, he couldn't concentrate to play *Dead Rising* for shit tonight."

"I'm brain damaged, asshole," Jake said. "What's...your excuse?"

"Ouch." Marcus laughed. "Brain damaged, my ass. All that bomb did was lower your IQ back into human range."

Adam chuckled and shook his head. He rubbed a hand over his hair and turned to Lizzie, looking suddenly uncertain. "So you're coming out tomorrow for dog training?"

Wait. Had she missed something? "Is that still okay?"

"Yeah. Of course. I wasn't sure…never mind."

He'd talked to her more tonight than he had in all the days they'd been training D-Day put together, and she wondered if he thought he'd somehow scared her off. Unfortunately for her and her libido, he'd done the opposite. She wanted to know more about what went on inside his head…and his heart.

For a moment there, before Marcus came outside, she thought he might even kiss her—but no, that was silly.

She cleared her throat. "I'll be here."

His face was dark, with both the moon and the house lights behind him, but she thought he smiled when he said, "Good. That's…consistency's important."

"Thanks for dinner," she said as she opened her car door and got in.

"You're welcome," he said, closing the door after her.

He looked like he might bend to say something to her through the open window, but then he patted the roof of the car and stepped back. She started the engine and backed up to turn toward the road and home, but then realized she hadn't thanked him for helping her save the pit bulls.

She stuck her head out of the window and called, "Hey!" at his retreating back.

"Yeah?" He turned to face her.

"Thanks for coming when I needed you today."

His expression was shaded by the night, but his words were bleak when he said, "Don't do that. Don't *need* me."

Chapter 11

A COUPLE OF DAYS AFTER THE GREAT DOG RESCUE, AS Talbott decided to dub the event, Adam parked his truck outside his sister's tiny cottage and took stock of his surroundings. D-Day waited impatiently on the seat next to him. The dog would be useless as a watchdog, would most likely drag a robber to the silverware drawer, but as a companion, it had potential. For whoever finally adopted it, anyway.

He got out of the truck and held the door, waiting for D-Day to stop bouncing before saying, "Come on." The dog jumped out and stayed right with Adam as he mounted the front steps.

Even stashed behind the Feed and Seed in the middle of a gray, dried-up downtown, Emma managed to bring a splash of nature to her digs. A hanging basket next to the front door spilled a waterfall of blue and white flowers nearly to the stoop. On the bottom step, a damned combat boot sprouted little cactus things from holes punched here and there in the leather. The little yard was surrounded by the backsides of the farm and hardware store to the right and a defunct bakery to the left. Mostly cinder block, the buildings were disconcertingly reminiscent of the villages Adam and Tank had regularly searched in Afghanistan. The dry, compacted ground, dust blowing in hot wind… it was hard to process. Being in town was always hard, but this place gave his brain mixed messages—home, danger, deserted village, innocent town. A bead of sweat slid along his hairline, and he once again found himself reaching to pat D-Day on the head.

Adam could hear Granddad complaining before he rang the doorbell.

"You're here! Good!" Emma said when she opened the front door. "The lawyer's gonna be here in a couple of minutes."

Hopefully in very few minutes. He forced a slow breath in and out.

"Don't let the air-conditioning out!" a querulous voice called from behind his sister.

Adam stepped into the cool interior, quickly scanning the room—kitchen area to the left, living room and hallway to bedrooms on the right. Well-lit, tidy, not many hiding places. D-Day pressed against Adam's legs, nudged his hand for a pet. He complied.

Granddad sat in a recliner near a small television. Every time Adam saw the man, he was shocked to realize his granddad was so old. Shrunken.

He peered at Adam, suspicion narrowing his cloudy eyes. "Who are you?"

"It's Adam, Granddad. He moved back to Big Chance," Emma said.

"Adam's in the army. Over there killing them Bin Laden assholes."

If only Adam *were* there right now. Not the first time he'd had that thought—Bin Laden was long gone, but there was still plenty of work to do. But no. He couldn't do it anymore. He was here with Granddad, having the same conversation every time he came to visit.

Emma shot him a sideways smile that reminded him she'd been dealing with this shit for much longer than the few months Adam had been back in Big Chance.

The room narrowed, and his vision darkened. *Crap.* He didn't have time for a panic attack right now. His breath stuck in his chest until he felt D-Day's ears under his fingers. He focused on the act of petting the dog, let the patchy fur anchor him in the present, where he was fine. Just fine.

"Are you okay?" Emma rested her hand on his arm, guiding him to a chair like he was a damned invalid, handing him a glass of iced tea.

Iced tea. Amber liquid, melting ice, fresh lemon. Sweet and cold, it chased the imaginary dust in his throat. He hadn't had Emma's sweet iced tea in the army. He was in Big Chance, here to sign paperwork to extend the time frame of their power of attorney for Granddad's care and finances.

Better. He couldn't be a basket case when the lawyer got there—he didn't want the man to think he wasn't competent. But wasn't that part of the reason he'd decided to sell the ranch? So he could make sure there was enough money to take care of Granddad and Emma. Put it somewhere safe so when Adam finally lost his shit for good, he'd know they'd be all right.

"What's that?" Granddad asked, pointing at D-Day. "You call that a dog?"

"Some people do," he said.

"What are you gonna do with it?"

Adam shrugged. "Teach it a few things so someone will want to adopt it."

"You should keep it. Since you don't have a girlfriend

out there to keep you warm at night." Granddad snickered, having shifted back to recognizing Adam. "Come here, dog."

D-Day looked at Adam and, at Adam's nod, approached Granddad and nudged his hand. Granddad rubbed the dog's head, and D-Day sighed with pleasure.

"There's a hole in the barn roof," Granddad said now, drifting back into some long-ago conversation. "Go find that ladder and put some plastic over the kennels on that side. That'll keep 'em dry until we get the leak fixed."

"Okay," Adam agreed. He could pretend he was going to fix a hole in the roof, just like he could pretend to be sane and sensible. "Anything else?"

"When did you get back?" Granddad asked now. "How many a' them Bin Ladens did you kill?"

"Hey, Granddad," Emma said. "I think Joe's here. Do you mind if we turn off *Judge Judy* for now?"

"I don't know why. Lawyers ought to love that show. Teach 'em all how to work right."

Thirty minutes and God only knew how much per hour for a house call later, Adam and Emma had their responsibilities squared away. Adam walked outside with Joe—who had not been Lizzie's boyfriend, ever. But still. Joe Chance was not only the mayor and a lawyer, he was instigator of the wonderful recycling program. Oh, and grandson of the bank president. An all-around good guy, Adam reluctantly admitted to himself. You couldn't hate him for being perfect. It wasn't his fault; it was genetics.

"Thanks for coming by, Joe," Adam said, shaking the man's hand as they stepped down from the porch. While Adam had been scowling around Big Chance his senior year, waiting for graduation and trying not to get arrested before he left for basic training, Joe had been a squeaky-clean freaking Eagle Scout. Even if Lizzie hadn't been his girl back then, he was single now. So why wasn't she calling *him* to help her rescue puppies and giving *him* the big sexy eyes? Joe would be a better choice for her.

Oblivious to Adam's inner dialog, Joe nodded. "Not a problem. I hadn't seen your grandfather in a while. I'm glad my dad talked him into putting this together when he started getting confused. It's difficult to let go of control. He must trust you two a lot."

Adam had never thought of it that way. He'd been focused on the burdens of the situation—mainly that the old guy was a cranky pain in the ass who needed constant supervision so he didn't wander into traffic.

"I wanted to talk to you without Emma," Adam told Joe. "This is between you and me for now. I haven't told her yet, but I'm going to sell the ranch soon, and I'll need to set up some sort of trust so Emma doesn't have to keep Granddad at home. I want to use the money to move him somewhere and give her some savings, too."

Joe nodded. "Okay. We can do that." He handed Adam a card. "Give me a call or come by later in the week. I've got to go right now—my cousin's new tattoo shop is having its grand opening today, and I promised to stop by."

Adam was surprised. The ultraconservative Chance family had spawned a rebel tattoo artist?

He might just have to stop by himself.

"Thanks, Rob. I'll be out tomorrow afternoon to pick them up," Lizzie told the veterinarian and then ended the call.

"Who's that?" Dad asked.

"Rob Chance. The veterinarian. Remember I told you about finding those puppies the other day? They're almost ready to come home...er, *go* to Adam's place."

"Oh yeah." Dad coughed weakly into an enormous red bandanna and then lay his head back on the headrest of his leather recliner, closing his eyes.

"Dad? Do you want some water?" She picked up the half-filled glass on the end table and held it out to him. A whiff of gin burned her nose. "Ohhhkay," she said, carrying the glass to the kitchen and dumping it. She found a fresh one and filled it with ice and water from the fridge.

"What did you do with my drink?" Dad bellowed but then modulated his tone when she reappeared with the water. He narrowed his eyes but didn't comment when she handed it to him. With a weak cough, he sipped and put it on the table, hand shaking.

Lizzie narrowed her own eyes. She suddenly had a sneaking suspicion that he wasn't feeling quite as miserable as he would have her—and her mother—believe.

"What have you been up to?" he asked her.

"Well..." In a perfect world, she'd do this all on her own and make it a fabulous, tear-jerking surprise with an *Extreme Home Makeover*-type reveal. But this was *her* world, and she needed help. "Remember Mill Creek, where all the kids used to go to have, um, picnics and stuff when I was in high school?"

"You mean the old Babcock place, where all the kids used to go to drink beer and make out?" he asked, straight-faced.

"Mmm, that's probably the same place."

"It's also where I think my grandfather had his claim, you know."

"I think you've mentioned that a time or two." *Or two million.* "Do you have any documentation about all that? I'm kind of interested in the history of the place."

He shook his head. "Nope. Just the stories Grandpa told."

"I wonder if there's anything at the courthouse." She'd already come up empty on current information, but maybe there'd be a clue in something from farther back—if she knew where to look.

Dad harrumphed. "I doubt it. Every time I've gone there to research a title or a deed, the file was conveniently burned in the Great Courthouse Fire or the Even Greater Sprinkler Disaster."

"That's what I was afraid of."

"You know, your mom and I used to go to Mill Creek to neck."

"Ew!" Lizzie clapped her hands over her ears, which she'd done every time he'd told her this her entire life.

"What's this about, anyway?" Dad asked.

She took a deep breath. "I think we should turn that land into a proper park, a kind of combination nature preserve, walking trail, playground, and local history center thing."

He raised both eyebrows. "That's a lot."

"I know. But it's a big place, and I figure if there's a lot to do there, more local organizations will be interested in supporting it. It would be a community thing and part of my new campaign to bring Big Chance back to life."

"You have a campaign?"

She nodded. "I do now."

"What's it called?"

"Well, it's not official or anything, but I guess it's called 'Bring Big Chance Back to Life.'"

He laughed. "Well, I can see the school system supporting the nature preserve idea, if you make it kid-friendly, and the town council ought to like the idea of a playground. But the entire Big Chance Historical Society is Mrs. Wells, the librarian, and the library closed three years ago, so she has the time."

The library was out of business? Lizzie put that in her mental "fix after the park" file. "I thought maybe you could help with the history part."

His face creased with pleasure. "I can do some groundwork." After a beat, he added dryly, "And I suppose Vanhook Realty could be another supporter."

She smiled innocently. "That's a great idea. And maybe I can reel in Chance and Sons Construction and any other local businesses that aren't going under."

Dad raised his brows. "Aren't you somethin', diving right into being a part of this town again."

"I think it was inevitable. But we have to find out who owns that land. If you don't know, who should I try next?"

"Have you run this by anyone from the town council yet? Like the mayor? Call Joe Chance. Kill two or three birds," Dad suggested.

"Did I hear you mention Joe Chance?" Mom asked, entering the room.

"Yes," Lizzie answered, flinching. Not a good idea to bring up the name of Big Chance's most eligible widower in Mom's earshot.

"Such a nice boy," Mom said.

"Yep. He's a good guy," Lizzie said.

"And such a sad story," Mom went on, shaking her head, "losing his wife so young. He has to raise those two little girls on his own now."

Mom was right, it *was* a sad story. Joe and his college girlfriend-turned-wife had been pretty happy, apparently. They had another baby several years after the first. But the woman died in a car accident. Joe, who'd been driving, escaped unscathed—physically, anyway. He'd come home to Big Chance to live with his family, where he was a busy lawyer, and—possibly because no one else wanted the job—had just been elected mayor.

"You know that the Hometown Independence Day celebration is coming up soon," Mom added. Some might hear that as a non sequitur, but Lizzie knew Mom was about to tell her to seek out the tragically single Joe Chance at the party, draw him in with her womanly wiles, and become the next—hopefully less tragic—Mrs. Chance.

Lizzie wasn't interested. Joe had been nice in high school—and definitely not unappealing, with his all-American blond hair and blue eyes—but the image of a tall, dark-haired soldier crossed her mind and eclipsed Joe.

Of course, with the way Adam had barely spoken to her in the days since their Dairy Queen chat, maybe she *should* aim her sights at Joe. Reliable, friendly Joe.

Chapter 12

Lizzie saw a familiar tricked-out Camaro in the parking lot of the veterinarian's office when Emma pulled her battered SUV into a spot and turned off the engine.

"What the heck is that thing?" Emma asked at the same time as Lizzie said, "Marcus is here!"

Emma looked confused. "Who?"

"Marcus. Talbott?" Lizzie reminded her.

"He's one-a them soldier friends of Adam's," Granddad supplied helpfully from the back seat.

"How do you know that?" Emma turned and looked at Granddad.

"I know everything," he said. "Mrs. King spends all day on Facebook and that Insta-whatsits. She doesn't even have to go out to the back fence to get her gossip anymore. Ain't that a thing?"

Lizzie saw Emma suppress a smile and nod in agreement. "That *is* something, Granddad. I don't hear half as much in the Feed and Seed."

"That's 'cause everyone goes over to that big place in Fredericksburg," he said sagely.

"God save us from Granddad and his 'good' days," Emma muttered as they got out of the car.

Lizzie thought the old man was pretty entertaining at the moment, but she also knew that his bad days were pretty darned bad, and he was a handful all the time.

Emma took Granddad's arm until he had his cane and both feet safely out of the car and steered him toward the entrance to the vet's office. "Let's go get these puppies," she said, squinting at the painfully bright glare from Marcus's white Camaro and raising her eyebrows at Lizzie in a *What kind of redneck throwback is this guy?* look.

Boy, was Emma in for a surprise, Lizzie thought. Meanwhile, she wondered what Marcus was doing here. Hopefully, there wasn't anything wrong with D-Day. If there was, surely Adam would have brought him here himself.

"Real Estate Lady!" Lizzie heard as her eyes adjusted to the dimmer light inside the cool waiting room.

"Marcus?" she asked. "What are you doing here?"

"We found…a dog." Jake's halting voice came from behind a bedraggled golden retriever, which shook its head and tucked its nose into the crook of Jake's neck.

The women followed as Granddad stumped over to the bank of chairs to inspect the dog on Jake's lap while Marcus stood to greet them. The dog wasn't interested in making new friends and tried to crawl under Jake's arm. "He's scared," Jake said.

"Okay, we'll give him a little space," Lizzie said, backing up a step.

After waving to the receptionist to make sure their arrival was noted, Lizzie provided introductions. She was shocked to see that Marcus's Schmooze-Master persona was nowhere in sight as he held out his hand to Emma and said, "It's nice to meet you," and gave her an almost bewildered smile. Marcus wasn't as tall as Adam or Jake, but he towered over Emma. He was built like a tank, and his dark skin and baby dreadlocks made an interesting contrast with Emma's pale, edgy femininity.

Much to his obvious disappointment, however, Emma barely gave him a glance and a two-millisecond handshake before moving on to greet Jake and the golden retriever.

"What's the deal with the dog?" Lizzie asked.

Dragging his gaze away from Emma, Marcus regained his composure and grinned. "Well, it's a funny story."

Jake ducked his head around the dog to look at Lizzie and shook his head.

"Not funny?" she asked.

Marcus rolled his eyes before sitting back down and putting a soothing hand on the dog's back. "I meant funny-strange, not funny-haha."

Jake shrugged.

Marcus said, "I went to get the mail, and this guy was sitting at the end of the driveway. Just sitting there next to the mailbox. I get up there and see someone *tied* him to the post."

"What?" Lizzie was stunned. "Why would someone just tie a dog to some stranger's mailbox?"

"I think they knew we've been taking in dogs. Decided to send us one more. He's good lookin', huh?"

Not really. Not only was the fur matted and filthy, but even through all the disgusting fur, it was clear the poor thing hadn't had a full meal in a while.

Emma, who'd been silent up to this point, said, "I bet Adam was thrilled."

Jake, once again invisible behind the dog, sighed.

Marcus smiled sheepishly. "Adam doesn't know yet. He had to, um, run some errands. We thought we'd bring him here, get him checked out, and see if he's got a microchip in case he's really lost and whoever abandoned him wasn't his actual owner. In the meantime, we'll keep him with us. Hide him between the puppies. What's one more?"

Emma snorted. Lizzie agreed. Adam was going to have a cow.

"Where's that other one?" Granddad asked.

"You mean D-Day?" Marcus asked. "He went with Adam."

That was interesting. Adam, who worked so hard to pretend like he couldn't stand the dog, had taken him for a ride?

"I'd like to be a fly on the wall when Adam gets a load of this addition to the family," Emma said gleefully.

"Right?" Marcus looked at Emma, and they shared an evil grin, which she glanced away from almost as soon as it started. "Hey, I have an idea," Marcus said, eyes still on Emma. "Why don't we do a cookout this afternoon? You guys are all coming out with the puppies and the mom, right? The weather's not too hot, and we can have a 'Welcome to the Big Chance Rescue Ranch' party. I'll see what grillables and drinkables I can come up with."

"Lizzie," the receptionist called, "Dr. Chance said you can come back whenever you're ready."

"Okay, thanks." Lizzie, who was always up for flame-broiled meat—and beer—looked at Emma to see what she thought about the party idea.

"What do you say, Granddad?" Emma asked. "Do you want to visit the ranch?"

"The ranch? My ranch? I thought you sold that money pit," Granddad said.

"I did. To Adam."

"Who?" He cupped his hand around his ear.

"Adam."

"Oh. But he's off fighting them terrorists in the desert."

Emma sighed and patted him on the shoulder. To Lizzie, she said, "We'll give it a try."

Plans agreed upon, Lizzie, Emma, and Granddad went through to the back rooms and found a much-improved mother pit bull and her now one-week-old pups in a small, hard plastic swimming pool.

The female stood awkwardly but looked rather piratical with her patched eye and splinted foreleg. Emma looked up at the tech to confirm, "She's friendly?" before holding her hand out a few inches from the dog so she could sniff her if she wanted to.

"Sweet as can be," the tech said. "Lets you pick up her pups, loves to get petted. She's a little hesitant on the lead, like she's been tied up or dragged, but she's so sweet, I bet she'll follow you anywhere."

"Pit bull, though," commented another tech. "You need to keep her restrained or someone will call the dogcatcher if they don't shoot her first."

"Every dog needs to be on a lead when they're around strangers," Granddad announced. "I used to train police dogs, you know." He began to regale the technicians with a story of his glory days while Lizzie guided the mother dog into the nearby crate.

Emma knelt, picked up a couple of puppies to hand in, and asked Lizzie, "What are you going to call them?"

"The mama is Loretta," she said. She looked under the

two nearly solid black pups that Emma handed her. "These guys are Garth and Travis."

Emma gave her two more, holding a black-and-white spotted one higher. "Girl." Then she raised the other, a brindle. "Boy."

Lizzie tapped her chin. "What do you think?"

Emma smiled. "Taylor and Lyle."

"Taylor Swift…who's Lyle?"

Emma shrugged. "Lyle Lovett. He was married to Julia Roberts for, like, five minutes, a long time ago."

"Okay. Lyle and Taylor, get in here with Garth and Travis."

"And here are the last two, both girls."

Lizzie looked at them, one mostly reddish, the other mostly white. "Reba and Faith."

Emma stood. "Come on, Granddad. You can come back here to tell dog training stories another day."

The tech smiled. "Visit anytime."

"Be careful what you ask for," Emma muttered.

"Thank Dr. Chance for us," Lizzie said. "We really appreciate his help."

"You're welcome," Dr. Chance said, coming into the room with a smile. "It was our pleasure."

The dogs securely settled in the crate, Dr. Chance hoisted it up and said, "Lead the way."

And Loretta and her band went to discover their new home.

"Why don't you at least get the prescription filled, and then you'll have it if you decide you need it?" Daphne asked Adam.

"Okay," he agreed with reluctance. He wasn't going to take the new antianxiety meds, but if it got his therapist off his back, that was one less person he'd disappoint this month. "Thanks for coming outside to talk. Maybe I shouldn't have brought the dog." He pointed at D-Day, who was snoozing in the grass, soaking up the sun.

"No problem. I'm sorry about the *service dogs only* rule," she said, gesturing at the building. "So I'll see you again at our regular time next month?" she asked, scrolling through her phone.

"I guess so," Adam allowed. He almost hadn't come today. That was one of the reasons he'd let D-Day in the truck this morning. He'd hoped that by "accidentally" bringing his dog along, Daphne would reschedule when he called her from the parking lot, unable to enter the building with a dog.

She'd laughed when he'd told her what he'd done and said, "Not many people would admit they accidentally on purpose brought their dog."

Now he rose and held out his hand to the middle-aged social worker assigned to him by the VA. She'd grown up in Dallas, had never witnessed anything more violent than a hockey game. And still she listened to his shit and, with very few comments, somehow made him feel better—for the first hour or so after their appointments anyway.

"I wonder something," Daphne said, looking at D-Day, who had risen to his feet with Adam. "There are more and more veterans coming in with PTSD service dogs, and it really seems to help."

Adam was already shaking his head before she finished her sentence. "This one's not suited for that sort of thing."

She raised an eyebrow. "He seems to be pretty in tune with you, and you know how to train dogs. Teaching him how to respond when you're stressed seems like a no-brainer to me."

Adam didn't tell her that D-Day already seemed to notice when he was getting agitated and would lean against his legs, asking to be petted. But he couldn't take care of another living thing. Ever. "It's an interesting idea, but I'm not going to be responsible for this thing's happiness," he said, turning to leave.

"I think you already are," Daphne said, letting her parting shot drift over him on his way to the parking lot.

It followed him clear back to Big Chance.

He eyed the dog, who sniffed with interest at the air coming in through the cracked open window.

Could D-Day learn to do things that a PTSD assistance dog would need to do? Turn on a light, fetch medication, interrupt the cycle?

Adam wasn't going to keep D-Day, because when he left Big Chance, he was going alone. But maybe he'd see what the dog could do, and maybe it could help someone else.

Chapter 13

"Thanks, Joe," Adam said. "Next Thursday should be fine." He held the phone to his ear with his shoulder and turned the truck onto Wild Wager Road.

"Great. I've got you down," Joe said. "Oh, hey. I have a quick question. Probably nothing, but do you know anything about some sort of extra life insurance policy or investment account that your grandparents might have stashed away?"

"What?" Adam laughed. "No. The only thing Granddad had was this ranch and a little social security income. Why?"

"Just something your grandfather said. Let me know if you think of anything."

"Will do," Adam said, then figured since he had the man on the phone, he might as well ask, "What's the deal with that Mill Creek property? Lizzie was asking about it, but I don't know anything except we share a fence line and Mitch Babcock lorded it over everyone that his family owned the coolest party spot."

"I don't know much more than that. Mitch's dad ran into some kind of financial trouble a year or two after we graduated from Big Chance. They pulled up stakes and disappeared almost under cover of darkness."

"Big scandal, huh?" Adam tried not to be pleased that overprivileged Mitch had been taken down a few notches.

"I guess. I heard a bunch of rumors. His dad had stolen

a bunch of money from the insurance company he worked for, his mom was having an affair with the principal of Big Chance...maybe Mitch's dad wasn't really his dad."

"Damn." He wasn't going to feel sorry for the asshole, but he did consider that maybe Mitch's life hadn't been as pretty and shiny as it had looked from the outside.

"Well, anyway, your grandfather keeps saying something about the extra money, but he's so confused, I figure it's something he's seen on TV or something."

"I'll be sure to let you know if I run across any secret hidey holes with keys to a gold mine," he said, and Joe laughed.

A noise in the background was accompanied by a muffled "just a second" from Joe's side of the line. "Hey, I've got to go. It's time for another Independence Day planning meeting, and I'm in charge of the dance contest."

Yeesh. Adam's money problems suddenly seemed more attractive. "You're the mayor. Can't you delegate that stuff?"

"Unfortunately, no. It's either the dance contest or the teenage talent contest."

Adam shuddered. "Talk to you later, Mr. Mayor." He hung up and turned into his driveway, looking forward to knocking out a few more home repair chores before collapsing on the couch and kicking some virtual zombie ass with Talbott and Jake.

Through his open window, he heard music and saw a speaker on the edge of the porch, near a small pyramid of beer cans. His right temple started to throb. Talbott sat on the porch steps, cooler at his feet, clearly the architect of the great Coors pyramid, talking to Emma. Whatever the topic, she wasn't buying his line of bull, because she shook her head and waved a dismissive hand his direction as she walked away.

Adam hoped there wouldn't be drama—it was bad enough that he had company. On the plus side, the scent of freshly mowed grass tickled his nose. The yard had been cut, and the fence line was clean.

Jake leaned on the handle of a rickety lawn mower that Adam didn't even know he owned, wiping sweat and grass from his face with his T-shirt, pulled up to expose his stomach. *Jesus.* One of them needed to start actually cooking, because the kid was looking better, but he needed to regain some of the meat that had fallen from his bones over the past few months.

And then Adam saw Lizzie. She stood in the paddock, a pair of filthy yellow shorts exposing miles of tanned, curvy leg, and an equally dirty white tank top clinging appreciatively to her torso. Maybe a little unexpected company wasn't so bad.

Then he saw the dog. *What the*—? A golden retriever, crouching and wagging in front of her, barking to encourage Lizzie to toss the tennis ball she held. Instead of throwing the ball, she aimed a hesitant smile in Adam's direction and picked up the leash dangling from the dog's side.

In the passenger seat, D-Day, already quivering with excitement, barked happily, because Lizzie was coming their way with another dog. D-Day tried to climb over Adam to greet Lizzie and the new arrival. Adam heaved the big lug back to its side of the truck and gave a stern, "No."

"Hi. We left you a parking spot." Lizzie pointed to the side of the barn, where her SUV and Talbott's ride rested. "We're having a party." Her wary smile tugged at emotions he normally kept deeply buried but that seemed to be reaching up out of the dirt in his soul more often lately. He wanted to tell her there was no reason to feel awkward, that even though he'd kind of avoided her for a few days after spilling his guts to her, he was thrilled that she'd come to the ranch.

Her uncertainty might have been more about the big hairy fluff ball than it was about him, though.

He was almost afraid to ask. "What's with the dog?"

Her eyes shifted from left to right, and she tugged the dog so it was behind her. "Dog? What dog?"

He suppressed a smile but rolled his eyes and let the truck roll forward to park next to the other vehicles. The ancient grill had been pulled out of the horse shed and stood next to the equally old picnic table. A few bags of groceries and a bag of charcoal sat waiting. They really were having a party. He shook his head and turned off the truck.

Whatever the deal was with the new dog, it was a chance for D-Day to practice restraint, so Adam gave a "stay" command and got out of the truck. D-Day stayed but worked the sad puppy look like a champion. Lizzie had followed the truck and now handed Adam a beer, all the while trying to keep the big yellow dog behind her.

"Thanks." He eyed the animal as he pulled the tab. He took a long swallow. His headache eased a little—until the dog nudged Lizzie out of the way and rose to its hind legs, nose to nose through the window with D-Day.

"What's with the dog?" he asked again.

"Get down," she hissed at the retriever. It got down but whined up at D-Day, who whined back. Lizzie's eyes widened in fake innocence. "I don't see a dog."

Lizzie's face bore almost as many smudges as her clothes, but her cheeks had been kissed by the sun, and she looked...happy. "How was your day, wherever you went?" she asked.

As distraction techniques went, it was pretty pathetic, but he gave her a pass while he let D-Day out of the truck. He choked up on the leash, since there was no telling how the two dogs would react to each other within touching—or biting—distance. He had to remind D-Day that when Adam stood still, dogs were supposed to sit, but after one quick correction, D-Day sat sniffing vigorously toward the other dog, which had wrapped Lizzie in a spiral of leash and sniffed back.

"Did you guys have a good trip?"

He ignored her blatant fishing trip for information—she wouldn't be interested in his trip to the shrink—and stayed on topic. "My day was fine. It might be better if you tell me you didn't bring another stray here for me to deal with."

In mock sincerity, she said, "I did *not* bring another stray here for you to deal with."

Hmm. Maybe *she* didn't. "Then who did?"

Jake sidled up and took the leash. He crouched down to pet the retriever. "We did."

"I found him tied to your mailbox this morning." Talbott had risen from the porch steps and ambled over. "You should have seen him before we got him cleaned up."

Lizzie nodded in agreement. "Ick."

Adam squeezed the bridge of his nose. D-Day took advantage of the lapse in attention to pull away and sniff exuberantly at the retriever, which accepted the other dog's interest with patience.

"No more dogs," Adam said.

He caught Lizzie, Talbott, and Jake exchanging a look that asked if he meant *no more after or before the retriever?*

"Did it have a collar?" he had to ask.

"Nope. We took it to the vet and no chip, either," Talbott said.

"Great."

"So anyway," Lizzie said, like the subject was closed, "I ran into Marcus, Jake, and Patton here when I went to pick up Loretta and the kids, and we decided to have a little celebration."

He didn't know which issue to address first. "Loretta and the kids?"

She pointed at a small kiddie pool that had been hidden behind a bush until he walked closer to the house. Granddad dozed on a rocking chair next to the dogs. "The pit bull," Lizzie said. "I named her Loretta, remember?"

Did he? It didn't matter.

"The kids are Taylor, Reba, Faith, Travis, Lyle, and Garth."

Vaguely aware that Lizzie was using names of country music artists he should recognize, he eyed the dusty cowboy boots on her feet. She probably knew how to line dance and would participate in Mayor Joe's dance contest next weekend.

"And now we have Patton, too." She smiled and pointed at the new dog, who was allowing D-Day to chew on its ears.

Adam said, "Leave it," and D-Day reluctantly sat. "Patton, huh?"

"I named him," Jake said.

Oh good. They probably got Jake to name the damned thing because next to Lizzie, Jake was the person Adam would have the most trouble saying no to.

"Oh, well in that case…" Adam didn't finish the sentence. He was so screwed.

Lizzie smiled and bumped Adam with her shoulder, a move that shouldn't have been so sexy, but the contact cranked up his awareness of her a few notches. "I think I need another beer," she announced, a little too emphatically. It dawned on Adam that she'd already had a couple. "Do you want another?" she asked him.

Adam shook his can and scowled. His first was already empty. "Yeah, I guess I do." Maybe if he had a buzz on, things would make more sense.

"What do people do for fun around here?" Marcus asked Emma while Lizzie picked at the tomato and cucumber salad she'd scooped onto her plate.

"Oh, you know," Emma said, not looking at him. "The usual. Watch haircuts. Listen to the grass grow."

"That sounds fun," Marcus said, not missing a beat. "Maybe you can show me where the barber shop is some day."

Emma did look at him then, raising an eyebrow at the baby dreadlocks sprouting from Marcus's head. "It's on Main Street, next to the tattoo place," she said, rising. "I'm going to get Granddad's meds."

Marcus just smiled and watched her walk away before tuning into a conversation Adam and Jake were having about something that had happened on a patrol while they were deployed together.

Adam took a big bite of the juicy hamburger while Lizzie tried not to drool on the burgers remaining on the plate. She shoveled in a bite of tomato, but it wasn't exactly satisfying. Not only was the salad less than filling, it was doing very little to take the edge off her three-beer buzz. She tried never to drink on an empty stomach—though to be honest, until recently, she hadn't had an empty stomach since breaking up with Dean. The first thing she'd done after leaving him was stop at Baskin-Robbins. She'd showed him, by God—gained ten pounds in two months. She pushed a piece of tomato from one side of the plate to the other before giving up and shoving the plate away.

She'd come home to find herself, but damned if she meant to find so *much* of herself.

Adam stopped talking and looked at her. "Why aren't you eating?" he asked.

"I ate," she said, pointing at her half-eaten salad.

"That's not food," he told her. "That's…filler."

She smiled. "I'm fine, really. I had most of today's calorie allotment about three days ago."

Adam frowned while he ran over her words, then shook his head and pointed at the platter of burgers, melted cheese singing its siren song in her direction. "Eat. Please."

"Oh, whatever," she said and grabbed the bag of buns from the other end of the table. Salad wasn't doing much to sober her up anyway.

After she'd eaten and listened to the umpteenth story about people she didn't know anything about, she decided it was time to go home. Lizzie wasn't an integral part of this gathering. If it wasn't for the guys adding "sorry" or "pardon my French" after every "motherfucker" or "cocksucker," she might have thought she was invisible. Good thing she'd stopped at home for her own car after fetching the puppies from the vet—she could leave on her own schedule.

D-Day, who lay on the ground between Lizzie and Adam, decided he'd had enough good behavior. He stretched and wiggled from beneath the table, rising to his long legs and giving a good shake, but was stopped short. He'd somehow managed to tangle his lead with Patton's. While the newer dog sat patiently waiting for rescue, D-Day limped in a circle and whined.

"Hold on, big guy," she told D-Day. She ducked beneath the table to unwind the nylon from the legs of the table and was greeted with three sets of long, human male legs. Adam was directly across from her, wearing jeans and work boots. Jake was next to Adam, in shorts and trainers, his thin legs pale and covered in dark hair—though the Texas sun and a fair amount of yard work did wonders to bring him closer to healthy. It was Marcus's feet, however, that drew her notice. One of them was discolored. Darker than the rest of his normally brown skin, it was almost purple. As though aware of her notice, he shifted his legs.

She quickly unwrapped the leash and straightened, her eyes automatically going to his face. He was pretending to pay attention to the story Adam was telling, but the lines of pain radiating from the corners of his mouth and eyes told another story.

"Marcus, your foot's purple," she blurted.

He jerked like she'd smacked him, which only made the pain on his face intensify.

"Dude, what the hell?" Adam asked, looking under the table. Marcus shifted as though to turn himself away from Adam's perusal but didn't get far.

"You've been sitting here too long," Jake said.

"I'm fine," Marcus shot back. "Keep track of yourself, would you?"

Jake was unfazed. "I'm trying. It would be…easier if you followed your doctors' instructions."

"What are you supposed to be doing?" Adam asked.

"Nothing."

"He's not supposed to sit for long without…walking, because of his…blood flow," Jake supplied.

"Jesus Christ," Marcus muttered. "It's not a big deal."

"Then let's get up and move." Adam rose, gathering a few empty beer cans. He took D-Day's leash in his free hand while Lizzie sat on Patton's leash and reached for the used paper plates. Jake shoved condiment bottles into a plastic grocery bag. Even Granddad, who had appeared to be napping, moved the container of cookies—onto his lap.

Marcus didn't move, other than to drain his beer and reach for another.

"Marcus?" Adam asked. It seemed somehow significant that this was the first time he hadn't called his friend Talbott—at least not in Lizzie's hearing.

"Yeah, yeah," he said, shoulders slumped as though his entire world—perhaps his façade of good health *was* his entire world—had been yanked from under him. "Give me a minute."

Lizzie felt terrible. The last thing she'd ever want to do was make someone feel bad about himself. She grasped for something to make amends—being useful usually helped her. "Can you hold onto Patton while I put these in the trash?"

Marcus reached for the leash, and the dog gladly moved around the table to a new sucker willing to scratch behind his ears. Patton sat on his haunches and raised a rear foot to swipe at his neck. "What's the matter, buddy? Collar too snug?" Marcus fiddled with the buckles, then shoved his hand under the nylon. "That's better." The dog stood, pulling Marcus to his feet as he moved.

"Hey," Jake commented. "That's the fastest…you've gotten up…in six months. Maybe you need…a dog to remind you to move."

Marcus regarded Patton. "So, what? I agree to take him for a walk every fifteen minutes, and he yanks me up off my broken ass?"

"Exactly," Jake said.

"There you go," Adam said. "Train it to be a service dog, and get it to earn its kibble."

"I don't need a damned seeing *eye* dog," Marcus said, stepping forward gingerly on the discolored foot.

"Not a seeing eye dog. Stability, mobility, whatever," Adam told him.

Emma, who had returned from the house, said, "Patton's a sturdy guy. I bet he could do it if the vet says it's okay."

"Dr. Chance said…he has good hips," Jake said.

"I've read about service dogs for veterans," Lizzie said. "They do a lot—from helping people remember to take medicine to easing anxiety issues from PTSD." She couldn't help looking at Adam when she said this, but he didn't return her attention.

"Wow, Sar'nt," Jake said. "You could train service

dogs…as easy as you trained Tank. Tank could even… help you."

Even the dogs froze under the immediate, oppressive silence. The crickets stopped warming up their nighttime instruments to hear Adam's response. He stared at Jake, jaw ticking, expression shuttered, before he took a breath and said, "Yeah, Lieutenant. Maybe he would." Without another word, he picked up the platter of leftover burgers in his non-leash hand and stalked to the house.

No one else spoke until the front door closed. Jake looked at Marcus and asked, "I messed up…again, didn't I?" Not waiting for an answer, Jake said, "Excuse me," then disappeared into the barn.

Marcus recovered and called, "It's okay, man," after Jake, but Jake didn't come back. "Shit."

Lizzie had no idea what had just happened. "Who's Tank?"

"He was Adam's last dog," Emma told her.

Marcus added, "He got blown up with the rest of us, but he didn't make it."

"Oh no." Lizzie looked at the house, as if it would spit Adam back out so she could see if he was okay.

"Here. This stuff needs to be refrigerated," Emma said, handing Lizzie a couple of grocery bags with leftovers. "I've got to get Granddad home. Tell Adam we said goodbye."

Lizzie appreciated Emma's obvious effort to give her an excuse to go after Adam but wasn't sure he'd welcome her presence. She went anyway and found him in the kitchen, fighting with a roll of aluminum foil. The foil, with a roll-hindering crimp along one end, was winning, and the sheet tore the wrong way. "God *damn* it." Adam wadded up the offending foil and slammed it into the trash can. D-Day watched with interest.

"Here," Lizzie said and put the bags she'd carried on the counter. "I'm good at this."

He looked like he didn't want to let it go—like he needed to prove his supremacy over inanimate objects—but with a disgusted sigh, he gave it to her.

"I brought in the rest of the food," she said, pushing at the bent edge with a thumbnail.

Adam didn't say anything but started taking things out of the bags and putting them in the fridge.

"Emma's taking your grandpa home. She said to tell you goodbye."

Nothing.

"I was thinking about entering the Miss Nude Big Chance contest next week. Do you think I should get a Brazilian first or go natural with a hint of landscaping?"

"Jesus Christ, Lizzie! Can't you tell when a man doesn't want to talk?" Adam crossed his arms over his chest and narrowed his eyes at her, but she could see that he was working to suppress a smile.

Trying equally as hard to hide the triumph she felt at getting through that tough hide, she said, "Well, I really can't talk to anyone else about this."

He snorted. "You really can't talk to *me* about it, either." But now his eyes twinkled.

"I don't know why not."

He scanned her from top to toe, and she thought his cheeks might be the slightest bit flushed when he shook his head and growled, "When are you going to sell this place for me?"

She had no idea whether the thought of seeing her as Miss Nude Big Chance grossed him out or turned him on, but at least he was talking to her. "I'll *list* this place when you finish the improvements I suggested." So far, he'd started several (probably unnecessary) jobs but had yet to paint the house, fix the roof, cut down the massive jungle that nearly overgrew the driveway, or shore up the sagging porch roof.

He scowled. "I'll start tomorrow."

"And then you'll talk to Emma?"

"I guess so."

Lizzie tried not to laugh at how much he sounded like a recalcitrant teenager. "Then I'll put some feelers out and see who might be looking for something."

He nodded. "Thank you."

She watched him for a moment. She wasn't responsible for whatever bad memories he was wading through tonight, but she also didn't want to leave him alone if he was in a bad place. "I, um, I should head out, I guess. Are you okay?"

He raised an eyebrow, no longer sullen or teenager-like and every bit the walking advertisement for hotness. "I'm good. Probably won't sleep much tonight, wondering what you decide."

Lizzie tilted her head, not sure what he was talking about but held captive by his laser-blue stare.

His smile was almost feral when he said, "I vote natural."

Chapter 14

THE DREAM THAT NIGHT WAS BAD. AFTER THE DAY HE'D had—seeing his shrink, talking about Tank—Adam expected it, had even considered taking some of the Ambien the doc at the VA had prescribed, but he'd had a few beers, and he didn't like the way it made him feel. He usually woke up in worse shape than if he'd forced himself to stay awake all night. But sometimes you just had to fucking sleep.

Last night, he'd managed to get over himself enough to go back outside and help Emma get Granddad loaded up and act like he hadn't just had a temper tantrum because poor Jake upset his delicate feelings. Before he told Lizzie good night, she said something inconsequential about putting out feelers to people who might be looking for land before officially listing the property. And then she gave him a damned *hug* before *kissing* the dog on the head and driving off into the night.

Talbott and Jake went to walk the new dog and the pit bull before it was completely dark, so he'd gone inside and up to bed. Didn't matter that it was only nine o'clock.

He told himself he was going to read for a couple of hours, but like anything else he'd tried to do for the last, *hell*, five years, his attention span was shit. He wound up staring at shadows on the ceiling. What was he doing, trying to fix things in Big Chance? He should leave now. And do what?

Maybe he should get a job driving interstate trucks. Be on the road for the rest of his life.

That had led him to thinking he might have to stay with his sister during holidays, and then he was somehow driving a tractor trailer full of soldiers—like a boxcar in a World War II concentration camp movie. They were in Afghanistan, and Lizzie sat next to him in the cab, telling him all the things she wanted him to help her with. He couldn't help her because there were soldiers in trouble, and he was responsible for them... A family of dogs blocked the road, strapped with explosives. He told Lizzie not to try to move them, but she just laughed and patted his leg and got out. He tried to stop her, but his door was locked.

The next thing he knew, he was sitting up, gasping for breath. D-Day straddled his chest, dangling a giant, slimy rope toy in his face.

He sat up and shoved his hands in the dog's fur, pulling him close, breathing in his relatively clean doggy smell. He let his own breath match the dog's rhythm until they were both panting less desperately.

D-Day licked Adam's ear and reclined next to him with a sigh. Adam rubbed his head, acknowledging—if only to himself—that he appreciated the dog choosing to sleep in his room instead of with his new best friend, Patton.

He lay back and tried to think about anything else, but the images from the dream, the sense of impending danger, were slow to leave.

The comforting murmur of faint curses and explosions from the living room beckoned, so he got up to join Jake and Talbott for the current zombie apocalypse battle. He wanted to bitch at them and blame the sounds of gunfire and death screams for his interrupted sleep but knew that was bullshit. Hell, the video game was practically white noise for him.

"Hey, man," Talbott said, scooting over to make room on the couch and reaching into a handy cooler for a cold beer, which he handed to Adam. "Take over for me. We've almost got that herd of zombies corralled in the school gym."

D-Day joined the retriever next to the plastic kiddie pool, which someone—probably Jake—had wrangled inside to serve as a nursery. The female pit bull raised her head to glare at the boys, then settled down with a sigh when she was sure they were there to keep her company, not harm her children. The damaged eye had been removed, but even with the splinted leg, she was doing surprisingly well.

Adam accepted a beer, joined the game, and decapitated a few gray monsters, but then Jake's character ran into a blind alley and got eaten.

"Aaah, hell," Jake said, throwing his controller down on the coffee table. "I can't even…kill zombies right."

"Dude, it's cool. I got your back," Talbott said. "Give it a minute, get your power back up, and we'll get 'em."

"No, man," Jake said, tossing a beer can at the trash bag across the room. He missed. "This…is bullshit. You can't take care of me…for the rest…of your life." The alcohol made him speak even slower than he usually did.

"Yeah, I can."

Adam tried to ignore the bickering and focus on the raging battle of pixels in front of him.

"You can barely…take care of yourself," Jake said.

"I'll be all right," Talbott said. "And you will, too. All we gotta do is stick together, and we'll be all right."

"How? I can't get to the…*goddamned*…grocery store… and back. What happens…when you have surgery? Who will drive you…places? I can't do that. I can't…find the… *fucking* driveway."

"You know, for someone who thinks he's not recovering, you sure can cuss me out better than ever."

"Don't change…the subject."

Adam recognized that they weren't talking about the video game anymore and put his controller down. "What surgery?"

"Nothing, Hoss." Talbott's normally "it's all good" expression was closed down tight, and his warrior mask was firmly in place.

"He's got to get…his back fused." Jake, on the other hand, had never looked younger than he did now, in the flickering light from the video monitor.

"No, I don't."

"If he doesn't, he's going to have…more problems than a…purple foot."

"It's not that bad," Talbott insisted.

"It's worse. You need…to…face reality, *asshole*. Where… *what* am I going to do…if you can't fun…function?"

"Damn it, Jake, shut *up*. You're going to jinx me."

"Enough!" Adam yelled. All three dogs raised their heads, but only D-Day moved, rising and padding across the floor to settle next to Adam's legs. Hand on the dog's head, he spoke in a lower voice. "Stop it, both of you."

The two men looked at him, and he saw two very different versions of fear staring back. He automatically entered Sergeant Collins mode. "I need more information."

Talbott shook his head. "You don't have to worry about it—"

Adam stopped him with a raised hand. "You didn't show up here for a little vacation."

Talbott shot a glance at Jake that said he was done looking out for his friend's feelings. "We came here because *Jake* needs help. Because *I* need help with Jake."

Jake didn't speak but shook his head wearily, aging a dozen years in the space of his friend's words.

"Bullshit," Adam said. "Jake might need a hand up, but I've seen the way you move when you think no one's looking. You're hurting. I've also seen that duffel bag full of pills you carry around. I'm going to help. One way or another, I'll make sure you have somewhere to go and something to do, and I'll fight the VA for whatever else you need."

"Listen," Talbott said, "I do still have a lot of pain. That's what the meds are for. But I'm going to be okay. I've got a workout regimen, and I'm getting stronger every day."

Jake shook his head almost imperceptibly but also shrugged. Adam got the message. They were fighting a losing battle on this front, so he made a decision and took another tack. "That's great, man. If anyone can do it, it's you."

"You know it," Talbott said, his easy confidence reappearing.

"But you still need help." He could see that Talbott was about to protest, so he said, "Just listen for a minute. What do you have the most trouble with?"

Talbott shook his head but then admitted, "*Some* days— not *all* days—standing up is hard, and getting up and down stairs can be a little rough."

"Okay. Here's what we're going to do. Patton, come over here."

There was no way the big dog had learned its name already, but it saw Adam gesturing to it and came to see what he wanted. He ran his hands over the dog's body, feeling big strong bones. "You had him checked out by Rob Chance?"

"Yep," Jake confirmed.

Talbott was silent, suspicious at this apparent shift in the conversation.

"I was half joking when I brought it up earlier, but if Doc Chance says it's okay and the temperament tests look good, I don't see why you can't train yourself a mobility assistance dog."

Talbott rolled his eyes, and his tone became all *duh*. "Because I don't *need* an assistance dog? And don't you have to be permanently disabled to get one?"

Adam had considered this. "Yep. But anyone can train one. You could train this one, and then if…when you're better, you can donate the dog to someone who needs one."

Talbott mulled this over, mouth pursed.

Jake, however, was grinning. "Cool. You're going to train dogs again."

"Just until Talbott has the hang of it. I'm *not* getting back into the dog business." Adam waved around the room to encompass all three adult dogs and the pups. "These things are all getting new homes. Don't forget I'm cutting bait here as soon as I can."

"What…about Lizzie?" Jake asked.

Adam froze with his beer can almost to his lips and said, "What about her?"

"She likes you," Jake said. "And she'll be...bummed out if you move away."

"You sound like an eighth grader, Jakey," Talbott said. "What he means is Lizzie wants to *get* with you. As in, *naked*."

Adam shrugged, trying to be nonchalant. "Lizzie likes me because I'm helping her with D-Day." But even as he said it, he knew what they said was true and, worse, that he wanted to get with her even more. He was going to have to make sure that he didn't leave Big Chance with more regrets than he'd brought with him.

Chapter 15

ADAM RETURNED TO THE RANCH AFTER HIS NEXT VISIT to the VA, half hoping, half fearing that Lizzie would be there. For the past couple of weeks, he'd managed to stay on the roof of one building or another until nearly dusk, replacing missing shingles and nailing down others that might think about wiggling in the next breeze. He'd shored up the rafters under the sagging porch roof, too, and cleaned out all the gutters. His theory was that staying on a ladder as much as possible would keep her at arm's length and prevent him from pulling her soft curves against him, from tasting her kiss. He had managed not to *do* it but couldn't seem to stop *wanting*.

And of course, she hadn't missed a training session. She was there every afternoon, working with one of the dogs, passing what she'd learned on to Talbott, who had reluctantly agreed to put Patton through his paces. She'd yell up through the sweltering summer heat to ask Adam questions about behavior and care every fifteen minutes, smile, and tempt him with promises of sweet, cold iced tea—which he'd refuse, pretending he was more than happy to parboil himself on the barn roof.

Except he wasn't happy. And Daphne, his VA shrink, had noticed, commented on his edginess, and then sat patiently until he confessed that there was this woman…

He'd come home with a new self-help suggestion—to

stop worrying about everything that could go wrong and appreciate what was going right. Like the fact he was working through his shit enough to notice the possibilities in front of him. He didn't have to act; he just had to notice.

Whatever. His opinion was that *noticing* how badly he wanted Lizzie and *noticing* the way she blushed while holding his gaze would only increase the amount of noise in his head.

Adam had stopped in town on his way home, even though he'd already exceeded his time-not-being-a-hermit quota for the day. He'd decided that if he broke out in a sweat while he was there—and not a nice lower-your-temperature type sweat, but a prickling-along-every-nerve-ending acid sweat—then fine. He'd go to town every chance he got until he melted or got better. He even reviewed the relaxation and desensitization exercises Daphne suggested. He couldn't very well expect Talbott to acknowledge and deal with his shit if he wasn't going to take care of his own.

Which brought his mind back around to Lizzie and the possibility that he might see her today.

D-Day began his wiggle and whine routine as they approached the house. There didn't appear to be anyone home. No dogs barking, no drunken soldiers lounging on the porch, nothing. There was no festive barbecue in his barnyard. As a matter of fact, it was eerily quiet when he parked the truck and got out.

"Hello?" he called into the house, but he already knew it was deserted—Talbott's car was gone from the side of the barn, and Talbott didn't go anywhere without Jake. D-Day gave an echoing bark, but it wasn't answered.

Where were the other dogs? Loretta and her crew had

been relocated to the barn during the day, because the puppies were starting to move around and needed more room. They normally made a ruckus when anyone pulled in.

Adam was getting used to the mutts, though, and that was a bad thing. As different as they were from the dogs he'd worked with in the army, they still panted, barked, and wanted their bellies rubbed, and every time he found one lying on his couch, he was reminded of Tank.

Fucking Tank.

Stupid. It was a dog. Equipment. Like his rifle or his helmet. Something to be inventoried, used, replaced when it couldn't be repaired. If his grandfather had taught him nothing else, it was not to get attached to anyone or anything. So why had his second stop today been at the new tattoo place in town? He rubbed around the edges of the plastic taped over the new ink on his shoulder. It would itch like crazy in a few more days, but right now, there was a burning ache. The pain was only skin deep—it didn't hurt nearly as bad as the hole the damned dog had left in his heart.

He led D-Day into the house and detached the leash. The dog trotted ahead into the kitchen and slurped up water from the big pan by the back door.

He flipped on the kitchen light and stared dumbly at the mason jar filled with weeds in the middle of the battered kitchen table. Who the hell would do that? Probably Talbott's idea of a joke. They'd no doubt come in with a whole field guide's worth of bugs. He picked up the jar and opened the back door. A gust of wind swept half of the petals off. Looking at the sky, he wondered if a storm was blowing in. There had been hazy clouds hanging around all day.

He bent to put the jar on the stoop.

"Are you allergic?" a voice asked from the side of the house.

Adam jumped and jerked, dropping the jar on the concrete step, where it shattered. "Damn it!"

"I'm sorry! I didn't mean to startle you." Lizzie apologized and stepped forward as though she'd meant to catch the mess before it hit the ground.

"Stop!" Adam held up a hand.

She froze, eyes wide.

He remembered too late that she was neither one of his soldiers nor one of his dogs. "I don't want you to get cut," he explained. "Where did you come from? I didn't realize you were here."

"I figured that out. I'll make more noise next time. I parked behind the barn." A half smile curved her mouth, and he wondered if she still used cherry Chapstick.

Fortunately, he was distracted by a rustling in the weeds beyond the yard and the joyful bark of the big yellow dog, who shot out of the field and headed straight for Adam and the broken glass.

"Whoa!" he shouted and jumped over the mess on the step. He caught the dog but landed on his ass in the process. Instead of squirming away, Patton thanked him with a big, sloppy kiss.

From inside, D-Day barked as though he were missing out on prime rib.

"Phew, you stink," Adam grumbled, pushing Patton's face away, but the dog wouldn't be deterred.

"Yeah, he found something gross and muddy to roll in while we were walking around."

"Don't let that happen," Adam warned, looking at the filthy dog. "You're supposed to be in charge."

"Yeah. He doesn't seem to be getting the message. Come on, Patton." It took everything in Adam not to smile while Lizzie laughed, pulling the dog away by the collar. Patton got in one more kiss before surrendering.

"What the hell?" Adam wiped his face on the shoulder of his T-shirt.

"He missed you, duh," Lizzie told him.

"I don't know why. Jake and Talbott feed and walk it."

"Well," she said, as though reading his mind, "some of us can't seem to take no for an answer."

He looked at her then, her rueful smile suggesting that she wasn't just referring to the dog.

"I—" What did he say to that? She clearly didn't think he wanted her around, which, he had to admit, wasn't strictly true, in spite of the way he'd been avoiding her lately. It was more that when she was around, he got confused. He started wishing for things that he knew he couldn't have, things he didn't deserve. And in spite of all his good therapy intentions, that pissed him off.

Unaware she'd tossed a verbal gauntlet, she tugged the dog's collar again. "Come on, Patton. Let's get your bath."

Holding onto the dog with one hand and her big beach bag with the other, Lizzie proceeded through the kitchen, toward the hallway, to the foot of the stairs.

"Wait a minute. What are you doing?"

"Taking Patton to give him a bath."

"What? In my house? In my bathroom? No. I don't think so."

"Well, where else do you think I should do it?"

"Outside. With the hose."

"What?" She looked truly confused. "But there's no hot water out there."

"It's a *dog*."

For a moment, Lizzie thought Adam was teasing her, but one look at that solid jaw convinced her that he wasn't planning to let her wash the dog in his bathroom. "But he needs a bath."

"So wash it outside with the hose."

"No way. That water's, like, fifty degrees. You must have a well that comes from the North Pole!" Okay, she was engaging in a tiny smidgen of hyperbole, but she'd had a shitty day, hitting dead ends everywhere she turned on the Mill Creek project.

Apparently, Adam wasn't in a mood to back down, either. "The hose is in the barn, which is, like, a million degrees."

"Oh, good idea. Let's get him hot, then freeze him, then cook him again. Pneumonia, anybody?"

Adam snorted. "Do you want me to tell you how many nights I've spent soaked to the skin in the middle of winter? How many nights my *dog* spent outside soaked to the skin in the middle of winter?"

"Yes, actually," she said. "You never tell me anything about playing army."

His eyes narrowed. "I wasn't *playing*."

"I'm sorry. I didn't mean to minimize—"

"I'll tell you this about the army," he ground out. "A dog is just a *dog*. It's not a baby, and it doesn't need to be treated like one. It doesn't even need to be in the house. Ever."

"Is that what they taught you in dog handler school? That your dog's nothing more than a big, hairy rifle?"

He took a deep breath and let it out. "Listen. I know you don't get this. Your life is all about being nice and sweet and good, and you probably carry spiders outside so you don't have to squash them. But you need to face reality. Dogs aren't people."

She'd address his comment about her relationship to reality later. Her own patience had thinned to the breaking point. "Patton is not a Bulgarian mani-whatsits!" she shot back. "And I'm not a badass Army Green Beret!"

Something she said must have gotten through to him, because his arms dropped to his sides and his mouth softened. Then one corner rose. His eyes crinkled—years of pain and unknown horror faded from his expression—and he grinned.

"What?" she asked, suspicious of this shift from verbal sparring.

"Ranger."

"Huh?"

"I went to Ranger school. And I was an MP, not a Green Beret."

"Oh."

"And Tank was a Belgian Malinois, not a—what did you call it?"

"A Bulgarian…um, I have no idea," she admitted. "But whatever he was, he probably didn't like being coated in stinky mud any more than Patton does."

Adam's smile grew. "There's nothing any dog loves more than rolling in stinky stuff."

Lizzie blew out a breath. She wasn't thrilled that Adam's cranky-ass demeanor only cracked because he was laughing at her ignorance, but the way he looked at her now was almost worth it.

Or rather, it *would* have been worth it if she still had a huge crush on him. Which, damn it, she did.

And that made her madder than this whole argument. She knew he didn't want her. He hadn't wanted her on his graduation night twelve years ago, and he didn't want her now. Hell, he hadn't even come off the roof to talk to her for, like, ever—she had to inadvertently ambush him with a dirty dog to get near him.

She looked down at Patton, who gazed up patiently, certain that Lizzie would fix whatever the problem was. How could such a neglected dog manage to trust again so easily?

Of course, what Patton didn't understand was that he was trusting her to get him an indoor bath. She suspected that to the dog, an indoor bath would only be horrible, as opposed to a *very* horrible hose bath. The trust he'd so easily given might be blown to smithereens.

"Come on, Patton," she said, clipping the dog's leash to his collar. "I guess you can make it another day until I can get you an appointment at the Perfectly Pampered Pooch."

"Oh, for crying out loud," Adam huffed. "You're really going to pay good money to get a stray professionally groomed?"

She looked at the knotted, muddy mess and said, "Yes."

Adam scowled, took two steps away, and muttered, "I shouldn't have replaced that water heater." Then he came back and hoisted Patton into his arms. "Come on, then, Princess," he said and proceeded toward the stairs.

Lizzie scurried to catch up with him. "Where are you going?" And who was he calling *Princess*? "Patton's a boy, in case you missed that."

"Just come on before I change my mind."

Chapter 16

"Thank you for this," Lizzie said, smiling at Adam when he came back into the bathroom with a couple of old towels.

All he could do was nod and say, "Sure," because the wetter her sheer T-shirt and lacy bra got, the less blood there was going to his brain.

He forced his gaze to the dog, who cowered in the corner of the tub, as far from Lizzie and the handheld spray nozzle as it could get. It looked up at him, imploring him to step in and save it from this torture.

"Suck it up," he told it. "It'll be over sooner." Then maybe he could get out of this bathroom without reaching for the cheerful woman who was up to her elbows in lavender-scented doggie shampoo, dragging the dog in question into her lap so she could gently wash around his face.

Adam draped a big towel over his forearm like a fancy waiter so he could seem to be ready to catch the dog after it was rinsed clean but more to hide how *hard* it was getting to resist the considerable charms of the nicest girl in town. Christ, he was like an eighteen-year-old kid again.

But really, what did he *think* would happen when he brought her upstairs and let her use his bathroom?

He hadn't. *Thought*, that was. Not beyond getting her to stop explaining why the stray needed to be bathed in luxury rather than hosed off outside like every other dog he'd dealt with.

A memory forced its way into his consciousness—a few years ago, spending his day off at Fort Hood, washing his new partner Tank, and then spending hours under a tree in the hot Texas sun, brushing then petting the damned thing in an effort to bond with it. Spending all that extra time working with a problem dog so it would trust him enough to stop growling at the wrong people. Thousands of dollars may be invested in the breeding and training of a dog, but the army wouldn't keep an animal that was handler-aggressive. And if it was handler-aggressive, it wouldn't be adopted out; it would be euthanized.

Another memory—his grandfather, expressionless, carrying his shotgun and a leash into the kennel to take Adam's favorite German shepherd, Thor, for one last walk into the brush beyond the barn.

He forced the memories away and focused on Lizzie. Better to die of unrequited lust today than think about any of that shit.

Patton squirmed again in Lizzie's arms while the last of the suds were rinsed away, and she said, "I give up. I think that's as good as it's going to get. Can you take him?"

Reluctant to move the towel away from his groin, Adam nonetheless stepped closer and ignored the way his pants tried to unman him when he squatted to reach for the dog. The second the water was turned off and it sensed its ordeal was over, Patton leapt from the bathtub and made for the open doorway.

Adam managed to grab the back half of the dog before it escaped. He put one hand through the collar, but before he could get the towel untangled, the dog wound up and shook like a spin mop, spraying half the water in Texas over his bathroom floor. Lizzie, still sitting in the tub behind him, laughed. He tried again to get the towel over the dog's body, but it wasn't any more interested in drying off than it had been in getting washed.

With a twist and hop any rodeo bull would have been proud of, Patton escaped. It took a mighty jump and landed with all four paws in the middle of the bed. On the clean sheets. Where it gave another wet shake.

"Damn it!" Adam dove toward the bed to try to stop it before it started rolling around on his pillows, too. He caught it, wrangled it to the floor, and held it still, soaking his shirt and pants. "Can you bring a couple of towels in here?" he called to Lizzie.

"Um…"

He glanced toward the open bathroom door. *Oh hell.* She stood in his bathtub, completely drenched, wet shirt molded to her amazing body, jeans clinging to every curve and crevasse of her lower half. Her hair hung in clumps around her face, framing her smooth, rosy cheeks.

She must have read his dirty mind, because she crossed her arms over her chest and seemed to shrink in on herself. Probably thought he was the world's biggest pervert.

"I don't think you want me walking in there right now," she said.

He didn't want her to feel disrespected, so he said, "Right. Just, um…" He rose and carried the soggy dog back into the bathroom with him, turning sideways so he wasn't staring at her body while he grabbed a couple of dry towels. Aaand there she was in the mirror.

He cleared his throat and reached behind himself to hand her one of the towels, waving his hand blindly until she snatched it from him.

"I'll just, uh, I'll just take the dog out here," he mumbled, trying to leave without embarrassing either of them any further.

"Wait—"

Crap. "Yeah?"

"Do you—do you maybe have a T-shirt and some sweats or something I can put on?"

"Yeah, just a minute." He resisted the impulse to smack himself in the forehead as he pulled the bathroom door shut behind him. Of course she'd need something dry to put on.

He rubbed the dog a few more times with the towel, soaking up as much water as he could, and then set it on the floor outside in the hallway, next to a pacing, anxious D-Day. Adam shut the bedroom door to block them from coming back in. Let the damned thing go crawl on Talbott's sleeping bag.

He found a pair of sweatpants and a tan T-shirt, which he carried to the bathroom door. Knocking, he said, "I've got some stuff here."

The door cracked open, and Lizzie peered out at him. "Do you even have anything that will fit me?"

Was she *trying* to kill him? "Of course I do." He shoved the clothes through the tiny space and watched the door snap shut.

He stood there for a minute, until he heard the sucking *sploosh* of a wet shirt being pulled away from her body. Would her skin be pebbled with cold or pink and smooth with heat? He walked away from the door, but that didn't stop him from wanting to touch her, either way.

The next sound he heard was a zipper, followed by some heavy breathing—probably her fighting to get the snug wet denim down over those hips.

No. No, no, no.

He tore off his own wet shirt and threw it onto the pile in the corner. He got to the mirror and saw that the plastic taped over his new tattoo was coming loose. He peeled off the remaining tape and threw the temporary bandage away. Niki Chance had done a good job. She'd welcomed him when he and D-Day stopped by her new tattoo shop earlier in the day, and the dog was more than happy to roll around on the floor getting belly rubs from the other artists and a few potential customers.

He grudgingly admitted that he was glad he'd let her work on him.

"Oh God!" The exclamation was soft, but the room wasn't huge, and Adam felt Lizzie's shock all the way to his boots.

He whirled before she could get a good count of the shrapnel wounds in his lower back. But when he turned and her eyes ran over his torso, he wasn't sure whether she'd been reacting with horror at his scars or something else—because the way her pupils flared right now, he thought she might just be impressed with his workout regimen.

She was wearing the clothes he'd given her and not a thing more. He could tell because her full breasts were straining at the fabric of the worn T-shirt, and the pants were loose at the waist but tighter at the hips, snugging into the creases at the tops of her thighs.

He swallowed and nodded, trying to speak. "You, uh, you got into the clothes all right."

She realized he was examining her and crossed her arms over her chest again. She turned slightly, shoulders slumping forward, as though that could make her body disappear.

Jesus. Who had made her so self-conscious?

He looked away. "I'm sorry. I…don't mean to make you uncomfortable."

"It's not your fault. I'm a wreck."

He looked at her then, but it was her misery that he was aware of now, not her dangerous curves. "I thought that was my job title."

She snorted. "Everyone has their own interpretation. I know I'm huge, and this stretchy stuff doesn't help things any. I'll try to keep some extra clothes in my car, in case anything like this happens again."

How could she not know how incredibly sexy she was? He remembered that in high school, she'd been insecure, and then she'd said something about that ex-boyfriend judging how much she ate. The asshat who'd let her believe she was anything less than perfect had found her weak spot, enlarged it, and left some pretty damned big scars. Adam wanted to kick his ass.

Adam had failed miserably at a lot of things—keeping his team safe, keeping his family financially afloat. If he could do one thing right, it would be to make sure Lizzie stopped hating her own body, because *damn.* He loved it.

Lizzie had been chilly when she'd peeled out of her wet clothes in Adam's bathroom, and his worn T-shirt and threadbare sweatpants hadn't done much to warm her up. But the way he looked at her right now sent shivers down her spine that had nothing at all to do with the temperature.

Of course, when she came out of the bathroom and saw all that tattooed skin-covered muscle, she had a hot flash. There was a red, white, and blue Celtic knot surrounding one of his biceps that ran up his shoulder, where it expanded and became an American flag most of the way across his back.

Then he turned to face her, and her brain short-circuited. While Adam stared at her, every insult her ex had ever hissed in her ear came flooding back. She tried to mentally sneer at Dean, the way her therapist had suggested—give it right back to him, because anyone who needs to control you with insults probably has a small penis—but she wasn't sure that was working right now. And yeah, her therapist was technically a hairdresser, but she'd talked Lizzie through some rough times and gotten her over a few really bad kitchen color jobs, and Lizzie trusted the woman. Why was she thinking of Dean when Adam freaking Collins was semi-naked right in front of her, anyway?

"Lizzie." Adam stepped closer to her. The heat from his skin radiated over her.

Had his eyes always been that *blue*? The air in the room thickened, and it suddenly became harder to breathe.

"Lizzie," he repeated. "I need you to know something."

"Um, okay," she croaked.

"You have no reason to hide your body. As a matter of

fact..." He hesitated, those eyes as sincere as she'd ever seen them.

Oh good. Here came a pep talk about how all she had to do was cut down on partially hydrogenated fats and carbs and then start doing CrossFit, and she'd feel a million times better and—

His lips pressed against hers as his hands came to rest on her hips, giving her the impression, for one brief second, of being cherished and safe. It was a little kiss, just a touch. His mouth was gone before she even had time to register what he'd done, but the...the...*after-feel* of it had her raising her fingers to her lips as he stepped back.

Stunned, she stared at him until he looked away— toward the window, and then down, his hands on his hips, blowing out a big breath.

This gave her a moment to look at him again, at the way he—*oh Lord.* He either had a banana in his pocket or... She looked back at his face, and his smirk told her that he'd totally caught her looking.

Well, fine. It wasn't like he hadn't been looking at her first. Not because he thought she was disgusting but because he thought she was *sexy*. That was what had started this whole...whatever *this* was.

It struck her suddenly that they were in his bedroom. As in the room where he slept, where he took off his clothes, where he probably slept without his clothes.

He cleared his throat. "So anyway," he said, "I think you're pretty hot."

Lizzie couldn't help it. She laughed. His little smirk became a real smile, and she realized that as weird as this situation was, she felt almost comfortable, for the first time in…she didn't know how long.

"Well, then, I'll have to ask if I can borrow this outfit for my next hot date."

He nodded. "It's yours."

"I'm not sure, though…pumps or flats?"

"Are pumps the ones with the pointy toes and the high heels?"

"Yes."

"Pumps all the way."

"I'll have to see if I have any that would go with these colors."

"I don't think the color matters all that much," he said with a gleam in his eyes that suggested it didn't matter what she paired the shoes with. Nothing at all might be even more acceptable.

Oh Lord. The idea of traipsing around naked in front of someone as hot as Adam was bad enough—stumbling around in high heels? Ridiculous.

She had to look away from the heat in his gaze before she was incinerated.

Then the atmosphere shifted again, growing increasingly awkward with each passing second. *What now?*

She blurted the first thing that came to her mind. "I'm sorry Patton trashed your bed. Do you want me to help you change the sheets or—" *Ugh.* Now he was going to think she wanted him to invite her into the clean sheets. Which she did, of course, but…

"No, that's okay," he said, turning to drag the top sheet up with a vigorous shake. "I'll get them later."

Lizzie noticed then the red area around a tattoo she

hadn't noticed before, on the shoulder without the flag. She reached to touch the undamaged skin next to the art.

He jerked around.

"Sorry. Does it hurt?"

"No. A little. You surprised me is all," he said, putting his hand over it.

"Can I see?"

He hesitated but then removed his hand and turned to give her a clear view.

It was a dog. She knew it was probably a Belgian Malinois—she still wasn't sure what made it different from a German shepherd. It was beautiful, at any rate. The dog stood proudly, wearing a doggie Kevlar vest, staring into the distance. Beneath the image was one word: Tank.

"Tank of the cold showers and rocky bedding. Will you tell me about him?" she asked.

He shook his head. "Nothing to tell." But the slight hoarseness in his voice and the way he ground his jaw spoke volumes.

Lizzie's heart clenched for his pain even as her frustration bubbled up and out. "He's just another piece of equipment, right?"

"Exactly."

Chapter 17

"What's on the agenda for today?" Talbott asked Adam when he came into the living room the morning of July 4th.

When had he been put in charge of the duty roster? Oh yeah. When he'd agreed to having Talbott and Jake as houseguests.

Talbott dropped the weight he'd been curling with a thud. Patton, who'd been sitting in the sun near the living room window, rose with a start but then sank back to his haunches when he saw everything was okay. "Sorry, dude," he told the dog. He sat on the window seat and wiped sweat from his face with the sleeve of his T-shirt.

Adam shoved the weight out of the middle of the floor with his foot. "What the hell, man? I'm trying to sell this place. It'll be a lot easier if there aren't big dents in the floor from shit being dropped on it."

"Yeah. I'll keep that in mind," Talbott said, looking askance at the pitted and stained hardwood, most of which was covered by D-Day, who, unlike Patton, preferred to lie on his back, limbs spread to the four corners.

"Whatever. Can we just not add to the amount of repair work I'm going to have to do?"

"Ask Jakey to help. He's out of weeds to whack."

Both men turned to look through the picture window at Jake, who'd traded his gardening tools for—

"What's he doing?" Adam asked.

Jake was bent over the frame of an ancient bicycle and seemed to be bolting an old baby stroller to one side.

"I think he's building a sidecar for a bicycle," Talbott said.

"Why?"

"To get around. He's tired of needing us to go everywhere with him." Talbott pulled on a T-shirt, then barely hesitated before bypassing his boots for easier to slip on flip-flops. Adam suspected the man would only fight his way into boots when he was alone, given how much he'd have to stretch and bend. It was a testament to Talbott's willpower that he managed to stay in such incredible shape, considering he had trouble even walking some days.

At least Talbott could get where he wanted to go without help. Adam understood Jake's need for independence. He couldn't imagine having to rely on his friends to take him every place he needed to go, but—"What's the deal with the side thing?"

"Balance. He tried to ride the bike by itself but kept falling over. I told him a giant tricycle might be kind of cool, but he rejected that idea. So he's putting that thing on and planning to let Loretta ride there."

"Loretta doesn't need a wheelchair. That leg's almost healed."

The dog in question lounged beneath a tree, pups staggering around like a drunken rugby team, able to form a scrum but with no idea where the ball was. Now four weeks old, their eyes had opened, and they were moving around on their own but not near ready to leave their mother.

Talbott shrugged. "He wants to train a homing dog."

"A *what*?"

"I don't know if there's a formal name for it. He wants a dog to help him find his way to places. Or at least to find his way home if he gets lost."

Not this again. Adam felt the walls of the farmhouse, which usually seemed snug and secure, closing in on him. He was never going to get out of this town if he kept getting sucked into more projects.

D-Day whimpered and opened an eye to watch Adam, who took a deep breath before he spoke. "I don't have time for this. You know you're on your own with Patton, right? You've almost got basic obedience down, but you're fig-uring out the stability thing and how to confirm service animal status. There are a ton of rules and shit." He winced, realizing that sounded as though he'd considered it. Which he certainly hadn't.

"You can do anything if you've got the internet," Talbott told him and dug a folded sheet of computer paper out of the side pocket of his cargo shorts. "Here."

There, in black and white, was the list of state and federal laws about what constituted a service animal. "Basically," Talbott explained helpfully, "you've got to have a dog that won't shit in an airplane and who will do at least one cool trick to help his person."

God help him. "It's a little more complicated than that. You've got to prove you're disabled to get a dog, and then your dog has to be *way* more than potty trained. It's got to be super-extra chill in all kinds of situations and still able to do its 'cool trick' to help you. It can take two years to get a dog that well-trained."

"Aha!" Talbott said. "You *have* been thinking about it, if you know all that."

Shit. "I looked it up, because I knew you assholes were going to be up in my grill about it."

"You could do this for him," Talbott said, no longer teasing. "I already said I'll work with Patton, but I'm going to get better. It might take a little longer than I expected, but I'll get there. I'm asking for Jake. Look at him."

Adam did. He watched Jake, sweating in the hot Texas sun, chewing his lip as he fought to get the buggy attached to the bike. The scar on his head barely showed, now that his hair was growing. But he rubbed that area occasionally, as if checking to see if the mark was still there.

The scar Adam was responsible for.

"Jake's getting better, too, right? Who's to say that he's going to need help forever?"

"Dude." Talbott shook his head.

Adam sighed. He'd looked up traumatic brain injury, too. He knew plenty of guys who'd been blown up—multiple times—and had problems stemming from their concussions. Jake was suffering more than memory loss and concentration issues, which were bad enough. He had been more than a little concussed. He'd had to learn to walk again. And talk, too. His speech was still stilted, especially when he was tired. Those issues were improving, if slowly.

It was the getting lost thing that was holding him back—the topographical disorientation. At least it had a twenty-dollar name.

Adam said, "I can train a dog to find things by scent, but I don't know if that's the same thing as finding directions or if Loretta would be a good candidate. She's been through an awful lot, and she's pretty attached to Lizzie."

Talbott leapt into the breach with both feet. "How do we find out what to do? What do you need from me?"

D-Day, who'd been snoring a moment ago, sensed a change in the air. He rolled to his feet and stood leaning against Adam's leg.

"We're not starting anything today," Adam said. "Right now, we've got a horse shed to decrapify. When Jake's done playing Chance County Chopper, he's on cleaning duty. You're on inventory management."

"What does that mean?" Talbott asked.

"It means my grandfather never threw anything away, and I have no idea what's trash and what's worth selling. You, Mr. I-Can-Find-It-on-the-Internet, are in charge of figuring all that out."

Chapter 18

"ELIZABETH? ARE YOU ALMOST READY?" MOM KNOCKED and called through the bedroom door. "Can I come in?"

"Yep. I'm fine," she said, letting her mother in. "I was getting dressed."

Her mother raised her penciled-on brows and asked, "Is that what you're wearing?"

"Yes?" She looked at herself in the full-length mirror on the back of her bedroom door. Even though she could barely breathe, she kind of liked the way the bright-red dress made her waist look tiny, in a retro pinup girl sort of way. Her boobs looked pretty good, too. Of course, her primary objective for the evening was to pin down Joe Chance and get him to help her with the Mill Creek Park project, not to impress anyone with her womanly self. She turned and looked at her reflection from another angle. Although, maybe…

Mom didn't speak, which had Lizzie rethinking her resolution to appreciate her own curves. Adam liked her body, right? If His Extreme Hotness thought she was sexy, who was she to disagree?

But then Mom walked to the jewelry box on Lizzie's dresser, started digging, and said, "You know, I do like that dress. It's patriotic."

"Good. Thanks." Lizzie nodded, deciding she'd be brave and wear it to the dance, which was the culmination of the

Independence Day celebration, though she'd have preferred to cap off the long day with a glass of wine and an hour sitting on the swing in the dark of her parents' yard. She'd been up since six this morning, helping with a parade, a picnic, old-time games like a three-legged race and a watermelon seed-spitting contest, and then helped the local social services group make balloon animals for the little ones. Thank goodness she'd been able to refill her water bottle about seventy times, because she'd definitely needed it.

But she'd been playing phone tag with Joe Chance. She needed to get the town council behind her before any of the local businesses would pledge funding. She also had to find out who the property belonged to and convince them to sell it.

"Is Dad coming?" she asked her mother.

"Here. These'll work," Mom said, holding up a string of big, fake pearls and the dangly earrings that went with it. Then she said, "No, your dad's a little tired, so he's going to stay home tonight."

A fist of fear clutched Lizzie's gut, and she said, "Is he okay? Should we call the doctor?"

"No," Mom said. "I think he had too much pie at the picnic. And he's too old to play cornhole in the sun like that."

"Mom, you guys aren't even sixty."

Mom smiled. "Thank you. But still, it was hot today, and I think he just got a little dehydrated. He's going to stay home and drink ice water and watch baseball. He'll be fine."

Ah. The Astros were playing tonight. And a little minor heat stress gave Dad a good excuse to skip the dance and watch baseball.

However, the reminder that her dad wasn't getting any

younger gave Lizzie renewed motivation to make this park happen.

"Will you join us in the organizer's tent for cocktails?" Mom asked.

"Oh jeez. I…" The thought of sitting under that sweltering tent to drink lukewarm whiskey sours with Ms. Lucy sounded horrible. "I'll try to stop by. I've got to talk to Joe Chance first."

Mom's face lit up like the sky would later with fireworks. "Oh, lovely! I'm so glad you've reconnected with Joe. He's such a nice guy."

Lizzie withheld her sigh. "Yep. Joe's nice."

"You should make sure you save a dance for him."

"Oh, I doubt that's going to happen."

Mom's face fell. "I just want to see you meet someone nice here in Big Chance. I hate to think of you using that Tender thing to meet another loser from Houston."

"Tinder. And that's not where I met Dean."

Mom waved her hand dismissively. "Whatever. I worry about you. You haven't done anything socially since you moved home."

"Yes, I have," Lizzie protested, but then realized that her mom probably wouldn't count training D-Day at Adam's ranch as a social activity. Still, she hated that her mom worried about her. There was enough to worry about with Dad's cancer. "I actually have a date tonight," she blurted.

Mom blinked. "Really? With who?"

"Adam Collins. You know, Emma's brother?"

"Huh." Mom's mouth turned down as she considered this. "Well, bring him by the tent for a drink, okay?"

Why had she said that? Now she had to come up with

a date or explain why she didn't have one. To Mom, Ms. Lucy, and all the other nosy ladies of Big Chance. There were good reasons Lizzie didn't lie much—she always made things worse.

Lizzie looked at her phone on her nightstand. This was going to be awkward.

She hadn't really spoken to Adam since the incident in his bedroom. The *kiss*. The kiss that nearly caused her to spontaneously combust, after which she'd grabbed her soggy clothes and escaped in his sweatpants with barely a goodbye.

She hadn't been avoiding him exactly, but she'd definitely been keeping herself busy—too busy to work with D-Day much.

She wiped her palms on her thighs or, more accurately, the skirt of the stupid dress she'd dragged out of the closet and squeezed herself into.

Just do it. No big deal. Call Adam, and ask him to come to the dance. He would say no. And she'd wind up trying to avoid being fixed up—if not with Joe, then with whatever other single guy Mom and Ms. Lucy could find.

She already had to find and corner the tragically single mayor to convince him to help her launch a pie-in-the-sky project. In her too-tight dress in front of everyone in Big Chance.

Screw it. Step one: Dial Adam's number. Done.

Step two: Figure out what to say when he—

"Hello." He sounded tired. Like she'd woken him from a nap. Great.

"Hi. Hey."

"Hi."

"It's Lizzie."

"Yeah, I know." Now he sounded like he was laughing at her with his just-woke-up-from-a-nap voice.

"Of course you do. I programmed my number into your phone myself, like the pushy broad I am. Anyway—"

"Why are you pushy?" He sounded weird, and that made her more nervous. Was he as freaked out by their kiss as she was?

"I'm pushy because I programmed my own phone number in your phone. Don't you think that's pushy?"

"Depends on your motives. Were you hoping I'd drunk dial you for a booty call one of these nights?" Now the voice was heavier on the drawl and lighter on the rust. And *not* Adam.

Oh God.

"Marcus? Is this you? Impersonating a Collins?"

He laughed. "Yeah, darlin', it's me. The good sergeant's in the bathroom with a magazine, and I don't think it was the kind you read while you're dropping—Hey!" She heard a scuffle, then Marcus's voice from farther away. "You were in the can. Who knows if you were jacking off or taking a dump? I was just taking my best guess!"

"I was in the shower, asshole," she heard Adam say, and then he was live on the phone. "Hello?"

"Hi. Adam. It's Lizzie." She took a deep breath and was struck with inspiration. "I'm calling because I wonder if you can help me with something. I've been trying to talk to Joe Chance about my thing—the park. He's always busy, and I know he'll be at the dance in the town square tonight. So if I go, at least he has to listen to me. But I need some moral support, and since you were so supportive when I suggested it to you—"

"Okay," he said.

"Okay?"

"Sure. I'll bring D-Day. He needs to spend time around people besides you, Talbott, and Jake. A trip to town would give you a chance to work with him and maybe find him a new home."

"Oh. I..." Disappointment flooded her. She wanted *Adam* to come to the dance. No way could she handle taking D-Day to something with a bunch of people. He'd jump on everyone, terrorize the food trucks, and drag her through the dust, probably make her too-tight dress fly up over her head, showing everyone in town that she was wearing white granny panties, and—

"What time are you going over? We'll meet you there."

"Really?" In her revised vision, her dress remained around her thighs, no children screamed in terror, and her mother couldn't throw her at Joe Chance. Best of all, Adam would be with her.

"Yeah. I'd like to see Joe, too."

"Oh...okay."

"So...time?"

"Well...eight?"

"Got it. Meet me near the statue of Emmit Chance."

"Sure."

They said goodbye, and Lizzie held onto the phone, staring at it for a long time after they disconnected.

Mom stuck her head back into the room. "Do you need to borrow heels?"

"Heels?" Lizzie looked down at the red sneakers she'd put on. They were okay but maybe not as glam as she wanted to look now. But heels? Yeesh. Adam was bringing

D-Day, and if she had on heels, she'd wind up facedown in the grass for sure.

"Yes. If you're wearing that dress, you should wear heels. I have some red ones you can borrow."

"You're right. Except I have something even better."

She waited until Mom shut the door, then went to the closet to dig out her good red cowboy boots.

And then she exchanged her granny panties for a thong. A red one.

What had he just agreed to? Adam cursed, rising from the couch and picking up an empty Mountain Dew can. "You guys finish without me. I've got to take a shower and find some clean clothes."

"But we've got the head zombie on the run!" Jake complained.

"Didn't you just come out of the shower?" Talbott teased. "Isn't that what you said when you came out of the bathroom? You were totally jacking off in there, weren't you? I knew it!"

"Jesus Christ, I was taking a leak, not that it's any of your business. And *now* I'm going back up there to take a shower."

"Why do you need a—holy shit. You've got a date, don't you? Hey, Jake, Collins has a date with Miss Lizzie!"

"What are you gonna wear, Sar'nt? Somethin' pretty?" Jake asked. His ability to crack jokes was improving, a sure sign he was slowly but surely coming back to himself.

"You should let him borrow your skinny jeans, Jake,"

Talbott said. "The hipster ones that make your ass look so good."

Adam snorted. "I've got pants, thanks. But it's not a date." Even though he was looking forward to spending time with Lizzie. At night. In the park. Where there would be music.

"What are you doing that requires a shower, then?"

Adam sighed. "I'm meeting Lizzie in town at a…dance. It's a community party with a band and shit. The mayor's going to be there." The mayor, who Lizzie's mom wanted to fix her up with. Because surely an unemployed soldier with PTSD was a much better choice than the mayor. Joe Chance was only a connected pillar of the community with a professional degree and a proven record as a family man. Nice guy, too. "We both need to talk to Joe, so it makes sense to go together." Besides, she had said she wanted his help. Before he knew what he was doing, he had opened his mouth and offered to meet her there.

"Anyway, the dog needs practice in town," Adam added. And so did he.

"Which dog?" Jake ran a hand over Patton, who had perked up at the conversation.

"D-Day."

"Oh." Jake tried to hide his disappointment, but Adam caught it.

Talbott must have, too, because he said, "You know, we don't know what Patton is like in crowds."

Adam almost groaned, then felt guilty. Marcus Talbott was a social beast, practically drying up out here on the ranch, and Jake was a people person, too. Or at least he had been. He would enjoy an outing, and they *should* see if Patton was mellow enough for big groups of people. Just because Adam couldn't deal with crowds, loud noises, or blonds with amazing curves and attitude didn't mean his friends wouldn't like to come to the dance.

"Why don't we all go and take both dogs?" Adam suggested. "If D-Day is too much of an asshole, one of you clowns can hang on to him while I do my thing, or I'll sit on a bench with the dogs while you two paint the town whatever color you choose."

"Oh, goody! Pa's taking us into town! I'm gonna put on my good overalls," Talbott said, clapping his hands like the dweeb he was.

"You put on whatever you want," Adam said, pointing at him. "But make no mistake: if you can't act your age, I'm not going to buy you any cotton candy."

"Hurry in the shower, then. The ladies are going to be *so* happy to see us, right, Jake?"

"Sure." Jake looked a little uncertain, but that was okay. Adam wasn't sure what he was doing, either.

Chapter 19

LIZZIE CHECKED HER WATCH AND SAW THAT IT WAS TWO minutes later than the last time. She looked up to find the statue of Emmit Chance staring down at her, his bushy bronze eyebrows furrowed in disapproval, which didn't help her nerves.

Adam most likely had changed his mind. He was late, and the Tommy Blue Orchestra was already halfway through their first set. She checked her phone again. Four bars of service. Well, maybe *his* phone didn't have service or battery or…

She decided to get on with it and find the mayor so she could present her idea to him. If Adam showed up, good for him. She rose on the toe of her shiny red boots to look over the crowd of dancers and dance watchers to see if Joe Chance was nearby.

"Lizzie! How's it going?"

She turned to see Emma approaching, holding her grandfather's arm. He wore stiff new overalls, a green plaid shirt, and white patent leather shoes.

"Emma, hi!" She gave her friend a hug.

Mr. Collins glared around the crowd and worked his jaw, a move that Lizzie recognized as one that Adam did when he was uncomfortable.

"I'm glad you're here," she told Emma. "Mr. Collins, it's nice to see you."

"I know your father," the old man said. "He's a shyster. Just like them Chance boys."

"Granddad, that's not nice," Emma chided.

"Anyone who'd try to take advantage of a sick man is no good in my book. I've got the last word on that, yes, I do."

"Um…" Lizzie didn't know what to say.

"And you make sure you watch yourself with that boy of mine. He's going to talk you out of your panties, mark my word."

"Granddad!" Emma shrugged apologetically and mouthed *I'm sorry*—though she did it with a twinkle in her eye.

Lizzie felt herself flush, which, added to the heat rising from the pavement, was less than comfortable.

"Oh, look. There's Mayor Chance. Let's go say hello," Emma said.

"I'm not going to talk to that sonofabitch. I want some waffle fries." Mr. Collins folded his arms and stuck out his chin.

"But Joe's our friend. Remember, he stopped over the other night?"

"Oh. I thought you said the mayor."

"I did. Joe's also the mayor."

A brief flash of frustration and fear flashed through Mr. Collins's eyes before he covered his feelings by reclaiming his mask of anger. "Talk later. Waffle fries now."

Emma was the poster child for patience. "Okeydokey. Do you want to share an order with me?"

"Hell no, I want my own. You'll hog them all."

Emma's laugh disappeared with them into the crowd.

Lizzie turned to see Joe Chance walking toward her, his blond hair neatly cut and shining in the lights that twinkled from the trees in the growing darkness. His shoulders were wide, if a little stooped from the weight of the world he no doubt carried around with him, but he smiled at Lizzie, and she recognized the all-American she'd been friends with when they were younger. She imagined meeting Joe here for the dance, but it didn't feel right.

"Lizzie, it's good to see you," Joe said, pulling her into a hug. "You look great!"

She blushed, especially when a group of women turned to see who Joe was complimenting. They gave her the once-over—from the top of her overdue-for-a-touch-up high-lighted hair, along the too tight and suddenly uncomfortable dress, down to the tips of her probably dumb cowboy boots. They turned away and put their heads together—to rip her to shreds, no doubt.

"I'm glad you made it out tonight. I'm sorry it's been so hard to get together, but the babysitter has the flu, and everything else that could've gotten worse, well, got worse."

"I'm sorry to hear that. I don't want to take up too much of your time."

He waved a hand through the air. "An audience with the mayor is first-come, first-served at the moment. I want to hear this great idea you emailed me about. Besides," he confided, leaning closer, "if I'm busy, maybe I won't have to judge the dance competition." He straightened and grinned with a mock shudder.

Now that the moment was here, she was terrified that Joe would laugh at her. It was such a weird plan. Then she thought about her dad and how his eyes lit up any time she talked to him about it. She took a deep breath and let fly. "I'm interested in buying some property out on Mill Creek

Road—you remember the old farm that Mitch Babcock's family owned? I want to turn it into a working historical park. Part education, part recreation, all good for the town."

His eyebrows went up. "A historical park. In Big Chance. Where did this come from?"

"My dad and your great-grandpa, actually." She pointed up at the statue of Emmit. "My dad's always been fascinated with the history of Big Chance—with the miniature gold rush that started things in the mid-1800s. The historical facts are yet to be confirmed, but he's told me a lot of stories."

Joe laughed. "I'll bet he has. I remember some of those stories. My dad said they were tall tales, but one of my cousins has a ring she swears was made with gold that Emmit found."

"I wonder if you heard the same stories I did."

"I don't know, but I bet the ones I heard weren't any more true."

Lizzie nodded her agreement. Not that her dad would ever lie, but as stories were passed down, the facts tended to shift. "I don't think it really matters if there was any gold. The whole Wild West gold rush thing captured my dad's imagination, and now he's…well, he's got cancer—did you know that?"

"Yes, I did hear that. I'm sorry. How's he doing?"

She nodded in thanks. "He seems to be okay, but he's been a little depressed, and I got this crazy idea, and he was interested, and now…well, now we think it could be a real thing, if we can muster community support. I drove out to Mill Creek a couple of weeks ago, and it occurred to me that maybe we could find a way to turn the area into something that would help the town—and make my dad happy at the same time."

"I'm listening." And he was. His intensity was a little disconcerting, actually.

"I know you've been starting some community improvement projects—getting the senior citizens and middle schoolers to run the recycling center is brilliant, by the way."

"Thanks. I told them they could sell all the scrap they gathered, and they've decided to turn around and start a community garden."

And didn't that add a little something to Lizzie's growing project idea…

"So anyway, there's this land just sitting out there," she continued, unable to stop now that she was on a roll. "It's not too far from town. What if we bought that land and started improving it, a little at a time? Maybe we can get someone with large equipment to donate time and get it cleared. Then the school kids can take on different parts of the work, like making paths and researching the history of gold mining, and turn it into a resource. Heck, your senior citizens could even put their garden out there if they want."

Joe pursed his lips in thought. "You know, you might be onto something here. Can you write up a proposal? There's nothing in the budget for this, but—"

He was going for it. Not sure she believed her luck, she said, "I think a few fundraisers and some business support might be enough to get it started. So we can start off small—with a community park—but then make improvements. Maybe even put in ball fields, a dog park, walking paths… Who knows? Maybe we can turn Big Chance into a tourist destination—rent a cabin for a weekend and do some old-time panning for gold?"

Joe gave her an admiring look. "I like the way you think."

Lizzie was thrilled. He liked the idea.

She began to let the little seed of hope in her chest take root. "The only problem here is…I can't figure out who actually owns the place."

"Adam Collins asked about that property, since it backs up to his. I couldn't remember anything, but surely there's something in the tax records."

She shook her head. "Nope. Dad said he remembers the Babcocks selling it right before they left town, though he didn't broker the deal, and there doesn't seem to be any record of who it went to."

Joe sighed. "I'll look into it. Not that collecting the back property taxes are going to put Chance County into the black, but there's got to be a record of something, somewhere."

"That would be great. And I'll work on that proposal. If I can get some sort of formal approval from you and the city council, I can start soliciting donations," she said.

"Sounds like a plan," Joe said. "I know a few people who might be willing to chip in."

"Terrific," Lizzie said, pulling out her phone to take notes.

She was so excited that she *almost* didn't notice that there was no apologetic text or missed call from Adam.

Adam had to park three blocks away from the square, and he was already late. He picked up the pace and tugged at the long sleeves of the button-up shirt he'd put on. It was all wrong for the sweltering night and his propensity for anxiety sweat, but Talbott had told him to wear it, and it was clean, so Adam hadn't argued.

It had been a pain in the ass getting everyone ready to leave the ranch, and his tension was sky-high by the time they passed the "Welcome to Big Chance" sign.

For such a tiny town, the gathering had attracted a lot of visitors. Always on the lookout for things that didn't belong—even here in Big Chance—he noticed several cars and trucks with license plates from out of state. People must be really hard up for entertainment. On the other hand, it should be good for Lizzie's plan to perk up Big Chance.

"Slow down, man," Talbott complained. "You don't want to seem too eager, do you?"

He eased up; he didn't want to be completely sweat-soaked when he got to the town square. But honestly? He *was* eager. Lizzie's call had ignited the first positive feelings he'd had in the week since she'd practically run from his house after they kissed, and he jumped at the chance to see her. He did have some papers for Joe, but that was an excuse. Nothing was earth-shattering enough to chase the man down on a holiday.

Lizzie's kiss had awakened something inside him—an aching need to know more of her soft, welcoming body and her kind, generous heart—though he reminded himself to keep his eyes on the prize. He was going to sell the ranch, satisfy his debts, and get out of town.

Meanwhile, he was here to make sure D-Day could

behave himself in town, not coax Lizzie to slip her fingers into the front of his jeans.

The sounds and smells of the party found him before they reached the town square. Music and the chatter of voices, a few children laughing and shouting, and the scents of fried pastry and smoked meat beckoned him forward.

The retriever was pretty mellow at the end of Talbott's leash, but D-Day was squirrelly, picking up on the energy of the crowd. He kept trying to tug at his leash. He had to learn to stay next to his handler no matter what the circumstances, so Adam had to stop every few steps to regain D-Day's attention. The closer they got to the square, the more kids showed up wanting to pet the dogs, which just stirred everyone up more.

It wasn't keeping the dog calm that twisted Adam's shorts in a knot; it was the kids. He was used to working with dogs who thought small humans were fair game for snacks. Tank had been nearly uncontrollable when it came to kids. He'd been the best explosives detector Adam had ever worked with—until he wasn't—but he required constant vigilance when Adam had him in public.

D-Day, on the other hand, seemed to want nothing more than to bathe every child he met with a long, wet tongue.

And the kids loved that shit.

Their parents, probably not so much, but Adam didn't see a whole lot of adult supervision occurring. Weren't American parents notorious for monitoring every breath their kids took? What was wrong with the people of Big Chance? Did they think it was some sort of magically safe place?

And when did he become the old lady on the corner who calls the police if you walk on her grass?

The streets next to the town square had been blocked off, and little kids ran around like rabbits, jumping and squealing. Two sets of teenagers—a few girls, and a few boys—faced off around the back end of a booth, the boys wrestling and impressing the hell out of the giggling girls. Or not.

The food vendors had set up here, at the south end of the square, and the band was at the north end, using the wide courthouse steps as their stage. The closer Adam got, the better the band sounded. They were actually pretty damned good. He couldn't see yet, but he could hear a guitar that would make Eric Clapton weep.

He emerged from between the frozen crap truck and the baked crap booth into a crowd of thousands—or so it seemed. The trees in the park were strung with twinkling white lights and multicolored lanterns, but the light barely touched the faces of the hundred or so people within spitting distance. How was he supposed to find Lizzie in this mess?

D-Day stopped, sat, and pressed against Adam's leg, apparently realizing this was way more people than he expected. Maybe it didn't know how to deal with them. Or maybe it just realized that Adam didn't know how to deal with them.

"It's cool, bud. We got this," he told the dog.

"Is that where we're supposed to meet her? Over by that mean-looking motherfucker?" Talbott asked.

Adam looked where Talbott pointed at the statue of Emmit Chance, town founder.

He didn't see Lizzie, but leaning against the base of the statue was the mayor himself. He was talking to a woman with her back to them. She was in a crazy-ass, fifties-looking dress. It was one of those things that tied around the back of her neck, leaving her round shoulders and soft arms bare. The dress dipped in to her waist before spreading out in a full skirt above a pair of gleaming red cowboy boots, sparkling with silver gemstones under the festive lights. The woman said something, and Joe laughed.

"Whoa," Talbott murmured. "Sexy. I wonder what she looks like from the front."

She was kind of interesting, Adam thought, but where the hell was Lizzie? Well, he might as well talk to Joe since he was here. Adam didn't want to interrupt the guy, in case he was trying to get lucky with Not Bettie Page, but he didn't want to lose Joe to the crowd, either. And Adam wanted to hand over the papers he'd found the other day cleaning out the horse shed. Probably nothing, but they sure looked official, and Adam needed to make sure they had everything together when he sold the ranch.

While he began to approach, a little girl in blond pigtails—probably about six or seven, wearing jeans, cowgirl boots, and a hot pink T-shirt—ran past Adam, yelling "Daddy! Daddy! Connor stole my ice cream!" She blasted straight into the long legs of the man Adam wanted to speak to.

Joe's smile was bigger now, completely real, and he swung the little girl up into his arms and gave her a big smacking kiss.

"Ewww, Daddy, that's gross!" She shoved at him, and he mock pouted. When she looked at her father's companion, her eyes grew wide as she took in the woman. "You're pretty," she told the woman.

The woman turned, blond ponytail swinging, and recognition brought Adam to an abrupt halt.

"Riley, this is Miss Lizzie Vanhook," Joe said.

"Lizzie?" Adam asked.

"Oh, hey." She spun the rest of the way around and greeted Adam. The hem of her dress twirled out, giving him a glimpse of dimpled knee.

Adam wasn't so busy ogling her, however, that he missed Joe giving Lizzie his own once-over. Somehow, he found his hand on Lizzie's waist, his fingers just barely touching her naked back.

She caught her breath and looked up at him, her eyes widening slightly.

Hell, he was surprised, too. This wasn't supposed to be a real date, and he had no business getting touchy-feely with a woman he wasn't supposed to be interested in.

"Are you her daddy?" the little girl in Joe's arms demanded of Adam.

"Huh?"

"Are you"—she pointed at Adam—"her"—she pointed at Lizzie—"daddy?"

"Uh, she means husband," Joe clarified.

Chapter 20

"No!" Adam couldn't have moved away from Lizzie faster if she'd been a radioactive porcupine. "No. I'm not her husband," he continued, as though he wanted to make sure his hand on her a moment ago had been a complete accident. "We're just, uh…she's my sister's friend."

From the corner of her eye, Lizzie saw Jake shake his head in disgust. She agreed.

Like she didn't already feel like an idiot in this dress. What had she been thinking? She knew she looked ridiculous. The little girl had said she was pretty, but chances were that meant she looked like a cross between Elsa from *Frozen* and Hello Kitty.

Oblivious to Lizzie's inner drama, Joe's daughter smiled at her. "Good. Then you can be *my* mommy if you want."

Joe, who had been smirking at the awkward moment, now began to cough.

"Daddy, are you okay?" Riley whacked her father on the back.

Adam moved in and took the girl from Joe's arms, while Jake took both dogs, and Marcus put his own hand on the mayor's back, ready to clear an airway if needed. Lizzie supposed this hero choreography was part of their megasoldier training. The kid looked perfectly comfortable in Adam's arms, giving Lizzie's ovaries a jolt.

"I'm okay," Joe finally gasped, his face red and shiny, the collar of his light-blue golf shirt looking a little tight.

"Do you want something to drink?" Lizzie asked, desperate for something to do.

"I wanna drink!" the kid said, squirming out of Adam's arms and marching toward Lizzie.

"Riley—" her dad protested.

"It's okay," Lizzie said. She needed a few seconds to regroup anyway.

Riley pointed at Marcus. "You watch the dogs, okay?"

Marcus, clearly surprised at the order, nodded with a half smile.

Riley took the equally nonplussed Jake's hand and said, "You come with me, too. My aunt Charley's the best lemonade maker, ever."

"Yes, ma'am," Jake said, handing the leashes over to Marcus, who stayed with Adam and Joe.

The little girl definitely had Chance genes—destined for leadership.

Lizzie found herself following Jake and Riley through the crowd, toward a tent hung with lemon-shaped party lights. A tall, slender woman seemed to be in charge of a crew of teenagers, laughing as she argued with a hefty young man about the best way to cut lemons.

"Aunt Charley!" Riley called. And then, like the undergrown adult she was, she said, "Lemonade for all my friends, please!"

"Hey, shortcake!" the woman said. "How many?" She smiled and nodded at Lizzie in greeting and then looked at Jake, her smile barely faltering as she took in the scar on the side of his head with interest. Jake didn't miss her obvious curiosity, and his hand rose to smooth the hair over the scar as he looked away.

Poor guy. His hair would grow to cover the marks of his injury, and he might even recover enough of his mental abilities to function in the world, but Lizzie wondered if his self-confidence would be completely annihilated by then.

Lizzie ordered six lemonades, and after making a significant contribution benefiting the Saint Bernardine Youth Group, the three turned back toward the men waiting at the statue.

Marcus stood a few feet away from Adam and Joe, enormous arms crossed over his chest, a leash in each hand. Joe's head was bent as he listened intently to what Adam was saying. Adam passed him a sheaf of papers, which Joe tucked into his back pocket.

She handed the men their lemonade, taking a giant slug from her own. After a brief, glorious hit of sweet and tart frozen goodness, her head throbbed in intense pain. "Owwwwww." She clutched her skull with her free hand and turned away.

"Brain freeze?" Adam laughed softly and put his hand on the back of her neck, the heat immediately counteracting the pain. "Better?"

She nodded, and after a moment, the hand trailed down her back to rest at her waist where it seemed to fit perfectly.

"Oh, hey. Maybe not such a good idea," Marcus told Riley, who stood in front of D-Day holding her lemonade cup within lapping distance.

D-Day certainly didn't mind, and Patton crowded in, hoping for a chance to dip his own tongue into the cup.

"Riley, yuck!" Joe reached for his daughter, but it was

too late. She'd put the doggy cup to her lips and took a big drink, then gave the golden retriever his turn.

"I'm sharing!" she told her dad proudly.

"Yep, punkin, you sure are. Sharing is usually nice, but maybe not with dogs, okay?"

"Can we get a dog?" she asked.

"Uh, maybe one day. After we've worked on who you can let drink out of your cup. Let's go find your sister, huh?"

"Where do the single ladies congregate?" Marcus asked Joe, scoping out the crowd. Jake, Lizzie noticed, glanced back at the lemonade tent.

Joe shrugged, and Lizzie suspected he spent a big chunk of each day avoiding the single ladies of Big Chance.

"I thought dogs were supposed to be chick magnets. You're not doing your job," Marcus told D-Day.

Jake had taken Patton's leash and was surrounded by a trio of preteen girls who oohed and aahed over him.

"These are not the chicks we're looking for," Marcus muttered under his breath as the girls turned to include D-Day in their cooing.

The band came back from their break, and they warmed up on the stage before launching into a fast-paced country classic. There was a makeshift dance floor in the middle of the courthouse lawn, and a group of people had begun to two-step around the space.

"We should dance. Don't you think we should dance?" Marcus asked Lizzie.

"Who, me?" she asked, a hand to her chest. "No…I don't—"

"Darlin,' you look hot enough to start a fire, and you need to be dancin.'"

"I...uh..."

She shot a look at Adam, who removed his hand from her lower back and said, "Don't let me stop you."

She suppressed a sigh, because she wasn't hoping he'd stop her but wishing he'd insist on being her dance partner.

"Miss Lizzie," Marcus said, handing D-Day's leash to Jake, "may I please have this dance?"

Halfway through the second song, Adam realized he was three steps from the dance floor. How had he gotten so close? He'd been watching Lizzie and Talbott dance—everyone had been. For someone with back and nerve issues, the man was light on his feet tonight, twirling her around the floor. Lizzie was a good partner for him, which made Adam grit his teeth.

D-Day whimpered, and Adam realized he had a death grip on the dog's collar. "Sorry, buddy," he said, loosening his hold.

"Who's that with Lizzie?"

Adam jumped and turned around, wondering why D-Day hadn't alerted him that someone was—"Oh. Hey," he said to Emma. "Hi, Granddad."

"You lettin' some stranger dance with your girl?" Granddad asked.

"Lizzie decides who she's going to dance with," he said before realizing he'd stepped into a trap.

The corner of Emma's mouth quirked up. "She can decide who to dance with," Emma said, "but it's nice if she has more than one choice. Did you even ask her?"

No. He sighed. "Fine."

Lizzie and Talbott moved within an arm's length, and Adam reached out to grab his friend's shoulder.

"What?" Talbott asked, separating from Lizzie to look at him, an eyebrow raised in mock challenge. Then he caught sight of Emma and smiled, smoothly transitioning Lizzie's hand to Adam's. "Hey, Emma," Talbott said. "Are you up to a turn on the dance floo—er, grass?" He held out a hand to her.

"Gee, thanks," Emma said, holding Granddad's hand, "but my dance card's full." Her words were sarcastic, but her cheeks turned pink.

Adam decided her flush was due to the heat and not a budding attraction. "Here," he said, handing D-Day's leash to Talbott. "Jake needs to be rescued, and this one could use a drink." He pointed to where Jake sat on a bench, the parade of little girls apparently never-ending as they stopped to pet Patton.

"I thought you'd never ask," Talbott said, and with one last look at Emma, he was gone.

The whole sweaty crowd seemed to disappear as Adam found himself standing under a tree full of twinkle lights, feeling awkward and shy in front of the prettiest woman in town. He stared at Lizzie, who gazed up at him, her skin glistening from exertion. She didn't speak, but her expression seemed to suggest that she'd been waiting for him to cut in, to ask her to dance.

The band switched to an old slow song—"I Swear," he thought it was called. The moment stretched, almost to a breaking point. Without a word, he took Lizzie's hand and led her into the swaying crowd.

He focused on not falling as they began to dance, the music, lights, and smell of her hair invading his senses and distracting him.

She felt *good*. He had one hand on her waist, just above her hip, and the other held her fingers against his shoulder. Her breasts brushed against his chest, and as he pulled her closer, her tummy pressed against his lower body, instantly making his jeans tighter.

"I didn't know you could dance," she said.

"I can't."

She raised an eyebrow and pulled away just enough to look down. He noted that the tips of her boots were on either side of his right foot, moving back as his own clod-hoppers shuffled forward, turning them in a slow circle.

Meeting his eyes, she said, "I think this is dancing."

He shook his head. "Nope. Can't be. If I got caught dancing—slow dancing with a *girl*, no less—I'd lose all the points I've got for my official Social Reject Club card. I'm just keeping you from running backward into those people over there."

"Ah." She nodded, her mouth curving up into an enticing smile.

Did she have lipstick on, or were her lips always that pink and tempting?

"I didn't realize you were a member of that particular group. You hide it fairly well, considering how nice you are to your sister. And you haven't been especially rude to me lately."

He considered this. "I *am* just a prospect. I won't be fully inducted for a while."

"Hmm. Well, maybe I can convince you to back out before it's too late."

How had her hand gotten behind his neck, and what were her fingers doing to the ends of his hair? He was going to have to get it cut soon, because that felt too good to be permissible.

"Why do you think I shouldn't join?" he asked.

"It's an ethical issue." A frown marred her perfect face, and she said, "My last boyfriend was secretly an A-hole level member—and I've sworn to screen everyone from here on out." She seemed to realize what she'd just said—her *last boyfriend*, as though there was another one in her near vicinity—and her cheeks colored, but she plowed ahead. "I mean, I can't share my dog with someone who might encourage crotch sniffing or leg humping."

Adam feigned horror. "Is that what A-hole level members do?"

"It's what their dogs do. I've never seen an actual human one do that."

"Thank God." He laughed and realized the music had changed again, to another slow something or other. It also occurred to him that he was having a really good time. He was in town, in the middle of a shit ton of people, and he hadn't reminded himself to breathe once.

Lizzie sighed and shifted slightly, her body pressing against his in a subtle, completely perfect way. Maybe he was just distracted by the woman in his arms. Maybe it was having a purpose—bringing the dogs to town, helping Jake and Talbott get their shit together. Helping his sister. Finding some level of peace with his grandfather.

Some combination of all of the above...

As though the universe was aware of his near contentment, it decided to make sure he hadn't been lulled into a false sense of complacency. He had guided Lizzie out of the middle of the crowd before he consciously registered the first *whoosh* and *thump* of the rocket. The brightly colored flashes of the fireworks were nearly gone before he computed that there was no threat.

"Oh!" Lizzie was among the enchanted. Through the haze of adrenaline coursing through Adam's bloodstream, he noted her shining eyes and parted lips. She looked like she was having an orgasm, while his heart was beating triple speed and his breath couldn't keep up—and didn't that just piss him off. He was ready to crawl under the nearest picnic table, and she was holding his hand, straining to get a better look.

He knew he was overreacting, that the fireworks were a trigger. His therapist had made him practice breathing through this shit, but he was still pissed off. He needed to leave.

As a few more fireworks filled the night sky, he reached for his phone with his free hand. He'd find Talbott and Jake and use the dogs as an excuse to leave. The problem was, they'd beaten him to it. There was a text telling him that they'd left, taking the car and the dogs, and hopefully he could get a ride home from Lizzie, since it sure looked like he was about to get lucky.

He cursed, shoving his phone back into his pocket. Maybe he could find his sister. He hoped she hadn't taken Granddad home already.

"What's wr—Oh." The knowing sympathy in Lizzie's eyes made the frustration and anger settle more deeply in Adam's gut. "Why don't we go?" she suggested. Or at least that's what he *thought* she said. He couldn't hear much over the buzzing in his ears, now that the explosions had ended.

"I'm okay. But Jake and Talbott bailed. Can you, uh, give me a ride home?" he asked, now feeling needy and pathetic in addition to chickenshit.

She was unfazed, though. "Of course. Let's go." She took the lead, holding tightly to his hand as she wound through the people on the lawn toward the food vendors that bordered the square. They squeezed between a funnel cake truck and a corn on the cob booth to the street beyond.

As they squeezed out of the lights and noise into the darkness, Lizzie nearly tripped over a pair of legs sticking out from under a food truck. She stopped in her tracks, and Adam nearly plowed her over as she bent at the waist to see what was going on.

"Get the fuck out here," came a harsh, muffled voice attached to the legs.

"What are you doing? Stop that!" Lizzie scolded.

"The dog won't come out," explained a woman standing nearby. Adam recognized the pregnant woman from the Dairy Queen. Crystal was even more pregnant, if that was possible.

"Get out here, you pussy dog." Clint scooted backward, a tree branch in one hand, yanking hard on the nylon lead he held in the other.

The blood in Adam's veins went nuclear when the asshole dragged a half-grown brown-and-white pit bull pup from beneath the truck, the metal spikes from its prong collar digging into the pup's neck.

Adam's vision narrowed to pinpoint, focusing squarely on the man and dog. Blood surged in his veins, flooding his muscles with a desperate need to move. He yanked his hand from Lizzie's and stalked forward, staring down at the now kneeling Clint, who blinked up in surprise.

"What the fuck do you think you're doing?"

Chapter 21

CRYSTAL SCREAMED WHEN ADAM GRABBED HER BOY-friend by the neck and jerked him to his feet. He slammed Clint into the back of the food truck and pinned him there with one arm, the other drawn back in a fist.

"Adam, no!" Lizzie leapt forward to grab his arm. He brushed her off with a jerk of his shoulder, but at least he didn't hit the guy. Instead, he got right up into his face. "*What* do you think you're doing?" he ground out between clenched teeth.

Clint's face was red, and his eyes bulged.

"Oh my God!" Crystal cried. "Let him go! You're killing him!"

Adam ignored her and growled into Clint's face. "I *should* kill you. Now talk."

Clint gasped and said, "Just trying to get my dog out from under the truck, man."

From the corner of her eye, Lizzie noted that the leash was slowly disappearing back under the truck. Crystal reached down to grab it.

"How would you like it if someone dragged you around by the spikes digging into your neck?" As though to demon-strate, Adam shifted his grip so his fingers pointed inward, where they could jab into Clint's throat, if he were so inclined.

"You've got to stop him," the pregnant girl hissed to Lizzie.

Lizzie agreed but also sensed any interference might push Adam closer to violence. Besides, a man who would get this upset about someone being cruel to a dog couldn't deliberately harm a human—could he?

Maybe. He'd been trained to protect those who couldn't protect themselves.

Apparently, Clint believed Adam could, because his voice quavered as he said, "Man, I'm sorry. I'm just trying to toughen him up."

Lizzie watched Adam almost vibrate with tension as he slowly released the guy and backed away. "Why does a dog need to be *toughened up*?" he asked. His jaw barely moved, his teeth were so tightly clenched.

Stupidity didn't scare easily, because Clint said, "He's a pit bull, man. Born and bred to kick ass. How's he going to learn to fight if he's too damned scared to come out from under a stupid truck?"

"You want to train him to fight?"

"Well…yeah." Clint looked doubtful. "There's good money in it."

Adam shot Lizzie a meaningful glance. When he appeared to relax and to speak again, Lizzie knew that he wanted her to go along with him. He nodded, as though in approval. "Have you been dogfighting for a long time?"

Clint looked at his girlfriend, then back at Adam. "Ah, no, actually. My cousin does. Or he did, anyway. He lost his dog a few weeks ago, though. It got beat by some cheating asshole who juices his dogs."

"People do that? Give them steroids?" Lizzie asked.

"Some do. It's bad for the dogs, though, so my cousin only fights with clean dogs."

"Honor among thieves, huh?" Adam chuckled, as though this was amusing.

"What?" Clint didn't understand the reference.

"Dogfighting is illegal, right?" Adam asked, acting like he thought Clint was cool for wanting to be a dogfighter.

"Yeah, but there're all kinds of places you can do it around here."

"No shit."

"Yeah, no shit." And good ol' Clint was back, hitching up his baggy pants, acting like the gangster he aspired to be. "You can win a shit ton of money if you bet on the right dog, even more if you own the dog," he said, then indicated the leash that Crystal still held next to the food truck. "I was thinking about training Bruce to fight, but he's a pussy. My cousin's bitch was tougher than this dog, and she got killed."

Or left for dead. Was he talking about poor Loretta?

"Oh, man, that sucks," Adam said, shooting Lizzie a sideways glance that suggested he'd had the same thought.

"Hey, man, if you're interested, I can call you next time there's any action. I'll get my cousin to take us out there."

"I'd like that," Adam said. He rattled off his number, which Clint entered into his phone.

Lizzie turned to the mother-to-be, unable to keep silent any longer. "Are you sure it's a good idea to have a mean dog if you're going to have a baby?" she asked.

Crystal cradled her belly and said, "Clint says if it's our dog, it'll protect the baby."

Adam put his phone away and shook his head at her comment. "I don't know much about fighting dogs, but I used to work with military canines, and—"

"No shit? Dude, that's so cool. Those dogs go after

terrorists and don't let go even if you hurt them." Clint bobbed his head, since he was *clearly* the authority.

Adam didn't dignify that with an answer but continued to address Crystal. "A couple things influence a dog's behavior—their genetics and what it's learned. Any dog can be mean if you treat it that way, but I wouldn't promise that even a really nice dog will never bite. It's instinct is to protect itself. But some breeds are more about biting and chewing. Not because they're mean, they just have big jaws with strong muscles that like to clamp down on things. If you train a dog with a bite impulse to fight, it's more likely to be triggered under the wrong circumstances. I'm not saying you can't do it, but I sure as hell wouldn't take a chance."

It was hard to tell if Clint was taking this in, but Crystal sure was. The dog was still under the truck, and she still held the leash, but she'd moved as far away from the animal as she could get.

"Well, this dog's obviously no good for fighting," Clint said, scowling. "Can't handle fucking fireworks."

Way to endear yourself to the veteran, Lizzie thought. *Point out something he's got in common with a frightened puppy.*

But Adam just nodded and said, "Good point." He squatted down to look at the little dog, whose curiosity had overcome its fear, and it had stuck its nose from under the truck. "And since you've been trying to teach it to fight, it might be unreliable."

"We're getting rid of it," Crystal announced.

"No way, babe. We'll breed him," Clint decided.

She opened her mouth to continue the argument but closed it again, apparently deciding to resolve that issue another day.

The dog crept closer and cautiously sniffed Adam's fingers. Adam carefully reached under, picked the little guy up, and tugged at the prong collar, which jingled around the dog's neck. "Whatever you decide to do with him, this collar is just going to make him more skittish if you don't use it right. Why don't you try keeping the regular collar on for a while, until he's more confident, and if you decide to keep him, I'll show you how to use the prongs right, if you need them," he offered.

"Sure, man, that would be cool."

Adam unclipped the leash from the prong collar then reattached it to the leather collar also around the dog's neck. With a final pat, he put the dog on the ground. "Oh. And if you decide you're not keeping him? Give me a call."

Lizzie's heart flipped upside down and inside out.

"Hey, you two have a good night, okay?" Adam told them. His stride was loose limbed and casual as they walked away, but Lizzie could feel every ounce of rage that still radiated from his pores.

—————————

Adam didn't pay attention to where he was going. He just held Lizzie's hand and walked, leading her away from that jackass and his future spawn. He had to get away before he lost his shit completely. He'd almost taken Clint's head off when he saw the little jerk trying to drag the terrified dog from beneath the truck—especially when that was exactly where Adam would have liked to be, too.

"I should have taken that dog away from him," he said now, stopping abruptly. Lizzie's forward momentum made her bump into his shoulder, and he automatically put his other hand out to keep her from falling. He released her, then paced a few steps before stopping to say, "I'm going to go back and get it."

"You can't do that," she said.

"I *can* do that. I can go back, find that idiot, take the dog, and—"

Lizzie walked toward him. "And *what*? Get arrested? Then he'll still have the dog, and you'll be in jail. What good will that do?" Her fingers, soft but firm on his forearm, cut through the haze. "You did the right thing."

"What? I almost killed him." He was contradicting himself—he *still* wanted to go back, knock Clint on his ass, and take the poor dog to safety.

Lizzie's smile was a little crooked when she said, "Well, maybe your method was a little extreme, but you got his attention."

"I wanted to kill him."

"But you didn't, did you?"

No. But the shit in my head…in my heart…

"You didn't hurt him," she repeated, taking his hand again.

How could she smile at him like that? And look at him with those big, soul-probing eyes? She now knew for certain that he was a basket case, and now he had even more proof he should stay on the ranch and away from actual people.

Always the mind reader, she said, "If you weren't here, God only knows what might have happened. He could have really hurt that poor dog. But you let him save face, gave him some good information, and we learned something about what happened to Loretta. We can update the sheriff with that, right?"

Maybe. Adam was so damned confused. He knew wrong when he saw it—abusing a dog was wrong—but how did he know what was right? The rules out here in the world were different. Too many shades of gray. "I don't know, Lizzie. I really don't know." Had he ever felt so hopeless?

How did he expect to hold it together long enough to make sure Emma and Granddad were okay when he couldn't handle simple human interactions? He'd even taken on more: Jake and Talbott, and all these dogs. He was supposed to be tying up loose ends, not creating more. And Lizzie was still here, by his side. *Caring* about him, for Christ's sake. There had to be something wrong with her.

Maybe he should just cut bait now. Leave tomorrow—no, tonight. Drive to the coast, walk out into the water until it was over his head and he couldn't come back to screw up anything else.

"Sit down."

"What?" He looked around. They'd walked a couple of blocks away from the center of town, past the Feed and Seed, and now stood by a picnic table in front of the completely dark Dairy Queen. *Why is it closed on a Saturday night?* he wondered absently. *Oh yeah. The thing in the square.* There had been an ice cream booth there.

He let her push him back so his ass landed on the edge of the table, but his feet remained on the ground. She wedged into the space between his knees and put her hands on his chest.

"Do you think I'm a good person?" she asked.

"Of course." She was the best person he knew, in spite of her poor taste in men.

"Then will you trust me when I tell you that what happened tonight is okay?"

"I don't—I don't think I can." What was wrong with him was deep inside, part of his structure. Like a dog that needed to bite things, his nature was hard-wired, and no amount of deep breathing or imagining his happy place or dog cuddling would fix him.

"Do you talk to anyone about this stuff?"

He didn't pretend not to understand what she meant. "Yeah. I see a shrink at the VA every few weeks."

She blinked.

"What? You thought I'd say I was too manly for that shit?"

"I...I don't know what I thought."

"I don't know if it's helping," he admitted.

"Do you talk to Jake and Marcus? They went through the same things you did. They understand."

"Only because the shit they went through was my fault. I fucked up, and they got blown up."

"What? It's not your fault."

"Yeah, it is. It was my mistake that got us blown up. It's my fault Jake can't think and Talbott's going to be paralyzed before he's forty. And it's my fault Celeste Garcia's kids don't have a father."

"Oh, Adam—" She put her hand against his jaw, the firm warmth of her skin a sharp contrast to the ice in his heart. He jerked away.

"Don't. I'm going to tell you what happened, and then you can tell me it's all okay, it was an accident, and blah blah blah."

She pressed her lips together, swallowing whatever goody-two-shoes protest she was going to make.

"We were following up on some intelligence about a guy who was making bombs. A really bad son of a bitch. I'd been out with Tank for three days, working with some SEALs who were looking for an arms dealer, and we were both exhausted. Dehydrated. Worn out. But this intel was ripe, and our commander was hot to chase it down, so I ignored everything I knew about taking care of my dog and agreed to go along."

He remembered the dust, the heat, the smell of that dark little house. Cooking odors, sewage, and something worse. Something evil.

"I took Tank in there, and he sniffed around but couldn't find anything. He sniffed the hell out of everything but didn't alert. He was supposed to lie down and stare at whatever he finds. But he didn't. I let the rest of the team come in, and when we went to bust in the door down the hall, the whole damned place blew up."

"Why is that your fault?" Lizzie asked.

She was so damned naive.

"Because if I'd kept my dog back and taken an extra day, he would have been sharp. He wouldn't have missed that trigger."

"You don't know that."

"I do know that. Tank was the best explosives detector in the army, and I let ambition and enthusiasm distract me from being careful."

"So if you hadn't gone, those guys—the insurgents— they probably would have gotten away. And they would have hurt lots of other innocent people."

"You don't know that," he threw her words back at her, but she caught them easily.

"Nope. I don't. But I do know this: You did the best you could with the information you had. Your motives were pure."

"Motives don't matter for shit. I got a good man and my dog killed, and I ruined the lives of at least two other men. I'm never going to know how to do the right thing. I never have."

"Oh, for crying out loud," she said, moving forward, wrapping her arms around his neck. He resisted her, drawing his head back because he wanted so desperately to bury his face in her shoulder. "The only thing *I* think you ever did wrong was push me away when I wanted you to make love to me twelve years ago. Let's see if you can't remedy that, and we'll worry about the rest of your character defects later."

That sounded good. *So damned good.* To lose himself in her sweet body for a while. But he didn't deserve it. And she deserved better.

In spite of his hesitation, Lizzie pressed her lips against his and nipped at his mouth until he gave in with a groan.

Chapter 22

LIZZIE PRESSED HER LIPS TO ADAM'S, SOFTLY, THEN MORE firmly. When he finally kissed her back, he was *kissing* her. His tongue tasted of lemonade and mint as it toyed with hers, stroking, sliding.

One of his big hands went around her waist while the other cupped the back of her head, angling her for kisses along her jaw, to her neck, which he nuzzled, driving her out of her mind with the need for *more*. More of his touch, more of his kiss, more of his hard body.

She may have whimpered, because he drew back and looked into her face with a shadowed, unreadable gaze. He was going to turn away from her. Again. He was going to kiss her gently, pull away, and say this wasn't a good idea.

But this time, she wasn't a simpering sixteen-year-old virgin. This time, she was—

He pulled her closer while rising to his feet, so their bodies were aligned, and she felt his chest against hers, his pelvis, and—*Whoa*.

"This is too…out in the open," he growled. "I want… more."

She laughed. "Me too."

Wordlessly, he wrapped an arm around her shoulders and guided her to the side of the building, into dark shadows that would conceal them from any passerby. She slid her arm around his waist as though it was meant to be there, his warm muscles flexing under her hand.

Nothing else existed for her in that moment but Adam. The sound of his breathing, the smell of his skin, the feel of him moving next to her…and his taste as he paused to kiss her again.

They reached the deepest shadows before he stopped and pressed her against the wall with his body and moved his hands over her. He palmed both of her breasts, and she nearly collapsed from the sheer pleasure of feeling his hands against her nipples, even through the fabric of her dress.

She was restless, though. Her feet moved apart, and one of his thighs slid between hers, pressing hard muscle against her core. She wiggled, and he chuckled softly but didn't move his hands from their exploration of her curves—from the outside of her dress.

She almost sobbed. "Don't make me beg, damn it."

For a moment, she thought she'd ruined things, because he froze at her words. But instead of coming up with some noble excuse, he laughed. "Yes, ma'am." Then, more seriously, "Lizzie, you deserve to get everything you want. You should never have to beg."

"I want you. I'll beg later, if that sort of thing works for you, but right now? Right now, I want you to touch me. Right here, right now, right next to the Dairy Queen drive-through window."

He chuckled, and his head dropped to her shoulder. He took a deep breath. Then, looking straight at her, he said, "Undo your dress."

Staring right back at him, she reached one hand behind her neck and tugged at the tie holding up the top. When it went slack, her breasts were still covered, but the fabric was looser, and he tugged it down. She hissed when the warm night air hit her swollen nipples, and again when he bent to take one in his mouth.

Her hands were in his hair then, on his shoulders, his back, everywhere she could reach. "Oh please, oh please," she repeated, needing more.

"I wanna take my time with you, I really do," he murmured between kisses and licks against her skin. "But I also said I didn't want you to beg, right?"

"Yes, you did," she agreed.

With a reluctant-sounding sigh—but a sideways grin—Adam straightened and yanked her skirt up. He ran one hand between her thighs and up, stopping when he got to the fabric between her legs. His rough fingers stroked over the silky material, then under it, slipping easily through her folds.

"Oh yeah," he muttered. "Yeah."

"Uh-huh," she answered, her voice rising, because he was stroking her right where she needed him. She was wound so tightly, she was afraid she might spin off into the stratosphere before she even got to touch him.

With a shaky sigh, she said, "Can we—"

"Yeah. We can." He fished in his pocket. "I swear to God I wasn't planning for this to happen," he said, "but Talbott shoved this at me when he took the dogs." He held up a small package containing, Lizzie assumed, a condom.

"You don't have to be apologetic," she said. "Since it *is* happening, right?"

He nodded and, with a note of wonder, said, "I think so."

"Good." She reached into the waistband of her dress and

tugged out a package similar to the one he'd produced. "You know, in case that one's not enough."

"Yeehaw," he said, and they laughed as they began to remove their clothes. He paused to run a hand over her backside, groaning when he reached her bare ass. He yanked on the elastic at her hip. She helped him, peeling the thong down her legs.

She watched breathlessly while Adam unbuckled his belt. She tore at the plastic covering of the condom while he popped the button of his waistband and unzipped. She reached for him, covering him, admiring the hard shape as she went.

He boosted her up while she wrapped one leg around his waist.

Finally, *finally*, he was there, just barely sliding into her slick heat. "Yeah, that works," he said, grabbing her thigh to hold her steady while he eased inside her, which was...

"Oh wow." Something about this angle really worked. He was both stroking her and filling her at the same time.

"Okay?" he asked.

"O-kay." She nodded, afraid she might break the connection if she moved. Adam seemed to have no such misgivings, because he smiled down at her, kissed her, and began to move.

And move.

Before she knew it, her body was tensing around him, lightning bolts of electricity running from the base of her spine to every nerve ending she had and back again.

She heard him groan, felt him tense, and everything went haywire as her nervous system short-circuited.

When it was over, when the aftershocks faded and he

slid from her body, she realized that not once, not for a second, even as she undressed in front of him, had she worried about her size.

———————————

Adam had never come so hard or so…completely. As the last waves of the world's most amazing orgasm faded, his knees buckled. Lizzie, God bless her, was ready and landed on her feet, needing only a hand on his shoulder for balance. Adam was nearly insensibly boneless, the top of his skull somewhere in the next county, the rest of his skeleton turned to rubber.

He somehow managed to drag his jeans back up around his ass but didn't bother to fasten them while he tried to figure out what to do with the condom—

"Here." Lizzie produced a tissue from somewhere, and he staggered to the nearest trash can while she fiddled with the skirt of her dress.

And then there they were, standing in the dark, staring at each other. His brain slowly came back online, but everything was skewed—shinier and softer at the same time. The past few minutes in her arms, in her body, had eclipsed everything he'd felt before that. Even now, he could barely remember what they'd been talking about, what he'd been so distressed over.

"How you doin,' soldier?" she drawled, wrapping her arms around his waist, smiling up at him. His arms slid around her shoulders, snuggling her against him so they leaned into each other, almost like they were dancing again.

"I'm doing...not terrible," he admitted. He scanned their surroundings and thought about what they'd just done, hard and fast against the wall of the Dairy Queen. God, he'd barely even touched her before he was slamming into her.

"I'm awesome," she told him, leaning in to nuzzle his neck. Her kiss-swollen lips quirked up. "But if you're not sure you did a thorough job, we can try again."

His dick agreed, but he looked around at the darkened, trash-strewn parking lot and decided that the next time he touched her, he wanted silk sheets, roses, champagne, the whole works. Or at least doors, so he could shut out the rest of the world and take his time to touch and taste every inch of her.

Meanwhile...what? "So, uh..." *Take the lead here, big guy, that's what.* "What do you want to do now?"

She sighed, though it sounded contented, not frustrated. "I suppose I should take you back out to the ranch?"

Ooh. A car had doors. "Yeah, if it's not too much trouble. Or I can always borrow Emma's car."

On cue, his phone buzzed in his pocket.

"Yeah?" he answered while Lizzie bent down and picked up some litter. Of course she would. Adam's mind was fogged with postcoital confusion, and she'd slipped right back into her superhero costume as Civic Responsibility Girl.

"Adam? It's Emma."

"Hey. What's going on?"

Lizzie gathered the litter—was that some sort of rag?— and began pulling at it. Wait. That wasn't litter. It was her damned thong.

"Are you still in town? I could use some help."

"Okay."

Lizzie lifted one boot-clad foot, then the other, and stepped into the thong. She met his eyes and began tugging the thing up to her knees, then her thighs…

"I'm being abducted by aliens, and they said if you bring them sixty pounds of whole wheat flour—"

He turned from the reverse striptease and said, "What?"

"I wasn't sure you were paying attention to me. You sound a little distracted."

He didn't have enough bandwidth for this. "Emma, what's going on?"

"Granddad's having a bad night. He's upset about something, and I can't make sense of it. I wouldn't bother you, but he keeps saying I have to tell you about whatever it is. Since I don't understand…anyway, can you come by and talk to him?"

Without thinking, he'd turned back to face Lizzie. He inhaled her scent. Lemon, something flowery, and, *Jesus*, sex. She stood close enough to touch, concern creasing her forehead.

Letting her know about his problems—and Granddad was one of them—didn't bother him as much as it might have an hour ago.

"Adam?" Emma prodded.

He closed his eyes, tried to focus. "Yep. Okay. I'll be there in five minutes." Putting the phone away, he told Lizzie, "I need to go to Emma's. Granddad's having some sort of dementia moment," he told her.

"Okay. Do you want me to come with you, or would that make things more chaotic?"

He *did* want her to come with him. She might not help

Granddad, but her pragmatic compassion grounded Adam. Just being near her evened out his blood pressure. She wouldn't stop the crazy from knocking on his door, but she'd definitely distract him from inviting it in for coffee.

Hmm. Frantic sex as treatment for PTSD—he wondered if he could get a prescription for that.

But no. He wasn't going to subject her to Granddad right now, not while he was feeling so...good. He felt *good*. It was such a foreign experience, he barely recognized it.

"Thanks for offering, but no thanks. I think I'd better deal with whatever this is on my own."

"Okay." She looked uncertain, and he felt the same way.

"I'll walk you home."

"You sure? It's pretty far out of your way," she said, laughing as she pointed at the fence between her family's backyard and the rear lot of the Dairy Queen.

He unlatched the gate and held it open, then followed her the few steps to her back door.

"So, I guess I'll talk to you later," he said when she had it opened.

"Do you want me to run you to Emma's? My car keys are right inside the door."

He shook his head. "It's only a couple of blocks away."

"Okay then." She waved her hands, clearly flustered. "I don't know what comes next. Do we hug goodbye from now on? Kiss?"

She was cute when she was at a loss, which had the effect of making him feel more in control.

"How's about this?" He leaned forward and pressed his lips to hers, and she hummed with pleasure. The kiss, which started out gentle and sweet, began to heat up, and he pulled away before he lost his mind again. "We'll worry about next time…next time."

"Okay. Good plan."

He watched her walk inside before turning toward the Feed and Seed and Emma's place. It seemed appropriate that Granddad picked tonight to have a meltdown, because Adam was feeling almost—normal? At least *human*, for the first time in a long time. Like a guy who'd met a girl for a date that had gone really, really well.

Give or take a near fight and some major anxiety.

He sighed.

He really had to get this ranch sold so he could get Granddad somewhere safe—for his sake *and* Emma's.

Chapter 23

"THANKS FOR COMING BY. I'M SORRY I INTERRUPTED your date." Emma stood on her front porch, biting the cuticle of her thumbnail. It was an old habit from when their parents died and they'd moved to Big Chance. Adam thought she'd given it up during grade school, but she seemed to have picked it up again sometime in the past few years. Because of losing her husband? Or because of having to deal with Granddad?

Either way, every time Adam saw her doing it, his guilt meter registered in the red zone. She shouldn't have to worry, and he should be helping more.

"I'm glad you called," he told her. "What's going on?"

She sighed. "I thought going to the square tonight would be good. Get Granddad to visit with more people than just me, Mrs. King, and you. He had a good time when we came out to the ranch a couple of weeks ago."

Seemed reasonable. It would be good for Emma, too, but he didn't say so. She got defensive any time he expressed concern about the fact that she went to work, took care of Granddad, and did little else. Some self-imposed punishment for Todd's death, he suspected.

Well, hopefully Adam could get the damned ranch sold, they'd get Granddad somewhere safe, and she'd be able to resume her life.

"So what happened?" he asked. "Granddad seemed okay when I saw you in town."

"Well, yeah, he was, at first," she said. "We had waffle fries and ice cream and watched people."

"And then the grease hit your gut?"

She smiled. "No, but I am glad I stocked up on antacids this week." Her smile faded. "He was cranky, but he's always cranky, bitching about how the funnel cakes weren't as crispy as when Grandma volunteered in the booth back in 1800-whatever."

They shared a chuckle over that. Granddad was notorious for comparing everything to the "good ol' days."

"But then we ran into Fred Chance."

"The mayor's uncle?" Adam tried to remember who was who, but he hadn't been back in Big Chance long enough to pass the "who are the Chance cousins" social membership quiz.

"Yeah. The great-uncle, I think. Anyway, he was there with his family and called to Granddad, and he just...lost it."

"Granddad?"

"Yeah. Mr. Chance was really nice—asked about everyone. Then he mentioned the ranch, and Granddad started calling him a lying, cheating scumbag, except he was calling the man Mike and not Fred. I got him to come home by telling him I wasn't feeling well, but when we got back here, he was talking to himself about bad decisions. He won't go to bed, he won't take his medicine, and he goes back and forth between paranoid outbursts and spaced-out silence. Says he's got to find out what happened to the proof."

"Proof? Of what?"

"That he's the legal heir to the throne of England?" Emma shrugged. "I honestly have no clue."

"Maybe he got confused between reality and something he saw on TV."

"Maybe." Emma didn't seem convinced, but the important thing was getting Granddad to chill out and take his meds so everyone could get some rest.

"Where is he?"

"On the sun porch."

"Let's go talk to him." Adam followed his sister to the door to the little screened-in area out back, just in time to hear the screen door slam shut.

"Shit." Adam followed. "Granddad, slow down!" The old man moved fast and made it to Main Street before Adam caught up with him.

"Hey, Granddad," Adam said. "Where you going?"

"I've got to find that Mike fella and make him give me back them papers."

"Mike who?"

"Oh, hell, boy," Granddad grumbled. "I'm old. I don't remember his last name. He's that one son of a bitch. Should be in jail, but we let him leave town instead. I've got to tell the sheriff."

"Ooookay," Adam said, trying to think. "You know, it's the Fourth of July, and people are all out celebrating. Maybe tomorrow would be a better time to sort things out."

Granddad stopped. "You don't believe me."

He knew the feeling—recognizing that your brain didn't work the way it was supposed to—so he tried not to be patronizing. "The sheriff's pretty busy tonight, with all the extra people in town."

"I know. That's why the son of a bitch won't be expectin' us."

"I tell you what," Adam said. "Tomorrow, I'll personally go to the sheriff's office with you and help you surprise this Mike. Would that help?"

Like a switch had been flipped, Granddad was suddenly all smiles. "That's a great idea, boy. You caught them terrorists well enough, I guess. You surely can't fuck up catching Mike."

Great, Adam thought as he successfully guided Granddad into a one-eighty turn and pointed them back toward Emma's house. Hopefully, the old man would forget his mission before he expected Adam to perform miracles and catch this imaginary Mike.

Lizzie collapsed backward onto her bed, arms outstretched, landing in the heap of stuffed animals her mom refused to throw away.

Adam. Collins. She'd just had mind-blowing sex with *Adam Collins*.

She sat up to remove her boots, appreciating the slight soreness that let her know she'd had not just mind-blowing sex but hard and fast up-against-a-wall sex. And she hadn't had to apologize for the size of her thighs or her soft tummy, like she had with Dean-the-Dick.

She spared Dean five more seconds—he'd once made a point of comparing his own ribbed abdomen to hers after making supposed love to her. On second thought, she was done giving him any more thought.

She'd come back to Big Chance for a fresh start, and she'd made progress, especially on the job and family front. She hadn't been quite ready to cast off all her old hang-ups, though, until now. It was time to be New Lizzie. New, improved, confident Lizzie who could *do* her long-lost high school crush and not fall apart or spend the next however many weeks wanting a do-over to get it right. That was how she always felt with Dean—whom she was *done* with and not thinking about anymore.

Because she had done it right with Adam. And he'd done it right with her.

How did Adam feel? Was he sorry? He'd looked a little shell-shocked before he left, but that kiss… She was a little annoyed that he'd probably been right; she'd been too young when they'd had that first chance, way back when.

They were both older and wiser now. Maybe even old and wise enough to climb over their separate piles of baggage and meet in the middle a few more times before—before what? Before she sold his ranch and he rode off into the sunset. Alone.

She wasn't going to think about that, either.

One thing that'd be okay to think about was Dad's historical park, so she grabbed her laptop and booted it up.

She spent an hour surfing through old online newspapers to see if there were any records of the sale of that farm on Mill Creek Road. It wasn't hard to imagine someone had misfiled the paperwork in the Chance County Clerk's office, but there had to be *some* record, somewhere.

Clint and Crystal crossed her mind, then. If Clint's cousin had used the place for dogfighting, maybe he knew something. Lizzie shuddered at the thought of approaching that person, whoever he was.

Adam might do it, though. Except that scared her almost as much, because he was likely to take on the dog-fighting guys single-handedly, like he was taking on everything else. She'd talk to him. Make sure he planned to get the sheriff involved.

Her phone chimed with an incoming text.

> **Adam:** Hey. Hope I didn't wake you. Just wanted to say...good night.

She smiled.

> **Lizzie:** Hey yourself. Everything okay with your granddad?
> **Adam:** Yep. He decided to run away from home and confront an imaginary enemy about an imaginary theft, but I convinced him to go home.
> **Lizzie:** How did you do that?
> **Adam:** Told him I'd help him talk to the sheriff tomorrow. Hopefully he'll forget about it by then.
> **Lizzie:** I'm sorry this is so hard for him. For everyone.

A pause.

> **Lizzie:** You still there?

Nothing.

Crap.

Five minutes later, long enough for her to reread their texts and worry about what she'd said wrong (ever in her entire life), her phone chimed again.

Adam: Sorry. Talbott fell. I had to help him get
       up off his ass.
Lizzie: Is he okay?
Adam: Yes. I think it was his pain medicine
       mixed with his messed-up back.
Lizzie: Oh no!
Adam: He'll just take another pill. He won't care
       again soon enough.
Lizzie: I'm not sure what to say about that.

She'd noticed that Marcus usually had a beer in his hand when she was at the ranch. Was he mixing that with pain pills? Surely, he knew better. It seemed that any comment was going to draw attention to the fact that Adam blamed himself for Marcus's situation.

Adam: Nothing to say. He does what he has to
       do to get through it.
Lizzie: What else is going on?
Adam: Are you trying to change the subject?
Lizzie: Unless you want to talk about it.
Adam: Change away.
Lizzie: What are the dogs doing?

Oh wow. That was dumb.

Adam: Is that your version of "What are you wearing right now?"

Lizzie: 😑

Adam: How did you do that? Lol is the extent of my text lingo.

Lizzie: There's a menu on your keyboard. I can show you later. So what are you wearing?

Adam: You first.

Lizzie: The same thing I had on the last time you saw me, minus the boots.

Adam: Nice. Unless you want to switch that around and send me a picture.

Her entire body heated. He wanted her to send him a naked picture of herself wearing boots? That was just...*no*. She found herself thinking about it anyway.

Lizzie: That might be something better left to your imagination.

Adam: I doubt it.

He did know how to make her feel sexy.

Lizzie: At least better left to naked eyes, not cell phone cameras.

Nothing.

And then her phone rang.

"He—hello?"

"Hey." His voice was all gravelly.

"Hey yourself."

"When can I get you naked again?"

Her stomach clenched—along with other parts of her anatomy. "That's very blunt."

"I'm not going to be around long enough to mess with fancy courtship crap."

She knew he meant to remind her that he was leaving Big Chance as soon he could, but it felt more…permanent.

It felt final.

Chapter 24

ALMOST A WEEK LATER, LIZZIE HIT ADAM'S NUMBER AND waited.

They'd spoken or texted several times since the Fourth, though she'd been so busy with real estate business, she hadn't been to the ranch. Each time she heard from him, she was pleasantly surprised that he wanted to talk to her.

"Hey." There was a little upswing on the end of the "hey," telling Lizzie that Adam was glad to hear from her.

"Are you busy?" she asked.

"I don't know." That was teasing. Her gruff, withdrawn soldier was teasing her.

She was out of breath and hadn't even gotten to the good part. She rushed on. "I'm working on my proposal for the mayor, and I want to take more pictures at Mill Creek, but to be honest, I'm a little too creeped out to go back there alone, knowing those dogfighting guys might show up."

"If you want to get me alone, all you have to do is say so," Adam told her.

"Oh! No. I mean, yes, but not—I don't—" Grr. She *did* kind of want to be alone with him. Correction: she *really* wanted to be alone with him. One world-record orgasm, and her brain was completely scrambled. All she could think about was having more orgasms with Adam. Soon. It had only been a few (long, lonely) days since Saturday night, and already, she was addicted.

"What time? Now?" he asked.

"Is it too early? It's only going to get hotter later."

"We're in Texas in July. When is it not hot?" He laughed. "Now works for me. How about you? Do you want me to meet you there?"

"Um, yes...it would be great if you'd meet me there, and yes, I want to go now."

Vibrations from his chuckle ran down her spine. *Now* might not be soon enough.

But it wasn't just about the possibility of sex. She desperately wanted to tell Adam her news, wanted to know what he thought. Even though he said he couldn't wait to get out of Big Chance, he'd listened to her ideas about the park and hadn't told her she was stupid or ridiculous.

"Okay. I've got to finish up a couple of things here, and I'll be there in...twenty minutes?"

She drove to the farm as slowly as she could, not wanting to seem too eager, but there wasn't much to slow her down. She'd already put a blanket in the trunk, filled her cooler with cans of lemonade, and there were condoms in her purse.

She should calm down. She'd already been up against the Dairy Queen wall with her dress around her waist, and that had been amazing. Spontaneous, in a twelve-years-in-the-making sort of way. This was *planned*. She was going to meet Adam, and they were going to hopefully, probably, have sex. In the daylight. Where all his perfect muscles and bronzed skin would be visible, and all her lumps and bumps and—no. *You're done with all that. Done.*

Still, by the time she crept out to Mill Creek Road and

eased down the lane, she'd only managed to spend fifteen of her twenty minutes.

When she topped the rise that overlooked the farmyard, there was already a vehicle parked there. A white truck with a bumper sticker that read "Freedom Isn't Free" and a long, tall cowboy in an army T-shirt leaning on the lowered tailgate, smiling at her.

She couldn't help but notice the cooler in the back of the truck and a sleeping bag conveniently laid out on the bed.

Would he laugh if she asked him if he had condoms in his purse, too?

She didn't get the chance, because she'd barely turned the ignition off before he'd opened her car door and pulled her out and into his arms. All her self-doubt and insecurities fled, because when he looked into her eyes, she *felt* the way he saw her and knew he liked it.

He held her gaze for a moment, but then he smiled, leaned in, and kissed her. Softly. Sweetly. So gently she would have thought she might not feel it, but for the way the warmth of his lips against hers stirred her senses.

"Do you know how glad I am that you called?" he asked after pulling back and looking into her eyes again.

She felt his lower body press into hers. "Oh, I think I have a pretty good idea."

He laughed. "Yeah. Well."

"I'm pretty glad to see you, too."

They were both quiet for a moment, smiling at each other, safe in the knowledge that they were on the same page, together.

"So, uh, do you want to take your pictures and stuff now?" Adam asked.

Oh yeah. That was technically why she'd come out here, wasn't it? She hadn't taken many shots the last time, because she'd found Loretta and the puppies. What she really wanted to do was to climb into the back of that truck and have her way with Adam, even if the ninety-five-degree morning would be magnified by sun and a steel truck bed.

But work first. She nodded. "Yeah, let's do pictures. Can we walk down toward the creek? I got the building and the hole in the ground last time."

They both looked toward the burned-out basement.

"Have you heard anything from the police?"

"When I first called the sheriff's office, a detective told me they knew there was dogfighting in the area, but every time they tried to bust a location, the ring had moved on. They said they'd patrol out here a little more, though."

"Should we tell them about Clint?"

He scratched his head. "Yeah, but I was hoping he'd call me—I gave him my number but didn't get his. I'd like to have a little more information before I talk to them again."

"I hope Clint calls you soon, then."

They reached a break in the fence line, where there would be access to the creek, but the closed gate was overgrown with brambles. Insects buzzed within the steamy tangle of branches, anxiously waiting for new victims. Lizzie's arms and legs itched just thinking about climbing through there. "Ick."

Adam didn't hesitate. "Hang on a minute," he told her, then turned and jogged back toward his truck.

It wasn't at all difficult to stand there admiring the way his body moved until he reached the truck and returned to her with...was that... "A scythe?"

"Yep."

"You just happen to carry around weapons of mass destruction?"

"If I'm hunting weeds, I do. We were clearing out some space behind the barn yesterday. Stand back." He proceeded to whack the hell out of the tangled branches and ivy, which also wasn't unpleasant to watch. In no time at all, he'd forged a mercifully short path to the other side.

"After you, fair maiden," he said, opening the gate and making a grand sweeping motion with his hand.

"Oh my. Aren't you fancy?"

"Yeah, I'm a real prince."

She didn't comment, just gave him her best under-the-eyelashes look and made sure to brush up against him when she walked past.

The air seemed to get easier to breathe when they reached the shade of the trees. Water burbled through stretches of wide, rocky creek bed, interrupted here and there by deeper, still pools. A frog, startled by their approach, leapt into the water and disappeared in the depths.

"It's beautiful," she sighed.

Adam didn't answer, so she turned to him for confirmation—but he was staring at her. "Yeah," he said. "It is."

A not-unpleasant heat burned her cheeks and warmed her tummy. She didn't know what to say, so she took the smart aleck way out. "You don't have to butter me up. I'm already a sure thing." She stepped toward him, but he backed up, holding up a hand.

"While I appreciate the sentiment—believe me, I *do* appreciate it—I'm a little sweaty."

"Hmm." She certainly wasn't bothered by a little good clean sweat, but he clearly was. She gently dropped her things onto the grassy bank. Reaching out for his hand, she said, "Well then, why don't you get cleaned up?" And she tugged him after her, toward the gurgling stream.

"Wait a minute," Adam protested as Lizzie took first one, then another step onto the slippery, mossy stones below the surface of Mill Creek. He followed her anyway but felt obliged to say, "I don't think this is really—Aaaah!" He cried out as his feet went out from under him and his hand slid free of Lizzie's grasp.

But when he landed, he barely noticed the big rock digging into his ass as the cool water hit his steaming skin.

"Oh no! Are you okay?" Lizzie didn't seem as concerned as her words might have suggested, especially when she splashed down next to him and grinned.

"I'm glad I left my phone in the truck." Even though it was already soaked, he pulled off his T-shirt and threw it to dry land.

Lizzie kicked her feet, sending a spray of water into the air and onto herself. Her wet top clung very nicely to her breasts, revealing the lace of her bra through the thin fabric. "Isn't this awesome?" she asked.

His mouth suddenly dry, he tried to answer her. "Uh-huh."

She caught him looking and laughed. She splashed water at him.

"Oh no." He smacked the surface of the water to return fire. "You don't want to mess with the master."

She raised one perfect eyebrow. "Ooh, I think maybe I do."

He cracked up, but instead of a splash, he got a flash of her creamy skin as she peeled that barely there top off and tossed it toward the bank, followed by her bra. It was good he was already sitting in the water, because she had a knack for keeping him off-balance.

"Jesus, Lizzie," he croaked as she rose onto her knees, water streaming down her bare skin. Her breasts were perfect. He'd touched and tasted the other night, but he hadn't looked. Now, he looked. Rosy nipples and full, creamy breasts rested above the golden tanned arms she wrapped around her waist against his perusal. He took her hands and tugged, urging her to reveal herself to him. Such a contradiction, this woman. So generous and giving and sure of her purpose—so insecure.

"You're so damned beautiful."

She was. Not just her body, which he loved, but the rest of her. Those big brown eyes narrowed slightly with doubt, but then, biting her bottom lip, she exhaled and relaxed, apparently deciding to accept his admiration.

He held her gaze and put her hands on his shoulders, then reached for her hips, urging her closer until she straddled his thighs.

He cupped her face, loving the way she leaned into his touch. He caressed the soft skin at her waist, then skimmed the sides of her breasts. He tried to savor this perfect moment, but the need growing in him was so strong, he was afraid he'd lose this sweet gentle thing between them if he gave in to it fully.

He had to kiss her, had to share the exact same air she

breathed. Slowly, their lips met, finding each other, tasting, teasing. Tongues brushing. Her breath stuttered—or was that his?

She pulled away, no longer self-conscious, and raised an eyebrow.

"What?" he asked.

"This." She scooted back a few inches and reached for the fly of his jeans, which was about to rip from the erection trying to fight its way to freedom. She struggled with the button, biting her lip with consternation at the water-logged denim. He leaned back on his hands, the sight of her golden head bent to her task giving him a jolt, leaving him paralyzed and waiting for the next thing. Which was the lowering of his zipper, followed by tugging at the fabric until he was free.

She looked up at him again, and his entire body buzzed with anticipation. She smiled, holding his gaze while she lowered her mouth to him, sexier than he'd ever imagined. The first touch of her tongue sent an electric jolt through his balls, up his spine, short-circuiting his brain as he gave himself over to her attention.

Oh God. She took him in as far as she could and used her hands where she couldn't, still looking at him, which was the hottest thing ever. Sensation pulsed through every cell of his body, and he knew he wasn't going to last. He couldn't. He should warn her that he was about to—

He groaned. She stayed with him as well as she could, until he eased out of her mouth while she stroked him through the final, fading contractions of his release. She smiled and leaned forward to press against him while they both caught their breath. Fortunately, they were in a fairly shallow section of the creek.

Her naked breasts against his bare abdomen made catching his breath difficult, as did the way she traced her fingers over his shoulder and down his arm. He caressed her in return for about five seconds before he had to have more.

"I want you. Go over there." He pointed to the grassy creek bank.

Her shocked expression was almost comical. "You don't have to—I mean—"

"I told you before, time is too short to beat around the bush."

She snorted. "That's an interesting metaphor."

He shook his head. "God save me from college girls who paid attention in English class." But he loved that she was so damned smart. It turned him on. "Get over there so I don't drown when I put my face between your legs."

"Oh." Something happened to her eyes then. Her pupils dilated, and her eyelids lowered.

His blunt speech turned her on. "Get over there," he directed with a chin jerk. "I'm going to make you come so hard, you won't remember your name."

She scrambled back then, splashing when she lost her balance on the slippery rocks. He laughed at her eagerness but rose more slowly, tucking himself back in as he yanked his jeans up and followed her to the edge of the creek. Instead of stepping onto the dry grass, she toppled forward and landed on her hands and knees.

He groaned at the sight of her fine, curvy ass and wanted those shorts off her. He imagined getting her naked, holding onto those hips as he pounded into her from behind. Christ, he was getting hard again.

She turned to look at him over her shoulder and gave him a sly smile. "Are you coming, Mr. Bushwhacker?"

He snorted and advanced on her—screw the slipping and sliding. "I think one of us is going to be coming really soon."

With a giggle, she crawled a few feet up the bank, but he caught her and flipped her over. Pinning her with his heavier body, he kissed the hell out of her until she was panting. He moved lower to worship those breasts, licking and kissing and nipping until she squirmed.

As much as he thought he could spend the rest of his life worshiping her nipples, there was something else he wanted his tongue on. He moved lower still, to kiss her belly just above the button on her shorts.

He tucked his fingers in the waistband on either side of the fly, finding elastic at her hip—another thong? "Undo 'em."

She obeyed with fumbling fingers, and when she finally got it, he yanked both shorts and thong down and off in one almost-smooth move. Well, if her foot was still in one side, at least she wouldn't have to look too hard to find them when it was time to get dressed.

If it was *ever* time to get dressed. Because there below him, her legs wedged apart by his body between them, lay sweet, glistening heaven.

Not looking up, he said, "I didn't shave today, and you're going to have beard burn, but you'll learn to like it." He lowered himself until he could taste her desire. He broke away, looked into her eyes, and said, "Damn, you're sweet."

Her gasp and the squirm of her hips let him know he'd once again surprised her—in a good way.

He slid his fingers into her—one, then two into the slick

heat. She clenched around him, writhing for more. So he gave her more. Her hands in his hair urged him on.

He lowered his mouth again until her legs began to twitch and shake around his ears. He ran his free hand along her torso, cupping a breast firmly, finding the nipple with his fingers and teasing until she came with a cry. Her body contracted around his fingers, again and again and *again*, flooding his senses with her release and nearly sending him off in his jeans.

"I want more," she growled when her thighs finally relaxed and he began to slide his fingers free.

"I'm gonna give you more, but I need my hand back to get a condom."

She laughed, spreading her arms and legs on the grass in a gesture of surrender. "Hurry. I'm dying here."

He did, rising to his knees, shoving his jeans down. And as soon as he had himself covered, he moved over her and into her, and they both experienced *more*.

They lay together afterward in the dappled sunlight, her head on his chest, which was full to bursting. He realized, as he listened to her tell him about the park she envisioned, that he'd miss this place. This town he'd hated since he'd landed here as an angry kid had slipped under his skin. Not only had he reconnected with his sister and Granddad, been able to help them a few times, to rejoin his family. Talbott and Jake and all those damned dogs had invited themselves into his life and into his plans, and Lizzie was edging her way into his heart.

This was not what was supposed to happen. He was selling the ranch, giving Emma the money, and getting away from anyone who might need him before he could disappoint them again.

The vague sense of uneasiness that was never far from his gut asserted itself, and its bigger, meaner sibling, panic, stood at the threshold, waiting to crush him.

Chapter 25

"I GUESS WE SHOULD GET DRESSED BEFORE THE BUGS EAT us," Lizzie said, reluctantly sitting up and reaching for her things. Was there anything less sexy than trying to put on a wet bra? She managed to get the straps straightened out and the girls adjusted in a semi-decent fashion. She'd thought about skipping the bra, but her shirt was too see-through. With her luck, she'd get pulled over heading back to town or caught by her mother on her way into the house.

Adam didn't answer as he turned his jeans right side out.

Lizzie wouldn't change the past hour—not even the soggy clothes—for anything in the universe, but something felt *off* now. She knew Adam wasn't here for good, and he was only passing time with her, but she usually felt connected to him when they were together. Even though she was dressed, she still felt naked.

She needed to keep this relationship in perspective, if that was even possible. Probably not. She was likely going to get her heart ripped out when he left, but damn it, she didn't see any way to stop that from happening. No point in backing away from him now.

"Are you okay?" she asked, because he wasn't even looking at her right now.

"Huh? Sure," he said, jamming his feet into his pants. He seemed to snap out of whatever mood he was in and asked, "What do you still need pictures of?"

Refusing to get sucked into old habits, like, playing Freak Out Until You Figure Out What Dean's Mad About, she said, "I want to get some shots of the creek and the meadow from both directions...from the fence toward the creek and back. I can use a satellite map to be more specific, but a person's-eye view will help Dad when we work on the proposal."

"How's your dad doing?" Adam asked.

"Not bad right now," Lizzie said. Especially since he had the Mill Creek project to work on. She didn't dare voice her hope, because God knew she'd jinx it, but he seemed to have a spring in his step now that he had an opportunity to apply all the information he'd gathered in a lifetime of wanting to tell everyone about the gold rush days of Big Chance, Texas.

"What does Joe have to say about it?"

"Oh!" She turned to him. "I didn't tell you, did I?"

"No..." He waited for her to talk. That was one of the things she loved about him. He listened to her, and he didn't tell her how to fix things or how she should do them differently, though he did ask pertinent questions that made her want to tell him even more.

"The mayor, the town council, and the county planning board met the other day. Joe gave them a brief rundown of what I'm thinking, and they all loved it! It turns out there are grants to help pay for infrastructure and equipment and stuff. I'm taking pictures to add to my formal plan so we can come up with numbers."

"That's great," he said. "You just...decided to do this thing, and you're doing it." He shook his head...in admiration, she realized.

This idea, which had felt abstract and hypothetical, even as she pitched it, was suddenly crystal clear and possible.

She nodded, confident in the knowledge that she *could* do this. "Yeah. We're getting closer to making this a reality."

"What's next?"

"We have to figure out how to buy the place. The county will file some notices about abandoned property, that sort of thing." She didn't want to go into how frustrated she was over her failure to find an owner. There were enough post-sex endorphins running through her bloodstream that she wasn't about to wreck her own buzz.

"I'm sure you'll be able to manage it," Adam assured.

"How's it going at your place?" she asked. "Things are easing up a little at Dad's office, so I can come out to work with D-Day later." *And to see you some more,* she almost said, but she wasn't quite *that* confident yet.

He shook his head. "The dog's fine." He hesitated before looking away and admitting, "He's turning out to be a great dog. If you can't find someone to take him, I guess I can hang on to him for a while if you want."

Lizzie's heart, already overflowing, nearly burst. Adam liked D-Day. Of course, she'd kind of known that for a while, but to hear him acknowledge that fact *and* use "him" instead of "it" was huge. Then he blew her away completely.

Before she could frame a response, he cleared his throat and said, "So, anyway, for a man who never had more than two nickels to rub together, Granddad sure had a lot of crap stored in weird places all over the property, but we're getting it cleaned up."

Reality crash-landed in the middle of her post-sex glow and optimism as she was reminded about the *other* reason she had for spending time with Adam. "Well, your place looks great. I'm sure we'll get some calls soon." *As soon as I start actively trying to find some interest.* "How's Marcus after his fall?"

His mouth twisted into a grimace.

"Uh-oh. Not good?"

With a shake of his head, he said, "I don't know. I can tell he's hurting, but he pushes himself too hard."

"And takes too many painkillers?"

Adam frowned. "I can't judge him for needing something strong. He's a physical wreck. Hell, I've got a pharmacy's worth of shit in my medicine cabinet, too. Of course, I hardly ever take any of it, because it doesn't work for me. But if it works for him?" He held out his hands in a gesture of surrender. "We do whatever we can to get through."

Lizzie needed to qualify her comment. "I didn't mean to sound harsh. I can't imagine what he's going through— what you all deal with. But you said he fell the other night because he'd taken too much of something."

Adam nodded. "Yeah. He scared me, but he'd worn himself out working around the ranch, topped with the trip to town, so he misjudged." He chuckled. "He'll be okay. He works too hard to be healthy to wreck himself."

Lizzie hoped he was right.

Adam went on, "And Jake's decided he needs a dog to help him find his way around."

"Is that a thing?" she asked.

He shrugged. "I don't see why not. His specific condition is kind of unusual, but I think he could get a kind of reverse-tracking dog. One that could find the way home if Jake got turned around."

"That's cool!"

The way he rolled his eyes said he wasn't convinced.

"Don't you think it's a good idea?"

"I think it's a good idea for Jake to have some help."

"But...?"

"It's kind of a rush job."

Of course. Because as soon as Adam sold the farm, he was leaving.

She wasn't enough to keep him here; she'd never harbored any illusions about that. But she realized she'd hoped that getting involved with dogs again might change his plans. Apparently not.

Maybe wherever he went after he left here, he'd find some dogs to work with. And some peace. A break from the demons that seemed to chase him almost everywhere he went.

She finished taking photos, and they walked back to their vehicles.

He held her hand to help her over a fallen log and didn't let go. Her fingers, intertwined with his, felt right. So damned right that her throat got tight.

Why couldn't he be happy here in Big Chance? What was out there in the big world that he couldn't get here?

Chapter 26

"Watch this, Granddad," Adam said. "Get the light, D-Day." The dog rose, looked around Emma's little living room, and trotted to the switches by the door. He rose onto his hind legs and pushed them with his nose until the lamp next to Granddad's chair came on. "Pretty cool, huh?" he asked, giving D-Day a congratulatory rub on the head.

Granddad sniffed. "What'd you waste time teaching it that for?"

"Ahh...you know. Sometimes I have nightmares. If the light's on when I wake up, I come out of it faster."

Granddad rolled his eyes, unimpressed. With the dog's abilities, or with Adam's nightmares? Adam tried to convince himself it didn't matter either way.

When she left for her doctor appointment, Mrs. King had told Adam that Granddad was having a good day. But he didn't seem interested in anything Adam tried to talk to him about, just stared off into space, at least until D-Day nudged Granddad's hand for a pet.

Two more weeks had passed since the day Adam met Lizzie out at the Mill Creek place, and his anxiety attacks had resumed. He'd thrown himself into work, hoping that when he got the albatross of a ranch from around his neck, he'd feel some peace.

He and Lizzie managed to spend a few hours together

every day—sometimes naked, sometimes not—but even then, he felt the edges of his serenity crinkle.

The silver lining of this was that he was able to work with D-Day, managing to hang onto enough sanity to show the dog what to do when that rubber band of fear tightened around his lungs. Usually, just having the dog asking to be petted was enough to anchor him in the moment and allow him to find his center again.

Nighttime, however, was as bad as it had been right after he'd come from the Afghanistan. The dreams varied. Sometimes his team was with him in Big Chance, clearing the high school, and sometimes he was with Granddad or Lizzie, stranded in the desert.

It was time to move on. He tried not to pressure Lizzie, but he needed her to sell the damned ranch. All she said when he asked about it was that she'd spoken to a few people and would follow up with them.

And he had to tell Emma what he was doing, because she was starting to talk about having Christmas at the ranch this winter. He'd talk to her today, he decided. She was due home from work in a few minutes.

"Turn on *Judge Judy*," Granddad said, searching for the remote.

Adam fetched it from beneath the footrest of the recliner and found the right channel. Could he teach D-Day to change channels? He'd have to get a remote with giant buttons, but it was possible, he supposed.

As Judge Judy was about to rule on the case of the tenant with the cannabis farm, the front door opened, admitting Emma and a blast of summer heat.

"Phew!" she said, crossing the room and flopping on

the couch next to Adam. "It's miserable out there, even for Texas."

"How was work?" Adam asked.

Emma shrugged. "Boring. Sold a hammer to Mrs. Davis. That's the fifth one this month. She keeps losing them."

"What's she hammering?"

"I have no idea," Emma said, "but I hear she's kind of a hoarder. I bet she's got more than five hammers under all that junk."

That gave him a perfect segue. "Speaking of junk—"

"Oh! That reminds me," Emma interrupted. "Do you still have all those plastic water bottles in the barn?"

"Yeah."

"I said I'd bring them to town this weekend. Charley Chance—you know, Joe Chance's sister? Well she's doing a community enrichment thing. Getting a bunch of trouble-making teenagers to work with senior citizens to make… bird feeders or something…out of plastic water bottles."

"Oh. Great. But I—"

"And I also told her that you've got puppies that are going to be needing a new home soon. Couple more weeks, right? I hope it's okay that I told her about them. She said she was thinking about getting a dog."

"They're seven weeks old now, so soon," Adam said. "Lizzie's been taking Loretta out with her, starting to get them used to being away from their mom." Jake would be bummed; he'd gotten pretty attached to the dogs, but there was no way they were keeping them. They weren't going to have a place to live soon if everything went according to plan. "So about the ranch—"

"You know who I saw the other day at the grocery store?"

"No, who?" Adam asked and decided he'd try to talk to his sister about selling her childhood home another day.

———————————

Lizzie went over some paperwork in the den with Loretta snoozing at her feet. Mom had reluctantly allowed the dog in the house, mostly because Loretta was very ladylike and nothing at all like D-Day. Or at least nothing like old D-Day. New D-Day, Adam's right-hand dog, was nearly unrecognizable from the out-of-control pup he'd been at the beginning of the summer. Lizzie rarely even worked with him anymore, since it was clear Adam would be keeping the dog. She still went out to the ranch to visit the dogs almost daily. And maybe she went because she and Adam almost always found an opportunity to be alone.

This morning, they were making out in the barn when Jake and the dogs barged in. "Oh, there's Loretta!" Lizzie said, pretending that she'd been looking for the mother dog. "I, um, I wanted to see if I could bring her to town with me for a couple of hours."

Adam smirked, but she'd thought that Jake believed her, because he agreed and said, "That's a great idea." But then she'd caught him high-fiving Adam when they thought she wasn't looking.

Lizzie blinked to try to clear her head and focus on the bids she'd gotten to demolish the old barn and fill in the basement from hell at the Mill Creek farm. As soon as the county seized it for auction, she wanted to be ready to start work.

Dad was across the room, clicking through something

on his laptop. He was deep into the plans for what they'd tentatively dubbed the Vanhook Historical and Recreation Park.

"I think I found something," Dad said now.

"What?" Lizzie needed to stretch her legs anyway, so she rose to look over his shoulder. "What's that?"

He was looking at a PDF of some sort of receipt.

"I talked Joe Chance into getting those old files scanned and inventoried. You know, the stuff that got wet during the courthouse fire and then sat in the school basement for years?"

"No."

Dad said, "Back in…well, it might have been after you graduated high school, now that I think about it. Right about the time the old mayor got himself in trouble for taking bribes. Anyway, a few years ago, the courthouse got a new sprinkler system, which immediately malfunctioned. Probably because that idiot Babcock gave the contract to one of his half-baked cronies and pocketed most of the money."

Lizzie was immediately on alert.

"The Babcocks owned that property, you know," Dad said.

Yeah. She knew.

"That sprinkler accident got every damned piece of paper in that basement wet. They moved everything to the old middle school for storage to dry out, but by the time the sprinklers were fixed, there was a new administration, and it seems everyone forgot about all that paperwork, which never got entered into the computer."

"Okay, so what's this?"

"A lot of stuff that didn't make it onto the computer."

"Is there something about the farm in here?"

Dad squinted at the computer screen. "Yep. Looks like a bill of sale. From Robert Michael Babcock III to Robert Michael Babcock IV."

"That's Mitch Babcock," Lizzie said. "The fourth. I remember, because in middle school, he tried to get everyone to call him Quatro."

"It looks like the old man sold it to the kid for a dollar."

"Why would he do that?" she asked.

"Because of all the fraud charges. If he sold the land to the son, it would stay in the family and couldn't be sold off to pay the dad's debts."

"So it's been sitting there, and Mitch has never even had to pay taxes on it, because it wasn't registered with the county. Joe said he thought Mitch's family had sold the farm, but he couldn't find a record of the buyer. I can't believe no one bothered to figure out all this stuff until now. What municipality doesn't do everything it can to collect taxes?"

Dad raised an eyebrow at her. "Really? The mayor before Joe Chance was a drunk named Billy Bob Wells. The only thing he ever did in office was fall down the front steps, break his leg, and sue the county for damages. Joe's done more in his nine months in office than the past six mayors combined."

"Okay," Lizzie mused. "So Mitch Babcock appears to be the owner of the Mill Creek farm. Does anyone know how to find him? Where did his family go after they left Chance County?"

"Houston," Mom said from the doorway. "At least that's what Faye Straub told me."

"So we need to see if Mitch is still there." Lizzie sat back down at her computer.

"You won't find him there," Mom said.

"How do you know this?" Lizzie asked.

Mom pursed her lips. "I don't want to gossip," she began. Lizzie and Dad just waited.

Mom continued, "But Faye's sister Joyce was friends with the wife, and she said that things went terribly downhill after they left Big Chance. The father drank himself to death, the mother died of cancer a couple of years later, and that boy of theirs never quite got his act together. Faye says he moved back to the area a few weeks ago and is living in a trailer his cousin's family owns out on Route 15."

"No kidding," Lizzie said, impressed with her mom's ability to assimilate random information. (Not gossip, of course. If it had been *gossip*, Lizzie might have heard about all this before now.)

"Nope," Mom said. "And Faye said the trailer's the biggest eyesore in the county. That Mitch painted it orange and blue for the Houston Astros, and he didn't do a very good job."

Wow. So Mitch owned the farm. Was that going to make it harder or easier to buy the property? She'd just to have go find out. "Come on, Loretta. We're going for a ride."

Chapter 27

"God *damn* it!" The first thing Adam encountered when he walked into the living room was a pile of dog crap, which was bad. What made it worse was that the pile happened to be on his dead grandmother's antique rag rug, which he'd rescued from the horse shed. He'd have to get it cleaned. Again.

"What's wrong, Sar—" Jake's voice cut off when he saw Adam standing on one leg inside the doorway. He began to back up the way he'd come, but the protesting squeak of a puppy had him toppling forward.

"Jake!" Adam forgot about his offended foot and ran across the room to keep Jake from slamming face-first into the coffee table. He barely managed to get the two of them onto the couch without landing in any more crap or causing new injuries. He pulled off his shoe and held it poop side up while he regained his equilibrium.

"Oops." Jake smiled his half smile and looked at the nasty footprints stretching across the room. "I'll clean that."

"What the hell, man?" A puppy crawled from beneath the couch and climbed on top of two others napping on a sweatshirt. One of *Adam's* sweatshirts, if he wasn't mistaken.

"They're gettin' big, aren't they, Sar'nt?" Jake lifted the nearest puppy.

"Where's their mother?" Adam asked, as though he could insist Loretta make her children behave.

"Lizzie has her."

"Oh. Right."

"I guess there wasn't much blood in your brain this morning, huh, Sar'nt?" Jake asked, referring to the way he'd almost caught Adam and Lizzie in the act.

Talbott clomped down the stairs, oblivious to everything but his phone, until the stench hit him. "Damn, Hoss, you forget where the outhouse is?" The look on Talbott's face might have been comical if Garth or Travis—Adam couldn't tell them apart—hadn't just left another deposit next to the stepped-on one.

"Have you guys seen any of these Facebook posts from Zimmerman?" Talbott asked, holding up his phone.

"Man, I barely use my phone as a phone," Adam said. "I don't even think I have that app on mine. What's going on?" He looked at the screen Talbott handed him, Jake peering over his shoulder.

There were a bunch of animated gifs showing things blowing up, cartoon characters running off cliffs or into walls. "So?"

"Don't you think that's strange?" Talbott asked. "No pictures of his wife and kid, no cute cat memes. Not even a political rant. I don't know, but this stuff seems weird."

"So call him," Adam suggested, hoping Talbott was reading too much into things.

"I did," Talbott said. "He's not answering."

"He texted me last night," Jake offered, pulling out his phone and scrolling through. "Here." He handed it to Adam.

The last message had come in at three a.m.

Zimm: You up?

Jake: No

Zimm: Then why did you answer

Jake: I was sleeping, but I'm awake now
        because you woke me up

Zimm: Fuck it never mind

Jake: What do you want?

No response.

"Why didn't he answer you? What do you think he wanted?" Adam handed the phone to Talbott so he could read the exchange.

Jake shrugged. "I think he was...drunk texting and went to sleep."

Talbott handed the phone back to Jake, his frown deepening. "I don't have a good feeling about this."

Neither did Adam. "Why don't you send him another text?" he suggested to Jake. "Find out how he's doing."

"What should I say?"

"Ask him where he's getting his crazy Facebook shit," Talbott offered.

Adam didn't have a better idea, other than coming right out and asking the guy if he was coming unglued, which didn't seem like a good idea.

Jake moved his thumbs over the screen while Adam got to his feet. He found a roll of paper towels and spray cleaner under the kitchen sink and then tiptoed across the living room to start cleaning up after the puppies. "These dogs have got to go," he muttered as he collected another turd.

Jake glanced up, stricken. "Max says he got them from a site called 'The Man Left Behind.'"

"Oh hell," Talbott said. "I heard about that. It's like a message board or chat room for veterans who are thinking about suicide. And it's not to talk them out of it."

"Jesus." Adam scrubbed both his hands through his hair but couldn't wash away the dread tightening his scalp. A few violent images didn't necessarily mean Zimmerman was in trouble, but if he'd been going to pro-suicide websites, he could be in a dark, dark place.

No one spoke for a long moment.

"You should call him," Adam said.

"Me?" Jake asked.

"Yeah, man. You have the best relationship with him."

Jake shook his head. "Not me. I don't…I won't say the right thing."

"We're right here next to you," Talbott said.

Looking doubtful, Jake pressed the buttons.

They watched the phone as though it were a live bomb with a short fuse.

"Yeah." The call was answered.

Jake put the phone to his ear. "Hey, Zimm. We want to know if you're okay…me and Sar'nt Collins and Talbott."

Adam could hear the response from where he stood three feet away. "You're talking about me? What the hell for?" Zimm spat.

Jake looked to Adam and Talbott, uncertainty creasing his forehead.

"Gimme that." Talbott grabbed for the phone and spoke into it. "This is Talbott. We were talking about you because you're posting messed-up shit on Facebook. What did you think would happen?"

Adam couldn't hear any distinct words after that, but

Talbott said a lot of things like "Uh-huh" and "Yeah, I get it" and "No, man, don't think like that."

Meanwhile, Adam sat down on the floor, where a puppy—Faith?—crawled into his lap while D-Day leaned against his shoulder. He fondled the little one's ears and considered what was happening on the other end of that phone line. He had a feeling he could fill in the blanks very easily. Zimmerman was lost. He didn't know how to be around people. Nothing made sense except the crap that pissed him off. He couldn't sleep most nights unless he took a pill, drank himself blind, or worked himself to exhaustion.

Talbott was doing a little more talking now. "You know, we're doing okay here. We've got all these dogs, man. You've got to see them. I don't care if you're a cat person. You'd love these little fur balls."

Zimmerman had come home to a wife, a new baby, and a job at the family trucking company. He had a big family in Indianapolis, and while overseas, they'd all written him almost every day, sending him emails with stupid-ass—but admittedly funny—cat pictures.

If a guy with everything going for him couldn't keep his shit together, what hope was there for the rest of them?

"Seriously, man. You've got to come down for a few days. Take a break... Yeah, maybe your wife could come, too? Okay, yeah, maybe she needs a break from you. Whatever."

What? Talbott was inviting more desperate people to the ranch. Adam's heart felt like jungle drums, beating in his chest, faster and louder, warning of danger. "Damn it, Talbott," he began, his annoyance loud and clear, but Talbott just turned his back and continued to talk to Zimmerman.

"Yeah. Call me back as soon as you get a chance. We'll figure something out."

Frustration, fear, and helplessness pushed Adam to his feet, and he headed for the front door as Talbott ended the call.

"Where you going, Sar'nt?" Jake asked.

"I don't know," he said. He stepped over a puppy on his way to the door and, God *damn* it, almost stepped in another pile of crap. "Jake, it's time for these dogs to find new homes."

He ignored the stricken look on Jake's face as he pointed a finger at Talbott. "And you. Hear this. I'm not running a halfway house for broken-down soldiers who can't keep their shit together."

Lizzie didn't have any trouble finding Mitch Babcock's single-wide mobile home that probably hadn't been mobile since it left the factory, at least thirty years ago. It was, indeed, blue and orange, but there was something decidedly *not* cheerful about the garish colors. They were almost aggressive, she decided.

A dented white pickup sat next to the sagging steps, and she pulled her car in behind it, under the unenthusiastic shade of a scrubby-looking pine. Loretta was curled into a ball in the foot well of the passenger seat.

"How can you sleep like that? Wouldn't you rather sit on the seat?" Lizzie asked but got no response.

She made sure the windows were rolled down before turning off the ignition. Somewhere a dog barked, a lonely sound. A whisper of apprehension skittered over her skin.

Maybe she shouldn't have come out here alone, but she'd known Mitch in high school. He was a spoiled jerk, but she didn't remember being intimidated by him. Still, as she approached the front door and looked for a clean place to knock, she wished she'd coaxed Loretta to come with her.

She found a spot, knocked, and waited. She was about to give up when she heard movement inside.

"Hang on, damn it," growled a voice from the other side of the door as it creaked open. "Yeah?" The person who stood blinking out at her only vaguely resembled the Mitch Babcock Lizzie remembered.

This man had the same ultrafine blond hair, though instead of being professionally cut and styled, it was greasy and flopped over his eyebrows. The whites of his blue eyes were streaked with red, and his face—from what she could see, his whole body, really—was puffy.

Mitch looked Lizzie up and down, grinned, and wet his lips. "Hey, darlin'. What's your name? Did Jorge send you?"

"No, Mitch, I'm—"

"I don't normally like so much meat on the bones of my dates, but you look kinda high class."

Dear God, did he think she was a sex worker?

"I'm Lizzie Vanhook," she said. Her phone rang, and she hit the button to send the call to voicemail. "Remember me from high school?"

His expression changed then, surprise replacing lust, followed by confusion. "I was just kiddin' about that Jorge thing," he said as he straightened. His eyes narrowed suspiciously. "I don't have much to do in Big Chance any-more. What brings you all the way out here?"

He looked toward her car, then scanned behind her, as though she might have someone hiding in the bushes on the other side of the road. Apparently satisfied she was alone, he stood back and opened the door wider. "Come on in." The odor of unwashed feet and stale beer wafted out of the humid darkness.

Lizzie shook her head. "No, thanks. I…my dog's in the car. She'll freak out if she can't see me."

"I don't see a dog," Mitch said.

"She's lying down, but believe me, she can see me." *Hopefully.* "So anyway, Mitch, I moved back to Big Chance a couple of months ago and was surprised to hear you'd moved back, too," she started.

"Yeah. Sometimes things just happen that way." He ran a hand through his stringy hair, but it didn't help. "This dump is my cousin's place, you know," he said, "I'm just staying here until my condo's ready."

Or maybe he didn't have anywhere else to go. "Is that right?" Lizzie asked, going along with his narrative.

"What are you doing these days?" Mitch asked her, as though they'd run into each other in the produce aisle.

"I'm working for my dad. Doing real estate. And I'm here because I want to talk to you about that land you own. The Mill Creek farm."

"Really?" His eyes took on a beady quality, making him look like an enormous white rat. "What about the farm?"

"I'm interested in buying that property—well, a group of us are interested—to create a new outdoor multiuse park."

"Oh, well," he said. "Aren't we fancy?"

Lizzie ignored the sarcasm and said, "We've been trying to find the owner for a while, because there were some problems with the paperwork, and we didn't know it belonged to you."

Mitch shrugged. "Well, you found me now."

"So I want to know if you're interested in selling that land," she said.

"Well, let me think a minute." His thinking seemed to involve staring at Lizzie's boobs.

She refused to do him the honor of crossing her arms over her chest, but she did turn slightly and brought her notepad up to use as a shield of sorts.

"How much are you willing to pay?" he asked.

"Not a lot," she told him honestly. "We're working with a very tight budget."

"That's too bad," Mitch said, shaking his head in a poor approximation of sympathy. "I've already had an offer on that land. Big development company wants to give me half a mil for it."

Lizzie coughed. "That's, um, surprising. It's kind of out of the way. What kind of development company?"

Mitch's sideways grin was nasty. "I'm obligated not to talk about it—confidentiality agreement, you know." His eyes raked over her body again. "But if you want to come inside and have a drink, I might be convinced to give you more information. I bet those lips of yours will feel real good coaxing *stuff* out of me."

Lizzie was off that porch and away from Mitch's disgusting presence so fast, she barely bothered with a seat belt before putting her car in gear.

The moment she was out of the drive, Loretta raised her

head from the foot well, turning her one good eye to look at Lizzie as if to ask, "Is it safe to get up now?"

"I think we've lost our park before we even had it," Lizzie told Loretta, who tilted her head sympathetically.

It wasn't until she was most of the way home, at a stop sign at the turn for Wild Wager Road, that she bothered to check her phone for messages.

"Hey, Lizzie, this is Rob Chance. The veterinarian? Yeah. So my cousin Joe said you might know of some property that would be a good fit for me. I'm interested in expanding my practice to large animals and could use a place not too far from town, with enough room for a barn or two, some paddock space, but not necessarily grazing land."

Well, didn't that just provide the icing on her afternoon? Someone who wanted to look at Adam's ranch. She'd call Dr. Chance back later. Right now, she'd take Loretta home, tell Adam about how she wasn't going to be able to get her park land after all, and by the way, she had a possible buyer for his ranch.

The sun chose that moment to slide behind a cloud.

Chapter 28

ADAM'S MOOD HADN'T IMPROVED MUCH IN THE HOUR since he'd been chased out of his own house by puppies and assholes, but at least it wasn't much worse.

Twilight pushed the last rays of sun behind the clouds lining the horizon, and night creatures began to stir. There was a thick, heavy texture to the night, and Adam suspected a storm was brewing. They were due. It hadn't rained in weeks. The air smelled of dried earth and dead grass—sure signs that summer had peaked and there was nothing left but to survive another month and hope to be out of here by fall.

Maybe once he'd gotten shit settled here, he'd head to, hell, Maine. Eat blueberries and lobster and look at the leaves, then hibernate for the winter. As long as he didn't have to stay here in Big Chance, trying to make amends and not ruin anything else.

Headlights cut through the deepening dusk, and Lizzie's car appeared, windows down and radio blaring some sort of ass-kicking done-me-wrong song. Lizzie sang along at the top of her lungs—and so did Loretta. Pit bulls were not bred for their vocal skills, and he refused to pass judgment on Lizzie's, but just knowing she was here evened out his rough edges. Adam smiled in spite of his crappy mood.

"Hey," he said, opening her car door. "Nice duet."

Loretta jumped over Lizzie's lap and into the yard. He

should correct that—Loretta needed to wait until she was invited to get out of the car—but something about the tightness of Lizzie's smile told him not to sweat the small stuff at the moment.

"What's the matter?" he asked.

She blew out a defeated breath. "Guess who owns the Babcocks' Mill Creek farm?"

"Who?"

She looked up at him. "Mitch Babcock."

It took a minute for Adam to connect her words to reality. "I thought they sold out and moved away a long time ago."

He stepped back as she climbed out of the car. Leaning against its side, she said, "Yeah, well, a lot of people thought they were done with Big Chance. But my dad found some paperwork that shows Mitch's dad sold it to Mitch for a dollar right before they skedaddled out of town."

"So where's Mitch?"

"He moved back here not too long ago, and he's staying in the skeeviest trailer you can imagine out toward Fredericksburg. He looks and smells like he's been living on Cheetos and vodka. Kind of acts like it, too."

"What does that mean? You saw him?"

She pursed her lips as though to resist a bad taste. "Yeah. I thought—I guess I thought he'd be just dying to sell me the land because he'd somehow become a great guy."

Mitch hadn't been a great guy when they were kids, and Adam didn't imagine having his family lose everything would have made Mitch suddenly humble and generous. "So what happened?"

"He said he wouldn't sell unless we could top the five-hundred-thousand-dollar bid some developer supposedly offered him. Then he offered to negotiate in exchange for a blow job."

Adam's stomach churned, and he had to consciously relax his hands. The disgust he felt knowing someone disrespected his Lizzie was tripled by the knowledge it had come from Mitch Babcock.

He'd never seen her look so…sad. He pulled her into his arms, all the while thinking about driving out toward Fredericksburg to *talk* to Mitch.

"Hey," she said, leaning back to look up at him. "I'm okay. He didn't touch me, and I'm never going there again."

"Damn," he said. "I'm sorry about this. What are you going to do next?"

She rose on her tiptoes to kiss him on the jaw. "I'm gonna thank you for *not* telling me what to do next, for one thing."

"Well, it's not like I'd have a clue," he muttered.

"I don't know what to do," she admitted. "If he won't sell, there's not much I can do. Maybe the county will charge him enough back taxes to scare away his big fancy developer, if such an entity even exists. Otherwise, I'll look somewhere else, I guess. Now that we've started planning, I really, *really* want to see this thing through."

"It's too bad this place wouldn't work for you. We could kill two birds with one sale."

She didn't respond, so he plowed ahead.

"I mean…we could get a bulldozer out here and build a fake creek," he said. "Invent some legends about stuff that never happened."

Her lips smiled, but her eyes didn't. "Well," she said, on a long, shaky breath, "that's another thing. I got a voicemail. It seems Rob Chance is looking to start a large-animal veterinary practice, and this ranch sounds like it might fit his needs."

"Really?" Adam didn't know why he was surprised. This was what he wanted, and Lizzie'd come through for him. This was good, right?

"No promises," Lizzie said. "I'll call him tomorrow and find out what he's looking for specifically."

His phone rang. "Crap. Hold that thought."

Lizzie nodded and led Loretta toward the barn to reunite with her puppies.

"Hey, Emma."

"I really hate to ask you this…" Emma began, which meant that she was about to ask him *this*. Whatever *this* was.

"Whatever you need, just say it."

"Yeah, you're going to take that back."

He couldn't imagine what she could ask that he'd deny, but he said, "Ask and we'll see."

"I need you to keep Granddad at the farm for a couple of days."

No. No, no, no. "Sure, Em. What's going on?"

"He got agitated today about that thing he keeps talking about. Our legacy. He knocked Mrs. King down when she tried to stop him from leaving the house."

"Is she okay?"

"She's still at the ER, but it looks like she's got a dislocated hip. She'll be out of commission for a while."

"Will she be okay, though?"

"They're transferring her to Austin to see a specialist. We'll know something in a couple of days, but the ER doc said it might have been easier to fix if the hip actually broke."

"That blows," Adam said.

"I'm really sorry," Emma said, her voice thick and rough.

He might have thought she was crying, except Emma was tough. She only cried at movies and the national anthem.

"I wish I didn't have to ask you, but the Sterns are out of town, and I'm running the Feed and Seed by myself this week," she continued. "I can't leave Granddad alone, and I can't take him in with me. He'll chase off the customers."

Adam rubbed his forehead. "It's okay. You want to bring him now, or you want me to come get him?"

"Can you come in the morning? He just took his medicine, and when he goes to bed, I'll get him packed."

"No problem. Damn. I'm sorry, Emma."

"What are you sorry for?" She sounded truly puzzled.

"That you've had to deal with all this. It's not fair."

She laughed. *Huh?* "You're such a dork. I'll see you tomorrow."

"Okay."

"Good night, Dipwad."

"Good night, Buttface."

She laughed again and disconnected.

He looked at Lizzie, who had returned from the barn and was leaning against her car again, looking at something on her phone. When she realized he'd ended his call, she put it away.

"Emma doesn't understand why I'd be sorry that she's stuck with Granddad," he blurted. He needed an interpreter for sister speak, because it sounded like she really didn't get it.

"She loves him," Lizzie said, shrugging. "She's lived with him for, like, ever, right? Even when she was married? He's been there for her, so she wants to be there for him."

Adam hadn't been there for anyone. "He knocked his caregiver down today, and she's pretty banged up."

Lizzie covered her mouth with her hand. "Oh no."

"Yeah." He rubbed his forehead again, which did nothing to stop the continuous loop of *It's all Adam's fault* running through his brain.

"No you don't," Lizzie said sternly, and he looked around for a dog until he realized she was talking to him. "You're not going to beat yourself up about Emma being okay with taking care of your granddad."

"But she should have a life. She should be out meeting new guys and buying shoes and shit. Instead, she's stuck working a dead-end job in this dead-end town and living with her *grandfather*."

"Seriously? You think she hates her life?" Lizzie huffed out a breath and held up a hand. "I'm sorry. It's really none of my business. I just hate that you take on so much."

He laughed. "You're the one who wants to save the world."

She put her hands on her hips. "And what are you trying to do?"

"Get through today, mostly."

"Yeah. And bail your sister out of some imaginary miserable existence, give your friends a place to figure out what to do next, and adopt a boatload of homeless dogs, and—"

"I did *not* adopt those dogs. They're all going to other homes. Except maybe D-Day. And Emma might not know she's miserable now, but when she figures it out, I need her to have choices. And Granddad does need more care."

Lizzie smiled at him and moved closer. Almost close enough to touch. And then...*yes*. She was right where he needed her to be so that, as he leaned down, he was able to plant his lips on hers. So that, as he kissed her, he could smell her hair, feel her sigh. *Be* with her. Let the world disappear for a few glorious moments.

When they separated, as humid Texas air refilled his lungs, he thought of a question. "Did good ol' Mitch say what these 'developers' of his want to do?"

"Nope." The way she popped that *p* sounded pretty definite. "Let's just hope they aren't putting in a strip club."

"Well, if I were building a *gentlemen's entertainment center*," Adam said, "the outskirts of Boo-Foo Nowhere is *exactly* where I'd start."

Lizzie snorted. "Gentlemen's entertainment center?"

"It beats titty bar. Or do you prefer exotic danceteria?"

She laughed outright at that one. "Danceteria?"

"Yeah. I made that one up myself."

"I can tell."

And there they were, smiling at each other again. He was starting to get used to the warm bubbly feeling he got when she was close.

"I really—" His phone rang again. Which was probably for the best, because he wasn't sure what he was about to say. Really enjoyed her company? Really wanted to razzle her dazzle?

He took his phone out of his pocket, surprised at the display. "Hello?"

"Hey, Adam. Joe Chance."

"What's going on?"

"Do you have a minute?"

He looked at Lizzie, who was busy with her phone again. "Yeah, I guess so."

"You know those papers you gave me on the Fourth?"

The stuff he'd found in Granddad's old bureau when he cleaned out the horse shed. He'd almost forgotten about that. "Sure."

"Sorry it's taken me so long, but I finally got a chance to go through them."

"No worries. I know you've got a few other irons in the fire."

Joe laughed. "You wouldn't believe." But then his voice sobered, and he said, "I had to do some research, because some of the writing on that deed was almost illegible."

"There's a deed?"

Lizzie looked up, listening to his end of the conversation.

"Yeah, it's a deed," Joe confirmed. "And here's the thing."

Something about Joe's tone… "Is this going to screw up my life?" He put his arm around Lizzie, tucked her close while he waited to hear the news. A cool breeze blew over them from the west, and lightning crackled in the distance.

"I hope you'll find this to be good news. That bill of sale and the other stuff? Your grandfather bought the Mill Creek farm from Mitch Babcock ten years ago, for fifteen thousand dollars."

"What?" Adam didn't understand. "*Granddad* bought it?"

Lizzie pulled away from Adam now, looking at him in confusion, so Adam put the call on speaker to let her listen.

"Yep."

"But Lizzie said that—"

"I know," Joe interrupted. "I heard from Lizzie's dad that they've got paperwork showing Mitch bought the place from his father for a buck on June 17, 2006. Well, it seems that Mitch turned around and sold it to your grandfather on June 18."

Lizzie grabbed Adam's arm and practically jumped up and down. A tickle of excitement ran down his spine, but he ignored it, because there was no way this was happening. It still didn't make sense. "But then why would Mitch think it's still his?"

"Well," Joe said, "these papers were all part of that freak accident at the courthouse—which I'm starting to believe wasn't so freaky or accidental. Anyway, there's no official record of the transfer of property. As far as county records go, it would appear to still belong to Mitch."

"So who actually owns it?" Adam asked.

"This deed's witnessed and notarized, so it's legal. I want to dot a few i's and cross a few t's, but your grandfather owns it fair and square—or rather he did until we signed this last batch of papers, where everything's in a trust for you and Emma."

"I'll be damned."

Joe kept talking, some mumbo jumbo legalese, but the take-home message was that it was Adam and Emma's. Not Granddad's. And not Mitch Babcock's.

"Thanks, Joe." Adam hung up and turned to Lizzie.

"Did you hear that?" she asked, eyes wide and excited.

"Yeah. I did. You're going to get to build your park." He kissed her, reveling in the knowledge that he could make both their wishes come true. "And after I sell Mill Creek farm and this place, I can get Granddad decent long-term care, put away savings for Emma to start a new life, and maybe get my ass to Maine before the first snowfall." As he recited his plans, he didn't feel quite as jazzed as he'd expected.

Lizzie's expression sobered, and she looked toward the house, where Talbott, Jake, and a few dogs were visible through the living room windows. She kept her eyes on them as she said, "Yep. You've got a chance now to do what you've been dreaming of."

Chapter 29

LIZZIE'S MIND HAD BEEN SPINNING FOR HOURS AND showed no sign of slowing down as the sun rose and cast long shadows through her bedroom.

Adam owned the Mill Creek farm. Not nasty Mitch Babcock.

She gave a passing thought to what Mitch might do when he learned his claim of ownership was invalid but then figured he must know this, since he was the one who'd originally sold the place to Mr. Collins. He'd get over it and slither off somewhere else. Blinking her gritty, sleep-deprived eyes, Lizzie decided to get up, shower, and face the day. She needed to let Dad know they'd be able to purchase the land and start on their park soon, and she had to return Rob Chance's call about Adam's ranch and set up a time to show it to him. She had to stop freaking *crying* about Adam's plan to leave Big Chance.

Maybe she should call him, just to check in, tell him… what? She was sorry for pooping on his happiness last night when he talked about his plans? She hadn't screamed and cried and begged, only failed to offer a "Go, Adam!" about bailing out of Big Chance. No, she decided. It was time to wean herself away. She wouldn't call. *Or* text.

Another stupid tear blurred her vision, and she wiped at it angrily. Why did she think for one second that he would do anything other than exactly what he'd said? He'd told her what he planned from the beginning—before she'd gone and gotten attached to his twisted-up, all-around good-guy-in-spite-of-himself self.

It had been crazy to hope he'd fallen so hopelessly in love with her that he'd forget how much he hated Big Chance. That he'd somehow see he could be complete and happy here, where people—not just her, but lots of people—wanted him, needed him, *cared* about him.

Loved him.

Oh, fine. She'd admit it. She loved him.

Whatever. She'd survive, and this time, she would *not* wind up with a schmuck like Dean as a consolation boyfriend. Time to stop crying.

Zzzzt. Zzzzt. She jumped for her phone. Maybe it was Adam... She checked the display as she hit Accept and—*Oh.* "Hey, Emma."

"Hey, Lizzie. Are you up? Of course you are. You answered. I'm sorry to bother you so early, but I wanted to call you before I got Granddad up and moving, and I need to ask you a favor."

"Okay."

"Can you check in when you go out to the ranch to work with the dogs and let me know everything's okay? I mean, I know it will be. I think. But Granddad's going to stay there today, and I worry he'll drive Adam up a wall or something, and—well, you know."

"Yeah. I..." She cleared her throat. "I'm not sure..." she tried again, but apparently, she *wasn't* done crying just yet.

"Sweetie, what's wrong?" Emma asked.

And as if her question was the key to the floodgates, Lizzie started to cry in earnest—and talk.

Amazingly enough, Emma understood enough of what Lizzie was telling her to say, "What the *hell*? He's blowing everything up because he thinks he needs to give me *money*?"

"I'm not sure *blowing up* is exactly what he'd call it," Lizzie hedged, feeling protective of Adam and his misguided motives.

"I don't care what he calls it," Emma fumed. "He's got a good life, right here, right now. His friends are here, and he's got a purpose, helping those guys and working with those dogs. If he'd just get out of his own way, he could really make something of all that. And then there's you. What does he think is going to happen between you two when he leaves? You'll just hang around until he decides to slide back through town?"

"I'm not sure there's supposed to be an 'us two.' And he wants you to have choices."

"What *choices* do I need money for? Which Prada bag to carry when I pick up Granddad's meds from the pharmacy?"

Lizzie couldn't help but laugh. Leave it to Emma to get pissed off at someone for wanting to be generous to her.

"All right, listen," Emma said. "Don't worry about me worrying about Granddad. You take care of yourself today. Get your nails done, binge-watch every episode of *Gilmore Girls*, or try one of every Blizzard flavor at Dairy Queen if you want. I'll worry about Granddad."

If only that were an option, Lizzie thought. Instead, she was going to call Rob Chance and help him buy Adam's ranch.

When Adam pulled his truck in front of Emma's little house, he had that anxious buzzing in his head signaling the start of a bad day. He'd gone to bed with the same feeling, and it had kept him company as he watched constellations shift through his window until dawn.

He reached over the center console for D-Day before remembering he'd left him at the ranch this morning to recover from Adam's sleepless night. It was disconcerting, how much he'd come to rely on the dog's steadying influence. Over the past several weeks, D-Day had become sensitive to Adam and his damned moods, and the dog had gotten plenty of practice trying to distract him during the past twelve hours or so.

Things had begun to get weird yesterday, sometime between sharing the good news about Mill Creek farm with Lizzie and when she'd driven off into the night. She was upset, even though she was going to get her park. It wasn't the Mitch Babcock thing, because that was all but over—someone would have to break the news to him, but what could he do? No, some kind of dark cloud had fallen over both of them when they'd discussed the sale of both properties. He refused to consider that the thought of his leaving Big Chance was a problem for either one of them. He'd never in his life wanted to stay here, and she had no reason to want him to. Did she?

God, did she have *feelings* for him? Of course she *liked* him. She wasn't the have-sex-to-scratch-an-itch kind of woman, but she also had standards, which she shouldn't consider lowering for an unemployed, washed-up cowboy-without-a-cow loser like him. Maybe after he was gone, Joe Chance or that veterinarian, Rob, could step in—

The growl that rose from his own chest startled him, and he decided not to think about who Lizzie might end up with.

"Are you coming in to help me, or are you going to sit there like King Useless all day?"

Adam was startled by Emma's sharp tone. He hadn't even heard her come outside, and here she was, right next to his truck.

The surprise didn't do much to ease the anxiety attack waiting to drag him under, and he didn't answer her as he opened his door to get out. He was even more shocked when she shoved him against the front bumper of his truck. "What the hell?" he asked.

She put her hands on her hips and glared at him. "You. Are. A. Dim. Witted. Jerkface."

"What?"

"I just got off the phone with Lizzie, and she told me what's going on. What exactly are you trying to accomplish?" She didn't wait for him to answer. "You have some nerve, marching into town like a—a monarch butterfly and trying to run my life!"

A monarch butterfly? He put that aside and focused on her complaint. "I don't want to run your life. I want to help you fix it."

"It's not broken!" She held up a hand to forestall the protest on his lips. "Lizzie told me what you think, and it's horse hockey. My mistakes are my mistakes. You already bailed me out once, and *that* was too much. I'm a grown-ass woman, not a helpless fawn."

He'd gotten so caught up in her animal metaphors that it took him a moment to realize she'd run out of breath. Then he had to process what she was telling him.

"You're mad at me for wanting to help you?"

"Yes!" She frowned. "Well, not totally. I'm grateful to you for helping when Todd and I got in trouble, and I can't tell you how glad I am to have you home in Big Chance."

He flinched. He probably should have been clearer about his plans to leave as soon as he could, but most of the time he'd spent with Emma, they'd been talking about Granddad.

"I wish I'd been here for you and Todd—I only talked to him a few times after he got out of the army, but I knew something was off. If I'd been here, I could have jumped in and—"

"And what? Made me abandon the love of my life? Talked me into reneging on that whole 'for better or worse' business?"

Whoa. It must have been bad if she'd even considered leaving Todd. "What exactly happened with him? You never really told me what—"

"Nothing. Don't worry about it. That's not what we're talking about."

He should have been here. Then he'd know. He could have—what, told her how to run her life? Like she thought he wanted to do now? He tried to explain. "You've practically been tied to Granddad since Todd died. He's getting to a place where he needs specialized care."

She shook her head, even as her shoulders slumped. "Maybe. But I like having him with me."

Adam suddenly wondered if she kept Granddad with

her as a shield. Maybe he wasn't the only member of the family who strove to avoid the rest of the world, but still. "When are you supposed to take care of *you*?"

Her expression softened. "I'm pretty low maintenance."

He laughed. "Then you shouldn't wear yourself out too much."

"God, you are such a dipwad," she told him, shoving him in the chest with both hands.

He pretended to stagger. "You wound me, Buttface. Go get Granddad, would you?"

"This conversation isn't over," Emma warned. "Come on. Let's get this show on the road before I decide to put you in adult daycare, too."

Chapter 30

"Where are we goin'?" Granddad asked for the third time since Adam pulled out of Emma's driveway and then onto Main Street.

"Out to the ranch," Adam said, stopping at the corner to wait for a truckload of cattle to cross.

"I don't want to live there anymore," Granddad said.

"You don't have to. We're just gonna hang out for a while."

Adam was about to move his foot from brake to gas when Granddad unbuckled his seat belt and said, "I don't think so."

Adam slammed his foot on the brake and grabbed the old man's shirtsleeve before he could get the door open. "Damn it, Granddad, don't do that!"

"I'm not moving back out there. Your grandma don't live there no more. I ain't gonna stay without her." He twisted, trying to break free. "Take me home."

"Okay, but wait a minute," Adam said, trying to figure out what to do. Fortunately, when he released the handful of shirt, Granddad stayed put. "Do you mind going to check out some property with me?"

Granddad ground his jaw but finally nodded. "I got nothin' else to do."

"Great," Adam said. "Could you put your seat belt back on please?"

"Fine." Granddad fumbled with the buckle, got it fastened, and they resumed their trip.

"Do you remember buying the Mill Creek farm from Mitch Babcock about ten years ago?" he asked.

"'Course I remember. But I bought that place from *Mike*," Granddad said. "Before he tried to cheat me."

"Mike? Mike who?"

"Bab-cock," Granddad said, drawing the word out.

"Are you sure it wasn't Mitch?"

Granddad shook his head. "It was the kid that brought the paperwork," he said. "But it was the old man who set it up, then tried to cheat me."

"How did he try to cheat you?"

"Sneaked out to the ranch and stole the bill of sale. Right out from under my nose."

And yet Adam had found the paperwork while cleaning out the horse shed.

"What were you going to do with the land? Put in more kennels?"

"Nah. There's more than enough room at the ranch for more dogs. I was thinking about putting a few head of cattle at the new place."

Interesting. For all Granddad's pride in owning a "ranch," he'd never wanted cattle or horses that Adam could remember.

"Where's that big black dog?" Granddad asked now, turning to scan the back seat in case the enormous dog was hiding.

"I left him at the ranch with Patton and Loretta."

"Who's Loretta? She some new girlfriend?"

"No," Adam said. "She's that pit bull with the puppies that Lizzie found."

"Lizzie that cute little blond gal?"

"Yep."

Granddad pulled his handkerchief from his pocket and blew his nose. "I helped her and Emma with them pups."

"Yeah," Adam confirmed. "The Mill Creek farm is where she found them. They were left to die by someone into dogfighting."

"On my land? I'll kill anyone tries to harm a dog on my property. You call the sheriff?"

"Of course."

"Good." Granddad leaned back in his seat. "I wish them assholes hadn't stole that deed, or I'd sit out here with a twelve-gauge and keep 'em away myself."

Adam didn't doubt it but instead asked, "When did this theft happen?"

"Right about the time your sister married that friend a' yours and rearranged all the furniture out at the ranch."

Which was about when Emma noticed Granddad was starting to lose track of time and forget things.

"Is it possible the papers just got misplaced?"

"Huh." Granddad pursed his lips while he considered this. "It's possible. I'm old. I can't remember everything, you know. But I never did trust those Babcocks. I think Mike was the third—he was the mayor for a while, you know. I think he stole it."

"Well, maybe you're right." Adam conceded the point for the moment.

They were quiet for the rest of the ride, and by the time Adam reached the turn-off to Mill Creek Road, Granddad was snoring softly, head lolling on his chest.

Adam drove carefully over the rutted lane, not wanting

to disturb Granddad, and when they reached the farmyard, he continued through the gate and under the trees next to the creek.

He turned off the ignition, rolled down the windows, and stared at the water burbling over the rocks. Even this far into summer, there was a decent stream of water. Lizzie's park would be a popular place, which meant that there wouldn't be any more making love on the mossy bank.

There wouldn't be any more of that for Adam, anyway. He'd be moving on soon enough.

His phone beeped, surprising him—there hadn't been reception when he was here before, but apparently there was enough of a signal for a text to go through, because Emma's message came through loud and clear: Have a good day. Call me if you have trouble. And by the way—we need to talk about Lizzie.

He thought of Lizzie's face last night when they'd talked about his plans. About the reproachful glare from Jake when he told the guys his news. Talbott had shrugged and said, "No problem, man," but Adam thought he'd seen a flash of panic in his eyes.

Uncertainty entered the picture and stuck around for the first time since he'd come back to Big Chance. He acknowledged that he'd be letting Jake and Talbott down after promising to help them. The rational part of his brain argued that he *had* helped. He'd let his friends move in and take over his life for a whole lot longer than he'd expected. He even let them—with Lizzie's help—talk him into breaking his *No Dogs Allowed Ever Again* rule.

And Lizzie. Damn him, he hadn't meant to get involved with her, but he'd gone and done it. Let her under his skin.

Leaving Big Chance was going to be easy as pie. Leaving Lizzie would hurt like hell. The only saving grace was knowing she'd be much better off without him and all his baggage. He'd just have to work hard and try not to think about how *much* better she'd be.

He tried to practice not thinking so much now, to focus on the outside world and not his inner combat zone. The stream gurgled softly nearby, and a few birds twittered. The morning heat was tempered by the hint of a breeze, and Adam willed himself to relax—just for a few minutes.

"I can meet you there in thirty minutes," Lizzie told Rob Chance as she rushed to swipe on a second coat of mascara. She pulled up her last clean pair of dress pants and found an unwrinkled blouse hanging over the back of a chair.

"I know it's short notice, but I had a cancellation this morning, and the next few days are totally booked," the veterinarian told her.

"Do you know where the Collins place is?" she asked.

"Wild Wager Road, a mile past Mill Creek Road, on the right."

"Sure."

After hanging up, Lizzie shoved her feet into a pair of low-heeled pumps and ran a brush through her hair, then looked around for her car keys.

"Aren't you going to have breakfast?" her mother asked as she buzzed past.

"I'll get something later," Lizzie promised.

It wasn't until she was most of the way to Adam's place that it occurred to her that (a) she should have at least grabbed a cup of coffee, and (b) she should have warned the guys she was bringing a potential buyer out to look around.

She picked up her phone and said, "Hey, phone. Call Adam Collins."

"Calling Adam Collins," her phone answered.

Miraculously, the call went through—right to voicemail. Well, she'd be there in a minute anyway and could help with any last-minute beer can removal, dish washing, or dirty laundry stashing herself before Rob arrived.

She could also cowgirl up and accept the inevitable—Adam was selling the ranch to move…somewhere, and she'd promised to help him. What had she said back in June? She'd sell the hell out of that place.

Adam's truck wasn't parked by Marcus's Camaro when Lizzie pulled up next to the barn. He was probably getting Granddad from Emma's, which would explain why he hadn't answered. He was either busy or in a dead zone.

When she got out of the car, she heard barking and saw D-Day on the other side of the front screen door. He rose onto his hind legs and hit the door handle. He and Patton charged out, knocking into each other in their haste to reach her. Loretta followed more sedately.

"Hey." She stooped to give hugs, scratches, and ear rubs in equal measure, appreciating the sloppy kiss from D-Day a little more. She would miss the big goofball when Adam left, because it was pretty clear they'd adopted each other. She was glad of that, even though her heart would be extra sore at the double loss.

Okay, none of that, she told herself, rising and heading toward the house. It would be really unprofessional to have tear-streaked raccoon face when her client arrived.

"Hey, Lizzie," Jake said, pushing through the front door. He stood on the porch in jeans and a Big Chance Independence Day T-shirt, holding a steaming coffee mug. He looked a thousand times better than when he'd arrived, and Lizzie could envision the broad-shouldered young man he'd been before the accident. He'd never regain the young part of that, though.

D-Day and Patton raced back and forth between her and Jake, herding them closer together, then dashing off to mark any territory that hadn't already been peed on that morning.

"Adam's not here right now," Jake said.

"I see that, but Dr. Chance is coming to look at the place."

"Dr. Chance?" Jake wrinkled his forehead in confusion. "The veterinarian?"

"Yes. He's looking for a place to move his practice."

"Why…here?"

Lizzie froze at Jake's hesitant speech, a sure sign he was stressed. "Adam told you he wants to sell the ranch, right?"

Jake's shoulders slumped. "I hoped…he was bullshitting."

"I know," she said. "I—"

"You hoped so, too…right?"

She tried to deny it. "I need the commission from this sale. Rob's gonna be here in a few minutes. Do we need to clean inside?"

"No," Jake said. "I've been up…for a while. Marcus is still sleeping. I'll throw…some cold water on him."

"Great. I'll visit the puppies." She could hear them beginning to bark in the barn.

"They can go in the paddock now," Jake said, indicating the fenced area before turning to go back inside.

The moment Lizzie opened the kennel, she knew she'd made a mistake. Still awkward and roly-poly at nearly two months old, the puppies were getting fast. Especially when all six ran every direction at once. She dashed after Garth first, who made a beeline for the driveway. She caught him just as Taylor slid under the front porch, and Lyle found something to roll in near the trash cans.

D-Day and Patton joined in the fun, each chasing one puppy or another.

By the time she had five puppies and one mother dog safely behind the fence, she was sweating and dusty, and Rob Chance was pulling into the drive, hitting the brakes just as Reba tumbled across his path.

Oh good, Lizzie thought, diving for the pup. She got a hind leg and only scraped one knee in the process. *I'm not only a consummate real estate agent, I'm a responsible dog carer, too.* "Hi, Rob," she said, rising to her feet with Reba in her arms. She reached around the squirming dog to shake his hand. "Let me just reunite this stinker with her family."

Rob, fortunately, didn't seem phased by the chaos. "Nothing like a good dog chase first thing in the morning," he said, giving Reba a pat. "You, little lady, are about due for some shots."

Reba licked his hand.

Lizzie added the puppy to the scampering crew in the paddock and asked, "Where do you want to start? The house? Or out here and the barn?"

The front door squeaked, and Marcus and Jake came outside. Both men stood, staring at Rob, arms crossed, eyes narrowed.

"Let's start out here," Rob suggested.

Chapter 31

ADAM DOZED BUT DIDN'T THINK HE'D ACTUALLY FALLEN asleep until something—a bang, like a door closing—roused him. He heard it again. A car door, from a distance. Someone was out in the farmyard.

Maybe Lizzie.

He grabbed his phone and saw a notification of a missed call from her. Anticipation fizzed through his veins. The patchy reception out here was on the not-happening side right now, but this was not a problem, especially if that was her car door he'd heard. He could walk a few yards through the trees and see her in person. He shoved the phone into his pocket and got out of the truck.

Softly closing the door so as to not disturb Granddad, he headed out from beneath the canopy of trees and across the meadow. He made it to the opening in the fence before he saw the vehicle in the farmyard. The hairs on the back of his neck rose. This was *not* Lizzie. He should have realized it was someone else—he'd heard *two* doors slamming.

Like every other truck in Big Chance, this one was white. There were metal boxes in the back, with grated openings in the sides. Crates for securing animals. A dog barked and scratched from inside one as the relentless summer sun beat down on the dull steel. It was too damned hot to keep a dog locked in what could very likely turn into its own coffin.

Obviously, whoever owned this truck wasn't out here to survey the property for park usability.

Before he went pit bull avenger on anyone, however, he needed to know what he was dealing with. Two men stood beyond the truck with their backs to Adam. They hadn't heard his approach, so he crouched down behind some bushes.

"All it'll take is some cosmetic work—patch the floor, fix the stairs, add lights, and you'd have a decent pit," the taller, thinner man said. "You've got space over on the north end to put a few cages, and there's plenty of room up here to watch everything. You have a better arena, you'll get bigger players."

Christ, they were talking about making improvements for more dogfighting.

Adam felt that familiar surge of adrenaline, but it wasn't here to give him a panic attack for a change. He checked his phone. Still no coverage to call 911, so he focused on gathering information. After he had some evidence, he'd rescue the dog in the back of the truck. He got his phone out and began to record video.

"Yeah, I can do that," the other guy said. This one was younger—probably in his early thirties, Adam guessed, with the build of a former football player—strong but not lean. The guy raked his fingers through thinning blond hair and looked around. "I'll get some porta potties out here, set them up by the barn."

A shock of recognition rocked Adam back on his heels. *Mitch Babcock.* Adam shouldn't have been surprised, especially after Lizzie's run-in with him yesterday. Mitch had owned the place, after all. Seeing the privileged prick from high school in person, a ball of anger started to shape in his gut as he connected this dirtbag to the dogfighting that had occurred on this property and pregnant Loretta, abandoned and left for dead. His rage intensified at this sleazebag who had tried to solicit a blow job from Lizzie for a property Granddad actually owned. Fury simmered in his gut.

The skinny guy said, "Start with basic improvements and go from there. But if you can't get some decent dogs out here, it's not gonna matter how fancy your pit is."

"See, that's where I'm thinking you can help me," Mitch said. "You've got the clout."

"I can mention you to some guys I know in Austin. But you've got to get something set up they can see before they're gonna drive all the way out here."

Mitch ran a hand through his nasty hair again. "I can do that. I've got this new dog." He gestured toward the truck. "I'll get him in there soon, have him tear up a few bait animals. Have my cousin record it."

"How soon can you do that?" Skinny asked. He put his hands on his hips, and the motion revealed the butt of a semiautomatic pistol tucked into his waistband.

Adam reconsidered his idea about confronting Mitch and his friend about the dog cooking in the back of the truck. He'd have to find another way.

Mitch shrugged. "I'll call my cousin now. He's got a dog. He asked me to show him the ropes, but it's a pansy-assed dog. I'll get him to bring it out here."

Mitch was talking about Clint. Adam knew this with a cold certainty, and his heart broke a little to think the young man had decided to move forward with teaching his dog to fight.

Skinny's smile was nasty. "Hope he's not too attached to it. Why don't you call him now?"

Mitch took his phone out and sent a text. "Calls don't go through real good out here, but a text should." He glanced down again. "Here we go. He says he'll be here in a couple of minutes."

Adam's phone gave a low battery warning, so he turned off the recording. He sent it to his cloud backup with a wish and a prayer for a signal, then, after a moment, sent it to Lizzie, too. She might not get it, but if she did, she could call the sheriff well before Adam could.

Meanwhile, he had to get that poor dog out of the heat. The truck was too exposed for him to sneak over and let the animal loose, which would be stupid anyway. He had no idea how aggressive the thing was.

Time to do some improvising, he decided. He had to be as nonthreatening as possible to make sure that pistol stayed where it was.

Straightening from his hiding place, he shoved his phone into his pocket, then grabbed a couple of handfuls of grass, which he rubbed on his shirt and into his hair. He took a few big, stumbling steps out into the open and groaned loudly. "*Damn*," he said, rubbing his face with both hands. Between his fingers, he saw Mitch and Skinny jerk and turn in his direction.

Dropping his hands, he staggered a step or two, then made a show of stopping, blinking, and realizing he wasn't alone. "What's goin' on?" He furrowed his eyebrows and looked around. "Wha—?"

"Hey, buddy," Mitch said, taking one menacing step in Adam's direction. "This is private property. You're trespassing."

Adam rubbed his nose. "Man, I'm sorry. I don't remember—were we partying here last night? Where's Jake?"

"Who's Jake?" Mitch asked, then said, "I don't know what you're doing here, but you need to make yourself gone, right now."

Adam looked around. "I don't know where I am, man. My friends must have left me here. How far is it to Austin? I'll call 'em, have 'em come back for me, 'kay?" He pulled his phone out of his pocket and tapped at it. "It's dead. I don't know Talbott's number."

"Shit," Mitch muttered, then, in a louder voice, said, "You're trespassing. You've gotta leave before I call the sheriff."

"Well," Adam said, arms out in a shrug. "I guess you're gonna have to call 'im, 'cause I don't know where I am or how to get anywhere else."

"Damn it," Skinny cursed. "Give him a ride somewhere. We can't have the law out here."

Mitch, who had come a few yards closer, peered at Adam. "Do I know you?" he asked.

Oh hell. Adam wouldn't have known Mitch if Lizzie hadn't described him. How likely was it that Mitch would recognize Adam? "I don't think so. I don't know you," Adam said, trying for a slack-jawed look.

"Well, I know who this moron is," growled a voice over Adam's shoulder. *Granddad.* "You're that little piece of Babcock shit."

"Where'd you come from?" Skinny asked.

"That truck back there," Granddad said, pointing over his shoulder to where Adam's truck was hidden by the trees near the creek.

Mitch, who'd been about to buy Adam's stranger act, looked at Granddad, back at Adam, and curled his upper lip. "Adam Collins. You were a loser before you joined the army, and now you're a drunk? Uncle Sam sure didn't get his money's worth, did he?"

"What's wrong with you, boy?" Granddad asked, shoving Adam's shoulder. "You day drinkin' already? Can't you see these idjits are the ones who've been dogfighting out here?"

As Adam looked from his grandfather to Mitch and then to Skinny, who had drawn his weapon, he wished he had a drink right about now.

A short beep heralded the arrival of another white truck, and sure enough, there was Clint.

"Thanks for taking the time to set this up." Rob did a slow three-sixty and nodded before opening his car door. "I think this might work for me."

"That's great," Lizzie said, almost meaning it. Rob had only blinked a little at the price she quoted, so he might be fairly easy to negotiate with. And if she kept reminding herself about the down-payment-on-Mill-Creek-farm commission, maybe she'd stop feeling so sad about Adam's defection.

"If we do this, how soon do you think I could take possession?" Rob asked.

Lizzie shot a glance toward the front porch, where Marcus and Jake sat in rocking chairs, watching and listening. At least they'd stopped looking like they were determined to defend the Alamo. "I'll double check with Adam on timing," she said. "Normally, it takes a few weeks to get financing in place and to schedule a closing and so forth—"

"I've got cash," Rob said. "And the sooner the better, so I can get out here and do a little remodeling and so forth."

Oookay. Not much time for changes of heart on anyone else's part. That was good, right? She *had* decided to face reality. She wouldn't have time to get any big ideas. "If you're ready to make an offer, I'll get you in here as soon as possible."

He laughed. "I may be getting a little ahead of myself. Give me a couple of days."

She was tempted to press Rob a little, because she didn't want to sit around on pins and needles, but that was part of the game, and she *didn't* want to scare him away. He'd already picked up on a little drama, with the two troubled amigos on the porch there.

"Okay," she agreed. "I'll check in with you in—" She was interrupted by the crunch of tires on the driveway as a small, dark-green sedan appeared.

She didn't recognize the car or its out-of-state plates. The wiry man who got out was a complete stranger as well, although with his long hair, long beard, and camouflage bandanna, he might have been an extra from that show about alligator hunting in the bayou.

"Zimmerman!" Marcus was off the porch, hugging the slightly shorter man and thumping him on the back. "You came!"

"Well, you said it'd be cool for me to bunk here for a while, and the wife just evicted me, so here I am."

Lizzie's *as soon as possible* got a little longer, and she

didn't miss Rob's slight throat clearing before he said, "Well, it looks like there're going to be some interesting conversations here, so I'd better head back to town."

"I didn't know anything about this," Lizzie said, which sounded desperate and defensive, but she was caught off guard.

"It's cool," Rob said, heading for his car. "Let me know what you find out, and we'll talk."

"Great!" She scrounged up her brightest smile and waved as Rob backed into a turn and headed toward town.

Jake joined the other two men, shaking hands with this Zimmerman guy, who now looked at Lizzie with curiosity. "This is Lizzie," Jake introduced her. "She's Sar'nt's lady friend."

Was. *Was* Adam's lady friend. Sort of. "Hi," she said, trying to act normal, whatever that was in this sort of situation.

"Anyone want some lemonade?" Marcus asked, heading back into the house. "I'm buying."

"Why not," Lizzie said as D-Day galumphed over, rose on his hind legs, put his front paws on her shoulders, and gave her a big, sloppy kiss before flopping to lie next to her.

Marcus came out with an armload of canned lemonade and passed out drinks.

"Adam's going to be so surprised," Jake said, leading Zimmerman to a chair on the porch.

"I thought you said he knew I was coming," Zimmerman said, forehead creasing in consternation.

"Eh, don't worry about him," Marcus said, looking over Zimmerman's shoulder and widening his eyes at Lizzie with a *please don't contradict me* expression.

"Where is Adam, anyway?"

"He went to get Granddad," Jake said. "He should be back by now. He left D-Day here."

D-Day sighed and rolled onto his back.

"You've sure got a bunch of dogs," Zimmerman observed. He was looking toward the paddock, where Loretta sat staring back at the group on the porch, as her pups either tried to nurse, chewed on her ears, or climbed over her.

"Yeah, we're like the Last Chance Ranch for dogs," Jake said.

"And soldiers," Marcus agreed.

Lizzie couldn't sit here anymore, listening to Jake name the dumb ranch. What were these guys going to do if—when—Adam sold the ranch? And she was playing a big part in this...this...betrayal.

"Hey, guys, I'm going to take Loretta into town. We need some girl time," she said.

"Yep, see ya," Marcus said, but the guys barely noticed her departure, they were so caught up in shooting the breeze with their friend.

Lizzie was halfway back to town when she picked up her phone, about to tell it to call her dad, when she saw she'd missed a text from Adam. She pulled over and realized it was actually a file.

It took her a minute to figure out what she was seeing and hearing, but then she recognized Mitch. He was talking with someone about the hellhole where Loretta had been left to die, and she made the connection. She checked the time of the recording. Almost thirty minutes ago. Adam *wasn't* at Emma's with Granddad. And if he hadn't come back to the ranch since he'd shot this video? He had a problem.

"Hold on, Loretta," Lizzie said, turning the car around to head toward Mill Creek Road.

"Hey, phone. Call 911."

"I'm sorry, there is no service here," her phone said helpfully. Too bad 911 couldn't receive texts.

With shaking fingers, she sent a message to Emma: Need help at Mill Creek farm. Can't reach sheriff. Call 911 for me? Dogfighting trouble.

She hit Send, then added, Call Marcus and Jake. Tell them Adam needs help.

Chapter 32

"BUDDY, IF YOU POINT THAT GUN AT ME, YOU'D BETTER BE ready to use it," Granddad told Skinny.

"Oh, I'm more than prepared," Skinny said as he gestured for Adam and Granddad to move away from the fence and toward the pit.

"Jesus, Mitch," Clint hissed as he got out of his truck and slowly approached the group. "What is this?"

Adam could see Clint's dog in the cab of the truck, jumping around with excitement and barking through the partially rolled-down window. The dog in the other truck answered but sounded hoarse, as though he'd been barking for days.

"You need to get that dog out of that crate before he dies of heat stroke," Adam said, ignoring the gun and moving toward the truck.

The dust at Adam's feet exploded, and he jumped back, bumping into Granddad as a shot rang out. As if in slow motion, he turned to see his grandfather fall almost straight backward, his rear end hitting the ground a split second before his head struck the hard dirt. Adam dropped to his knees to see to Granddad, and he heard Mitch say, "What the hell, man? You shot the old man!"

"No, I didn't. The old guy just fell when I shot at your friend."

"Dude, you can't just shoot at people!" This was Clint,

wide-eyed and pale, standing back from Mitch and Skinny and looking like he wanted to turn tail and run.

Adam took Granddad's wrist. His pulse was steady, unlike Adam's, which galloped with fear for the man who'd raised him. Granddad was still and silent but breathing, thank God. There wasn't any blood, but he'd whacked his head hard. "We need to get him to a hospital," Adam said.

"Yeah, sure, we'll get right on that," Skinny sneered. "Right after we make sure you're not going to the police."

"Okay, yeah," Adam said, hands out in a gesture of surrender. "I won't say anything to anyone, I swear. I don't even know what you're doing out here. Just let me get my granddad to a hospital."

"How do you know this guy?" Skinny asked Mitch.

"We went to high school together, but I haven't seen him in years."

Adam thought maybe Mitch would be asked to vouch for him, but Skinny put that wish to bed when he looked at Adam. "You said you've been staying in Austin?"

"I, ah—" What to answer? Try to keep the drunken loser charade going to lull Skinny into a false sense of security?

Skinny took a few steps toward Adam, waving the gun around. "You work for the Ambrose brothers, don't you?"

"Who?" Adam shook his head. "I don't know what you're talking about."

"You just happen to be from Austin, and you just happen to interrupt my plans to expand into Ambrose territory?"

"I don't think he's from Austin." Clint stepped forward. "I've seen you in town, haven't I?"

Adam grabbed the life preserver. "Yeah. I live here. I was partying in Austin with some friends."

"And there just happened to be an old man in a truck nearby? Bullshit," Skinny said. "Too much of a coincidence."

"Seriously—" Clint tried to protest, but Skinny swung the gun around in his direction. Clint raised his hands and backed up a step.

"Get that rope out of the truck," Skinny told Clint and Mitch. "Tie up your friend and the old man. Make it good, too. This wouldn't be a good time to give an old friend a break."

"He's not an old friend of mine," Mitch told Skinny as he took the rope and squatted next to Adam.

Adam thought about fighting—if he'd been alone, he would have. But Skinny stood with his gun pointed at Granddad's head.

As Mitch bound Adam's wrists behind his back, leaving no room for blood circulation, Clint worked on Granddad, who appeared peaceful.

"Don't move him!" Adam pleaded.

"I won't." The kid shot an apologetic look at Adam but crossed Granddad's arms over his chest and looped the rope around his hands. Adam didn't blame him. Clint hadn't asked to drive into the middle of a hostage situation.

"Now that we have that taken care of, let's get on with the business at hand," Skinny said.

"Wait," Mitch said. "What are we doing with these two?"

Skinny shrugged. "There aren't too many fast-running rivers around here this time of year, but there are plenty of caves," he said. "Coyotes will clean up the evidence before anyone finds them."

"You're going to kill them?" Clint's eyes showed white, and he'd lost color.

"Naw. We'll just tie them up really well and let nature take its course."

There was just enough crafty evil in Skinny's eyes to tell Adam that he wasn't blowing smoke. And Adam wasn't delusional enough to believe he'd be able to get himself and Granddad free before dehydration killed one of them.

"You. *Cuz.* I hear you got a dog you want to train to fight," Skinny said to Clint.

"Uh, I was thinking about it," Clint hedged, shooting a quick look at Adam.

"Well, go get him. Mitch, you get your dog, too," Skinny instructed. "I'll keep an eye on our spectators."

"Now?" Clint asked. "Why?"

"We need to make a little demo video of Mitch's setup here, and your dogs are going to be the stars."

Clint shrugged and moved toward his truck, clucking to the half-grown pup, telling it to sit and wait while he opened the door.

Mitch had his dog on a leash and stood away from the others. The thing was huge, growling and straining, especially once it saw Clint's dog hop out of the truck.

"Okay," Skinny said. "Get 'em in the pit."

"What?" Clint took a step back. "You're really going to set them on each other? Bruce is still a puppy!"

"What did you think we were going to do?" Skinny asked, laughing. "Do an agility course?" He shook his head. "Nope. I want to see some blood."

"I thought you just wanted to have some dogs to show how—I don't know." Clint shook his head. "I'm not doing this."

"Damn it, Clint," Mitch said. "You said you wanted to see how it all works. Now's your chance."

Clint shot Adam another look and said, "I changed my mind."

"Oh, for Christ's sake," Mitch said. "You don't know what you're missing. There's a lot of money for a man with a strong stomach. You've got a baby on the way, you know."

"Yeah," Clint said. "I know." But he didn't back down, and Adam silently applauded his backbone.

Mitch's big dog started to growl and bark in earnest now and turned toward the lane leading from the road.

"What the hell?" Skinny growled.

Adam looked up to witness the arrival of the absolute last person in the world who should be here right now. It really was true that there were no atheists in foxholes, because Adam began to pray like he'd never prayed before.

As Lizzie pulled up in her SUV and opened the door to get out, Skinny put one hand on his hip. "Well, how about this?" he said.

Lizzie had just tried to call 911 again when she heard the gunshot from the road and decided not to wait for Marcus and Jake or the sheriff. Adam wouldn't sit by while *she* got murdered.

When she stepped out of her car, however, she realized she might have only delayed the inevitable as she took in the bizarre scene. A scrawny older guy pointed a gun at her as Mitch fought to control a drooling, growling pit bull.

Granddad was lying in the dirt. Adam, bound and sitting on the ground nearby, was clearly not happy to see her. He wasn't just mad, he was livid. His nostrils flared, and his jaw had never looked more rigid. She decided not to take it personally.

Clint was there, too, holding his young dog's leash, looking like he might pass out at any moment. She didn't blame him—it was hot as hell out here.

"Hello, bayyyybee!" the gun guy sang. "Thank you for coming to our party!"

"Hi there," Lizzie said and made a dramatic swipe at her drooping hair. "Hey, Mitch. How are you doin' today? It sure is hot out here. I'm sorry to interrupt your gathering, but I'm a little lost. Didn't there used to be a creek around here somewhere? It sure would be lovely to take a dip on such a hot day, don't you think?"

"Stop talking," Gun Guy said. "There's no creek here."

"Oh, shoot," she said. "I wonder—does your phone work out here? Maybe I can call my friend and ask—"

"Stop. Talking," Gun Guy repeated. "Get over here."

"What? Why?" She looked at Adam and saw with a jolt of fear that Granddad hadn't moved. Was he dead? She pushed the terror deep down inside and asked, "Why are those men tied up? Were they *trespassing*? Would you like me to drive them to town for you? I know where the sheriff's office is."

"No. Shut. Up."

Okay, she hadn't really thought it would work, but she was flying by the seat of her pants here.

"You know this one, too?" Gun Guy asked Mitch.

"Not really. Same high school, but she's younger'n me."

Interesting that Mitch didn't mention Lizzie's interest in buying the property.

Gun Guy smiled. It wasn't a nice smile. He told Mitch, "I have an idea. Let's take this young lady for a tour of your establishment."

Huh? What establishment? Lizzie wondered.

"Why don't you walk on over that way?" Gun Guy said, gesturing with his weapon to the other side of the former basement, where the broken concrete steps led down to the unfenced side of the cellar.

Lizzie stalled. "You want me to go into that...*basement*? I know it's open to the sky and all, but it's burned out, and I'm a little more dressed up today than I would be if I were going to go—"

"Now," Gun Guy ordered, pointing his gun at her again.

Shouldn't the police be here by now? Where were they?

For all her rambling, Lizzie was telling the truth about one thing. She was *not* dressed to run around dangerous places. It was hot as blazes out here, and she was sweating through her clothes. And these *shoes*. She picked her way carefully over the debris-strewn ground and made a mental note that if she got out of this, she'd carry a pair of sneakers everywhere.

How *was* she going to get out of this? Where was her cavalry? Marcus, Jake, and Zimmerman should be here by now, surely. The ranch wasn't that far.

When she reached the far side and looked down into the basement, she paused.

"Now down the steps and get in there," Gun Guy said, pointing to the open door of the caged area.

That cage hadn't been opened when they were here

saving Loretta, had it? Poor Loretta. She was terrified to be here. She'd curled up on the car's passenger-side floor, just like yesterday when she'd slept all the way to Mitch's... Realization hit her. Loretta hadn't been sleeping yesterday. She'd been hiding when they got to Mitch's place because she remembered him.

Before she took a step down, a crack of sound startled Lizzie at the same time as something thudded into the dirt next to her.

"You son of a bitch!" Adam shouted, struggling in his bonds, rising to his knees before Gun Guy swung around and whacked him in the face with his gun.

"Oh!" Gun Guy said, looking back and forth between Adam and Lizzie. "Do you two know each other?" He pointed at Lizzie. "Holy shit. Are you from Austin to get up in my business, too?"

What?

Adam glared at Gun Guy, blood dripping from a cut on his cheek. Clint's dog disappeared beneath her SUV in a flash of leash. Then Clint shifted, watching Gun Guy.

Mitch and that terrifying dog followed her to the basement rim.

"Girl, get in that basement before I start the blood flowing early."

Oh God. *Ohgodohgodohgod.* She was going to get eaten alive by a dog in front of Adam.

She looked down, heat radiating up from the pit. Lizzie felt like she was about to walk into her own personal crematorium.

Taking a deep breath, she looked up and caught Adam's gaze.

Adam had never felt such helpless terror. Of all the things he'd failed at—and there were more than he could count at the moment—failing to keep Lizzie safe was the one that he'd never be able to survive. She met his eyes across the distance, and Adam couldn't look away from her damp, flushed, *beautiful* face.

Her lips moved, and he could have sworn she said, "I love you."

He couldn't say anything back to her, didn't want to give Skinny and Mitch any more ammunition to hurt her, so he only nodded. If she was as terrified as Adam was, and if believing Adam loved her back could give her peace, then he wanted her to have hope.

He tried to tell her, with one long look, how much she meant to him, how much more meaning his life had with her in it. Three months ago, he'd been a broken loser, with no sense of purpose other than repaying a debt to his sister and riding off into the sunset. Lizzie brought him that big goofy dog and gave him a reason to get out of bed in the morning. Lizzie, with her optimism and trust, had helped him find his way back to work that he loved. He once again related to humanity in a way he hadn't believed possible.

Turning away, she swiped a sweaty strand of hair away from her face and took one step down into that deathtrap of a basement.

He couldn't let her go like this. He had to tell her. "Lizzie, I—"

Lizzie saw a flash of movement in her peripheral vision and looked up. Someone was in the bushes lining the lane from Mill Creek Road. Marcus, Jake, and Zimmerman must have arrived.

Unfortunately, Mitch's dog noticed them at the same time as Lizzie. It turned from watching her to strain toward the road, sniffing and snarling. *No.* He couldn't alert Mitch and Gun Guy that help was here.

Mitch gave the dog's leash a yank. "What the hell—"

Lizzie hoped the guys in the bushes were paying attention. Turning, she yelled, "I can't die like this!" and lunged away from the basement.

Mitch tried to grab her, losing his balance in the process. With a grunt, he fell on her, releasing the dog's leash as they toppled into the dirt. From beneath two hundred and fifty pounds of stinky idiot, she heard gunshots and watched the pit bull take off for the bushes where Marcus, Jake, and Zimmerman hid.

Chapter 33

BULLETS FLEW AS ADAM FOUGHT TO FREE HIMSELF AND get to Lizzie. His hands were still bound behind his back, and he twisted his arms, trying to loosen the ropes for everything he was worth. He'd rip off a hand and do somersaults to get to her if he had to. He'd protect Lizzie with his last, dying breath.

She screamed and shoved at Mitch, who flailed like an upended turtle, while his dog sprinted away and dove into the bushes.

Meanwhile, Skinny turned in maniacal circles, pointing his gun randomly, seeming unable to fix on a target. He sent a couple of shots into the air.

Adam renewed his struggle to get free.

"Hold still, man," came a voice from behind. Clint. With a couple of sharp tugs, the rope was cut. Blood and pain rushed into Adam's hands, but he didn't give a shit. He reached for his ankles.

"Wait," Clint said tightly. He scooted around and put his Leatherman to work on Adam's feet. Both men kept an eye on Skinny. The shooting had stopped for the moment, while Skinny tried to jam a new magazine into his gun.

On the other side of the basement, Lizzie managed to get out from under Mitch. She glanced at Adam, then kicked off her shoes and ran toward the dog in the bushes.

Oh hell no. She couldn't possibly be planning to try to rescue that dog in the middle of this mess.

But then a deep bellow from the bushes made it clear what—or who, rather—Lizzie was trying to help. The dog backed up, dragging a man with him—shit, was that Zimmerman? Here?

Jake and Talbott followed. Both men tried to grapple with the dog, but it wasn't giving up on its prey, who tried to curl into a fetal position on the ground. The shouting and general chaos only served to firm its resolve, and it clamped its jaws deeper into the man's leg. Lizzie screamed at the dog to let go and looked like she might try to dive in and help.

"You get her. I'll take this one," Clint said, nodding toward Skinny.

Adam nodded and ran across the farmyard while Clint tackled Skinny.

Adam reached Lizzie and pulled her away while Jake and Talbott tried to get the dog away from Zimm. He checked on Mitch, but the man was still floundering on the ground. Jake let out a yell, and by the time Adam turned back around, Talbott was pulling an unconscious dog away from an unmoving Max Zimmerman.

Jake crouched next to them, holding a heavy branch and breathing hard. "I'm sorry," he said shakily. "I hit it."

"Watch out," Talbott said. He pulled off his T-shirt to wrap around the wound in Zimm's leg, which pulsed with a steady stream of dark, red blood.

Adam looked at the dog, now a few feet away. It was still breathing but unconscious. For how long?

Zimmerman moaned. He was in bad shape.

Talbott said, "Come on, Zimm. You with me, buddy?"

Adam looked at Jake, who was staring at the ground, panting. "Jake, don't lose it on me, man."

He looked at Adam. "I hit the dog."

"You saved Zimmerman. The dog's okay. See? He's breathing." He nodded at the dog. "But we don't know when he'll wake up. Put him…" He looked around. "Can you take him over there, tie his leash to that tree, and keep an eye on him while I check on Granddad?"

With a big breath, Jake shuddered and seemed to come back from wherever he'd been. "On it, Sar'nt." He crouched and lifted the dog.

Granddad still lay quietly on the ground, oblivious to all that had happened.

Adam saw Clint finish tying Skinny's feet together. He was bound just as Adam had been. Silently, Clint held up the gun to show he'd also been disarmed. Good. One asshole down.

Adam turned to find Lizzie just in time to hear her yell, "Let me go, you dickwad!" Mitch Babcock had her by the arm and was trying to wrestle her into her SUV.

God. Could this day get any worse? "Let her go, Babcock!" he yelled.

Lizzie looked up and was knocked sideways when the car door blew open with a burst of fury.

Loretta charged past Lizzie and latched onto her former master's arm, taking Mitch to the ground in a flurry of fur and screams.

Adam made it to Lizzie's side and wrapped an arm around her as he backed them away from the carnage.

"Get this bitch off me!" Mitch howled in panic.

Loretta squatted on Mitch's torso, her jaws clamped tightly on his upper arm, her single eye fixed on his. He tried to pull away from her, but she just bit deeper. Jake stepped forward to grab for Loretta's collar, and she growled around the arm in her jaws. Jake raised his hands and stepped back.

Mitch lifted the hand of his uninjured arm in supplication and begged, "Don't let her kill me."

Snarling, Loretta released him but snapped at his face. Mitch froze, wisely averting his eyes from the dog.

Lizzie pulled away from Adam. "Come on, Loretta," she coaxed, standing a few feet away. Adam stood at her back. She didn't think she needed protection from the dog but was grateful to Adam for not trying to take over, even as he made her feel safer.

Lizzie was dimly aware of approaching sirens but stayed focused on the scene in front of her. "Loretta, you've got babies at home who need you," Lizzie said softly. The words wouldn't make any sense to Loretta, but hopefully the sound of her voice would register. "The police are here, Loretta. Let them take over now."

Loretta didn't look away from her captive, but she did step off him and back away.

"Here, Loretta," Jake said, moving forward slowly with a leash, which she allowed him to clip to her collar.

Adam pulled Lizzie in close, grasping her hand.

Loretta stood stiffly next to Jake, watching Mitch try to struggle to his feet. "Stupid dog," he muttered, one hand clamped over his arm. There didn't seem to be much blood.

"Wouldn't fight back to save her life a few weeks ago, and now she's gonna turn on the hand that fed her."

"You've got to be kidding, right?" Lizzie asked, incredulous. "You let another dog try to kill her and then left a pregnant dog for dead."

Adam squeezed her hand, and she appreciated the unspoken support, especially because she was a little wobbly at the moment.

"She was *pregnant*?" Mitch said. "Son of a bitch. I shoulda kept her. How many puppies?"

"None that you'll ever see," Adam told him.

"Which of you is Adam Collins?" A man in a brown uniform walked toward them, a hand on the pistol in his holster. A couple of Chance County Sheriff's vehicles were parked behind him, and an ambulance was pulling behind them. The deputy wasn't looking at the humans, however. His eyes were on Loretta, who was still intently watching Mitch.

"I am," Adam confirmed.

"Can you secure that dog, please?" the deputy, whose name tag said Red Diamond, asked.

"She's okay now," Jake said.

Adam shook his head, though, and said, "He's right. She's already on edge. Why don't you put her in Lizzie's car? Mitch isn't going anywhere."

Indeed—Mitch was still on his backside in the dirt, holding his arm.

Jake saw to Loretta as another officer dealt with the dog that had attacked Max Zimmerman, and one stood over Mitch's friend, unloading the gun he'd had. An EMT jogged toward Zimmerman, while another attended Granddad.

It wasn't getting any cooler out here, Lizzie noted. She

used her free hand to tug at her blouse, hoping to move some air in and out and cool off a bit. She wondered if the cop carried cold water in his cruiser. Wouldn't that be a nice thing for a Texas policeman to carry?

"Hey, Jake," she called as he coaxed Loretta into her car. "The keys are in the center console there. Go ahead and turn on the air-conditioning for her, would you?" She would really love to be in that car with the air-conditioning but knew she needed to stay out here and share her story when it was time.

"Your sister contacted us, but it looks like we missed most of the excitement. Could you tell us what happened here?" Diamond asked Adam.

"I'm fine," Granddad croaked at the EMT trying to assist him. "Just get me untied. I've gotta take a leak." Clint sawed at the ropes with his Leatherman.

At hearing Granddad's voice, Lizzie felt relief flow through Adam's fingers into hers.

"I need help," Mitch whined.

"We'll be right with you," the paramedic with Zimmerman called.

Maybe there was a cooler full of water in the ambulance, Lizzie thought.

Diamond took a notepad and pen out of his pocket. "Okay." He looked expectantly at Adam. "Tell me what happened."

"These two"—Adam indicated Mitch and the other guy—"are the ones running the dogfighting ring here."

"That's a lie," Mitch protested.

Adam ignored him and went on. "And they were here making plans to expand their operation."

"Bullshit." Mitch's protest lacked conviction.

"What were you doing here?" Diamond asked Adam.

"We own this property."

"The hell you do," Mitch said with a little more spirit. "This is mine."

"Did you forget selling it to my grandfather a few years ago?" Adam asked.

"There's no proof of that," Mitch said.

"Yes, there is, but we'll deal with it later," Adam told him. Adam released Lizzie's hand. The few inches he moved away felt like miles. He went on, "They also had a dog locked in a metal crate sitting in the sun. I don't even want to think about how hot it was in there. I took some video of Mitch and Skinny over there making plans and sent it to my—I sent it to Lizzie and asked her to get help."

Lizzie watched waves of hot air rise from the roof of her SUV and listened as Adam described her arrival and everything that happened after that. And through it all, she could only focus on what Adam had almost said. *I sent it to my... to Lizzie.* He'd nodded after she'd mouthed her dying confession to him...*I love you*...but what did that nod mean?

He understood what she was telling him, that was all.

By the time Adam finished speaking, another cruiser had arrived. Lizzie was dimly aware that Gun Guy was loaded into the back of one and Mitch put into another. Lizzie could hear him complaining about how much pain he was in from the dog bite. The deputy in charge of Mitch grinned. "Don't worry, sir. We'll make sure you're treated appropriately."

"Excuse me," Lizzie said, walking toward Deputy Diamond. "Do you happen to have any water in your car?"

"Lizzie?" Adam's voice came from a long distance, even though she could see him standing a few feet away. "Lizzie!" His face was the last thing she saw as she collapsed.

Chapter 34

"I'LL SEE YOU LATER?" LIZZIE ASKED AFTER SHE WAS loaded into the back of the ambulance between Granddad and Zimm. She'd been down for a few moments that lasted seven lifetimes to Adam. She seemed better, had complained that she didn't want to take up valuable space, but the medics thought she needed to be checked out by a doc—and Adam agreed. Her forehead was creased now, and she said, "I need…" Then she shook her head.

"What's wrong?" he asked. "What do you need?"

"You?" She said it like a question, as though she wasn't sure she had the right to ask.

It took everything he had to remind himself that she was going to be fine—better—without him. "I'll come by after we finish up here," he found himself promising. Granddad, who was complaining about being strapped into a seat, and Zimmerman, on a second stretcher, took up every extra inch in the vehicle. The medics promised they'd call her parents. They'd take good care of her.

Heat exhaustion. That was what the medic said when Lizzie collapsed. Adam knew what that was, had seen it in the desert. A few days into his first deployment, he'd watched a man *die* from the heat and made it his mission to always see that his soldiers were hydrated at all times.

"We radioed dispatch, and they called your sister. She'll

meet the ambulance and see to your grandfather," one of the deputies told Adam.

"Thank you." The doors were closed and the lights and sirens turned on. He watched until the ambulance pulled away, then turned to the remaining group of people.

"Just a few more questions, and you can all go." Deputy Diamond beckoned to Clint, who loitered in the background, tightly holding the leash of his dog.

"Yes, sir?" Clint stepped forward, eyes down, resigned to...something.

"Can you tell me what your part was in this?"

Adam forced himself to pay attention, not to worry about Lizzie.

Clint took a deep breath and said, "I came out here under the pretense of bringing my dog to fight."

"I see," Diamond said.

"But I wasn't really going to do it. I knew my cousin Mitch was involved, and I thought it was cool when I first found out he was doing it. Badass, right? I got a dog and everything. Then Crystal—that's my girlfriend—she made me watch this documentary about dogfighting, and I knew I couldn't do it. We're going to have a baby, you know? I can't have a vicious dog around a kid."

Diamond scribbled something in his notebook. "So why didn't you say no when you were invited?"

Clint looked at Adam then. "Because I knew you were going to try to get them busted, and I wanted to help."

Adam shook his head, confused. "What?"

"After we saw you on the Fourth of July and you gave me your number, Crystal said you were going to set me up to get busted. She could tell you weren't interested in dogfighting, at least not in *doing* it."

Adam chuckled, the first thing he'd had to smile about all day. "Smart woman, your Crystal."

"Yeah, she's the best," Clint said, grinning. "Even though she has to put up with a loser like me."

"Well, she must see something worth loving," Adam told him.

Diamond cleared his throat. "Okay, so you were only here to rat on your cousin?"

Clint looked a little guilty then. "Well, maybe not Mitch. I was hoping I could find out who the ringleaders were and keep him out of it. He is my cousin, after all. But he didn't exactly act like he gives a shit about me, so I'm glad you got him." His phone chimed, and he looked down. "Oh wow," he said. "Can I go? Crystal's water just broke."

"Go," Diamond said. "Good luck."

"What about us?" Adam asked. "Do you need anything else?"

Diamond shook his head. "Not unless you want to come help with the arrest report back at the station. Your friends and your lady did the hard work."

And wasn't that the truth. Lizzie had been through hell today, while Adam watched from the sidelines.

"Loretta helped, too," Jake added. He'd coaxed the dog out of Lizzie's car, and she was glued to Jake's leg.

"That's one hell of a dog," the deputy said, eyeing her with one eyebrow raised, as though he didn't believe that an animal could have acted so confidently to protect her mistress.

"She is," Adam agreed. "She'll get extra kibble tonight for sure."

"What's going to happen to the other dog?" Jake asked.

Diamond said, "One of the other deputies is our part-time animal control officer. He'll take the dog to town and keep it there until its disposition is determined."

Adam knew—and he could tell by Jake's face that he also knew—the dog would most likely be put down.

"Can we—" Jake began, but Adam cut him off, knowing he was about to ask if they could take it in.

"No. We have to let the law deal with it." The last thing they needed was another dog—a volatile, vicious dog—to be responsible for.

The last official vehicle finally pulled away, leaving Adam alone with his two best friends.

"How'd you guys get here?" Adam asked Jake and Talbott.

"Zimmerman drove—he parked on the main road. And he has the car keys," Jake said. "Can we ride to Last Chance with you?"

"Last Chance?" Adam asked.

"Yep," Talbott said. "We decided that's the ranch's name, since so many down-on-their-luck dogs and soldiers have shown up."

"I wonder if Doc Chance will keep the name when he takes over," Jake said.

"What?"

"Yeah, Sar'nt," Jake said. "He came out this morning. That's why Lizzie was dressed up. She said he likes the place and will probably make an offer."

Adam's heart sank at the news. He couldn't think of anything to say, so they walked back to his truck together, quiet and tired, like the team they'd always been.

Lizzie shifted restlessly on the narrow hospital bed. Even with extra pillows and the ability to move the various parts up and down, she couldn't find a comfortable position, but she had to *rest* before they'd let her go home.

Unfortunately, every time she closed her eyes, she saw Adam's face as she was lifted into the ambulance. That was a goodbye face if she'd ever seen one. And since he'd made it at her a few times, she should know.

"I thought you'd be home binge-watching *Extreme RVs* by now," Adam said as he entered the room, wearing neither his goodbye face nor his I'm-glad-to-see-you face. This one was completely unreadable. He did, however, come bearing a gift. He put a potted plant on her tray table. It was some kind of fern in a blue, baby hippo–shaped planter, bearing a sign that read "It's a boy!"

"Wow, thanks," she said, smiling in spite of her nervous stomach.

"They were all out of regular sick-people flowers," he said, shrugging. "Oh shoot," he said, reaching to peel off the yellow *CLEARANCE* sticker from the side.

"I can't imagine why they haven't already sold that," Lizzie mused. "All any new mother needs is another living thing to take care of."

Adam chuckled, and Lizzie got a zap of pleasure from making him laugh. Then it was gone, and Adam stood next to her bed, hands in his pockets, looking as uncomfortable as she'd ever seen him. An uneasy silence fell between them, filling every available space.

He cleared his throat. "So you're still dehydrated?" He nodded toward the half-empty IV bag.

"Nope. I've been peeing the right color for an hour," she

told him, because she felt ornery and wanted to jolt them out of this awkward place. "I've got to get some IV antibiotics and some *rest* before they'll let me go home."

"Antibiotics?" He asked. "Why?"

She pulled the sheet back to display her bandaged feet. "I picked up a few thorns and bits of broken glass on my dash across the barnyard. My park is going to have to have a 'No Bare Feet' rule until it's really cleaned up, I'm afraid."

He didn't smile at that. "Damn it," he muttered.

"What? I'll live. Honestly."

"Yeah, you will," he told her, nodding decisively. "You're going to be fine."

"What does that mean?"

"It means you're going to be *fine*," he told her, doing the deliberately obtuse thing.

"Fine," she repeated. "F.I.N.E. Effed-up, insecure, neurotic, and...whatever *E* stands for."

"Emotional," he supplied. "That sounds more like me. You'll be the real kind of fine."

Although her stomach burned with an anxiety that belied her words, she said, "I'm the real kind of fine now, I'd like to point out."

"Yes, you are. And you'll be even better after I'm gone." He put his hands on his hips and stared out of the window instead of at her.

Her whole body flushed with a kind of pain she'd never felt before. She'd been preparing for this moment, knew it was coming, braced for it, and still, it knocked her over and shook her like a rag doll.

"So you're really going to leave."

He nodded, still not looking at her. "Yep."

"Even after everything that happened today." *After I bared my soul to you, told you I love you.*

He looked at her then, and his next words burst from his lips with startling force. "What the *hell* were you thinking this morning? Why would you show up out there like that?"

"Oh, I don't know," she said, welcoming anger to edge out the hurt, making her bold and direct. "Maybe I got a video that scared the crap out of me, and maybe I love your stupid ass and didn't want you to die!"

"Why the hell would you *do* that? Love *me*? You don't *look* like a stupid person."

"Maybe I am dumb, but I need you in my life. You make me feel like...like I matter."

Adam didn't blink, just came right back at her with, "Bullshit. Don't love me. Don't need me. I told you not to need me." His hands were balled into fists now, and his eyes flashed danger.

"Well, guess what, soldier," she shot back. "I do anyway. But that's okay. You don't have to love me back."

Adam didn't respond, which was good, she supposed. Memories of her last fight with Dean came crashing back, the one where he told her it didn't matter how thin or successful or fashionable she got, she still wasn't what he wanted. *Why?* What was wrong with her?

She said, "Look at it this way. At least you'll still get to make your stupid amends to the people who don't want or need them."

Adam inhaled deeply and then exhaled. He looked calmer, but Lizzie could see his hands shaking. "I'm gonna check on Granddad and Zimmerman."

He didn't wait for a response but turned and left the room. He didn't get far.

"Hey, there you are," came Emma's voice from right outside Lizzie's open door.

He must have still been radiating distress signals, because Emma said, "Are you okay?"

"Yeah. How's Granddad?"

"Fine. CT scan was perfect. He's sleeping now, and they'll evaluate him again in the morning and probably release him then."

"Good."

"How's Lizzie?" Emma asked in a not-exactly-low-enough whisper.

"Pissed off." Adam's almost whisper was even louder.

"What did you do?"

Lizzie had a moment of gratitude that Emma thought this was all Adam's fault, too.

"I told her I'm leaving. It's not new information."

"Dagnabbit, Adam, what is *wrong* with you?" Neither of them was bothering to speak softly now.

"The best army brass in the world have wondered the same thing," he said.

"Oh, horse butts." Emma did have the best noncurse words ever. "You were a great soldier. One of the best. I've seen the medals and commendations."

"*Was.* Was a good soldier. I'm not anymore."

"You're a good *man*, Adam. A good man wearing blinders and earplugs, but still good. Even if you threw yourself to the wolves today like so much raw meat. Taking on those guys by yourself, what were you thinking?" The same question he'd asked Lizzie a few minutes ago and one she wished she'd asked right back.

"I was thinking I had to get that poor dog out of the heat. That if those assholes killed me, maybe then you'd accept the money from the sale of the ranch or at least use my life insurance money to take care of Granddad and give yourself a new start."

"*What*? I don't *want* a new start," she said, frustration clear in her voice. "And if you died, what would happen to Jake and Marcus? And those dogs?"

"Maybe you'd let them stay on the ranch a while. Maybe you'd give them some of the money."

"And what about *Lizzie*?" Emma hissed. "She's in *love* with you!"

"She'll get over it. All of you will."

"How can you say that?" Emma asked. "We're your family."

"I don't care, Emma. Don't you understand? I...*can't* care. I'm broken. I can't be responsible for other people. Not anymore."

"Oh, Adam," Emma said.

He must have walked away then, because in the next moment, Emma appeared in the doorway to Lizzie's room.

"Did you hear that?" she asked.

Lizzie nodded.

"I'm so sorry," she said. "He didn't mean it."

But Lizzie knew that he did. And she understood why he had to leave. He felt responsible for taking care of everyone he cared about, which was why he wouldn't accept her love. She would just be one more burden for him to carry.

Chapter 35

"Here he is," Jake said when Adam entered Zimmerman's room.

"How you doin'?" he asked Zimm, leaning over to clasp his hand and give him a soft clap on the shoulder in an abbreviated bro hug.

"Pretty good, right now," Zimmerman said, smiling woozily. "But in between shots, my leg hurts a little."

"What's the prognosis?"

"Don't know." Zimmerman shrugged. "They did this remote video feed thing with a surgeon in Houston. He's going to review things and come back with some suggestions."

"Did you let your wife know what happened?"

"I left a message. Not holding my breath that she'll return it." Zimm's laugh was bitter. "Maybe I should ask her to check if my life insurance is paid up."

Life insurance. Adam didn't laugh, since he'd just spouted off about the same thing to Emma.

"Where's Talbott?" Zimmerman asked.

"He stayed home to rest," Jake said. "He strained his back rolling around on the ground today."

"I guess I chose a bad day to show up, huh?" Zimmerman said.

"You could have had better timing," Adam agreed. "But we do like to entertain our guests. Maybe not so much all at once, but…"

"I'm sorry, man," Zimm said. "My wife took the baby and left. Told me to be gone when she got back."

"I'm sorry." Adam didn't ask what Zimm had done to chase her off. He wasn't really sure he wanted to—

"We had a fight. I lost my shit and tore up the house." Zimm banged his forehead with his fist. "I scared the crap out of Shelley and the baby. Hell, I scared myself."

Jake was quiet, and Adam followed his lead. The only thing he could do right now was listen and offer compassion instead of judgment.

Tears ran down Zimm's face. "Shelley got mad at me because I didn't do something. I don't remember what, not that I blame her. She never gets a damn break. I wasn't there when the baby was born, and she dealt with all that newborn shit alone. She thought it would get easier when I got home, but I've just made everything worse."

Jake said, "I know what you mean. You had a job where you knew what to do. And then you come home, and you don't…fit in your old space."

Yep, Adam thought. That was it—what was happening for all of them.

Zimm said, "I tried to work for a while—my dad had me doing all kinds of stuff for his company—but sometimes I'd get up in the morning, grab my coffee, and keep going past the office. It would be five o'clock, time to come home, and I'd been sitting in the car in the parking lot of some random grocery store for eight hours. Finally, I quit going in.

"Anyway, she asked me to do something, but I forgot, and then she had this sad look on her face like she knew I was worthless, like she didn't even care enough to fight anymore. I started yelling, trying to get a rise out of her, and she finally started giving it back, telling me how she was faithful to me and couldn't have loved me more while I was serving but started to hate me since I got home."

He banged his fist against his head again. "So we're in the living room fighting, and I picked up the damned coffee table and threw it against the wall."

Adam couldn't breathe.

Jake sat with both hands over his mouth, listening.

Zimmerman's voice broke. "The table crashed into the wall, where the TV is. And the TV fell and broke, and everyone was screaming and crying... Shelley said maybe I should go somewhere I'd be out of everyone's misery." With that, Zimmerman put his head against his knees and sobbed.

Adam rubbed his hands over his face, wishing he knew what to do to help this damaged soul.

A snuffling, scratching sound drew Adam's attention, and he turned to look at Jake, who had drawn a puppy out of the tote bag he'd insisted on bringing with him. He put the little guy on Zimmerman's lap.

After a moment, Zimm looked up and tried to understand what was happening. He wiped his eyes as the little dog clambered around and put his paws on Zimm's chest. Zimmerman smiled hesitantly and lifted the puppy to peer into its face. Garth—Adam was pretty sure it was Garth—licked Zimmerman's face with enthusiasm.

Within a couple of minutes, both Zimm and the puppy were asleep.

Adam looked at Jake, who shrugged innocently. "I don't know how it got in there, Sar'nt."

Adam snorted.

Jake grinned, and pretty soon, they were shushing each

other as they cracked up, trying not to wake up Zimm or alert the nursing staff.

Once they had both regained their composure, Jake said, "They're both sleeping kind of nice together, aren't they?"

"Yeah," Adam said. "I guess we can sit here a little longer until one of them wakes up."

"Or we get evicted," Jake said.

The bout of euphoria brought about by the laughing fit was squashed by the weight of everything Adam was carrying around with him.

He carried a financial burden for his granddad's care and his sister—whether she wanted him to or not, he was going to help her. He felt responsible for his friends' physical and mental conditions. Even if he hadn't intentionally— even neglectfully—missed that bomb, even if it had been a complete freak incident, Adam had been the man with the detection dog. The one everyone trusted to clear a room. They were all taught that they had to be able to count on the soldier next to them.

Then there were all those dogs. As he and Jake were turning from the ranch onto Wild Wager Road on the way to the hospital, Adam could have sworn he saw a black-and-white-spotted something move through the brush. With his luck, there'd be another damned dog on his front porch when they got home tonight.

And then there was Lizzie. Who was so smart and funny and beautiful and caring. And for some crazy reason, she loved Adam. He wanted to deny it, had tried like hell to convince her and himself it wasn't happening, but there it was. And damn it, since he was exhausted and without defenses, he'd admit it. He loved her, too.

As though he were following Adam's train of thought, Jake, in his incomparable, straightforward style, said, "I wish I knew what was going to happen after you sell the ranch."

Adam sighed. "Jake, you don't know what'll happen in the future no matter what."

"Maybe, but I really like it here. I like doing all the work and taking care of the dogs. I feel…okay with you and Marcus."

"Really? You must be hard up if you like hanging out with me."

"Sometimes you're even fun," Jake told him, then grinned.

"Jake, you're gonna be okay. You're getting better all the time, right?"

"I don't know, Sar'nt. It's like…I'm not a real person anymore. I say shit I shouldn't say, and I get lost. I'm like… Forrest Gump without Jenny."

Adam snorted. "Well, you've got a great Lieutenant Dan in Marcus Talbott."

"Yeah, like he wants to babysit me for the rest of our lives." Jake shook his head. "I don't know. Maybe I should let my parents find me some place to stay where I can't cause trouble. I don't think I could even get a job right now."

Adam's heart clenched. No. Jake couldn't give up. What did he say he looked forward to? Working at the ranch. Taking care of the dogs. Being part of a team.

Adam waited to feel the weight from that realization press him down, but either he was at maximum capacity or something had changed. It occurred to him that he'd been planning to give up, too. He thought taking care of those to-do items would fulfill his duties, and then he could float through the rest of his life in a way that no one would give a shit, untethered, going with the flow.

But these people he insisted on feeling responsible for—what would happen if they were no longer in his life or he in theirs? A strong, stubborn part of him wanted to believe that he was more expendable than Jake—and more blame-worthy. But he realized they were all part of one big crazy team, all working together to keep one another's heads above water.

Jake, Talbott, Emma, Granddad, even Clint and Zimmerman. D-Day—the dog who made it possible for him to manage everyday activities, for crying out loud. And God help him, Lizzie. Most of all, Lizzie, who loved him, even as she saw everything ugly inside him—and made him look, too.

Well, damn. This clarity thing was painful.

Adam had enlisted in the U.S. Army because he wanted to train dogs to find terrorists, because he knew how to work with dogs and wanted to get better at it.

Because he wanted to do something that mattered.

After his first deployment, his goals shifted, and his sole purpose was to keep the soldier next to him alive. He thought he'd failed on that last mission, but for the first time, he understood that he'd done his job. He'd kept a hell of a lot of soldiers alive, on a lot of missions. And now he had a chance to keep them alive, here in Big Chance, with his messed-up family and broken-down brotherhood. It might not be perfect, but it was a home and a family none-theless. A team. He had people who could need him, if he'd let them. A purpose, if he'd accept the call.

A future appeared in his mind's eye—fuzzy in parts, but

the first few miles of the road visible. A lightness started to dawn within him as a plan took shape.

He got to his feet. "Jake, slide that pup away from Zimmerman. Let's head home. There's something I need to do."

Within minutes, they were in Adam's truck, and a few more things had become clear. "Hey, Jake, what if I told you that I could get you a job for as long as you wanted it?"

A spark bloomed in Jake's eyes for the briefest moment before it fizzled and his expression fogged over. "Don't mess with me, okay?"

"I'm not messing with you." Adam began to talk.

Reluctantly, Jake listened. "I'm not sure I can—"

"Yes, you can. And we're all gonna be there to make sure, because we've still got one another's backs, right?"

Jake blew out a breath and ran a hand over his head, barely even hesitating over his scar. Finally, he nodded.

"Great." They'd reached the ranch, and Adam jumped out and jogged to the house, calling to D-Day as he went. "Put on your nice collar," he told his dog. "We've got a mission."

Chapter 36

"Thanks, Mom," Lizzie said and shoved the last of her toiletries into the zipper bag, ready to head home. "It's just until I can get my own place."

"I still don't want a dog, but I understand it's not up to me whether you choose to have an animal as a significant other or not."

"Um, I'm not sure 'significant other' is the term I'd choose," Lizzie said, although she fully expected to use Loretta to fill the Adam-shaped hole in her heart.

Mom waved her hand dismissively. "You know what I mean. Companion, life partner, whatever."

"Well, anyway, I think you and Loretta will get along fine." Lizzie had decided that the pit bull was coming home with her, as soon as those puppies were old enough to find new homes. When Adam left, he'd take D-Day with him, Marcus would keep Patton, and the puppies would be easy to re-home. Jake would surely take one. But poor Loretta, so afraid of everyone, needed a family who understood her, and Lizzie wanted to provide that.

"Are you ready to leave?" Mom asked. "I do wish they'd keep you overnight," she said for the eleventh time.

"I'm glad they're letting me go tonight," Lizzie said. Again.

"Okay, I'll go down and watch for your dad."

Lizzie thanked the nurses for taking care of her and

gingerly moved to the wheelchair a nursing assistant brought. Her feet still hurt like hell, so she'd be moving slowly for a few days at least.

"Let's hit it," she told the assistant, who pushed her toward the elevators.

She planned to go to her room at her parents' house, crawl under the covers with a laptop and the Netflix password, and stay there for a long time. Like until Adam left town, so she wouldn't have to run into him.

She'd be okay. She really would. She'd started over when she'd come back to Big Chance, and this broken heart thing was just a tiny blip. She had plenty to keep her occupied. She would throw herself into the Mill Creek project. Learn to make sushi. She'd buy a used guitar on eBay and teach herself protest songs.

"Did you say your mom and dad were meeting you here?" the assistant asked her when they approached the automatic doors.

"Yes. They've got a big blue Buick. Aren't they—" She broke off when she saw the vehicle idling at the curb.

It was not a Buick. There was a big, white pickup truck parked at the curb, with a long, tall cowboy leaning against it. He seemed to be staring through the glass doors, but his eyes were shadowed beneath the brim of an old cowboy hat. His arms, crossed over his chest, strained the sleeves of his black-and-gold T-shirt, and his boots were dusty.

How was this happening? She hadn't even started her Adam-free life, and she was off the wagon. He was probably here to pick up his granddad or Zimmerman. She made a mental note to write a letter to the hospital staff suggesting staggered release times so patients could avoid running into former lovers.

The doors slid open, and Lizzie pretended not to notice Adam as she peered off to the side, looking for her parents. Mom and Dad were nowhere to be seen, and the well-lit parking lot was nearly deserted.

"Are you sure this is the right exit?" she asked the assistant.

"Mm-hmm."

Her wheelchair stopped right in front of two long legs. Looked like this interaction wasn't avoidable. Looking up—way up—she met Adam's eyes. "What brings you here?" she asked.

"I came to see you." His gaze suggested that he had things to say to her, but what hadn't already been said?

"Don't you have things to do? Like pack for parts unknown?"

He shook his head. "Not right this minute."

No, of course not. She hadn't even brokered the sale of the ranch with Rob Chance, and she didn't have anything in writing about Mill Creek farm. She was going to have a tough time instituting her Adam-abstinence plan.

"Can you give us a minute?" he asked the nursing assistant, who moved around the wheelchair to look at Lizzie with a questioning glance.

"I'm fine," Lizzie assured her. "Thank you."

The doors opened and closed with a whoosh, and then it was just Lizzie, Adam, and a few thousand flying insects trying to commit suicide by light bulb.

Adam watched Lizzie with an intense focus that made her shift uncomfortably.

"What are you looking at me for?"

"I like to look at you," he said.

"Take a picture. It'll last longer," she told him.

"The real thing's better."

She rolled her eyes. "That's going to suck for you in a few weeks."

"God, I hope not," he said.

That stung. A lot. She took a deep breath, channeling the anticrying anger gods, and said, "Listen. I'm at a distinct disadvantage here. I'm tired, my feet hurt, and my parents don't seem to be here to drive me home. Oh. And I got my heart broken today. Can you tell me what you want?"

He blew out a breath. "This shit's not easy for me, you know?"

"No. I don't. Because you're not telling me."

He smiled then. "You're amazing."

She tried to ignore the nice little wiggle that went through her soul, because it didn't matter how *amazing* she was, she needed to *not* be another brick in the burden that Adam insisted carrying around.

"Fine." He uncrossed his arms, shoved his hands in his pockets, pulled them out again, finally rested them on his lean hips, and said, "Today was nuts."

"To say the least."

"And I still had a lot of time to think. Usually, that's not a good thing."

"Usually?"

He shrugged. "I guess it depends. I got out of bed this morning with every intention of doing the right thing. You know, help Emma with Granddad, find out about selling the ranch, try to talk to Jake and Talbott about their plans, maybe teach D-Day to fold laundry."

At the sound of his name, a black head appeared over the side of the truck bed.

"Hey, D-Day," Lizzie said.

"Shhh," Adam said. "Not yet."

D-Day's head disappeared again.

"Anyway, the point is," Adam continued, "I try to do the right thing most of the time. Unfortunately, that doesn't always work out."

"Don't beat yourself up about today," Lizzie said. "You *did* do the right thing. It's not your fault that everything went wonky. It turned out mostly okay, right?"

"That's what I'm trying to say. I *do* try to do the right thing, but stuff doesn't always work out."

At her blank look, he went on, "After we got blown up, everyone said it wasn't my fault. Emma says it's not my fault that Granddad's a challenge, and whatever went wrong with Todd wasn't my problem."

If he was going to tell her, again, how he was responsible for fixing everything, she was going to scream.

Instead, he said, "For some reason, I think I finally got that today."

Lizzie felt a smile break out. Her heart was still leaking all over the place, but she was glad Adam had found a little closure.

"But that's not all," he said. "I'm responsible for everyone I care about."

Okay, maybe the *It's not your fault* lesson hadn't sunk in.

"I don't want to add to that burden you feel," she said.

"Understood." He nodded as if to himself. "But here's

the thing. The more people I care about, the more people I'm responsible for, the more people who are on my team. They're also responsible for me."

"Whoa," Lizzie said, absorbing this line of thinking. "That's kind of deep."

"Right?" He outright laughed now. "I see now that Emma needs me—my help with Granddad—more than she needs money. And I've got a chance—a big one, if you'll forgive the pun—to do something good here for my guys. Something I know how to do, and something they can help me with."

She felt her mouth tilt up at the corners. "What, exactly, do you have in mind?"

"Well, I seem to have a ranch full of army veteran, wannabe cowboy dog trainers."

"That's quite a job title. 'Army veteran wannabe cowboy dog trainers.'"

"Yeah, I might leave the 'wannabe' part off after a few weeks. They seem to be settling in fairly well. Not sure I'm ready to turn them loose with any steers or horses, though."

"Especially since you don't have any. Maybe let them practice on dogs?"

"Something like that. We got lucky, and a few good dogs found us. That doesn't happen much. But there are a million dogs out there who need homes. A lot of them get ditched because they have simple-to-fix behavior problems, and some of them just get thrown out for no good reason. We can take some of them in, rehabilitate the ones who need work. Some might be able to work as service animals or emotional support dogs or therapy dogs to serve other vets. Hell, we can even have the guys come out and stay for a while, do some of the basic training themselves."

"Basic training. You are punny."

"And you're beautiful," he said, leaning over to kiss her.

"Oh." She pulled back, startled. "What was that for?"

"I'm sorry," he said. "I guess I left something out."

She just looked at him, at his strong, lean jaw, at the deep blue eyes, so full of emotion. How could she have ever thought he was remote? Or maybe he'd just managed to open up recently. With her.

"I'm sticking around for another reason. There's this girl I kinda have a crush on."

"A crush?"

"I met her a while ago, and I think she was into me, but it wasn't the right time. Then I ran into her again, and at first, I still didn't think it was a good time, but now I'm reevaluating my options."

"You are?" She crossed her arms.

"Yeah."

Adam crouched in front of Lizzie. "Listen, I know you're going to be really busy with your job and the Mill Creek park, but I wanted to ask you—"

"Okay."

He raised that eyebrow again. "Okay? You don't even know what I'm going to ask."

"I don't really care," she laughed. "If it's you and me, I'm in."

"Damn, I love you," he said.

"Oh." Lizzie's heart, which had felt so empty a little bit ago, was overflowing now. She was short of breath and feeling flushed.

"Ah, hell," Adam said, looking at her with concern, taking her hand in his. "Are you okay? Are you having more heat exhaustion?"

"No, no," she reassured him. "I'm fine. The real kind of fine."

"Yeah," he said, "you are." He looked down at their clasped hands, then up into her eyes. "I do, you know."

"What?"

"Love you. I don't know—" His breath caught, and his eyes took on a suspicious sheen. "I don't know if I'd have figured any of this shit out on my own, but I do know that if it weren't for you, it wouldn't matter so much."

Lizzie's throat was so tight, she could barely breathe, much less speak.

"It's okay if you need to think about it for a while. If, you know, if you're not sure about what you said earlier."

"I love you, too," she said.

"Oh, thank God."

She laughed, and then he did, too. He straightened, turned to the truck, and snapped his fingers. "D-Day, come here, buddy."

The dog leapt over the side of the truck and stopped, grinning and drooling, next to Adam. From his back pocket, Adam produced a piece of red cloth.

D-Day took it in his mouth and brought it to Lizzie, dropping his giant head in her lap.

"What's this?" Lizzie asked, accepting the slightly soggy fabric and giving D-Day a pat. She straightened it out and untangled the straps. "Big Chance Support Dogs" was embroidered across the back, and one side said, "D-Day."

"Talbott ordered it from the internet," Adam said. "He

might have been a little premature, but he did have the right idea. We need you to be a part of this. Jake's on board, and I'm pretty sure Talbott will help when he's feeling better, and maybe we can get Granddad settled and free Emma up to do stuff if she wants, but you're the one with that thing we need."

"That thing?"

"Yeah. That get-it-done, figure-it-out, make-it-work thing."

She didn't think she could smile any wider, but she did.

"Would you do the honors?" Adam led D-Day closer to Lizzie, and she put the vest on the dog. He looked quite dapper.

"So, Big Chance, not Last Chance?" Lizzie asked.

"Yeah, I guess so," Adam said with a wry smile. "Turns out Big Chance isn't so bad after all."

Chapter 37

LIZZIE STOOD IN FRONT OF THE MAYOR WITH HER DAD ON one side and Adam on the other.

Joe Chance bent his head to the certificate on his desk and signed it with a flourish, then looked up with a grin and said, "I now pronounce you Big Chance, Texas's new director of parks and recreation."

Joe rose to shake Lizzie's hand and then handed Adam a fat envelope.

They'd managed to get everything squared away on the same day: Adam and Emma closed on the sale of the Mill Creek property to Chance County, Lizzie signed a contract to not only oversee the creation of the Vanhook Historical Recreation Park but also to supervise rehabilitation of a playground next to the courthouse and to head up the Big Chance Convention and Visitors' Bureau.

And Adam had himself an official nonprofit corporation: Big Chance Ranch Rescue and Support Animals.

"Joe, we're having lunch at Dairy Queen, if you'd like to join us," Dad told the mayor as they filed out of his office.

"Thanks, but I promised to take the girls Halloween costume shopping," Joe said with a grimace. He pushed the front door of the courthouse open, and everyone filed down the steps into the still-hot October afternoon.

"Do you want to ride with me?" Dad asked, digging his car keys from his pocket.

Lizzie looked at Adam and said, "No, I think we'll walk."

"Okay, see you there in a minute." Dad, who was doing incredibly well now that his chemo was done, still needed as much air-conditioning as he could get and drove the few blocks to the restaurant.

"How are you doing?" Lizzie asked Adam when they were alone on the sidewalk. He took her hand as they walked toward Dairy Queen.

He shook his head. "I'm not sure. I really appreciate your dad helping me put together the business plan, but I can't help but think we've missed some details."

Lizzie nodded. "I know. Me, too. But I also know that we've got a huge group of people pulling for both of us, so if we stumble, someone will help get us back up."

"You're incredible," he said, leaning in to kiss her.

"Right back at you," she said, still pinching herself over the fact that this guy was in love with her and making plans for a long, happy future in Big Chance.

It hadn't been too hard to convince Mitch to relinquish his claim on the Mill Creek property, since the mayor informed him that he owed thousands and thousands in back taxes.

Mitch and his gun-wielding friend were both in jail, each awaiting trial on a variety of charges, from kidnapping to fraud to cruelty to animals. It seemed like justice that both men were going to be spending a long time in cages.

"I can't believe I've got a new job," Lizzie said. "I love working at Vanhook Realty, but now that Dad's doing better, he really doesn't need my help that much. Besides, this feels more like a big-girl job, since I got it on my own. Now, I've just got to find a big-girl place to live." It had gotten really difficult to find time and space to be alone with Adam over the past few weeks, and she was pretty desperate to find some digs of her own.

"I'm sure you'll find something soon," Adam said.

As they approached Dairy Queen, she saw Marcus and Jake sitting at one of the outdoor tables with Patton, Loretta, and D-Day on leashes. The puppies had been dropped off at the vet for checkups and shots.

"Come on, Hoss, Hossette," Marcus urged. "They're gonna run out of ice cream."

"We're coming," Adam said, rolling his eyes. He reached to open the door for her, and as the first gasp of air-conditioning reached her skin, Lizzie and Adam were hit with a giant, "Surprise!"

A crowd of people spilled out of the restaurant, carrying balloons and signs that said "Congratulations" and "Welcome Home For Good!"

"Wow," Adam said, blinking. "This is…"

"Nuts," Lizzie finished.

Mom, Dad, Emma, Granddad, and Mom's party planning ladies all crowded around Lizzie and Adam to offer congratulations and good wishes. A couple of Big Chance sheriff's deputies were there as well.

After a moment, however, the Dairy Queen door opened again, and a giant ice cream cake appeared, carried by a woman—

"Is that you, Crystal?" Lizzie asked.

"Yep," she said, putting the platter down on a picnic table and grabbing the plates and knives that were already there. "Clint got laid off from the tire plant over near Fredericksburg, so he's home with the baby."

"Well, it's good to see you," Lizzie said, "but I'm sorry Clint's out of work."

Crystal shrugged. "It's good for him to be with the baby."

Within minutes, everyone was digging in to ice cream cake.

"Where's your other friend?" Deputy Diamond asked. "How's he doing?"

"Zimmerman's doing better," Adam said, though Lizzie noticed he didn't smile when he said it. "He's staying with his parents while he recuperates from his last surgery, but I think he might come back to stay with us at the ranch for a while soon."

"That's…good?" Diamond asked.

"It is," Marcus, who was sitting nearby, said. "It's not good that his life is pretty messed up right now, but it's good that there's someplace he can come to get his head together."

And it was, Lizzie thought. Adam planned to take in as many rescue dogs as he could afford to and train as many as possible to work as support animals in some capacity, and he wanted to populate the ranch with veterans who needed a hand up. Marcus and Jake would help with the ranch operations while Marcus worked with Patton to train him to be a mobility assistance dog and Jake tried to find a dog who would help him with his directionality issues.

Emma stopped by the table, holding Granddad's hand. He'd recovered physically from the incident at Mill Creek, but his dementia seemed worse, and Emma finally agreed that an adult day center was necessary. "We're going to get back to Bright Days," she told Lizzie and Adam now.

"How's your ice cream?" Adam asked Lizzie once they'd said goodbye to Emma and Granddad.

"Oh!" she said, digging her spoon into the softened mess of gooey awesomeness. "I don't know."

"Hey, Adam," Jake said, holding up his phone. "I think we need to find another bed or two."

"What?"

"I just got a text message from Zimmerman. He's coming back to the ranch next week and bringing a friend."

"Oh," Adam said. "That's, um…great."

"Where are you going to put them?" Lizzie asked. "The barn?" The farmhouse was already bursting at the seams with just the three men and a few dogs.

"I guess the first order of business is to expand the horse shed into a bunkhouse," Adam said. "Hey, Crystal," he called.

"Yeah?"

"Do you think Clint wants a job doing some construction?"

She nodded emphatically. "Yes. He does."

Adam laughed. "Well, tell him to call me. I need some help on the ranch." To Lizzie, he said, "Eat your ice cream."

"Are you trying to keep me fat?" she asked but dug her spoon in again anyway.

"I'm trying to keep you perfect," he told her, putting an arm around her and pulling her close, just as her spoon hit something hard at the bottom of the ice cream.

She dug through the mess and came up with a couple of flat metal pieces. There were two, and they looked like dog tags. *What the heck?* With a suspicious glance at Adam, she swished them through a cup of water that a grinning Crystal slid toward her.

One of the tags read, "D-Day, Property of Adam and

Lizzie, 9873 Wild Wager Rd." The other had Loretta's name but was otherwise the same.

Lizzie looked up at Adam, who gazed at her with a hell of a lot of love and a smidgen of uncertainty. "I know a really wonderful house you can move into if you're interested," he said.

"Hey, Crystal," Lizzie said. "How soon do you think Clint can start working on that horse shed?"

Acknowledgments

Writing is considered a solitary job, but wow—there are a lot of people to thank once the book is all ready to head into the world!

My family is first. Thank you for understanding why I don't cook or clean, and that sometimes I flake out completely. I love each of you way further than to the moon and back.

I'd like to thank everyone at Sourcebooks who has worked so hard on the Big Chance Dog Rescue series, especially Cat Clyne, for believing in this project and having the patience to see it come to fruition.

Thanks to Nicole Resciniti for being the best agent ever and having all the faith—especially when my own well was running a little low.

We each write our own stories, but other authors are critical: Dawn Alexander, thanks for being at the other end of emergency "I have a Texas question" texts. To Kari Lynn Dell, for sharing real cowgirl stuff—I'm gonna work that cow-cam in somewhere. To my Passionate Critter peeps, thanks for welcoming me into your system and holding me up through the last few rounds of edits—seems like someone's always on the Facebook chat to offer a "You can do it!" Watch out, girls—there are more books to come!

To my friend Dave S., who shared a lot of painful, scary

stuff and gave me a glimpse into the heart and mind of a vet. To every other veteran and service member—saying "thank you for your service" isn't enough, but I'll keep trying to figure out what is.

Author's Note

In Romancelandia, it was easy to miraculously find a couple of stray dogs for Adam and crew to train as service dogs, but in real life, it takes a lot of hard work, money, and time to find the right dog to do the amazing things a service animal can do. As research for this series, I decided I should try to get my dogs to do more than simply come when I call them and not poop inside. I now have one dog who can also shake hands—impressive, right?

A few years ago, I was fortunate enough to spend a week with a PTSD service dog, Goose, and her trainer, Cole. I was blown away by how well this dog handled herself (and by all of her cool tricks). A few days into our trip, my dad passed away after a long illness. I had been prepared for that day, although I'd hoped it wouldn't happen while I was away with no immediate flight home. When I ran into Cole and Goose after getting the news, the first thing Goose did was rise onto her hind legs and lick my face. Several times that day, stuck in Las Vegas and far from my family, Goose came to rest her head on my lap and asked to be petted, reminding me I wasn't alone. So, yeah—I'm a believer in what these dogs can do. If you'd like to know more, visit http://gotyoursixsupportdogs.org/.

And a note about pit bulls: Few would argue that pit bulls are among the most controversial canine breeds in the world—many areas have laws against owning pit bull–type dogs—even though there's no across-the-board agreement on what makes a dog a pit bull. I did an informal survey and found that 75 percent of the dogs in a nearby large-city shelter are pit bulls and pit-mixes. Too many are euthanized because they are not adopted. Most are sweet, gentle creatures, although some have been treated horribly and can be aggressive—as can any breed. While I don't suggest everyone go out today and adopt a pit bull, I will say this: please support your local animal shelter and rescue groups!

About the Author

When Teri Anne Stanley isn't working as a professional science geek, she's usually writing, though sometimes you'll find her trying to convince her rescue dogs that "sit" doesn't mean on the couch. She's definitely *not* cooking or cleaning.

In her endless spare time, she's the human half of a therapy dog team, an amateur genealogist, and a compulsive crafter. Along with a variety of offspring and dogs, she and Mr. Stanley enjoy boating and relaxing at their estate, located in the thriving metropolis of Sugartit, between Beaverlick and Rabbit Hash, Kentucky.

Visit her at teriannestanley.com.

PUPPY
Christmas

LILA WAS GOING TO KILL HER SISTERS FOR THIS.

"Lila! Lila Vasquez!" A voice hailed her from across the crowded ballroom floor. It was followed by the bustling of a woman in a tasteful two-piece dress suit. A pang of envy flooded through Lila for that neat, pearly-gray fabric, but it was a short-lived sentiment.

Mostly because it was immediately replaced by embarrassment. And despair. And the overwhelming urge to throw herself out the nearest window.

She changed her mind. Death was too good for her sisters. Nothing less than lifelong torment would do.

"Aren't you so brave," the woman cooed as she came to a halt. Her sweeping gaze took in the full glory of Lila's billowing bubble-gum-pink ball gown. If the color wasn't bad enough, the fact that she was followed by a trail of sparkles everywhere she went was. She'd left the ladies' restroom looking like a glitter bomb had gone off in one of the stalls. "I wish I could wear something like that, but at our age, you know…"

Yes, Lila did know. No one over the age of twenty-one should ever leave the house in this shade of pink. Unfortunately, Sophie and Dawn had interpreted the Once Upon a Time theme literally. Instead of the costume party she'd been assured awaited her inside these doors, Lila had found herself inside a nonprofit event as upscale as it was elegant. She stuck out like a sore thumb.

A giant, pink, puffy thumb.

"It's so nice to see you, Kathy," she said, forcing a smile. It probably looked about as plastic as she felt, but she was determined to stay put. She'd been invited to this ball as an established and vital part of Spokane's hearing services community. Its purpose was to raise funds for the hearing impaired, largely for the purchase of medical equipment, implants, hearing assistive tech…and service dogs.

Lila might look silly—and feel just as ridiculous—but her dogs deserved a seat at the table, metaphorically speaking. She'd give them that even if it meant she had to stand here all night, shedding glitter into fifty-dollar glasses of champagne.

"I'm excited to hear who will be getting our puppy donation," she said in what she hoped was a casual tone. "So are my sisters. I'm supposed to text them the moment I find out. Do you know when they'll be making the announcements?"

Kathy waved an airy hand. She was one of the ball organizers, but she had less to do with the details and more to do with squeezing large donations out of the city's finest.

"You'll have to ask Anya. She has the full schedule. I only came by to ask where you got that gorgeous dress. My daughter's winter formal is coming up, and they're doing Candy Land this year. That's exactly what we've been looking for."

It was enough to send a lesser woman fleeing for the nearest hiding place. Lila had spotted several already, each one more appealing than the last. There was a huge banquet table she could crawl underneath to wait out the evening's events, or a swan ice sculpture dripping in the entryway that might provide an adequate shield. In a pinch, even that pair of waiters with giant silver platters could help her make a quick getaway.

But Lila stood her ground. Lila *always* stood her ground. Neither snow nor rain nor heat nor extreme social embarrassment—

"Oh God." Catching sight of a familiar man by the entryway, she whirled around, her skirt ballooning around her legs. "This can't be happening."

"What can't be happening?" Kathy asked, her brows raised. She took a sip of her champagne, a wayward piece of glitter clinging to her upper lip. "Are you sure you're all right?"

No. Lila wasn't sure of anything except that no number of waiters with silver platters would be able to help her now. What she needed was for the ground to open up beneath her, for the world to swallow her whole. Risking a quick peek over her shoulder, she scanned the entryway again and… Yep. It was happening. It was happening, and there was nothing she could do to stop it.

She dashed a hand out and grabbed Kathy's forearm. "Quick—what's the easiest way out of here?"

"I think maybe you should sit down," Kathy said, frowning at where Lila was crushing the silk of her suit. "You look as though you've seen a ghost."

On the contrary, it was no ghost that had caught Lila's eye. That flash of white coming from the opposite side of the room was blinding enough to be supernatural, but Lila had never believed in that sort of thing. Ghosts weren't real and bogeymen were make-believe, but a smile as toothy and brilliant as her *ex-boyfriend's* had caused her plenty of sleepless nights.

"The kitchen?" Lila asked, mostly to herself. "No, I'll never make it that far. It'll have to be the emergency exit."

She knew she was babbling, but she could no more stop the words from leaving her mouth than she could still the sudden thumping of her heart. *Patrick Yarmouth.* Of all the men to saunter through the door looking as though he'd dropped in straight out of a toothpaste ad, it had to be him.

She could brazen this dress out for the sake of her company, Puppy Promise. She could smile and sparkle for as long as it took to woo the people who had the power to take that company to the next level.

But she could not, would not, *dared* not risk exposing herself to the man who'd accused her of perfection like it was a four-letter word. Especially since he hadn't spotted her yet. *There's still time to make my escape.*

"I'm sorry, Kathy," she said as she lifted her skirts and headed for the bright red exit sign. "I have to leave."

"Does this mean you aren't going to tell me where you got the dress?" Kathy called, watching her go. "My daughter will be so disappointed."

"I'll email you the details tomorrow," Lila promised as she pushed through the door to safety. *Better yet*, she thought as she navigated the steep flight of steps leading down, *I'll shove the dress in a box and mail it to you.*

After tonight, there was nothing on earth that could induce her to wear sparkles again.

It was only cowardice if she hid *behind* the potted plant.

"I'm standing next to it," Lila said to no one in particular, if only because there was no one in particular to say it to. She'd escaped the emergency stairwell to find herself on some kind of first- floor landing. It offered a fountain and a ficus and a complete absence of other people—all three of which were serving to calm her rattled nerves. "I'm taking a break, that's all. Getting away from all those dark suits and demure gowns. I'll be back to my usual, capable self in a few minutes, and then I'll be able to face him."

Her attempt at boosting her own confidence failed. In truth, it was only her inability to pull her skirts in far enough that kept her where she was. There was no way she *could* fit behind that plant.

A soft sniffling sound stopped Lila before she could make the mistake of continuing her one- sided conversation. It wasn't like her to flee at the first sign of danger; even less to self-soothe with a running dialogue. She was supposed to be the unflappable Vasquez sister, the one everyone else turned to in times of emergency.

In other words, the *perfect* one.

The sniffle sounded again, this time accompanied by a hiccupping sob. Her own worries cast aside, Lila picked her way out from her hiding spot next to the plant and surveyed the room. As far as she could tell, it was still empty. There was a possibility that sound might carry through one of the vents, but—

A small voice sounded behind her. "Are you a princess?"

For the second time this evening, Lila found herself whirling around, startled. This time, however, her gaze landed on a small girl standing just a few feet away.

The first thing she noticed was that the girl appeared to be wearing a dress that was identical to her own. Bubble-gum pink. Sparkles. Tulle. All things that made a grown woman look like she was one magic wand away from a starring role in *The Wizard of Oz*, but looked perfectly at home on a six-year-old.

The second thing she noticed was that the child had a pair of twin cochlear implants, one on either side of her elaborate updo. The small, purple-colored plastic pieces behind her ears attached to even smaller nodes via looped cords. They were, in Lila's line of work, a fairly common sight. They were also a clear sign that this girl's parents couldn't be too far away.

Upstairs in the ballroom, probably. *Where Patrick is.*

"Oh, hello," Lila said, somewhat taken aback. Surprise rendered her voice harsher than usual—a thing she regretted as soon as the words left her lips. The poor girl was obviously lost, staring up at her with wide, blue eyes that were swimming in tears. "I didn't know there was anyone in here with me."

The girl didn't respond, her breath once more catching

on a sob. Lila's experience with children wasn't vast—she was much more of a dog person than a kid one—but even she could tell that a situation like this one called for tact.

She fell into an unladylike squat so they were level with each other. Not only was getting down the first thing a puppy trainer did when approaching a wary animal, but the girl was watching Lila's mouth with the intensity of long practice. Lila had enough experience with hearing service dogs and their owners to recognize that the girl most likely used a combination of her cochlear implants and lip reading to communicate.

"Are you lost?" she asked.

The girl nodded, her arms wrapped protectively around her midsection.

Lila held out a hand with her palm up to show she meant no harm and held it there. That was another good puppy-training trick. Maybe this wouldn't be as difficult as she'd feared. "Then you're in luck. I'm not lost at all."

"You aren't?" the girl asked, blinking at her.

"Nope. I have an excellent sense of direction." She held a finger straight up. "You go thataway."

The girl's gaze followed the direction Lila was pointing, but she had yet to take Lila's hand. "Through the ceiling?" she asked doubtfully.

"Well, no. You have to take the stairs, I'm afraid. There's an elevator around here somewhere, but I'm not sure where to find it."

That caused the doubt in the girl's voice to increase. "You mean this isn't your castle?"

The Davenport Hotel, where the event was being held, was about as fancy as Spokane architecture got, but it was hardly what Lila would call a *castle*. "Oh, um. No. I think it's owned by local real-estate developers, actually."

Apparently, that was the wrong answer. The girl's arms clenched tighter around her stomach, a fresh bout of tears starting to take shape in her eyes. "I thought it was your castle."

Lila had no idea how she was supposed to respond. It wasn't in her nature to lie to small children, but she didn't know what else to do. Her sister Sophie would have been able to comfort the girl with kind words and a smile, and Dawn would have had her laughing within minutes, but Lila had always been better with adults than children.

Then again, she'd also always been the kind of woman to dress sensibly and stand her ground when faced with an unexpected encounter with an ex-boyfriend. Clearly, today was an anomaly.

"My castle is much bigger than this one," she said, casting her scruples aside. "And it's located in, um, a faraway kingdom?"

It was the right thing to say. A look of relief swept over the girl's face, the beginnings of a smile taking shape in the perfect bow of her mouth. "You *are* a real princess," she said. "I knew it."

She finally slipped her hand into Lila's. For some strange reason, Lila had expected the girl's hand to be sticky— children were usually sticky, weren't they?—but the palm pressed against hers was perfectly clean. And soft. It was a nice surprise.

"I'm not allowed to talk to strangers," the girl confided with a shy smile. "But a princess isn't a stranger."

"Oh dear," Lila murmured. It wasn't her place to lecture

children on stranger danger, but for all she knew, the girl would take this one successful venture and run off in the future with anyone claiming to be royalty. "Actually, I *am* a stranger. It's important to be wary of grown-ups no matter what they're wearing. You know that, right? A fancy dress doesn't automatically make someone a princess. Just like a tuxedo doesn't automatically make someone a prince."

In fact, now that she thought about it, there were lots of warning signs that could be worn on the outside. Take, for example, a man's blinding smile across a crowded ballroom floor.

"It's all too easy for a person to hide their true nature behind clothes," she added. "Clothes and makeup and shoes and a smile you know better than to trust, if only because no man has teeth that white unless there's something wrong with him. I don't care what anyone says or how many times they say it. You shouldn't be able to see your reflection in someone else's molars."

The girl tugged on Lila's hand, pulling her attention down. She pointed first at her own ears and then at Lila's lips before blinking expectantly.

"Oh," Lila said, dismayed. "I went on a bit of a tirade there, didn't I?"

"Emily might not have had the privilege of catching all that, but I sure did," a male voice sounded from behind them, causing Lila to jump. Again. "And I, for one, am dying to meet this man. Does he gargle with bleach, do you think, or is it that new charcoal toothpaste everyone is going on about?"

COMING SEPTEMBER 2019 FROM
SOURCEBOOKS CASABLANCA

COWBOY TROUBLE

Joanne Kennedy's Westerns will leave you wanting to wrangle a cowboy of your own!

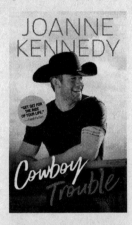

Her latest love-life disaster behind her, Libby Brown flees to the Wyoming countryside to fulfill a childhood dream by starting her own chicken farm from scratch. But the West is wilder than she expected, and while she's determined to succeed on her own, the sexy, sturdy cowboy next door sure is helpful...

**"Refreshing and different...
Ms. Kennedy's novel is a winner."**

—*Night Owl Reviews* Top Pick, 4.5 Stars

CAUGHT UP IN
A COWBOY

USA Today bestselling author Jennie Marts
welcomes you to Creedence, Colorado,
where the cowboys are hot on the ice

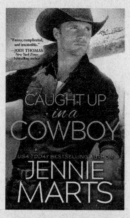

After an injury, NHL star Rockford James returns to his hometown ranch to find that a lot has changed. The one thing that hasn't? His feelings for Quinn Rivers, his high school sweetheart and girl next door.

Quinn had no choice but to get over Rock after he left. Teenaged and heartbroken, she had a rebound one-night stand that ended in single motherhood. Now that Rock's back—and clamoring for a second chance—Quinn will do anything to avoid getting caught up in this oh-so-tempting cowboy...

"Funny, complicated, and irresistible."

—Jodi Thomas, *New York Times* bestselling author

For more info about Sourcebooks's
books and authors, visit:

sourcebooks.com